D1263078

HIGH TREASON

Center Point
Large Print

Also by DiAnn Mills and available from
Center Point Large Print:

Deadlock
Deadly Encounter
Deep Extraction

**This Large Print Book carries the
Seal of Approval of N.A.V.H.**

HIGH
TREASON

DiANN MILLS

CENTER POINT LARGE PRINT
THORNDIKE, MAINE

This Center Point Large Print edition
is published in the year 2018 by arrangement with
Tyndale House Publishers, Inc.

High Treason is a work of fiction. Where real people, events, establishments, organizations, or locales appear, they are used fictitiously. All other elements of the novel are drawn from the author's imagination.

The text of this Large Print edition is unabridged.
In other aspects, this book may vary
from the original edition.
Printed in the United States of America
on permanent paper.
Set in 16-point Times New Roman type.

ISBN: 978-1-68324-715-9

Library of Congress Cataloging-in-Publication Data

Names: Mills, DiAnn, author.
Title: High treason / DiAnn Mills.
Description: Center Point Large Print edition. | Thorndike, Maine :
   Center Point Large Print, 2018.
Identifiers: LCCN 2017056283 | ISBN 9781683247159
   (hardcover : alk. paper)
Subjects: LCSH: Government investigators—Fiction. | Attempted
   assassination—Fiction. | Large type books. | Romantic suspense
   fiction. gsafd | GSAFD: Christian fiction. | Love stories.
Classification: LCC PS3613.I567 H54 2018b | DDC 813/.6—dc23
LC record available at https://lccn.loc.gov/2017056283

ACKNOWLEDGMENTS

A huge thank-you to Alycia Morales, Edie Melson, Lynette Eason, Emme Gannon, Mary Denman, Vonda Skelton, and Linda Gilden. You are the best!

Todd Allen—Your edits, suggestions, and encouragement helped detail my story. Thanks so much.

Connie Brown—Thank you for brainstorming illnesses for Monica.

FBI Special Agent Shauna Dunlap—Appreciate how you help keep my writing credible.

Beau Egert—Thank you for helping me with the research and always answering my questions.

Audrey Frank—Thank you for sharing your wisdom about Muslim culture and patiently answering questions.

Julie Garmon—You read every book and provide me with valuable suggestions. Thank you.

Karl Harroff—I so appreciate your weaponry knowledge.

Mark Lanier—Your Sunday morning series of "Why I'm Not Agnostic" was a tremendous help in writing Kord's search for God.

Richard Mabry—I couldn't write a book without your medical knowledge.

Dean Mills—Oh, the hours you spent with me researching, editing, and listening to my ups and downs.

James Watkins—Your brainstorming ideas for my plot inspired me to give this story a twist.

HIGH TREASON

1

FBI SPECIAL AGENT KORD DAVIDSON had survived missions in the Middle East, been detained in Iran, escaped an ISIS death trap, and still walked and talked. His past kept him fueled for the future while adrenaline flowed whenever he recalled the danger—and the victories of working Houston's terrorist division.

Early Tuesday morning, Kord sat in a Mercedes limo with Saudi Prince Omar bin Talal, his longtime friend and a grandson of the royal Saud family, en route to the Saud mansion in River Oaks. The prince's mother, Princess Gharam, and his two sisters rode in a limo behind them. Prince Omar had requested Kord for protection detail as an olive branch to the Americans. Smart move, in Kord's opinion. The strained relations between Saudi Arabia and the US resulting from falling oil prices and the US having less dependency on foreign oil was only part of the problem. Despite being a strong ally to the West in the fight against terrorism, the Saudis disapproved of how the US was handling the ongoing tension in Iran, Syria, and Yemen, and the list went on.

Kord shook off those bleak thoughts and turned his attention to the security detail. "I'm looking forward to catching up with your family," he said to the prince. "I appreciate the e-mails with your sons' photos, but I want to know all about them from their father."

Prince Omar grinned like a boy himself. "They study hard and work even harder at mischief. You and I will have hours of coffee and conversation." His expression shifted to lines that aged him. "I wish the circumstances regarding my mother were more pleasant."

"MD Anderson is the best medical center in the world to help her."

"And Houston has the only facility conducting a clinical trial for her type of cancer. I keep telling myself she'll be fine, trying to be hopeful. I have an appointment with her team of doctors after she's admitted to the hospital this afternoon. They want to review the testing from her doctor in Riyadh and explain their proposed method of treatment." He paused. "I'm glad you're with me. In case Mother's treatments aren't successful, I'll need a friend."

"Princess Gharam's a strong woman."

"She's determined to fight the cancer."

"I see your business plans aren't on the schedule."

Prince Omar turned to him. "I'll give you that once I know about Mother's treatment."

"My job is to ensure your safety."

"We'll discuss it later. On Wednesday week, I'd like for you to accompany me to Saudi Aramco."

He responded respectfully. How many of those at the family business were supportive of Prince Omar's plans to lease ownership in Saudi oil reserves to Americans?

Prince Omar tapped his driver on the shoulder. "Wasi, don't forget we're stopping at the Frozen Rock."

"A little early for ice cream," Kord said.

"Not on Riyadh time."

The prince's press secretary, Malik, laughed. "Prince Omar, I reserved the shop for 9 a.m. before we left home."

The moment the limos pulled off Westheimer into the busy shopping strip housing the Frozen Rock, uneasiness crept over Kord. A sensation he couldn't shake and one he'd learned to trust. He scoured the area looking for potential danger. "Prince Omar, I don't think we should do this."

"This is one of Mother's favorite excursions, and my sisters enjoy it too."

He glanced at his friend. "Zain and I can take orders and deliver them. My gut tells me this isn't safe, and I can't give you a solid reason why."

"I know your gut talk," Zain, the head Saudi bodyguard, said. "Kept us from getting killed a couple of times."

Prince Omar sighed heavily. "We have eight armed men. This is a go."

Wasi drove the limo to a far corner beneath

an oak where both limos had room to park. The Frozen Rock sat midway in the retail center.

Zain turned to the prince. "Kord and I will make the initial trip and ensure the area is secure. After I talk to the owner and pay him per the conversation Malik had yesterday, I'll call you. If I detect anything risky, we can cancel."

The prince lifted his phone and frowned. "My battery is dead. Must have used it up at the airport. Call Malik if there's a problem."

Per the State Department and HPD, the bodyguards, all dressed in suits, were permitted to carry weapons in case of an attack. But Kord couldn't shake off the wariness. Only Zain and Prince Omar wore white cotton pants and shirts under their *thobe* and *ghutra* with a black *mishlah*. The men shared a remarkable resemblance, but having Zain disguised as the prince gave Kord little relief. He surveyed the area, noting teens from the high school across the street, two women in workout clothes, and others who gave no apparent reason for the hesitancy in his spirit. "Would you like for Wasi and Malik to join us?"

Zain laughed. "You and I have faced a lot worse than a store owner forgetting to open early."

"True." No talking down a stubborn Saudi when he'd made up his mind.

Wasi placed the limo in park.

Kord exited the limo and walked around the

14

front, his attention focused on every conceivable point where danger could be lurking. Finding nothing, he opened the door on Prince Omar's side, and Zain stepped out, his slender body wrapped in centuries-old culture and tradition. The two strode across the parking lot toward the window-walled Frozen Rock, painted in vivid orange and neon green. A Closed sign on the door met them, but lights were on inside the shop. Good. The reservations were intact. Now to get the prince and his guests fed and out of there. Was Kord crazy to be so apprehensive?

He knew Zain had his eyes and ears on what was happening around him while his fingers were inches from his weapon. A few feet from the glass door of the ice cream shop, Zain broke his stride.

He fell against the glass door.

The pop of a rifle sounded.

Kord grabbed him, pulling out his Glock with his other hand. Shouts in Arabic alerted him to bodyguards emerging from the limos close behind him. Time hung suspended. Zain's body slid to the sidewalk facedown, the *ghutra* soaked in red.

Kord bent to his friend and felt for a pulse. "Zain," he whispered, "this isn't the way it's supposed to happen." No response or faint heartbeat. Blood oozed from the back of his skull, draining a Saudi life onto US concrete.

Screams rose from nearby women and children. The man who'd shared Middle Eastern danger and saved Kord's life was dead. No doubt mistaken for Prince Omar. How did the sniper know about the stop at the Frozen Rock?

Monica poured a large cup of the Arabic blend for a regular customer. "Chicken-bacon wrap too?"

"You bet. Add a bag of chips and a banana."

She peeled off a label containing a quote, sealed it onto the side of the cup, and handed it to him before bagging his lunch order to-go. "Been to the rodeo yet?"

"Taking the family on Saturday. The crowds will be crazy, but that's part of it. What about you?" He gave her a polished smile, one he used for her and every person he met there. Dressed in a dark suit and a two-hundred-dollar tie, he looked every bit the successful lawyer.

"Sunday afternoon."

He turned the cup to read the quote. " 'Be sure you put your feet in the right place, then stand firm.' Abraham Lincoln. Good one. I'll remember it in court this afternoon."

"May you win all your cases." She laughed and pointed outside to dark, gathering clouds behind him. "Don't forget your umbrella."

He left the café and dashed down the sidewalk. She continued to serve coffee, specialty drinks, and deli sandwiches to the remaining patrons in line. An easy part of her life, but not her mission, her calling. Passing on smiles and encouragement provided optimism for her day and hopefully for the recipient.

A black man in his mid- to late thirties sat at a small table in the corner and sipped a double dry short. He'd spoken in a Nigerian accent, piquing her interest. The man's cell phone rang, and he snatched it. Frowning, he spoke low. She scanned him for recognition while reading his lips.

"I have no idea when he's arriving, but he'll have the rest of the money." The man listened. "We have to be careful." A tall black woman entered the café and seated herself beside him. He nodded and smiled. "I have to go. She's with me now, and we'll figure out how to surprise Father with a birthday party even if our brother doesn't get here in time."

Monica's cell phone vibrated twice, paused, then three more times, signifying a notification from her handler.

"Lori, can you take over?"

Her friend gave a quick nod. Without a word, she moved to the register. No questions asked. Monica had told Lori months ago when she was hired that personal family issues could demand her attention at any time. Yet Lori kept her employed at the coffee shop. With Monica's commitment to the CIA, she was forced to lie to her family and friends, but the cover kept them safe. If the truth ever surfaced, the betrayal might destroy the relationships she treasured. Would they ever understand her commitment to keep their country safe?

With no time to waste, she locked herself inside the restroom, knowing she had less than two minutes to read and respond. Her mental clock counted down to thirty seconds remaining. If she missed confirming the secure notice, it would repeat until she responded. A nagging headache didn't help the urgency.

Safe House ASAP
OMW

2

AT 12:30 P.M., Monica pressed on the radio in her car before she clicked her seat belt. News was her go-to station, and she wanted to know what stirred media juices in case it reflected on the reason she'd been contacted.

". . . tragic shooting this morning of Zain al-Qureshi, bodyguard of Saudi Prince Omar bin Talal. The victim was shot and killed at the Frozen Rock Ice Cream on Westheimer. He was part of a royal entourage that arrived from Riyadh earlier today. Investigators are on the scene. No arrests have been made."

The commentator moved on to sports, and Monica silenced the radio. Not good. The relationship between Saudi Arabia and the US didn't need a weak link. Many of the Saudis, especially the conservatives, would want to hold the US responsible. Most likely why her handler wanted to see her ASAP.

Within fifteen minutes, she'd parked her Honda three blocks away from a safe house east of the Galleria area.

Before emerging from her car, she swallowed two Tylenol with half a bottle of water. Dratted headache attempted to distract her. For a moment, she admired the peaceful setting, basking in the

19

tranquility as though it were sweet nectar, hoping it would chase away the pounding in her head. The weather had coaxed pink azaleas into bloom, and the lawns and shrubs wore a vibrant green like a new spring dress, fresh and welcoming after the sporadic rains.

Danger often didn't wear a disguise.

She walked up the sidewalk to the traditional style, two-story faded brick home built in the eighties. A dog barked. A red cardinal called out from the top of an oak tree. A ten-year-old Ford sat in the driveway—no other vehicles in sight. Seemingly safe, yet her Smith & Wesson was a touch away in her shoulder bag.

The CIA could send her anywhere. The assignment and the person or persons detailing it waited inside. She'd been at Coffee Gone Dark for over a year, longer than she'd been at any undercover job.

A momentary snippet of doubt robbed her determination and caused her to tingle. She'd vowed not to allow the past to dictate the future.

Monica rang the doorbell to the home where she'd find answers. The door opened slightly to reveal Jeff Carlton, her handler. Clad in his usual worn jeans and a black T-shirt with a sports jacket, he offered neither a smile nor a greeting but merely stepped aside for her to enter.

He closed the door and she eyed him. "Are you going to tell me what's going on, or are you being all clandestine on me?"

He smirked. "You have a new assignment."

Her heart sped. "What about the weapon sales to Boko Haram? We're getting close to the dealer. She's a regular at the café."

"This won't take but a few weeks."

Logic told her she'd been working four months on arresting those responsible for illegal gun sales. Someone else could take a short-term assignment. Questions slammed against her mind, but she'd hold back until Jeff offered more information.

"What else can you tell me?"

"The info is in the kitchen."

Typical all-CIA Jeff. She followed him down a chipped, tiled hallway to a clean but dated kitchen in drab shades of brown and tan. The aroma of freshly brewed coffee met her nostrils— the kind that was ground, packaged, and set on a warehouse shelf for months.

She hid her startle—Houston's FBI Special Agent in Charge Ralph Thomas. He straightened after leaning over a glass-topped table beside a second man. At six foot three and dressed in a dark suit, white shirt, and conservative tie, he easily towered over her.

Jeff led out. "I'll get the intros out of the way before I explain why we're here. Special Agent

21

in Charge Ralph Thomas, I'd like for you to meet Operative Monica Alden."

He grasped her hand. "It's a pleasure. Jeff has told me a lot about you. He speaks highly of your skills. Your exemplary record in the Middle East is why you've been asked here today."

A second man scooted back his chair and stood. "This is Special Agent Kord Davidson," SAC Thomas said. "He works the terrorist division."

She did a quick once-over of the agent to note he was hostile. Unhappy about something. Clad in a navy-blue suit, he reached for her hand, but his dark-brown gaze, veiled in thick lashes, was icy.

Jeff gestured to the table. "Have a seat, and we'll get Monica up to speed. The FBI initiated this meeting, so SAC Thomas will conduct the briefing."

The only chair available closed the distance between her and the unhappy agent. A sneaking suspicion said they would be working together. She slid into place and focused on the FBI's SAC.

"You probably heard the news about a sniper taking out Zain al-Qureshi, one of Saudi Prince Omar bin Talal's bodyguards."

"Yes, sir."

"Kord was with them. The Saudi prince arrived on his private jet early this morning. His plans are to oversee the care of his mother at MD Anderson. She's suffering from an aggressive type of breast cancer and will be participating in a clinical trial. His sisters are also with him. Prince Omar has an agenda other than his mother's health. He's here to negotiate with oil and gas companies to lease Saudi oil reserves to Americans."

That was a significant step forward in Saudi and US relations. The White House had been holding meetings regarding business between the two countries. "Were threats made about the prince's visit?" she said. "Specifically the opposition within Saudi Arabia concerning his business plans?"

"Definitely. We haven't detected an outbreak of violence here or a carryover from Saudi protests."

The incomplete information bothered her. Was this truly all they had? With the bodyguard's assassination and no arrests, the US was embarrassed and had to regain its position in the international community. She gave SAC Thomas her attention. "Surely the CIA or FBI have leads. Could Iran, Syria, or ISIS be spearheading the assassination plot?"

"All possibilities. Prior to his arrival, Prince Omar requested his friend Special Agent Kord Davidson for protection detail. Kord met him at Hobby Airport and joined the entourage. The prince brought eight bodyguards, three servants, one office staffer, two sisters, his mother, but neither of his two wives. Prior arrangements had been made for a 9 a.m. reservation at the Frozen Rock on Westheimer. There a sniper killed a bodyguard who looks like the prince. Which means his schedule was leaked." He turned to his agent. "Kord, I'm sorry. I know you and Zain were friends. The critical factor is an assassination took place on American soil, indicating a plot has Prince Omar's name on it. It could also extend to his family. The prince has questioned our security methods and indicated a possible leak to the media about his arrival. Due to the serious ramifications of this issue going unresolved, I felt it was in the best interest of national security to bring in the CIA. We can't lose Saudi Arabia as an ally."

Kord raised a brow. "I still question whether a task force is necessary."

Now she understood—Kord had a personal stake and wanted to handle the mission himself. Did he have a case of guilt in the bodyguard's death? Later she'd offer condolences. Right now it would sound canned, non-caring.

"The decision's been made," SAC Thomas said. "I requested an operative to work with you on this assignment. However, if you feel you cannot remain unbiased or work with the CIA, then I will replace you. We have a powder keg here, and a lit match just waiting to fall." His silence punctuated the seriousness of the earlier tragedy.

Kord bored his gaze into his boss's face. "My

allegiance has always been to the FBI and the United States. No one knows better than I do that the US is being held partially responsible."

Monica studied him. How did his priorities fit into his friendship with the prince?

"You've stated Prince Omar is like a brother," SAC Thomas said. "I'm concerned about your loyalty to him versus the United States. What if you learn info that's contrary to the FBI mission and the good of the American people?"

"I resent the implications. But for the record, I'd report the findings to you immediately."

"Thank you." SAC Thomas turned to Jeff. "What would you like to add?"

Jeff paced the small room. He looked like a scruffy-faced kid, but he had a mind like a roomful of computers. "Forming a protection task force is the best course of action to keep the prince and his guests safe while maintaining diplomatic relationships between the US and Saudi Arabia. The US needs them on our side, especially in view of the hostile forces in Iran."

"Has Prince Omar provided names for us to investigate?" she said.

Agent Davidson gave *stoic* a new line in the dictionary. "If Prince Omar had a suspect, we'd all know about it."

Monica sorted through her intel and experiences in the Middle East. "Wouldn't he want to change his plans, possibly have another male

25

family member oversee the care and well-being of his mother while the prince handles business transactions from Saudi Arabia?"

"He has a genuine concern for his mother," Kord said. "And a desire for his country to grow economically. He's chosen a face-to-face with oil and gas executives."

"That's commendable. But what about the danger to himself and all those in his company?"

"I've talked to the prince at great length about the danger of his staying. He claims running back home only postpones the reasons for his trip. And it doesn't solve Zain's murder. If you think about it, that's why you're here: to help oversee his protection."

If Agent Davidson's words were intended to sting, he'd better brush up on his tactics. She held back a retort. Did he want to discuss the implications of losing Saudi Arabia as an ally?

Monica wished she had the agent's résumé and could speak to his expertise. "How long has the trip been public?"

"Two and a half months," Agent Davidson said.

"Time to put an assassination attempt into action. Just as Prince Omar flew to the US, so can his enemies. We know it was a security leak from somewhere, whether the plot is based here or abroad."

"Operative Alden, you're not as close to the situation as I am."

3

MONICA HAD ANGERED AGENT DAVIDSON with her perspective. Not a good idea when they would be working together. While SAC Thomas voiced a concern about Kord's relationship to the prince, Monica viewed the connection as a plus. If the two men were like brothers, then Kord had gained the prince's trust. She'd worked enough in the Middle East to understand trust held the most weight.

"Agent Davidson, it's not my intention to undermine your skills or your relationship with Prince Omar. Today has been filled with tragedy. I'm trying to compile information while looking at the current threat."

"Bringing you into a task force wastes time when the case is fresh," Davidson said.

"I'm a fast learner." She poured pleasantries into her words with the realization he had already decided her help wasn't an asset.

Jeff stepped in. "Unfortunately, the prince's agenda strays far from his mother's health. My guess is his interests also include the purchase of another race car to add to his fifty-million-dollar hobby. Or acquiring another string of hotels. Benevolence tours have never fallen into his behavior patterns in the past."

"Take another look at the man," Agent Davidson said. "I've found him honorable in his personal and professional dealings. Right now he's grieving the loss of a good friend, and so am I. While I'm positioned to help protect Prince Omar, I'd rather be working on finding who murdered Zain."

Silence hung in the air like a bomb waiting to explode. Monica waited for the varying personalities to simmer.

"We all want the same thing," SAC Thomas said. "Flying by the seat of our pants is not our preferred mode of operation. But until we have facts, all we can do is investigate and query informants. We have no idea who's behind the plot, but we're moving on it. Other agents are exploring any local leads, but you, Operative Alden and Agent Davidson, are assigned to the security detail. Kord will work as an assistant to the prince's media secretary, Malik al-Kazaz, for US communications. Operative Alden, you'll pose as Kord's assistant. You now have credentials to show you're FBI. Only Prince Omar knows your CIA status. Besides protection, you can be keeping an eye out for any internal leaks."

"I don't need a partner." Kord's words rumbled low.

Ego had roots in her new partner's attitude. She'd have felt the same way. Almost a slap in the face that he wasn't doing his job. She'd been there.

"We're all sweating this. Are you on board with Operative Alden, or do you want to be replaced?"

Second time the question had been posed to him.

Kord swung to Monica as though he were sizing up her potential as his partner.

"What's it going to be? I haven't time to waste."

"I'm in."

Jeff faced the table. "You two can get started here. No time to waste. Kord, your car is parked two blocks south, and you will use it to transport Monica to the Saud family estate in River Oaks. Everything you need will be brought to you. Monica, your vehicle has been removed."

SAC Thomas handed her a copy of Prince Omar's itinerary. His agent must already have one. "You've been given access to a secure site for all communications. I don't care if the prince is heading to the bathroom, we want to know what he's doing. Operative Alden, Prince Omar's sisters may have info, and they'd be hesitant to talk to a man. Kord has Middle Eastern experience working undercover and has knowledge of the language, culture, and familiarity with the Saud family. Use it. Kord, your partner has completed two missions in Iran and one in Iraq. She speaks Farsi, Arabic, and

Swahili. She has a photographic memory, reads lips, is a bomb expert, and is superior in pulling info from unsuspecting targets."

Jeff cleared his throat. "Nine months ago, Monica believed a terrorist planned to bomb the city's underground tunnels and was right. We'd discounted the scheme while she pursued it."

Kord raised his right index finger. "The family has state-of-the-art security equipment ensuring the premises are protected. Have we detected any weaknesses within our control?"

Jeff deferred to SAC Thomas. "You have that covered."

"It's solid," he said. "Not much we can do about preventing an attack via a drone."

SAC Thomas pulled two phones from his pocket and slid them across the table along with an ID naming Monica as FBI. "Use the FBI badges and IDs. Are there any questions before you two read the intel sent to your new secure phones? Kord, most of it is redundant."

"Will local agents be aware of a new agent bearing her name?" Kord said.

"Have it handled," SAC Thomas said.

"How long will Prince Omar's mother be here for treatments?" Monica said.

"Approximately four weeks. If she survives."

She rose from the table. "I'd like to make a phone call to secure my cover. It should take all of five minutes."

"Go ahead," Jeff said. "That has to stay intact."

Reaching inside her handbag, she pulled out her iPhone and listened to SAC Thomas talk to his agent before she left the room. "The urgency of a task force and the work ahead is your style. Behave yourself and get the job done."

"The prince will object to any American on his protective detail but me, especially a woman."

"It's not your call."

4

MONICA TAPPED HER FOOT and waited for Lori to answer her cell phone at the Coffee Gone Dark café. The time registered at 1:35, and the shop didn't close until 3 p.m. Few customers ventured in midafternoon, making the last hour easier to prepare for the following day.

"How's everything?" Lori said, a bit breathless.

"Okay, I think. Were you running?"

"Took a late delivery order and left my phone in the office. You didn't answer my question."

A heavy shot of remorse hit her. "I'm going to be out of pocket for the next few weeks, maybe a month. I'm so sorry."

"Forget it. Don't worry about your job. Take care of what's pressing, and I'll get my niece to fill in until you're back."

"Are you sure?" Monica enjoyed working at the café, although she could be whisked away at any given moment.

"We're sister-friends, aren't we? Just call me when you can."

"You're the best." Soon enough she'd have to quit her job and move on to wherever the CIA sent her.

"What can I do to help? I understand family and personal issues, and I'm praying, but what else?"

She'd have an ulcer soon. "I wish I could talk more. Just impossible."

"No worries. You've had to take off before, and it always works out."

"Lori, a shipment of coffee beans is coming in. I'm sticking you with roasting them."

"Who showed you how to use the roaster?" Lori laughed rather musically, and Monica bathed in the temporary relief. "When you're ready, I'd like to hear what's going on with your family."

"No big thing." Monica's family had no clue how she occupied her time.

"My worry is the sacrifices you're making. I hope your family appreciates you. Anyway, I'd like to think you're on your way to Costa Rica. Some gorgeous Latin guy is waiting to sweep you off your feet."

Monica sighed. The CIA was her family, and there was no gorgeous hunk in her path. "How did you guess?" Her five minutes were nearly up. "I have to run. Are we okay? I mean, I'm saddling you with all this extra work."

"You deal with your problem. Prayers headed your way."

Regret swept through Monica for hiding her career from Lori, the dear friend who sat beside her in church, where they sang praises and prayed together.

Pushing her cover life to the side, she needed to focus on the new assignment and process a ton of data. Add to the mix a partner who'd voiced his opinion about the two of them being a lousy fit. This had disaster written all over it. Working alone was her preference. Taking on a partner complicated her trust issues, but she'd give it her best.

She dropped her phone inside her bag and stepped into the kitchen. There she eased onto the chair beside Agent Davidson.

The idea of Jeff entrusting her to a task force meant he had more confidence in her than she had in herself.

Jeff caught her eye contact. "You and Kord have notes to compare. We all do. Talk through the police and FBI reports sent to your phones while SAC Thomas and I continue our discussion in the sitting room. In five minutes, you two are to head out to investigate this morning's crime scene. FBI and HPD are on it, but we want your perspective. Initial reporting confirms a sniper fired from the roof of Paramount High School."

"Did anyone get my change of clothes from the trunk before taking my car?" she said.

"No. I'll get what you need later."

She'd deal with it. "Yes, sir."

The two men left the room. She took account of the time. Davidson sat at the table poring over his phone.

"What can you tell me about Prince Omar?" she said. "I've heard the media claims of his extravagance, appreciation of beautiful women and fast cars. But who is the real man, the one you call friend?"

His gaze swung her way, not as harsh yet still chilly. "He's a strong and powerful man. Outstanding speaker. Successful businessman. Excellent father. Media claims miss the mark of the real man. And he loves his country and mother."

In which order? But she'd hold her tongue. All good stuff, except Kord had a bit of prejudice in his eval.

He pointed to her secure phone on the table, and she picked it up. "The last several hours are documented. With your memory, shouldn't take long for you to answer your own questions."

She slid him a sideways observation before navigating her phone. "Special Agent Davidson, do I hear sarcasm?"

He sighed and leaned back in the chair. "Call me Kord. And nothing personal against you, but this won't work for Prince Omar's protective detail."

"Because I'm a woman. I get it. Experienced it all in the Middle East." She returned her attention to reading about Princess Gharam. His mother had not responded to typical treatments. Neither was she a candidate for a stem cell transplant. Sadly enough, she didn't have the rank of the favorite wife. In fact there were rumors of a divorce. Poor woman. Monica hoped to befriend her. Knowing the prince cared for her raised his status from the tabloids.

"We need hours to analyze intel and process Middle East chatter, and we don't have it," she said.

"Can you only work with precise organization?"

"No. But it helps." The report about Kord fascinated her. "You've worked a few impressive missions in Prince Omar's part of the world."

"I gain a lot of satisfaction from what I do. And I'm at my best working solo." Not a single involuntary muscle twitch.

"So you've said. For the record, I'm not a partner kind of operative either." She noted his black hair held a slight wave. Unlike her, his looks gave him the ability to pass for one of the prince's team. "I learned a long time ago that life often tosses rancid garbage. Deal with what's presented."

His face reddened. "Ralph spoke of your missions in Iran and Iraq. What's your experience with Saudi culture? Haven't had time to read it yet."

"I can handle myself."

"You'd better if you want to stay alive."

For over a year, she'd served coffee to customers while monitoring and recording conversations. When he read her résumé, he'd see her background. His objections should dissipate with her experience. "The real question is who's behind the attempt on the prince's life today."

"Rhetorical, don't you think?"

She read on. A description of Prince Omar's private jet played into his reputation for being extravagant: a Boeing 747-400, $500 million. She couldn't imagine such luxury, a flying five-star hotel.

Did she really have the confidence for this assignment? Never mind. If she wanted to raise her status and prove her value to the CIA, then she had to give 200 percent. But how quickly could she grasp the unique skills to help keep the prince and his family alive?

God, while I'm giving the impression of knowing how to handle Prince Omar's security with my confidence at zero, I need You desperately. Poke my heart when I'm about to mess up. And please pick up the pieces when I fall.

5

KORD WHIPPED HIS CHARGER into the parking lot of the retail shopping strip housing Frozen Rock and parked next to an HPD barricade. Officers covered the area, lights flashing. A TV van with a camera crew and reporter were live on the scene. Monica appeared to take in every detail of the gathered crowd and investigators, her face a mass of concentration.

He fought the frustration inching up his spine about the ludicrous situation between the CIA and the FBI. Did they believe Zain's death was his fault? And it was Kord who'd not stopped Zain's killer? Were his thoughts his own insecurity about not following his instincts this morning and avoiding Zain's death?

Kord had the ability to protect Prince Omar and didn't need anyone to help him. The prince would not be pleased with the arrangement. His—

Kord halted his thoughts midstream. Why waste brain cells? Prince Omar would ignore Monica and rely on him. She might have impressive skills, but she was still a woman, and the Saudis lived in a gender-segregated culture.

Under normal circumstances, he'd be attracted to the little woman beside him with the long blonde hair. Blue eyes. Super hot. Super smart or she'd not be in her position. But the situation was super irritating.

"The elephant between us refuses to eat my peanuts," she said with her attention on the phone.

"The elephant is a Saudi prince who has a distinct opinion about a woman's role."

"He's in the US. Our turf. Our terms."

"Can't change his beliefs because he has a temporary address."

"Look. I'm aware of Middle Eastern culture. For the record, I've used it to my advantage. Makes me wonder who has the biggest problem with it, you or Prince Omar?"

"A man would have his respect."

"And yours?"

"I'm not sexist."

"Are you sure?" She dropped her phone into her bag. "Both of you will have to get over it. I have the assignment, and I intend to work it."

He scratched the back of his neck. "You have no idea how hard this will be."

"I'll manage."

He sensed her eyes drilling a hole into him. "Are you planning my demise?"

"No. We have our differences, but I'm thinking about the day. I'm sorry your friend Zain was killed."

"Thanks." Later he'd manage his grief. He'd been assigned to Prince Omar before Zain was

39

killed, and he wanted to see the case to the end, find the killer, and protect the prince on his own terms. Not necessarily the best attitude, but he owned it. Mr. Ego himself.

Monica would learn in a few short hours about Prince Omar's beliefs. Kord banked on her quitting before the day was over—unless she was made of tougher stuff.

The House of Saud had a hierarchy according to each family member's status. Prince Omar's ranking fell in the middle range of importance. His life and experiences were worlds apart from Kord's, but they remained solid friends, a man whom Kord had trusted in the past. Western media depicted the prince as always in search of a good time. When Kord had been in Riyadh, he'd experienced a caring side of the prince with his immediate family and regard for those he met. He showed devotion to his two wives and seven sons.

"Kord, what's your gut take on the prince's agenda?" Monica said. "Are his plans contributing to what happened?"

"It's more about which one of our joint enemies pulled the trigger today."

"Should I ask who despises us and the Saudis this week?"

"Who doesn't?"

"Right. What else are you thinking?" she said.

"What do you mean?"

"I sense there's more."

"Are you a mind reader? That isn't on your bio."

"Intuitive. So, partner, what's spinning in your head?"

She had a quirk or two. "If I were in Saudi Arabia, I'd be following up different leads. Prince Omar's designs to negotiate with American oil and gas companies to lease oil reserves is a shrewd business move. Oil demands are declining, and better to conduct the business now than when the country has little choice."

"How are the Saudi conservatives handling the leases?" Monica said.

Kord breathed in deeply. "They're furious. They believe the oil reserves are given by Allah to the Saudis and therefore for the wealth of the kingdom. A dangerous move for Prince Omar and those who support him, but if the conservatives wanted the prince dead, they'd have made the attempt there."

"The oil leases could get him killed," she said. "Or one of Saudi Arabia's spiderweb of enemies is using the controversy to eliminate him. Is he wanting the negotiations to be completed before the Offshore Technology Conference in May?"

"Most likely so. He's on the roster for this year."

"Why is Prince Omar the one escorting his mother instead of his father? Then he could tend to business while she received care." When Kord didn't respond, she dove in. "Is he using his mother's medical condition as a smoke screen?"

"He's keeping the media at bay."

"How much are they aware of his plans?"

"Viewed as rumor. Fear missed Prince Omar's DNA, and what happened today was unfortunate but not a barrier to his plans."

"Before we check out the crime scene, I want to hear the reporter," she said.

He couldn't argue the point. Actually a good one. They clipped on their FBI IDs and moved to where a solemn-faced Hispanic woman took a deep breath before speaking into the live feed.

She repeated information that Monica and Kord had been briefed on. "Police officers and the FBI are combing the area for information leading to the sniper's identity. No other details are known at this time."

Neither Monica nor Kord said a word, instead continuing to the Frozen Rock, where a team of FBI agents were investigating the crime scene. Eeriness clamped on his heart, a vise of grief and dread. Zain had taken this same path earlier today. Nothing justified the murder of a good man.

One of the agents, a man with premature gray hair, recognized him.

"Davidson, you're on this one?" the agent said.

He nodded. "Richardson, this is my partner, Monica Alden."

Richardson reached out to take her hand. "We haven't met. Keep this guy in line. He can be a maverick."

She laughed, and Kord liked the sound. "I will," she said. "Good to meet you."

Kord got back to business. "Anything additional you can tell me?"

"Clean kill. Professional hit. You already know that. We're looking for anything left behind."

"I hear the shooter was across the street on the roof of the academic building at Paramount High School."

"Take a look at this." Richardson pointed to the hole in the glass door facing the parking area.

Kord followed the trajectory from where Zain had stood to the bullet lodged lower in the opposite wall of the store, an angle indicating the sniper had been positioned several feet away and higher at the high school. He should have concluded the sniper's location this morning, but his attention had been diverted to the prince's and his entourage's safety.

"We dug a round out of this wall. It's mangled, but I'd say possibly a .300 Win Mag."

"Has security footage given us a lead?"

"The owner here gave us permission. But we found nothing. City cams might show something."

"Thanks. Call me if you find anything."

"Will do. Good to meet you, Agent Alden."

Kord walked outside with her. "Those kids were in school when the shooting took place. This could have been a bloodbath. Makes me sick thinking about it."

"My thoughts exactly," Monica said. "A student or a member of the faculty could identify the killer. Another course of danger. Has anything turned up in the interviews?"

"Nothing solid yet. The arrangements to visit here were done in Riyadh. How did the sniper know the exact time we'd be there? That's the big question."

"Not if Prince Omar has someone on his team who betrayed him."

"The prince has conducted extensive background checks on his bodyguards and staff. Impossible."

"Anyone can be bought," she said.

"Prince Omar's men are loyal. Zain died for him today."

"Really? Money talks big."

Her cynicism brought out the worst in him. "I told you this partnership wouldn't work. You know nothing about a brotherhood of loyalty."

For a fraction of a second, a flicker of anger crossed her eyes. Monica instantly reverted to her professional mode, the one they all practiced consistently. No emotion. End the crime. Do your job.

"Don't pitch your chauvinism at me. I've

been where I wouldn't want anyone to go." She crossed her arms, then dropped them at her sides. "Ninety percent of our discussions are arguing. We can verbally kill each other or try to get along. Which will it be?"

An hour at the prince's home, and she'd resign. "We could be more civil."

"Thank you," she said.

They walked to his car, where privacy was their closest companion. "I'm listening," she said.

"ISIS, al-Qaeda, and every terrorist group in between are supporting or taking responsibility for what happened." He hesitated. "Someone paid for precise results. Once we know why, then we can nail the who."

"Or the other way around." She sighed. "Think about where we'd be right now if the sniper had been successful and killed Prince Omar." She shook her head. "That was unfeeling when your friend is gone."

He peered into her blue eyes. She looked the farthest from a CIA operative, more like a J.Crew model. If he wasn't careful, she'd be in the thick of his thoughts. "Every national security agency in the country is on this—checking through data on those with known terrorist affiliations." But she knew that. "The high stakes of an operation like this point to a disaster of not only alienating Saudi but also their publicly joining some of our growing list of enemies."

"We're on the same page."

"We'll know more after we talk to investigators across the street. Later on we'll have a security meeting with the prince at the Saud home. Prince Omar could very well have a suspect in mind by then and give us a name to question and end the killings. Are you familiar with Saudi etiquette?"

"Enough to get by."

He smiled, couldn't help himself. "I was afraid of that. Follow my lead, and if in doubt—"

"Women aren't equal to men. I know my place."

"You're left-handed?"

"I'm ambidextrous. Kord, I'm familiar with how Muslims view left-handed people. I know to use my right. Your second-guessing my skills is getting old."

If Kord was to work with Monica on any level, she deserved his respect. "Just being sure."

"I'll do my best to take a crash course in appropriate manners. My first priority is Prince Omar's safety. What I don't want is to discredit the US in his eyes."

She'd learn the realities soon enough. He almost felt sorry for what was about to transpire. Not her fault. Convincing Prince Omar of her abilities meant combating hundreds of years of Muslim culture derived from a literal translation of the Quran. Impossible.

Kord noted HPD had swarmed Paramount

High School, and several officers were on the roof. He doubted the sniper had left any casings. A new school was being constructed on the east side, making it easy for someone to move about.

"Ready to check out the high school?"

"If any of the students, staff, or construction workers witnessed the shooter, they might speak up."

"We'll assure them protection," Kord said.

"Doesn't always work that way."

6

MONICA AND KORD WAITED at the busy intersection until the traffic allowed them to drive across the street to Paramount High School. Before exiting his car, she dug into her shoulder bag for her Glock, then inserted it into her back waistband. She hung binoculars around her neck and stuffed latex gloves into her jean pocket. They walked to the front entrance of the original school. Silent. At least they weren't arguing.

Two TV vans and several media representatives stayed behind HPD's barrier.

Monica's thoughts exploded with the implications of today's crime, grim, and yet if the dead man had been Prince Omar, the whole world would be in an uproar with talk of the US's lack of security. And worse. The greater good crossed her mind, and acid rose from her stomach. No one had the right to choose one man's life over another.

The sniper had needed time to plan the kill, which meant he'd learned about the prince's schedule early on—not followed the entourage from the airport. She assumed the killer had military training. Sounded to her like the prince had an enemy within his household. She could only imagine his response. He'd demand proof without a loophole and blame US security before looking at his own people.

"What are the chances the sniper got in and out of the school without someone seeing him?" Kord said.

"Kord, you and I could do it and few would know we were here."

"Unfortunately you might be right. Whoever pulled the trigger has *professional* stamped on his training. Look at the strategic planning and accuracy."

"We'll get it figured out." Zain was his friend, and she kept discounting how the impact of his death had to be weighing on him.

"I want the investigation reports now."

She hadn't decided if they could work together amicably. One minute he seemed human and the next unpredictable. She'd been accused of the same characteristics. If she'd lost a good friend today and another friend's life was in danger, she might be crabby too. Given the tragedies, she'd try to curb her tongue.

An HPD officer met them at the school entrance with a middle-aged woman who trembled as though she might fall. "I'm the principal here." She clenched her fists, and instead of reaching out to shake their hands, she fished through her purse and produced a prescription bottle. Being in charge of a high school and knowing a sniper had fired from the roof of her building might cause the most sane to consider unorthodox coping mechanisms. The woman tapped the prescription bottle into her hand—a green capsule resembling Prozac. "It's for my heart," she said.

"We're from the FBI," Kord said. "We have a few questions about the crime committed here today."

"Have you read the police report?" the principal said. "It's all there."

"Yes, ma'am. We'd like to talk privately," Kord said. "A bodyguard from the Saudi royal family was killed."

The principal's eyes widened. "I thought it was a random shot, not a murder. I should have paid better attention. Are you certain?"

"It's a confirmed hit."

The principal glanced away, then back to them. "This is devastating news. Identification, please. She looks like a reporter to me. And we can talk out here in the open."

Monica and Kord displayed their FBI IDs. She didn't mind wearing her earlier work clothes. It simply deepened her cover with the public. Luckily this wasn't her or Kord's first rodeo—respecting others' positions, responsibilities, and emotions were part of riding the wild bronc while ensuring critical situations were handled.

"Today must have tested your stress level," Monica said. "I'm sorry."

"It's been trying." The principal relaxed slightly.

"Did anyone report an unusual occurrence, see someone on campus who alarmed them?"

"I repeat. I've given my report to HPD." She blinked dramatically. "Nothing confirmed. Some of my students want to be in the middle of this, while others are afraid to step forward. That goes for teachers, staff, and workers too." She pointed to the construction of the new building. "I have no idea if they saw anything."

Monica smiled into her pale face. "We'll receive a copy of the reports and base our interviews on those. When were you aware of the shooting?"

"Police officers arrived about fifteen minutes after it was determined someone had fired from the roof."

"What happened then?"

"We went into lockdown mode for two and a half hours, even those working on the new facility. Students and faculty stayed in their respective rooms while officers searched the building. Afterward they suggested we evacuate the building. No one exited without identification, and every student and faculty member met with the same scrutiny and questioning before leaving the grounds. The procedure took an extremely long time. We barely finished before you two arrived."

"How is the roof accessed?" Kord said.

"I've already given the information to HPD."

The principal lifted her chin at the officer standing nearby. "Would you escort these two investigators?"

"Yes, ma'am. Which of the two routes do you recommend?"

"Both," Kord said before the principal opened her mouth. "Has there been a report of anyone attempting to access the area after the shooting, other than law enforcement?"

The principal and officer responded negatively.

Monica lent a gentler tone to her words—despite her growing impatience with the principal. "We'd like to see the video surveillance over the past three days, inside the building, parking lot, and construction site."

"We'll need a search warrant. A very specific one."

"It's been ordered and signed. A sniper just killed a man, and that someone is on the streets, perhaps ready to strike again."

"My students need protection."

"That's exactly what we're talking about," Kord said. "Do you want another death on your conscience related to your school?"

"We have guidelines. Until I have the signed search warrant, no one sees a thing."

"We're all fortunate the sniper didn't open fire on the students and faculty," Kord said.

"You're right." She inhaled sharply. "I doubt the footage will do much good. The building is to receive a refresh of the security system. Some of the areas are not covered."

"The roof?"

"No." She moistened her lips. "But the parking lot is adequately monitored."

Monica tamped down her irritation with this woman. "You understand the media has already splattered the story all over the country. Needless to say it's an international incident. The whole world is looking at your school and the retail strip across the street. We're all concerned about the students and faculty. So have you spoken to the school board or superintendent about closing tomorrow? I'd think it would be imperative."

The principal tensed again. "The announcement will be made shortly. Our schools must be safe for our students." She touched her heart.

More dramatics or a serious health issue? "Are you okay? Do we need to call 911?"

The woman drew in a breath. "I'm all right. Just shaken."

Maybe the woman was nearing shock, and she and Kord had pushed her too hard. "Would you like to go inside, where you can sit?"

"I'd rather finish our conversation so I can rest alone."

Monica needed to put herself in the woman's shoes and stop judging. "We simply want to make sure the killer is apprehended before another tragedy occurs."

"We all want to think our country is safe for visitors. I'm sorry for my rudeness. The nightmarish incident has me worried about all those within my responsibility. I'll show you the stairways. No need for this officer to extend his duties."

They followed the principal through the school's main entrance. She escorted them to a door labeled Roof Access and indicated the location of the other door.

"I assume the stairways to the roof are normally locked?" Kord said.

"Yes. Except they're open now with HPD's activities. Once you're atop, you'll see the stairs on the north side."

Monica opened the door and flipped on a light. She snapped pics of dirty footprints on the stairway but doubted it would lead them anywhere. The sniper had far too much intelligence to leave a trace of evidence.

With the sniper's success today, what awaited them an hour from now? Tonight? Tomorrow?

7

THE MARCH WIND BLEW with its typical fervor on the school rooftop, and gray clouds gathered like soldiers readying for an attack. Kord glanced at Monica to make sure she hadn't been tossed off. "Need help?" he said.

She shook her head. "If I can't manage a little breeze, I might as well pack up my toys and go home. I've tracked the storm heading this way, and it's a biggie. We're lightning rods up here." She laughed at the wind, and it blew her hair back.

Model perfect. She didn't take trash from anyone. Kord caught his thoughts before they ran wild.

"I want us to find evidence before the rain washes it away." She shrugged. "My optimism is showing through."

"We need it."

They greeted the officers and learned nothing had been found.

"We're not giving up, considering the international spin," an officer said.

Leaving a casing behind would have been a generous touch, but the sniper had no reason to be obliging. Kord and Monica made their way to the north side of the roof, where the sniper had waited for the right moment to pull the trigger. There, the officers left them alone to resume their own sweep.

Monica spent several moments with binoculars focused on the crime scene across the street.

"Anything?" he said.

"Maybe. I'm thinking about it." She panned the area. "Doesn't take much to pick a lock to get up here, but I've calculated the distance, and we're looking at over six hundred feet. That wouldn't take a professional, but assembling and disassembling a weapon with precision and pulling this off is another matter. If he posed as a kid, then a backpack would be a perfect cover." Her attention swung from one entrance door to the other. "Want to know the odds of us finding a trace of evidence after HPD and the FBI have spent time on this roof?"

"No. Might be depressing."

"If it's here, we'll find it."

There went her optimism again. Sorta balanced his grief and frustration. Later when they were alone, he'd ask about her past assignments, take the time to get to know her better. . . . Maybe he'd been too rash, judgmental. Maybe she could handle Saudi opposition.

"The sniper wouldn't have taken any chances of being seen," she said. "Walking across the roof or stooping to avoid detection is an amateur's method."

"So he crawled from the southern entrance, which is closer than the northern." He eyeballed an imaginary line from the shooting point to the southern door in question. Dropping to his knees, he moved along the sniper's probable path, dragging his fingers and palms over every inch and looking for whatever he could find.

Thunder rumbled from the west.

Monica pulled the pair of latex gloves from her pocket and scrutinized a few feet in every direction.

"Sealing this in your memory?" he said.

"Yep." She silently imitated him, covering twelve feet of width between them. He observed her meticulous examination. She drew her hands over the roof, hesitating in some areas and picking through debris, stones, dirt, dried bird droppings.

Thunder cracked louder.

She coughed lightly. "I found what I think is clothing fibers, possibly cotton."

He crawled her way.

"Here's a jagged piece of the roof, enough to tear clothing." She gathered up the fibers and dropped them into a plastic bag before handing them to him.

"Good one, Monica."

"Depends if my find belongs to the killer or a kid who sneaked up here with his buds or a girlfriend. DNA testing takes a while, and even so, there may not be a match in the system. Which means you pocketed a long shot. We can put a rush on it."

"It's a start."

"Two things would help me feel better—our sniper caught on camera and a witness."

"Add a third—who turned on Prince Omar?"

"I'll take that. Does he interrogate his own like others in that neck of the woods?" she said.

"Skillfully if he's angry. Dicey no matter how it pans out." He paused. "It's not one of his. I know every person he brought with him."

Lightning cut across the sky.

Thunder split his eardrum.

HPD cleared the rooftop.

"I want to finish up here," she said. "And hope our bosses won't be replacing our fried bodies with another team."

Within minutes, the clouds exploded, raindrops pelting them like tiny stones. They spent a few more minutes on the roof. The clothing fibers were all they found.

Once they descended the stairs to the ground floor, they shook off the water drenching them and walked a hallway leading to a side entrance. "The interviews won't be released until late tonight or tomorrow, and we won't be the ones conducting them," he said.

"What do you say about checking out the physical fitness building behind us?"

"Any particular reason?"

"A hunch. Saw cars parked beside the building when we arrived."

The closer they walked, the more the sound of voices and the rhythmic pounding of a ball captured his attention. "Why are kids in the gym if the school was evacuated?"

"Good question."

They walked to the gym door, and he opened it for her to enter. The scent of sweating teen boys playing basketball brought back memories, the steady thump of the ball and sitting on the bench. Two coaches worked the boys on either end of the court, one layup after another.

Kord and Monica walked the sideline to one of the coaches, a man built like an outhouse. "My partner and I are investigating a shooting from the school roof. Is there a reason why the boys haven't been dismissed?"

"We have permission from HPD. This area has been cleared." The coach never took his eyes off the players. "We have play-offs and gotta have the practice if we're going to walk away with a trophy."

If Kord hadn't needed info, he'd have questioned the coach's priorities. The players' parents would handle his stupidity of putting their kids in potential danger. "Mind if we talk to the boys?"

"We're almost finished. Fifteen more minutes."

Great. School pride wins.

Monica strutted her wet stuff onto the gym floor. She waved her hands. "Hey, guys, can I have your attention for a few minutes?"

Every boy and two coaches were glued to the petite blonde. Admiration rose for his partner. Not that he doubted her abilities—she was quickly earning his respect.

"Y'all are aware a hit man found a way to the roof of your school and murdered a man across the street. Did any of you see anything? A stranger on the grounds carrying the means to assemble a rifle?"

"Listen up," a second coach said. "This is important. Police officers asked us the same things, and none of us came forward. Think about this morning. Now's the time to speak up."

The boys shook their heads. One continued to bounce a ball.

"Have you talked to the janitors?" the second coach said to Monica.

"We will. Wanted to check with your players first."

A leggy boy stepped forward. "I might have information for you. I had an orthodontist appointment this morning and got to school late. I saw a man carrying a toolbox. Not walking toward the construction site. He asked me how to find the janitors' office. Probably nothin'."

"Can you describe him?" Kord said.

"Jeans, baseball cap, button-down shirt. Maybe five foot seven."

"Race?"

The kid hesitated. "Kinda Hispanic, but not black. Slight accent."

"What kind?" Kord said.

He shrugged.

Middle Eastern? He didn't want to put words into the boy's mouth.

Monica spoke up. "Were his jeans torn?"

"I don't know," the boy said.

Kord recalled the fibers in his pocket. "How old was he?"

"My dad's age maybe. Or yours."

Kord had officially climbed over the hill. "Can you describe the toolbox?"

The kid did an assessment with his hands, approximately two feet long. "Black. Metal."

Kord made his way to the boy and shook his hand. "Thanks. We appreciate it." He nodded at Monica. "Other than determining where the sniper entered the school, do you have any more questions?"

"Just one more." She waved at the group of players and coaches and reverted her attention to the boy. "Which way did he go?"

The boy dragged his tongue across his lips. "Outside and down the hall to the left."

Kord and Monica followed the boy's directions and entered the office. An older man sat at a desk filling out some kind of paperwork. Kord explained why they were there. "We know you've been asked the same questions, but repetition often sparks our memories."

"Sure. I don't mind. I came back on my own after the kids and teachers were evacuated. Police said it was okay for us to use this building. Work goes on. Didn't see nary a thing."

"We're interested in a man dressed in jeans and carrying a toolbox," Kord said.

The man tightened his brow. "Didn't see any strangers."

"Are all of your fellow workers accounted for?"

"All but Chip. He must have gone home." He paused. "I know he missed an interview from HPD, and an officer requested his number."

"Can you call him?" Kord said.

"Sure." The man pressed in a number on his cell phone. After several long moments, the man offered Kord eye contact. "Chip, would you give me a call? You left without signing out." He laid his phone on the desk. "He must be busy."

"Sir—" Monica leaned in closer—"I'm sure there are areas of the school where only janitors are permitted. Can we take a look?"

"You're worried about him, aren't you? Me too. Not like Chip to disappear." He stood, his metal chair scraping across the tile floor. "I'll show you."

"We're interested in supply and storage closets too."

"The largest closet is really a room on down from my office. Got to keep chemicals and things away from the kids. Some of 'em would be snorting and making drugs if we didn't." He unclipped a ring of keys from his belt and led the way. "Are you thinking the killer could be hiding in there?"

That wasn't what Kord feared, but his mind usually took the worst chain of events.

They approached a door labeled Keep Locked at All Times. The older man handed Kord the key. But the door was unlocked. He stepped inside and flipped on a light. Monica followed behind him.

Navy knit shirts with *Paramount High School* stitched on the left front pocket hung on hangers from pegs. Industrial-size cleaning products lined metal shelving. Five-gallon buckets with an assortment of mops and wet and dry vacs looked like statues. The pungent odor of the afternoon cleaning, a mix of orange and something he couldn't identify, assaulted his nostrils. But he'd smelled much worse.

"Chip?" the older man said. "You back here, buddy?"

Kord walked deeper into the storage room.

A man lay flat on his back next to the wall, his neck slashed. Blood covered the floor near his head, and he wasn't wearing the navy shirt for janitors.

Kord touched his fingers to the side of the man's neck. No pulse.

8

THE SNIPER could have passed for Chip. Hispanic. Similar height. The dead janitor had been targeted long before today.

Kord and Monica stayed with the janitor until the medical examiner and FBI arrived to scour a crime scene—again. Monica seemed glued to the janitor's side, as though her presence comforted him.

Kord hoped the first day of Prince Omar's visit held no indication of what the remainder of the trip would entail. But he'd be a fool to believe otherwise. As a case of mistaken identity, Zain's death couldn't be the work of the Saudi conservatives. They'd have fired the kill shot on their own territory . . . unless they wanted to discredit the US. Then who? Iran despised the Saudis. So did others. What about those within the US with motive?

Twice in one day, Kord had witnessed a murder victim inside yellow crime scene tape. The sniper had killed Chip and worn his shirt while he slipped through the school to the roof. Why hadn't he grabbed one of the shirts hanging in the supply closet? Perhaps he'd already taken Chip's before discovering the others or Chip surprised him.

The killer had then assembled his weapon and pulled the trigger on Zain, shot in the line of protecting the prince.

Zain, Kord, and Monica walked with danger and understood the downside of their roles. So did anyone who put his or her life on the line for others. But the janitor had gone to work this morning with the goal of helping to keep a high school presentable, operable, and clean. At this point, only the basketball player offered any clue to the killer's appearance and the black metal toolbox in his hands.

The janitor drew a tissue from inside his desk and wiped his nose. "Chip Garza was a good man. Never late. Jokester. Good family. Never forgot any of our birthdays. We'll miss him."

"I'm sorry." Monica sighed. "That's a textbook response, when losing a friend to violence is horrible. I pray God gives you peace."

He pressed his lips together, no doubt to block the tears. " 'Preciate your kind words. My dad always said when we take a hard hit, turn to God."

She touched his arm. "Hold on to that. Do you have a church family, anyone I can call?"

"I'll get ahold of my pastor once I settle a bit. Thanks, though." He swiped beneath his eyes. "Bless you, sweet girl."

Kord hadn't taken Monica for a God person. Not what he'd originally sized her up to be.

Maybe she only said the words hurting people wanted to hear. He'd not speak to her about it unless he sensed a problem. He hadn't decided about God, an all-powerful being who created and destroyed in whatever order He desired.

How did she rationalize Zain's and Chip's senseless murders?

Monica swung her gaze around the supply closet. She excused herself and walked to a far corner, where she bent to examine a bit of dust. Although neither of them had found anything substantial, she'd doggedly persisted by retracing every inch of the closet. Kord joined her.

"The killer's skilled with a knife and a sniper rifle. He's calculating, intelligent." She peered at him as if he were going to comment. "This confirms military training, and a run through our databases with specifics could give us a range of suspects."

"The boy who gave us the lead is aiding an FBI sketch artist. My thoughts are Middle Eastern, but he could be Hispanic. Some pass for either race."

"Is today political, religious, or oil related?" she said. "Or all of them, depending on the origin?"

"That part of the world uses all three. Toss vengeance into the mix."

"We have a can of worms and no hook."

He resorted to a huff instead of sarcasm. "The

real bait is a Saudi prince with a price on his head."

By the time Kord and Monica dodged traffic in the downpour and drove back across Westheimer to the Frozen Rock, the barricade had disbanded. He phoned Prince Omar and told him they'd be there shortly. The prince still needed to admit his mother into the hospital and meet with her doctors. Kord and Monica would be part of the group driving her to MD Anderson.

Prince Omar had experienced a grand US welcome. Kord sensed determination rising above his own grief to protect those within his responsibility. Too many enemies wanted the prince and his family taken down. Until the US had those responsible in custody, the prince was walking a shaky path.

Kord pulled onto the busy street, his thoughts flying at the speed of lightning.

"Tell me about Zain," Monica said.

Frustration swirled in his gut. "I don't need a shrink."

"Right, and I'm not a hold-your-hand kinda girl. I asked a question, so suit yourself."

Maybe he was edgy. "Here's the CliffsNotes. Some years ago while in Saudi, Zain and I were on a joint forces rescue mission together. Prince Omar's second wife and his son had been kidnapped. We got them out of the terrorist camp. You get to know a man real well when facing life and death. Zain's killer is living on borrowed time."

On the way to the Saud home, Monica used the secure phone to text Jeff with a list of toiletries and clothing items for him to retrieve from the trunk of her car. She cringed at the thought of only a pair of jeans, a T-shirt, and toothpaste being there. Once she learned the attire required as Kord's assistant, she'd make additional requests.

Kord's reputation and what she'd seen in action impressed her. He'd completed several successful missions in the Middle East and escaped death against tremendous odds. The right man for her to be working with as long as he didn't have an arrogant streak. At this point, she hadn't detected one, only a bit of an ego. Now to figure out why his enemies would fear him. His skill set? Daring? His alliance with Prince Omar and his family? Or information she hadn't acquired yet?

Kord turned his Charger down a driveway that led to the iron-fenced grounds of the Saud family estate. He stopped at a sixteen-foot-high metal gate separating the rest of the world from the prince and his guests. She studied the house, or rather the mansion, unlike anything she'd ever seen. The neoclassical style in stone and stucco displayed the wealth to maintain the property. According to her report, the home was thirty-two thousand square feet and presided over three manicured acres. Seven guest suites, eight additional bedrooms, eleven full bathrooms, and five half baths. Monica could only imagine the interior design.

Kord lowered his window and pressed the button to the home's alarm system—monitored live by a private security firm around the clock.

"Kord Davidson and Monica Alden," he said. "Prince Omar is expecting us."

"Yes, sir," a man said. "Your license plate is not in our system. This will take a few moments to verify you and your passenger. Our facial recognition doesn't have either of you on file."

"Since when? We were given authorization this morning."

"New measures have been instituted. I'll do my best to expedite the matter. Each of you will need to exit the vehicle, approach the kiosk for a facial and retinal scan. Then a fingerprint check. Expect ninety-second delays while your identities are confirmed and filed into our system."

"Check your records. We've been cleared."

"How long would you like to sit outside the gate?"

He muttered a few choice words and grabbed a baseball cap from the backseat to prevent recognition from anyone spying on the home. She didn't have a thing with her to shield her identity.

Monica bit back a laugh. Obviously the man at the security company had spoken with Kord types before. "Want me to go first in case you open fire on the monitor?" she said.

"I'll restrain myself." He planted the hat on his head and exited the car.

While Monica waited for her check, she took in the exterior of the grounds and the street for signs of potential problems. Although law enforcement patrolled the area and kept constant surveillance, small inconsistencies could mean unwanted casualties. The neighborhood boasted of quiet affluence. Those who held the highest ranking were of old money, certain to frown on international visitors invading their empires. Massive oaks hid what residents wanted disguised and showcased what they wanted others to believe.

Hovering gray clouds indicated more rain. Flash flood warnings affected the low areas of the city, making some streets, roads, and underpasses impassable. Her T-shirt offered little warmth since it had been soaked while on the roof of the high school and clung damp to her skin.

Kord gestured for her to take her turn at the security camera. She left the car, and he joined her on the left side, blocking her from the street view.

"Oh, to have changed clothes before Prince Omar arrived."

"Nothing we can do about how you look."

She took a cursory look at herself and cringed. Her stained brown T-shirt and tattered jeans made her look like a reject from the cleaning crew. With what she'd been briefed about Prince Omar and his extravagance, he'd regard her with less than an ounce of respect or brains. But regrets never solved anything, and she'd been given this assignment because of her experience and abilities. What did Kord or the prince expect when she'd been pulled from an undercover job?

When she passed the security procedures, the gate opened. His frown annoyed her.

"What's wrong?" she said.

"We'll talk later. A word of advice—don't expect a welcome committee."

"I'm CIA and I've faced these people before. Play your intimidation games somewhere else."

He chuckled. Who was this man?

9

IN THE CIRCULAR DRIVEWAY of the Saud family home, Monica exited Kord's Charger, a new model and spotless. A great ride. But his car would have been better suited in the rear service area. Prince Omar had probably offered a more luxurious vehicle, but that could have been interpreted as a bribe, a career breaker for law enforcement.

She couldn't imagine living in a home this huge. A perfectly groomed landscape in tiered layers of green looked as though an artist had used a brush to paint the scenery. A marble fountain caught her attention, and she allowed the aesthetic experience to momentarily dispel her misgivings about her ability to work the case. She and Kord needed answers and an arrest. After that, protection detail should be less stressful. Maybe.

And Kord's attitude would not dampen her mood or run her off. He didn't want a woman working the task force? Get over it.

He joined her. "I'm a jerk," he said. "You're good at what you do. How did you pass for a local in the Middle East?"

"Wig, contacts, makeup."

He gave a thumbs-up.

"We could be a daunting team."

"Daunting?" A slight grin met her. She'd take a human response. They walked to the heavy wood-and-glass double doors of the home's front entrance. "Ready to meet Prince Omar?"

"By all means." Her thoughts dwelled on her gender being a massive communication barrier. The prince was highly traveled and well versed in Western practices. Perhaps being a woman was a moot point.

Get a grip, Monica. You know the odds against you are stacked higher than Mount Rushmore.

Two bodyguards stood by the entrance and greeted Kord. From the report and photos sent to her phone earlier, the taller man was Karim and the squarer man must be Fares.

Kord touched a speaker button, and a man from inside responded with an Arabic accent. "Saw you pull up."

"Figured so. Is Prince Omar available?"

"He is. Making arrangements for Zain. Guess I should let you in."

Kord shook his head. "Probably a good idea. Ali, FBI Agent Monica Alden is with me."

Women's roles varied in Muslim countries. Some women dressed modestly and colorfully with a scarf to hide their hair, while others were covered from head to toe in black and possibly revealed only their eyes. Saudi Arabia fell in the cover-everything mix. If she'd been given advance notice, she'd not be risking embarrassing the US in front of Saudi royalty. She craved a shower, clean clothes, a toothbrush, and clothing that met Saudi approval.

She'd follow Kord's lead.

The door opened to a broad-shouldered man dressed in a suit that cost more than her car.

Kord introduced her to Ali Dukali, one of Prince Omar's bodyguards. He had the blackest mustache she'd ever seen. The man nodded without eye contact, exactly what she expected. His attention focused on Kord, and it was her partner who was invited inside. She must be along for the ride.

The invisible women of the Middle East.

At first glance, she believed this world had landed in Houston from a royal palace. She positioned herself a half step behind her partner in a two-story foyer fit for a king. Her assessment wasn't that far off. A six-foot-wide crystal chandelier cascaded from the second floor like a waterfall. Cream-and-black marble floors and a winding, intricately etched metal staircase added to the opulence. Wealth was no shield to crime—quite the opposite, and many times the motivation.

Prince Omar and three more bodyguards descended the steps, reminding her of a scene from *Arabian Nights*. She'd only seen photos of the prince, but reality was impressive—huge

75

nearly black eyes, smooth nose, and a short beard with neatly trimmed sides. He and the others were clothed in Western attire.

The three bodyguards were easily recognizable from their photos. Inman had a deep scar below his left eye that disappeared into his beard. Saad was a younger brother of Karim, tall and slender. Wasi's eyebrows seemed knit in a permanent frown.

Kord strode to Prince Omar and kissed him once on the right cheek and twice on the left. "Amir Omar, *as salaam alaikum.*" Kord took his hand.

Monica interpreted the words: "Prince Omar, may peace be with you." This was the proper way for Kord to greet the prince. But she'd refrain.

"*Wa'alaikum salaam,*" the prince said. "Thank you for all you've done today on my behalf. I'm glad you're with me during this time of grief."

"It was an honor to call Zain a friend. Memories of him will live with me always."

"Allah will bless him for his sacrifice. Consul General Nasser al-Fakeeh is making arrangements for his body to be flown home for the funeral."

Kord pressed his lips together before speaking. "Please give my condolences to his family."

"I will. My family and staff landed this morning with hope, and now we mourn the loss of an honorable man. The day has been a burden of

76

confusion and questions. You, Zain, and I thought our time together would involve business, my mother's medical care, and sharing good times."

"Yes, Amir. I feel the same. How is Princess Gharam?"

"Weak. Emotional. She loved Zain as one of her own and blames herself for his death. She believes her need for medical care brought us to Houston."

Monica observed the conversation. The prince's mother must not be aware of her son's business affairs. No wonder she blamed herself for the death.

The prince continued. "My sisters are comforting her. I will escort her to MD Anderson as soon as a motorcycle escort arrives, arranged by your police department."

Monica had seen the text confirming the motorcade.

"Prince Omar—" Kord gestured to her—"I'd like to introduce a skilled FBI agent, Monica Alden. She is my assistant, supporting my role." He turned to her. "His Royal Highness, Prince Omar bin Talal."

Before she could speak, Prince Omar gave her a cursory glance, a momentary flash of disapproval, and immediately back to Kord. "All good men require an assistant. I'm sure she will be an asset to your work. Interesting that she makes coffee too."

Monica inwardly cringed. The prince's treatment wasn't a surprise—she'd been treated as poorly in Iran and Iraq. No mention of putting her life on the line for him. He simply snubbed her and reduced her status to serving coffee.

She was better than a rude greeting. This was her life's calling, keeping others safe, not nursing ruffled feelings. Determination to prove herself sped.

What else happened those years ago with Prince Omar, Zain, and Kord? She'd known nothing about the incident until Kord gave a brief overview. Could there be a link to the problems today? Who were the players then?

How could she do her job without needed intel and a dose of courtesy?

"Kord, I'll have Ali show your assistant to the front sitting area until the escort arrives," Prince Omar said. "Until then, perhaps we can talk about today."

Monica trailed after Ali . . . like an obedient dog. One look at the sitting room's extravagance made her uneasy. The royal-blue tufted chair didn't need the wet stains from her jeans. The Persian rug atop wooden floors held more gold thread than Fort Knox. Maybe not, but close.

Rather than sit, she faced the front grounds from behind a wall of windows and watched the motorcycle security arrive. Outside, Ali talked to Karim and Fares. She pulled her binoculars from her shoulder bag and read his lips. Later she'd ask Kord about him.

Two Mercedes limos pulled into place. According to tradition, each consecutive car lessened in luxury based on the passengers' status. Which high-dollar limo transported a possible traitor? It made no difference which vehicle Prince Omar rode in when someone he trusted might have designs to kill him.

She replaced her binoculars and processed the case. So many questions and she refused to see another dead body. Unfortunately the body count usually rose before it leveled off.

One step at a time, and most likely behind the men.

10

ON THE WAY TO MD ANDERSON, Monica rode in the second limo. Ali drove the first car with Prince Omar and Kord. Wasi was her driver, Saad rode in the front, and Princess Gharam slept on the opposite side. Monica had wanted time to chat with the woman, but it didn't happen. Her noble features matched the photo in her file, a beautiful woman with high cheekbones and large brown eyes, yet so fragile.

Monica read a briefing on hospital policy for non-US patients and the documents related to Princess Gharam. Dr. Wesley Carlson, a highly acclaimed cancer specialist, would be in charge of her treatment. The prince had preregistered his mother prior to US arrival and faxed signed documents. MD Anderson provided interpreters, if needed, to help the prince and his mother understand medical language and procedures. The hospital adhered to Muslim dietary requirements and offered a prayer room. If the prince needed restaurant recommendations, housing, the attention of Consul General al-Fakeeh, or transportation, the hospital offered resources to help make the stay easier. That had to offer a measure of comfort to the royal family in the midst of uncertainty.

Princess Gharam, a thin woman, used a wheelchair to enter the hospital. Her diagnosis was grim, but the clinical trials gave her a chance to send the disease into remission. She had a serene look about her, but when she stared ahead, her dark eyes emanated fear. While she and the prince met with hospital personnel behind closed doors of the international patients' office, Ali and Wasi stood guard outside. Monica had no plans to irritate either of them, especially Ali, who kept glancing her way.

She sat across from Kord in the waiting area, the best position to see those walking by. She observed the movement of everyone around her—doctors, nurses, staff, and visitors.

No one escaped her inspection. The killer had been successful twice, and she doubted that person had any thought of giving up. Kord appeared on alert too. Not one glimpse at his phone or an indulgence in conversation.

When the waiting area was empty, she moved to his side while keeping her focus around them. "I have a few questions," she whispered.

His gaze never wavered. "Figured you would."

"Actually, a lot of questions."

He swung his brown eyes her way for a brief second, and she caught their intensity. Definitely a distraction from her responsibilities. "My relationship with the prince? My escapades in the Middle East?"

"So you have a sense of humor."

"Light side is rare. Usually nose to the grindstone."

"In our business, that can keep us alive. Is Princess Gharam a fighter?"

"She's an exceptional woman. Courageous."

"From experience?"

"Yes."

"Good to know. Tell me about Ali."

"He and Zain are cousins. Grew up together. Why?"

"While waiting for the motorcade earlier, I read his lips when he talked to another bodyguard."

"What did he say?"

" 'This is over when I say it's over.' "

No signs of concern creased his features. "Could be legit, spoken in anger about the murder."

"True. Or it might be an admission of guilt."

"Impossible." Kord never looked her way. "I told you I know these men."

"I'm checking backgrounds on all of them. Are you going to ask Ali what he meant or am I?"

He glanced at Ali. "You're right. All bases need to be covered. I'll handle it now."

She hoped his friendship with Prince Omar and his men didn't sign a death warrant for all of them. But she'd been there. Knew what it was like to be betrayed by someone she trusted. "We can make this task force work," she said. "It's not my intent to be difficult—just do my job. You have the advantage in your relationship with Prince Omar."

"Are you trying to placate me?" But his words weren't harsh. "Monica, we have the weight of two agencies on our shoulders. Intel drips into our phones like water, and while we need to read it, it's not up to us to decipher every piece of info. The world is watching the US to see how the tragedy sorts out. You have your methods, and I have mine. In the meantime, we have to work together." He stood and walked to Ali.

Monica sat alone in the hospital lobby for nearly two hours while Princess Gharam was being settled into her room. Prince Omar had requested Kord to join him on the floor where his mother would be staying. A little difficult for Monica to befriend the woman when she was barred from the scene.

She had no idea what Kord said to Ali about his earlier statement. Neither did she have Ali's response because both men had their backs to her.

If not for her vigil on the elevator door and checking her phone for updates, she'd slip off to the ladies' room to wash her face and brush her teeth. Kord . . . he could have dumped acid on her outside Prince Omar's and the doctor's meeting or with her question about Ali. She respected, valued his treatment of her. Maybe they were off to a semi-good start.

Finally Prince Omar and his chosen men exited the elevators to drive back to the Saud mansion. Again she'd ride in the second limo with Wasi and Saad. Traffic had thinned with rush hour behind them.

The lights of the mansion signaled Monica's weariness. Evening shadows crept across the grounds and blanketed the beauty, like the *hijab* Princess Gharam and the other women from Saudi Arabia wore. A quick power nap sounded tempting, but it would be hours before she gave in to any semblance of sleep. Too many specifics to work out.

The limos stopped in front of the home, where Karim and Fares stood guard, and passengers left all vehicles. Jeff and SAC Thomas emerged from their cars, where they'd been awaiting the prince's arrival. New intel or a formality?

Once inside, Prince Omar requested a meeting with those involved with his security while dinner preparations were under way. Right now she'd take a BLT—well, maybe a turkey, lettuce, and tomato, since the Muslim diet refrained from pork. She hadn't eaten since half a bagel with blackberry pecan jam this morning, but she'd consumed more cups of coffee than she cared to count.

In the foyer, she waited with Kord for instructions. She scrolled through intel on her phone for updates while Kord studied his. She assumed he was catching up too.

He glanced up. "Want to talk?"

"I prefer privacy."

"The sitting room?" He gestured the way.

"Been there before."

The open windows of the sitting area ushered in darkness, and she closed the drapes while Kord snapped on a light. Once they were seated on chairs more comfortable than the mattress on her bed, she formed her words carefully with the knowledge of hidden recording devices. "How long have you known Prince Omar?"

"Over six years."

"And the man who was killed today, Zain, you've known him equally as long?"

"I have."

She added kindness to her words. "I need to get my interrogation hat on. You don't offer much info. Thanks for telling me about the danger you two experienced."

"Not the first time."

He'd reverted to his stoic mode. "Perhaps when we have a spare moment, you'll tell me more stories."

"Maybe," he said.

"I thought if we discussed what happened, something might trigger an idea about who is at the helm."

"Fire away."

She gave him a half smile for his pun. "Have you considered how the situation six years ago with Prince Omar and Zain could have influenced today?"

"I doubt the crimes are connected because the killers from back then are dead, but a formidable enemy waits for an opportunity to strike. Here are the details on what I told you before. Six years ago, I had an assignment in Saudi that involved US holdings. Bombers killed two American businessmen and kidnapped a third along with a Saudi government official. Within twenty-four hours, the two kidnapped victims were beheaded. The bodies were hung outside Riyadh. Although diplomatic relations between the two countries seemed to be worsening, the US and Saudi Arabia wanted the crimes rectified. We believed ISIS was responsible. I look Mideastern and grew up in Iraq, so the language and accent were familiar. I posed as a naturalized American citizen with a military background who was discontent with US policies. I asked questions and voiced my discontent with the US. I got inside the terrorist group."

Impressive. Kord just added another rung to her ladder of respect.

"Shortly afterward, members of ISIS kidnapped one of Prince Omar's sons and his second wife. I promised Prince Omar I'd return his family. Zain and I worked to free them. We were chased into a cave in the middle of the desert and managed to hide there."

He spoke as though giving directions to the nearest McDonald's. "We needed water. I knew of a well near the camp. Took the risk, not knowing Zain had followed me. Got myself caught by two men. They were ready to behead me when Zain arrived and ended their plans. We slipped back to the cave with water and a little food until the Saudis rescued us and killed the terrorists. Zain and I remained fast friends, and Prince Omar and I have kept in contact ever since. He's as close as a brother."

Did the CIA or FBI have reservations about Kord's alliances? "You saved a young prince and his mother. You infiltrated ISIS. Are you certain the past isn't linked to the present?"

He leaned his head back on the chair. "I've thought about it. Like I said, that retaliation would have happened a long time ago. Doesn't mean I'm not burning brain cells looking for leads. Since this morning, I've mentally checked off some people and highlighted others. Right now I need a one-on-one with Prince Omar."

"When?"

"First chance I get. Sometime tonight."

"I'd like to be present, but I also know he won't be open to having a woman there. I'm counting on you to brief me." She wanted the info now, but they both did. "What did Ali say?"

"He wants revenge for Zain's murder. And he saw you at the window with binoculars."

She expected it. "Do you believe him?"

"In our business, everyone is a suspect. He's a good man."

She'd keep her thoughts to herself for now until she had Ali's background.

"Monica, there are others who despise us and the Saudis."

"An internal attempt by the Sunnis?"

"Wahhabism is the practicing form of Islam. Doesn't prevent the Sunnis from protesting."

She'd considered the same. "I've seen the list of names. If we narrow those down to Houston with possible terrorist affiliations, we have a half dozen who could be in the middle of it or have information."

"The FBI is engaging them in interviews as we speak. Terrorists' cells seldom leave a cyber or paper trail."

"Except on the deep web," she said. "ISIS has recruited those with computer skills."

"The FBI and CIA are digging into encrypted networks." Kord looked at her, but his gaze was distant.

"What are you thinking?"

"I have a call in to an informant to see if he can learn the killer's identity. He has a family and wants them safe in the US."

"I'm suspicious of a fistful of countries as well

as factions within the US," she said. "Maybe I'll learn something when I talk to the princesses. Anything there?"

"Could be."

"What about the other bodyguards and the press secretary or entourage?"

"One."

"Who—?"

Ali filled the doorway, his massive frame like a grizzly. "Prince Omar is ready to see you now. I'll escort your assistant to the women's quarters."

"Ali, I respectfully request that Prince Omar allow Miss Alden to be a part of this discussion. SAC Thomas and Jeff Carlton value her expertise."

"I'll request permission." The bodyguard disappeared.

"Thank you." She was starting to like Kord.

"I may owe you a favor before we're finished."

Ali returned in less than ten minutes. "Miss Alden is permitted."

11

MONICA FOLLOWED KORD AND ALI down a wide marble hallway hosting alcoves containing gold-etched vases and ancient swords, priceless collector items from around the world. They continued to a massive natatorium. She clamped her mouth shut to keep from gawking.

Above the Olympic-size pool with a huge fountain were rooms with ornate metal balconies, possibly guest suites. Who had three crystal chandeliers overlooking a swimming pool? Four tiers of candle-like lighting were a bit more than she was accustomed to.

Around the pool were seating areas situated for privacy, reminding her of a five-star hotel. Maybe six. To her right, SAC Thomas and Jeff were talking with two bodyguards. She should be aware of their conversation. This boys-only club needed to end. For that matter, she hadn't seen the princesses. No surprise. Been caught in the middle of cultural differences more than once.

A long, glass-topped table had been set with bowls of fresh fruit, dried dates, and nuts. Two Saudi men in traditional white brought trays of coffee and cups, the nutty aroma of the brew tugging at her senses. Food and drink would energize her mind and body.

Prince Omar took his place at the head of the table with Ali on his right and Malik al-Kazaz, his press secretary, on the left. Kord managed a coveted spot beside Ali. On the remainder of the right were Jeff, Inman, and Saad. On the left beside Malik sat Wasi, SAC Thomas, Karim, and Fares, which meant the front door was armed with technology and not physical men. Monica squeezed into a chair on the far left. That was fine—allowed her to observe every man present, specifically the Saudis. Her gut told her one of them despised Prince Omar and helped plot his assassination. All trails led to a hole in the prince's security. She'd be observing all of them until she figured out which one was in the same bull pen with a killer.

Ali clenched his jaw. His stiffened body indicated bitterness, anger, or possibly something else.

Inman's scar had her attention. How had he gotten it?

Saad appeared too young to be a bodyguard. But looks could be deceiving. A pretty-boy type who could be deadly? He'd been with the prince's bodyguards less than a year.

Malik al-Kazaz focused on the prince. The press secretary knew every detail of the prince's life, a man whose background was squeaky clean.

Wasi had yet to show any pleasantries. His background indicated a quick temper.

Karim kept his attention fixed on the entrance into the natatorium. According to her report, more than once he'd stopped intruders from gaining access to the prince and his family.

Fares reminded her of a bulldog, and she sensed he didn't appreciate sitting next to her. A barrel chest bulged through his suit.

The bodyguards were trained to protect at all costs, experts in hand-to-hand combat, weaponry, body language—just as she and Kord were.

"Appetizers have been served. Then we'll exchange information," Prince Omar said. "The day's been too long."

A man poured coffee, beginning with the prince. Monica absorbed it all like a dry sponge. Her past missions in the Middle East had been in pits of poverty among those who wanted her—and everything she stood for—to die. This might not be any different.

Prince Omar turned to Kord. "My oldest son texted me and asked about you."

The relationship between the men, brought on by danger, had produced a close friendship. Unique and logical. Kord had referred to Prince Omar as a brother, so what about his own family? She'd ask when given the opportunity. Analyzing a person's behavior always began with a thorough knowledge of background and family history. She needed to trust him, but that might be impossible.

"Hard to believe he's seventeen now," Kord said.

Prince Omar chuckled. "My son would like to take you riding. He has quite an interest in the Arabians."

Kord smiled, and it was genuine. "Tell him I'd be honored. He showed much bravery back then for a boy of twelve. I'm sure his horsemanship reflects it. When this is over, I'll visit Riyadh."

"Good. You're not married, my friend. Come to my country, and you can have four wives."

Those at the table laughed, but Monica found nothing humorous in the statement. What woman in her right mind wanted to share her husband with three other women? For that matter, why would a man want to deal with four wives? No doubt the more women, the more sons. Heirs.

"Been too busy to look for a wife," Kord said.

"Ah, another reason to live in Saudi Arabia. I'll find a suitable woman for you."

"I'm picky."

"No problem. Give me your requirements."

The men finished their coffee, which was an outstanding Arabic blend, brewed strong. A few swallows and zip bolted into her veins.

While they ate, Monica again contemplated each Saudi in the entourage. She wanted to know their friends, family, siblings, immediate family members' occupations, health history, blood type, school records, grades, teachers, professors, everything.

Two cups of coffee and a small plate of dates and nuts later, her attention shifted to the prince, who announced his readiness to begin the official meeting.

"Ali, we're saddened as you are for Zain's death. Heartbreaking to lose a friend and cousin." The kindness in Prince Omar's voice touched her. Unexpected. "We all grew up together, and I grieve with you." He leaned toward Ali. "I vow vengeance."

On American soil? That hit a sore spot.

Ali lifted his chin. "Thank you, Amir. Whatever you need, consider it done."

That hit a worse spot.

"Gentlemen, we have much to discuss," the prince said. "I thought my trip here to tend to my mother's care would be uneventful. Someone alerted an assassin of my arrival, and his actions have greatly saddened us. My close friend gave his life for me. I would have suspected this in other parts of the world, but not in the United States. Who has crafted murder and why?" He stared intently at those around the table. "I accused the Americans of disclosing my affairs, while the Americans question the loyalty of my trusted men."

The Saudi men vehemently opposed the idea of a traitor among them.

SAC Thomas secured the prince's attention. "There's no point in dancing around the issues.

The world's watching, which means our allies and enemies. We all want the killer found and justice served for those involved who plotted the killings. It's no secret there are factions within both our countries who are against your policies and trip to the US. Pointing fingers doesn't solve the problem. Only unity. The US is actively pursuing any threats linked to what happened today. Our responsibility is ending the tragedies and keeping you and your companions safe while you're on US soil."

The prince folded his arms over his chest. Denial of emotions or a personality quirk? "The US was provided my goals for entering their country, and the problem erupted here." A labored breath disrupted the flow of words. "This has me baffled too. Although we are at odds on many levels, the seriousness of an assassination attempt has critical worldwide implications. Dare I remind you of terrorists infiltrating both of our countries?"

"Prince Omar," SAC Thomas said, "we're looking into a computer hack. That might explain how the information was transmitted. The name of the person or persons will take time."

"Leads? Suspects?" the prince said. "I refuse to hide like a coward."

Kord captured the prince's attention. "I may be able to offer assistance. Can we discuss my thoughts later on this evening?"

"Then we are finished until Kord and I have talked this through." He nodded at Malik. "Consul General Nasser al-Fakeeh and I will meet here in the morning, a schedule and location change due to today's attack. Please ensure our US friends are aware. Under no circumstances is the media to learn about my business meetings until I'm ready."

The secretary e-mailed the security team a list that included a trip to the hospital after the consul general's visit, then business matters at home. No mention of the oil leases.

The prince lifted his cup. "Enjoy your time together. Dinner will be served soon."

Monica studied her partner. Could he have discovered the enemy?

12

BEING INVISIBLE HAD ITS ADVANTAGES. No one spoke to Monica at dinner, not even Kord, but she'd been on the invisible front before. For Prince Omar to have shaken her hand or given her eye contact would have disavowed hundreds of years of established beliefs. Her very presence with the men this evening went against their practices. This arrangement would not happen in their homeland.

When the prince's sisters were absent from the meal, she assumed it was another boys-only-club affair. But she had no intention of cowering. Ali did little to hide his anger, but if he'd betrayed Prince Omar, he wouldn't be visibly upset with Zain's death. Unless Ali had been trained to mask his emotions and what she saw revealed careful orchestration. Possibly a dangerous man.

Monica enjoyed Middle Eastern food and recognized tabbouleh, a salad made of parsley, bulgur, tomatoes, garlic, and lemon. The hummus and pita bread were mouthwatering, along with a chicken, rice, and vegetable dish called *kapsa*.

When the meal ended, Prince Omar addressed Kord. "I'll have Ali escort Miss Alden to the women's quarters. Then we can resume our discussion."

"Good night," SAC Thomas and Jeff said to her.

She hated being left out of the loop. "Thank you for the excellent meal."

Ali stood and she followed him to a stairway off the kitchen.

"How long have you known Prince Omar?" she said.

He kept on walking. "Years."

"I want you to understand I have a job to do." She spoke to his back.

"As well as I."

Aggravated, tired, with a persistent headache, and burdened with way too much work, she entered a common sitting room of a marble-floored suite. Two Saudi women stared out over the grounds. One wore a floor-length skirt in emerald and gold, embroidered and embellished in soft layers, topped with a flowing silk blouse. Monica recognized her as Fatima, the twenty-two-year-old princess. Her seventeen-year-old sister, Yasmine, wore a red-and-white long dress that looked like a T-shirt in silk. From the shimmer and style, Monica guessed the gowns were Louis Vuitton or Chanel or . . . Didn't matter. Beyond her budget. They glanced at her and then reset their attention on the exterior. So there was a girls-only club too.

A second grand reception. After she showered, she'd approach the princesses clean and smelling better—hold on, she had nothing to wear unless Jeff had arranged an earlier delivery. Great.

She'd learned the women's quarters had three bedrooms, each with its own bath, and this central, lavishly furnished common area.

"Excuse me—which bedroom is mine?" Monica said.

The women turned to her but said nothing. She repeated her question in Arabic.

Fatima pointed to a bedroom decorated in brilliant blues and yellows, a common color scheme in the home. Monica thanked her in Arabic and excused herself.

She closed her bedroom door. The first thing that caught her eyes was a familiar small bag. Inside, she found toiletries and intimate clothing. Jeff knew what to grab, even a separate cosmetic bag with items used only in undercover work. Sorting through the clothing, she found her bullet-resistant vest, navy-blue slacks and a jacket, white blouse, and sensible shoes still with the tags. Also with tags were pale-pink pajamas in XS. Good ole Jeff. What a relief. As soon as she worked through her to-do list, she'd shower.

Some blessings came in store packages.

First on her agenda came an inspection of the room. Audio and video devices were always hidden in unusual places. She felt along the baseboards, ceilings, furniture, and light fixtures. She removed outlet covers and searched the plumbing—even the bidet. The ornate crystal chandelier above the bed caught her attention—an easy spot to hide just about anything. She pulled a chair beneath it and gingerly explored the fixture. Sure enough, a listening device set in a mass of ornate glass on one side and a camera on the other. Okay, she'd play their game. They knew she was aware of their toys.

For certain, other surveillance devices watched and recorded her every move. Until she located them, she'd be careful. With the same resolve mustered in every new case, she triggered her internal buttons to keep her eyes open, speak carefully, and text beyond a camera's sight. Nothing from this home would reveal the workings of her mind. Her search in the bathroom revealed nothing. Hopefully it offered her privacy.

Beside her bed was a royal-blue sofa. There she sat and read the background on Zain, the prince's bodyguard, driver, and friend. He'd been cleared by the US weeks ago. Her attention turned to Saudi culture, from religion to politics to food and drink. Every Middle Eastern country had its own fingerprint. Quickly she updated her previous knowledge of the country.

While some Saudis clung to the traditions of the past, Prince Omar had become more Western, especially with his views on growing his country. But from his actions, he hadn't advanced his opinion of women. How strange he supported female education. Women in Saudi Arabia had recently been given the right to vote and held about 20 percent of the political offices. Although not unlawful, deeply held religious beliefs forbade women from driving. Traditionally their bodies had to be covered in black in public, yet great strides had been made. Some advances were becoming acceptable as long as women understood they lived in a man's world.

Monica texted Jeff:

Thanks 4 dropping off my things. I need suitable clothes around the prince. Long-sleeved blouses. Dark colors. Another jacket. Scarves.

He quickly typed back. Still in meeting. Not sure ur idea is smart.

Monica had already debated the potential problem. The prince has no respect or value 4 me. When possible, I'll dress according 2 his preference. Need his confidence 2 do my job.

His response flew into her phone. Part-time hijab won't make a difference.

Handlers had a way of looking at things differently. Have 2 try. Refuse 2 have an international incident on my record.

OK. Remember ur job comes first.

I'm requesting 4 more bodyguard history. Will send in a minute. Need ASAP.

OK

She typed in questions and sent them to Jeff. A couple of things about the prince's itinerary were inconsistent. Some days were absent of hospital visits. And some hours were blocked with no explanation. Had the CIA or FBI questioned this? Or were the unaccounted hours designated for business?

She added a message to Kord. Text when u r free. I request an audience w/ Prince Omar later, and I need u 2 escort me.

Less than ten seconds passed before she was alerted to his response. OK. Just began w/ prince. Matters 4 u & I 2 discuss b4 then.

Closing her eyes, she prayed for wisdom. She must find a way to reach Prince Omar on his own turf.

A shower was in order and clean clothes. Her nose had reminded her more than once. Nothing Jeff brought would cover her head if the prince approved a meeting. Her attention settled on the closed bedroom door leading to the princesses. What did she have to lose by asking his sisters for their help? Gave her time to speak their language and start building trust.

The two women hadn't moved from the common seating area when Monica stepped in.

"I have nothing suitable to cover my head that would meet Prince Omar's approval. Can I borrow a scarf?"

"My name is Fatima. My sister's name is Yasmine. We speak English, and we can help you."

One point for Monica's side.

13

PRINCE OMAR'S PANELED OFFICE glistened with cherry hardwoods. L-shaped bookcases and cabinets lined a twenty-foot wall and around a corner. A white marble fireplace stood between the shelves of books. More gold trimmed the room than Kord would earn in a lifetime. His feet sank into a handmade cream-colored Persian rug woven with pale blue and green flowers. Instead of the prince sitting behind the elaborate desk, the two sat in companion chairs.

"Prince Omar, we've talked for twenty minutes."

"And nothing is resolved."

Memories of the past in Saudi Arabia and beating the odds in insurmountable danger were favorite topics. Prince Omar said their survival was the provision of Allah, but Kord had never been a believer in anything but himself. Not an atheist but rather an agnostic. Truth was, he'd like to find something to believe in when the world seemed so crazy. "We could keep this up until the sun rises and not grow tired of the stories. But right now we've got to figure out who's responsible for the deaths, and who wants you dead."

The prince steepled his fingers. "Our lists grow by the minute."

Kord clenched his fist. "I refuse to see you end up like Zain."

"Then where do we begin? Syria? Yemen? Iran? The oil situation that fuels power and hatred? The constant actions of ISIS? The Sunni? Those in Iraq who side with Iran? The protesters in your country?"

"What's changed?" Kord said.

"There are no fools in this game. All roads lead to Iran, and our sources are on it. Just who is carrying the smoking gun, only Allah knows. We'll hunt down all those involved and execute them."

Kord understood a nation's pride and how the prince believed his country deserved the distinction of eliminating the killer. "Are you ready to exchange names?"

"I gave those to Carlton and Thomas."

Kord believed he was holding back, but why? "You have more. When will you share what's really happening?"

"I'm waiting for a report inside Iran. If correct, then we can move forward. You stated earlier you had an idea."

"I'm also waiting on info—from a man inside Iraq. Politically connected, and I trust him implicitly. He's helped the FBI many times, but his concern is for his family. I didn't want to mention it at dinner and expose his cover. As soon as he calls, I'll relay the information."

"We could help him get out of Iraq or protect his family."

"I'll make sure he's aware of your generosity."

"Is he a friend from your upbringing there?"

"No, my work with the FBI. It's been too many years since I lived among the Iraqis to have a reliable informant from that time."

"Ah, weak men sway with the wind. Do you suspect a man here or in the Middle East?"

Kord wished he could give him a name or a group. "If I did, he'd be dead or in jail."

"Saudi eyes miss nothing."

"Do you trust every man in this house?"

He pressed his lips and nodded. "It makes this conversation difficult. But someone leaked information about my arrival."

"Do any of your men side with the conservatives?"

"No. That bunch is in Riyadh."

Kord took a sip of coffee. "Amir, I see your schedule is blocked for personal time."

"I need to ensure my mother's care and possible surgery can be done with my presence. Business meetings will occur then too."

Kord knew the prince far too well, and idleness wasn't in his vocabulary. "When is the first meeting with oil and gas executives?"

"Tomorrow afternoon with Shell. Also talking to Exxon the end of the week."

"Who's aware of the meetings?"

"Malik and Ali."

Monica had jarred loose his investigative skills. Unless a hacker had been successful in obtaining Prince Omar's schedule, a traitor roamed the house. "You'll keep me posted on all developments?"

"You are my ambassador to the Americans." He smiled. "Tomorrow is a busy day and we need our rest."

"Before we head to bed, may I ask two favors?"

"Of course."

"Trust me. I will do all within my power to keep you and your family protected."

"I have no doubt."

"The second is Miss Alden would like a word with you. I'll accompany her."

"Can't you relay her thoughts?"

He wanted to laugh. "Possibly, if she'd shared them with me."

"For you, my friend. A few minutes by the pool where we met earlier."

Kord thanked him and texted Monica to meet him in the foyer.

At the foot of the massive staircase, Kord breathed in admiration for the operative who'd chosen her job over defying culture. She wore a black scarf around her head, covering any semblance of blonde hair. If not for her ocean-blue eyes and pale face, he wouldn't have recognized her.

He liked her. Strange for him to come to a conclusion so quickly.

"Wasn't expecting a transformation," he said. "But your reputation states an identity change at a moment's notice."

"This is the only way I know to get Prince Omar's attention. It's not the Saudi black from head to toe, but hopefully he'll see this as a positive step."

Her dilemma touched him, a pleasant surprise. "Monica, your skills are indispensable."

She blinked.

Where did this about-face reaction come from? He'd been less than cordial when they first met. How strange in the course of the day, he'd learned to appreciate her skills.

"Thanks for requesting I be a part of the dinner meeting tonight."

"You needed to hear the conversation."

"What did you want to discuss before talking to Prince Omar?"

"Basically he believes Iran is behind the murders. Until he reveals what he isn't ready to share, we keep investigating. He'll tell me more after he hears from his sources." He shrugged. "I'm waiting on my informant inside Iraq."

"Has the prince shared how he plans to avoid the media while negotiating oil leases?"

"Managing his mother's care."

"That's a change in his habits when his visits in the past have been more . . . colorful."

"Depends if you know him or listen to media hype."

"Kord, are you friends with any of the other bodyguards who might have insight? Someone we've missed?"

He could use Monica's help with his problem. "Not a man. The prince's sister, Fatima."

"What kind of a relationship?" She eyed him with a twist of her head.

"Friendship, one established five years ago."

"Who was the male chaperone?"

He scratched the back of his neck. "Wasn't one."

"How could you speak to her without a male present? Or is the prince unaware?"

"He doesn't know. We weren't involved, but the fact we spoke privately might force me into marriage."

She bit back a grin, but he saw it. "Or get your throat cut."

"Hard to choose which could be worse."

"Sure enough, Romeo."

"Not funny."

They walked to the natatorium, where the prince awaited them with Ali. The prince shouldn't be annoyed with her dress. Although the damage had already been done.

Kord and Monica seated themselves on a

gold tufted sofa across from the prince. His old friend's eyelids looked heavy, aging him way beyond his forty-two years and cementing the need to keep the conversation short. A tray of coffee had been delivered. More caffeine would keep Kord awake when he needed rock-solid sleep, but respecting the hospitality guidelines was more important. Ali poured three cups. Kord waited until Prince Omar grasped his before he and Monica took theirs.

"Prince Omar, I appreciate your taking the time for Miss Alden to have a word with you," Kord said.

"Yes, of course. Miss Alden, what can I do for you?" As expected, he offered no eye contact.

"I appreciate this opportunity in light of today's tragedies. It's an honor to be a part of the team to protect you and your family. You were briefed about my Middle Eastern experience. I also have the ability to read lips and a photographic memory. I have a mental snapshot of every detail about today: where your bodyguards were positioned, the exterior of the Frozen Rock, and how investigators have swept the crime scenes. While on the roof of the high school, I zeroed in on the surroundings there as well. Each man or woman who passed us at the high school is in my head, those at the hospital, and the description of each man at dinner tonight." She lifted her chin, a little risky if the prince viewed her boldness as disrespectful. "I regret my first impression on you, and I don't have an excuse. In your travels, you've been to many events in which Western dress is prevalent and appropriate. I will do my best to honor your preference of a woman's appearance whenever possible. Please note, your safety is my priority. I want to assure you of my commitment to the mission and to help prevent another death."

Kord turned to the prince for his reaction.

"Did you read the lips of any who might be a suspect?" the prince said.

"Possibly. I'm researching all those, including Americans and Saudis."

"I want your conclusions."

She didn't dare implicate Ali with him standing there.

"As soon as I can verify them. I refuse to cast suspicion until I have facts."

"You carry a weapon at all times?" he said.

"Usually two."

"Now?"

"Yes, Prince Omar."

"Are you accurate?"

"My record states so."

"You're a follower of the book?"

He meant Jewish or Christian. "I'm a follower of Jesus."

"If given the time, I'd very much like to discuss your faith."

"I'd be honored."

"Do you enjoy your work at the coffee shop?"

"Yes. I like people." Monica's face showed no emotion.

"And what kind of coffee do you serve?"

She smiled. "Arabic."

"Why?"

"Smooth. Strong. Less bitter. Balanced taste."

He nodded. "Thank you for your time. Sleep well."

Kord took his cue and escorted her to the stairway.

"You made a step forward," he said. "Nothing can change his mind about women because it's in his DNA. His asking if you were packing was a positive sign."

"Interesting. He's as hard to read as some CIA operatives." She said good night without another word.

He rejoined the prince, who stared out over the pool.

"Water calms me," the prince said. "When worries stalk my waking and sleeping hours, the sound of trickling water helps me think more clearly." Prince Omar stood. "Kord, your assistant is a righteous woman. I believe she has a good heart."

Kord nodded.

"Have a restful evening, my friend. Morning always brings light to problems."

14

MONICA WOKE FOR THE THIRD time since she'd fallen asleep, a habit when in the middle of an assignment. She listened and heard nothing. Tossing off her blanket, she walked to the common area, where a dim lamp bathed the room in an amber glow. She retrieved a bottle of water from a small fridge masked as a cabinet and took a long drink. A bit of a scratchy throat bothered her, and the cool liquid felt good.

Beside the door rested a tote bag with her first name on it. Jeff's handwriting. Surely the bodyguards hadn't allowed him to leave this here? But no other women were in the house. She carried the bag into her room and pulled out a few clothing items that would help in her pursuit of acceptance—two pairs of dress slacks, one black and the other charcoal gray. Two long-sleeved blouses, one in cream and another in navy. All had Dillard's tags. He'd stuck in additional cover items from a previous job. She laid the clothes aside.

Now to see what went on while the rest of the household slept. She grabbed her binoculars and crept back to the common area. Snapping off the lamp, she tiptoed to a window facing the side grounds. The beauty soothed her soul.

Majestic. Peaceful. Unfortunately looks could be deceiving.

Two men in Saudi dress talked near a rear fountain, but their backs hid their faces. She waited about five minutes until the men walked away in opposite directions. A side view of each man indicated one was Ali, who had lost a cousin and friend in Zain. The second was the press secretary, Malik al-Kazaz.

Loyal members of Prince Omar's entourage deep in conversation in the dead of night. Or part of a conspiracy to kill him?

Monica woke at 6:00 a.m. As usual, questions fought for space in her mind, and she craved answers. None of the intel analyzed during the night had produced a solid clue.

Before rising, she praised God for His gift of life and asked for wisdom in all she attempted. Her prayer always settled on the same truth. She'd killed a man. Was her deed vengeance or duty? Guilt and shame were cruel partners.

Refusing to think about it any further, she walked to the bathroom for a shower.

Fatima and Yasmine had already prayed the *Fajr*, the predawn first prayer of the day, and would soon be in the midst of the sunrise prayer. The *Dhuhr* was the noon prayer, the *Asr* in late afternoon, the *Maghrib* at sunset, and the *Isha* in the evening. So glad she'd invested in learning about Wahhabism, so different from her own beliefs.

Glancing at the clothes, she questioned again who'd delivered them. Waking for every sound was part of her MO. She texted Jeff.

Were u inside the women's quarters?

His response flew into her phone as though he'd been waiting for her. I gave them 2 Kord.

OK

She liked the idea of Kord slipping inside the women's quarters even less. She texted him.

Thanx 4 taking the delivery from Jeff. How did u get inside?

Door unlocked. Problem?

No

Kord gloated over his ability not to wake her, and she refused to respond.

Get over your ruffled feelings, Monica. From now on she'd make sure her door was open at night.

Today began early. She must react efficiently and effectively. The prince's schedule started at eight, when the consul general arrived for an hour-long meeting. She doubted her attendance would meet the prince's approval, but Kord might hear the goings-on and relay the conversation. Perhaps the bodyguards would speak to her. Sounded good in theory.

After buttoning the blouse's high neckline, she opened the door from her bedroom to the common area. She heard Arabic conversation, and then Fatima and Yasmine greeted her. Again they were dressed in runway attire.

A large silver server held a feast. Fatima rolled it near a sofa and two chairs. The sights and aromas tempted Monica—fresh coffee, a carafe of hot water, a chest of assorted teas, dates, olives, various cheeses, and hot breads.

"Breakfast has been brought to us this morning," Fatima said. "My brother would like for you to join us."

Being a woman on this assignment left her out of the loop. Yet getting close to Prince Omar's sisters meant learning their opinions about the events besieging their family.

A few minutes into the meal, Monica turned to the sisters. "Thank you for including me. The prince's invitation to share breakfast with you is a beautiful way to start the day. The cheeses and hot breads are delicious." She poured another cup of rich coffee. She must find the source of these beans. "Prince Omar is a good brother."

Seventeen-year-old Yasmine smiled, her face bathed in youth. "Omar takes excellent care of us."

"I wish your visit to the US was not laced with tragedy."

"We're optimistic the clinical trials for our mother will be successful."

"I wish healing for Princess Gharam too,"

Monica said. "This is a trying time for all of you."

"Thank you. Fatima and I are glad to be here."

So proper. Monica turned to the older sister. "Do you have special interests or hobbies?"

"I sketch landscapes," Fatima said. "I find it relaxing."

"That's wonderful. Perhaps I can observe your techniques while you're here."

"If there's time." Fatima took a bite of warm bread.

"Yasmine, what about you?" Monica said.

The younger sister's dark eyes sparkled. Her thick hair hung below her shoulders, and her delicate features gave her an exotic look. "I play piano."

"I'd love to hear you."

Yasmine blushed. "There's a music room on this floor. Perhaps I can play for you."

"Excellent. What do you want to see and do while in Houston?"

"Shopping at the Galleria. A trip to Starbucks. I'd like to see horses, and I know the Houston Rodeo is an attraction. Once Mother makes progress, I'll ask Omar what we can do."

"You would love the rodeo. One of my favorite events is the livestock show that allows boys and girls an opportunity to earn money for their education. Some are able to display and compete with their animals. Bull and bronco riding is a thrill. Were you wanting to attend a concert?"

She nodded. "My brother would have to select one he feels is suitable."

In their culture, men protected the women. "My father gave me strict rules to live by while growing up. At the time, his demands angered me, but then I realized his guidelines were because he loved me. After I came to my senses, I listened and obeyed." Monica recalled a bit of rebellion. "Not all the time, but I did better."

"What caused you to be obedient?"

"I rode in a car with an intoxicated driver. We were in an accident, and my arm was broken. The pain and close encounter with death served as a reminder of my father's words to never ride in a car when the driver had been drinking."

"I see. Why did you decide to work with an assistant press secretary who is really FBI?"

How did she answer that? "Kord is an excellent teacher, and I'm learning much from him."

Fatima coughed. Fake. Okay, what did the older sister know? Or had Monica's nearness to Kord prompted the green monster into action? Fatima was a lovely woman, a mirror of her mother. "What would you like to do while in Houston?"

"What do you recommend?" Hostility brewed stronger in Fatima's words than the coffee.

"The options depend on your interests."

Fatima stiffened her back. "Yasmine and I are

to assist in Mother's care. Entertainment has not been discussed."

"But I've spoken to Omar, and he's planning outings for us." Yasmine's voice grew shrill. "Must you always spoil things because you're angry with our brother?"

Monica mentally highlighted the question.

Fatima rose from the elegant sofa. "Hush, Sister. Miss Alden dare not hear your immature whining. She is not one of us."

"I apologize for upsetting you," Monica said. "Can we enjoy our breakfast and each other's company?"

"I think not." Fatima whirled around and walked away. The door to her room slammed shut.

Monica questioned the anger again. "Yasmine, I'm sorry."

"No need. She's grieving a loss."

"Your mother? MD Anderson is highly successful in treating cancer."

"Another matter. She's not happy one of Omar's friends is here."

"A bodyguard?"

Yasmine sighed.

"Who? Can I help?"

Yasmine moistened her lips and reached for a date. "Are your parents in the city?"

Maybe Yasmine would open up at another time. "They live in Ohio, as well as my four brothers."

"Do you miss them?"

"Yes, but my work is here." Or wherever the CIA sent her.

Yasmine chatted on about her brother assuring her of seeing the sights of the city. No more mention of Fatima.

The animosity between siblings raised some questions, but Monica doubted she'd get answers from Fatima. Last night, the older sister displayed hospitality and a willingness to help Monica dress appropriately. What happened between then and now?

Monica kept a pleasant demeanor intact. The problem lay with Kord. He'd neglected to tell her a few things about him and Fatima.

15

KORD QUESTIONED THE SURFACE TALK between Prince Omar and Consul General al-Fakeeh. Malik typed notes on an iPad while the two men discussed diplomatic relations between the two countries. All pleasant, as though for Kord's benefit, which exasperated him. He wanted names and motive, not useless words.

"You're aware of the changes to benefit our country. All will have a positive impact on every citizen," Prince Omar said. "Education for women, less of a dependence on oil, and strengthening our military."

The consul general frowned and reached for his coffee cup. "Be careful, Amir. There are those who prefer the old ways. I've heard rumors that you intend to lease Saudi oil reserves to Americans."

"Who told you that?" the prince said.

"My sources."

"Let me just say, my enemies are many, but they won't succeed. I'll inform you of any important business decisions. I ask that you come to me with any unconfirmed statements."

World politics were unpredictable, with simmering disagreements between Saudi Arabia and those who wanted the country out of the hands of the Saud family. Kord lived with the burden of which country had designs to blow up another. Too many people had no thought of the innocent killed in the name of power and ideologies. A reason why he'd dedicated his life to protecting others from power-hungry predators.

Kord disagreed with many of the country's practices, but Prince Omar knew and respected his beliefs—not a typical response from a man who lived and breathed his culture.

"Prince Omar," Consul General al-Fakeeh said, "how can I help you with the attempts on your life?"

"Report every detail to me. Release a statement that indicates the killer has been arrested and is willing to give up all accomplices."

Not a good idea, but first Kord would listen to the prince's analysis of the situation.

"What else would you like for it to say?"

"The US and Saudi Arabia refuse to give up the name of the killer or his motive." The prince turned to Kord. "Does my plan meet with your approval?"

"Will the announcement prompt the real killer to strike again? Or will he shut down until the media reports fade to the next sensationalism, then strike again?"

"Nothing the FBI has done before or after my arrival stopped the murders."

Kord chose his words. "Prince Omar, this has the possibility of blowing up in our face. We—"

Prince Omar lifted a finger. "We all manipulate media for our benefit. If it serves a purpose, what's the difference?"

"How will your suggestion help us find those responsible when we're giving them time to regroup?"

"It buys time, my friend, and informants."

Kord's secure phone alerted him to a text—his contact from Iraq. Perfect timing. He captured Prince Omar's and the consul general's attention. "This is important. If you gentlemen will excuse me, I'd like to take the call in private."

"If it relates to Zain's death," Prince Omar said, "you can talk while we're here."

Choose your battles. "Would you do the same for me?"

The prince hesitated, then smiled. "Take the call wherever you choose. If there's one man I can trust, it's you."

Kord thanked him. The recording devices located all over the home would hear the one-sided conversation, so he walked through the foyer and onto the front grounds. He touched Nasim's number, and the man greeted him in Arabic.

"I received your text," Kord said in Nasim's native tongue.

"I have little information, my friend. The plot

123

you are seeking against Prince Omar didn't originate in Iraq or Iran. Neither do I have a leader's name or those funding the scheme. From what I've learned, Prince Omar has an enemy in his house."

"What's your source?"

"Iranian intel. Secure."

"What else was said?"

"The enemy in Prince Omar's house would destroy him."

"Keep searching. Anything you can find, no matter how minuscule."

"I give you my word. How is my father?"

"Spoke with him two days ago. He likes Seattle, but the cold and wet bother him. Says he can't get warm."

"Very good." Nasim laughed softly. "Give him my best. Tell him I look forward to the day when we are together. Tell him the children are growing."

"Every time you help me is documented for your benefit. If you fear for your family's safety, the Saudis will help as well as my contacts."

"Good. I'm pleased. I'll call you again soon."

Kord phoned SAC Thomas and relayed the information. "Sir, the new piece is possible betrayal from among the prince's trusted men. If true, it narrows our scope. But the prince won't be convinced easily. His men are like brothers."

"The situation needs to be addressed."

"I'll pull him aside as soon as possible."

"What's your take?"

"If someone in the prince's house is behind this, then a killer was hired to carry out the assassination."

"I'll look into the cartels and put out feelers for hired assassins. See what surfaces."

"Appreciate it. I'm with the prince and Consul General Nasser al-Fakeeh. Prince Omar has requested the consul general release a statement to the media about an arrest made."

"Snuff that out. This is our jurisdiction," SAC Thomas said. "The prince knows more than he claims."

"He'll share details when he's ready to."

"You're blind when it comes to him. Don't let it get you or others killed."

Kord gripped the phone. "Yes, sir." Prince Omar had placed his life in danger and those around him, and Kord was well aware of the precarious situation.

The call ended and he rejoined the prince. "Amir, may I have a word with you in private?"

The consul general and Malik stepped into the hallway. Kord relayed the conversation from Nasim but didn't give his informant's name.

"Can you trust him?" Prince Omar said.

"He's not failed me in the past."

"I'll have Malik send the information home.

Tell them to search until they have suspects to question."

"You won't release news of an arrest?" Kord said.

"Consul General al-Fakeeh agrees with you, so I'll postpone the report."

Kord doubted any of the crimes would have *closed* stamped on them today or tomorrow. The players had strategized their plot to ensure success. Those who'd committed their lives to keeping the prince and his family safe were seemingly handcuffed with no idea of the next plan of attack. "I'm waiting on security camera footage from yesterday. Once I'm able to—"

"What's the delay?"

Kord grimaced. "I know a judge signed the search warrant. I'll check again." He texted SAC Thomas. A response buzzed his phone—within the hour.

"Are we ready for the drive to MD Anderson?" Prince Omar said. "The consul general will follow us in his car to the medical center."

Kord had no idea the man planned to visit Prince Omar's mother. What else had transpired in his absence?

16

IN THE PRIVACY OF HER bedroom, Monica used her laptop to study security footage from the cameras located near Frozen Rock. Unfortunately nothing showed evidence of anyone involved at the crime scene. Kord had been the first to rush forward when Zain stumbled and fell. The camera caught the anguish on Kord's face and the way his reflexes swung into action. She paused the video and peered intently into her partner's face. A scowl etched his features. The anger that motivated him to find the killer was equal to his responsibility as an agent. A double hit for whoever was behind the attack. She had her own reasons to ensure no more victims, and hers were about redeeming her past mistakes.

She moved on to what needed to be probed— every angle of activity inside and outside Paramount High School. Although Kord and other investigators were reviewing the same footage, each had a different perspective. Teachers, students, and construction workers had been interviewed, but none had anything more to report than what they already knew. All the remarks and opinions would be tossed into a pot of ideas until something substantial surfaced.

Theoretically it all sounded good.

Techs would take hours to scrutinize each moment, but she could scan through it now for her own take. The time stamp on the school footage in the parking lot began two hours before the crime. She zoomed in on every face—a professional hit man had his plan memorized, reviewed it mentally, and put it into action. High probability the shooter worked alone on the rooftop to carry out the assassination. But he could belong to a terrorist group, and pulling the trigger was his role.

She paused the video overview and closed her eyes, putting herself into the mind of the killer. . . . He'd parked a vehicle that had easy access to the side street of the school. Exited, grabbed a toolbox, panned the area for police officers, and walked toward an entrance. On the way, he asked the teen for directions to the janitors' office. Made his way there. Met Chip inside. Lured him to the back room, probably by force. Took his shirt and keys. Murdered him. Unlocked the door leading to the rooftop. There he assembled the sniper rifle and pulled the trigger on Zain, thinking he was the prince. Monica calculated twenty to twenty-five minutes if the killer knew the precise time the prince's entourage planned to stop for ice cream. Impossible to follow the limos and position himself before Zain walked toward the shop.

Her phone alerted her to a text.

Ready 4 MD Anderson?

Monica had lost track of time. She closed her laptop and locked it in a metal case. Shoving the device into a closet, she grabbed her weapon and tucked it into her back waistband. After slinging her jacket over her shoulder, she ensured her earbud was in the pocket and hurried down the stairway.

Outside, three bodyguards stood beside Prince Omar's limo. Monica wanted to question them, examine their answers, but the prince and body-guards might not value her conversation unless they initiated it. Consul General al-Fakeeh waited with them, and he offered her a nod. Points for his side.

She rode in the rear of Prince Omar's second vehicle with Wasi and Saad, leaving Fares and Karim to protect the Saud home. The Lexus behind them transported the consul general. He'd requested to see Prince Omar's mother, and once he visited her, he'd leave for his office with Prince Omar.

Later she'd tell Kord the consul general had been most respectful, obviously well-versed in Western ways. He could be a liaison in working through the protection detail.

In the eighteen-minute drive to the hospital, she studied the vehicles around her, memorizing license plates out of habit. The vehicles reached the medical center, renowned for its advances in technology to promote healing. Perhaps the professionals here could help Prince Omar's mother.

This afternoon during the prince's downtime, she had many things to confirm with Kord, beginning with whom he or the FBI suspected of carrying out the plot to kill the prince.

As they turned onto Holcombe, she texted Kord. Would u ask Prince Omar if I can visit Princess Gharam?

Her question wasn't inappropriate as long as she filtered it through Kord. A few minutes later, he responded.

A brief mtg 2 introduce yourself as my assistant. Nothing else.

Ok. Thanks.

She is unaware of ur protection detail.

At the hospital, Monica sat outside the office door where the other men gathered with Dr. Carlson and two other physicians. She stepped into her people-watching mode. At times she wanted to say, "Stand up straight" or "Cute children" or "Great smile." Tough habit to break. She continued for thirty minutes until Kord exited.

"I'll escort you to see Princess Gharam," he said. "The prince has another meeting for a second opinion on her condition."

She joined him en route to the elevator. "Bad news?"

"The cancer has metastasized to other organs and her brain. This morning they started testing her body's ability to handle the trial drugs. Dr. Carlson recommends a double mastectomy. He doesn't sound very optimistic about her recovery. Just buying time." He sighed. "Prince Omar wants to be sure he's making the right decision."

She mulled over how the culture protected their women, made sure they were properly taken care of. "I assume he'll determine the treatment, perhaps without consulting her."

"Possibly so."

"What if she believes the surgery is necessary and he thinks otherwise?"

Kord glanced at her. "What do you think?"

"I wouldn't survive under his rein, and I do mean *r-e-i-n*."

"The truth is, if the surgery and treatments lengthen her life for one day, she wants it. Her children mean everything to her. The prince has seen her suffering, and it's a tough decision."

"When is the surgery scheduled?"

"Monday—if she gains strength."

The elevator doors opened, and they entered what looked like a hotel suite. The prince had spared no cost for his mother's stay. The furnishings and traditionally styled decor in soft shades of cream and healing shades of green caught Monica's attention and calmed her.

The princess definitely needed an environment conducive to healing.

"Before we talk to her, I need to update you," Kord said. "My informant heard there's a mole in the prince's house."

"Betrayal fits with how the sniper knew when to be in position."

"I agree."

"How did Prince Omar respond to the possibility of one of his men being a part of the assassination plot?"

"Staunchly denied his men's involvement."

"Not surprised."

Inside Princess Gharam's room, a nurse wearing a *hijab* tended her. The familiar clothing and another woman to possibly share prayer times must be comforting.

Kord approached her bed. "Princess Gharam, it's good to see you. *As salaam alaikum.*"

She returned the greeting. Exhaustion deepened the lines around her eyes.

"I'd like to introduce you to my friend, Monica Alden," he said. "She's my assistant."

The princess turned to Monica and held out her hand. Monica held it gently. "It's a pleasure to meet you."

"I apologize for sleeping yesterday in the limo."

"Not at all. You need rest."

"My son said you'd be helping Kord."

"I'm honored," Monica said. "It's a wonderful opportunity to learn from the best."

"He's been such a good friend to Omar."

"We all need friends to walk through life."

"I will remember your words."

"Princess Gharam, I'm praying for you." Healing, physically and spiritually.

"Thank you." A wisp of Fatima and Yasmine graced her smile.

Monica sensed relief the woman hadn't questioned the origin of her beliefs. So hard to choose when to announce her faith in Jesus and when to establish friendship.

"Princess Gharam," Kord said, "we can stay but a few minutes. You need your rest, and Prince Omar will be here soon. Promise me you'll do all you can for the days ahead."

"I'm fighting. I want to look happy for Omar and my daughters. It saddens them when I'm weak and in pain." She hesitated and a wave of discomfort passed over her face. "I want to hear what the treatments will be. Not knowing is a little frightening. I'd rather be prepared for what's to come."

"Overseeing your care shows Prince Omar's love." Kord spoke tenderly. "If you like, we can visit you another time."

"I'd enjoy that very much. Perhaps I'll feel better when you see me again. I miss my daughters today. Every moment is precious."

Monica kept her composure despite the sadness and ultimate reality of the woman's illness. What would she do in the same situation? She thrived on good health and despised the idea of being bedridden.

17

THE MOMENT PRINCE OMAR entered the room, Monica sensed his presence, an essence of confidence and authority. He moved to his mother's bed, and Monica and Kord stepped back with Consul General al-Fakeeh and three bodyguards. Princess Gharam's eyes glistened in pure adoration for her son, and the sight gave Monica pause to observe the power of love. Since the beginning of time, families had shared a bond that stepped beyond the boundaries of culture to a special place in their hearts.

Monica waited for Kord to act. He excused himself from the room, and she followed. Two additional bodyguards were posted outside the door, and a third stood near the elevator. Kord chose seating where they could keep an eye on anyone exiting the elevator or moving toward Princess Gharam's room.

"You put on a good show." His tone cut like a razor.

What had crawled under his skin and laid eggs? "Excuse me? A show?"

He glared at her. "Your statement about praying for Princess Gharam. Were your words supposed to put you into the inner circle? I heard you speak the God thing to the prince and the janitor. But trust me, Prince Omar's God and the janitor's aren't the same."

Was he grieving Zain's death, tired, or an atheist who'd just confirmed his new partner placed God in the center of her life? He could deal with it. "You're mad because I told a sick woman I'd pray for her. I have been and will continue to pray for her healing, not to Allah but the Judeo-Christian God. If you have a problem with my faith, that's your issue, not mine."

"Am I talking to a God-fearing Texas gal?"

"Is this a stumbling block for you?"

"Only if the God thing gets in the way of job performance."

She longed to laugh, yet how regrettable he didn't know the God who ruled the universe. "Faith just might be in your best interests considering what's happened in the last twenty-four hours."

His features tightened. "Let me get this straight. A shooter has a weapon aimed at you, and you're going to ask him to prayerfully think before pulling the trigger?"

"Take another look at my résumé." She pointed to the phone in his hand while a rush of memories punched her hard. "I can hold my own in a firefight. We had this discussion earlier. Nothing stands in the way of my job performance." She wished she believed her own words.

His scowl seemed permanent while he scrolled

through his phone. Ignoring him, she calculated how many steps from the elevator door to Princess Gharam's room and how fast she could intercept a potential shooter. Although her legs were short, she had the marathon-running gene, a trait she shared with her four brothers that was handed down from a dad who played pro ball for the Yankees.

From the corner of her eye, she saw Kord continue to read. She might have exaggerated her qualifications, but she had a few accomplishments under her belt.

"Monica."

She turned to him.

"I owe you an apology. Originally I skimmed your résumé. I've been a jerk. Again."

"No problem. I'm good. Try explaining it to God since He's the one you've offended."

He groaned.

"I'll give you a little slack. We have two murders hovering over us, and your friend Zain is one of them."

"That doesn't justify my actions."

"Right. I gave you a break." She couldn't resist a grin. "Next time is another matter."

"For the record, I'm a proponent of only sure things."

"Me too. Has the prince released his intel?"

"Still waiting. While we have a little time, let's look at the security footage. The sound of the elevator will alert us to anyone." Kord bored his attention into his phone while she did the same to hers.

She logged on to the secure site and found where she'd left off.

"Take a look at 9:35 a.m.," Kord said.

"I looked at this earlier." She found the footage. "The man rotated his body in the opposite direction whenever cameras could have captured his face. The only thing he couldn't avoid was his height." She paused the screen and studied it. "I'd say approximately five-six or -seven like the young man at Paramount High School said. The killer is scary skilled. Before it's over, I want to find out who trained him. And where."

"Right. None of the footage gives us the ability to run him through facial recognition software." He stretched his neck.

Her mind spun back to who could be behind the attempted assassination. Suspicion crept into her processing. While she'd assumed a member of the prince's entourage was responsible for the deaths, what about Americans who were upset with Prince Omar's visit? Those who thought they were doing the world a service? She'd check backgrounds on every person she could think of before she and Kord compared notes.

No more murder cases with her name on them.

18

PRINCE OMAR AND CONSUL GENERAL al-Fakeeh
exited Princess Gharam's hospital room with
their bodyguards. Kord stood and Monica joined
him. A light floral scent gave no doubt to her
femininity. Trying to figure out the woman from
her background proved more difficult than he
imagined. Her Middle East missions proved her
ability to outthink the enemy. But how did he size
up a determined operative? But her innocent face
and Jesus-freak attitude completely threw Kord
for a loop.

He could trust her to have his back. No
problem. But having her on a detail with an Arab
prince who believed it was a man's world . . .
Could Kord work effectively when he might
have to run interference between Monica and
Prince Omar? And she'd already compiled
distrust against Ali.

"She's either very good or will disrupt all we
do," Ali had said when confronted with what
she'd lip-read. "Your government shouldn't have
assigned a woman."

Kord valued loyalty. "Or her gender could be
an asset."

Now Prince Omar approached him. "Kord, the
consul general is leaving. My plan to join him at

his office has been postponed. Dr. Carlson wants to speak to Mother and me together."

"I'll escort Consul General al-Fakeeh to his driver." Kord needed to explore the two conversations he'd missed between the prince and the consul general.

The consul smiled his thanks. "A limo is waiting outside. My driver texted earlier to arrange for a replacement."

"Is he ill?" Kord said.

"A family emergency." He reached for Monica's hand . . . in front of the prince.

Monica grasped it. "It's been a pleasure to meet you. Have a good day."

Kord turned to her. "I'll keep you posted on our wire."

She reached inside her jacket and positioned the earbud before taking a stance between the elevator and Princess Gharam's room.

The elevator opened, and Kord gestured for the consul general and his two bodyguards to enter. The door closed with the protectors shielding Consul General al-Fakeeh.

"How was your time with Princess Gharam?" Kord said.

The white-haired man grimaced. "As well as can be expected. The surgery and clinical test is her last chance to lengthen her life. The prince said longevity is more important to her than quality, and her condition grieves him."

"I have no idea how I'd feel in her position. Has to be different for each person. The doctors here have worldwide distinction for their success in treating her type of cancer. I hope they can bring her and the prince promising news. Strength and optimism are a disease's enemy."

Consul General al-Fakeeh stared at the descending elevator numbers. "I understand she doesn't know about the threats to the amir, only about Zain's death. She expressed her sorrow in the loss."

"Princess Gharam is an intelligent woman. I'm sure she's aware of danger wherever the royal family travels."

He turned to Kord. "For his own safety, the amir must return home and allow another family member to oversee her care."

How well Kord knew Prince Omar's stubborn stance. "I've tried, sir. But he insists on fulfilling his responsibility."

"I gave him my most convincing speech while you were on the phone this morning."

"And?"

"He believes the attempt is for any male member of the Saud family, and he refuses to subject others to an assassin's hand. He also has business matters, but I have no idea what."

"Noble but deadly." Kord carefully worded his thoughts. "Has he mentioned a name?"

Consul General al-Fakeeh said nothing.

"I can't help the prince if I don't have a suspect."

"He hasn't mentioned anyone specifically. My plans were to persuade him to listen to reason. For now he has this appointment with Princess Gharam's doctor. He assured me we'd talk soon. But each moment that passes, I'm fearful for his safety."

"I understand."

The elevator door opened, and the consul general's phone rang. He glanced at the caller ID. "My office. I'd better take this. Kindly wait for me, as I have another matter to discuss with you."

Kord waited in the foyer while Consul General al-Fakeeh strolled about twenty feet away with his bodyguards. What was on the man's mind? Had the prince said more in Kord's absence? Moments later, he returned, his face a mass of lines.

"Are you all right?" Kord said.

"No." He shook his head. "My original driver was found dead. His replacement must be an impostor. Call the police."

"Usher the consul to hospital security," Kord said to the two bodyguards while pressing in 911. "One of you alert security. We need HPD." He hurried through the hospital entrance, quickly spotting the limo. Kord approached the driver, an olive-skinned man wearing an expensive suit that appeared tailor-made—more reason to suspect a considerable amount of money had been tossed at this plot. A beard, kaffiyeh, and sunglasses completed his appearance. Kord noted the gloves, no fingerprints.

The driver eyed him and hurriedly slid inside the limo.

Kord raced toward him. "Stop! FBI." He pulled his weapon.

The man sped east on Holcombe, tires squealing into traffic. Kord fired into the passenger-side window, making a dent in the glass. He'd banked on the limo not being bulletproof. Fat chance.

He fired several more shots. The vehicle disappeared through a red light. Horns blowing. Brakes protesting.

An HPD vehicle sped around traffic after the limo, and it too vanished.

Kord clenched his fist. Prince Omar originally intended to accompany the consul general to his office. The mole must be one of the bodyguards or house staff. Who? And why?

Monica heard multiple police sirens outside the hospital. A normal occurrence, but caution moved her to contact Kord.

She touched her earbud and brought the mic on her wrist to her mouth. "Everything okay?"

"Had a close call with Consul General al-Fakeeh. I'll be there in a few."

"What happened?"

"His replacement driver could be our sniper."

"I'll keep my wire on."

She stepped in front of the elevator. Ali was positioned outside Princess Gharam's room, stone-faced. He called her name, a first. Actually his first real acknowledgment of her existence, other than annoyance last night. Whoa, she needed to get over that.

"What's the problem?" His English held a thick accent as he strode her way.

"A confrontation involving Consul General al-Fakeeh. All I know is he's all right. Kord will be here shortly. Please inform Prince Omar to stay in his mother's room until we know more. I suggest canceling Dr. Carlson's visit for now."

He stiffened. "Prince Omar had planned to leave with the consul general."

She'd already considered that. Focusing on the elevator, she listened for the announcement of its arrival and watched for the light above it.

"Miss Alden."

She whirled to Prince Omar with Wasi and Saad behind him. She was uncomfortable he'd left his mother's room. "Yes, Prince Omar."

"What's the problem?"

"There's been an incident with Consul General al-Fakeeh. He's safe, and the police have been called."

"A shooting? What happened?"

"I don't want to give you an inaccurate report.

144

Kord will be here soon, and he'll have correct information."

"Has something happened to Kord?"

"He's all right."

The prince stood before her. She could feel his presence like before, not menacing but commanding. A jolt, a chill and a flush, swept through her. Prince Omar must be protected without question, regardless of culture or gender. She avoided eye contact. "If a hostile is on the elevator, he could open fire. I urge you to consider moving back."

Wasi took a deep breath. "Prince Omar, there is truth in Miss Alden's words."

"Very well. I wish to speak to Kord the moment he arrives." He turned abruptly and walked back to his mother's room.

Monica longed to be with Kord—in the middle of the action and adrenaline flow. Anywhere but with two burly bodyguards, Ali and Inman, suffocating her on both sides. Forcing relaxation into her body, she replayed what she'd told Kord yesterday about the killer—skilled with a knife and sniper rifle, trained to eliminate his victims with precision. He was cold-blooded, calculating, and had obviously murdered before. She'd contacted the CIA for updates in the investigation, and dozens of terrorists and questionable characters from around the world had made the list.

She trusted no one until they proved themselves. The fact Kord had a solid friendship going
with the prince and now the current infraction
gave her pause. Was he concealing information?
She wasn't paranoid, only playing all the cards.

Ali's words from yesterday, the ones said
outside the mansion, rolled across her mind:
"This is over when I say it's over."

19

MONICA NOTED EVERY FACE on Princess Gharam's hospital floor. She looked for those using their phones or having a private conversation. Instead she viewed somber men standing alone and alert. Ten minutes had passed without word from Kord. Where was her partner?

With one eye on the elevator monitor, she contacted Jeff. He answered on the first ring. "Just getting ready to call you. Can't believe our luck on this case. Someone called 911 about a dead man. HPD responded and found a man strangled in an alley. Initial ID looks like the consul general's driver. Apparently the killer replaced him with a scheme to abduct the consul general. No leads at this point."

"Thanks, Jeff. Keep me updated." She dropped her phone inside her jacket pocket. Was the killer after those of Saudi descent? Or was this another plot to assassinate Prince Omar while the two men rode to the consulate?

Ali moved her way, the one man she wanted to analyze. "What have you learned?"

"The consul general was unharmed."

"I have that information."

No harm in revealing info since the attempt was foiled. "His original driver was found dead, and the man posing as his replacement got away."

"The impostor needs his throat cut."

"We'll find him."

"And do what? Slap his hands and send him back out to kill again?"

"He'll be processed according to the law."

"We all know he's the man who killed Zain." Ali's nostrils flared. "You Americans have no regard for a dead man. One more Arab is eliminated with no thought about his family and friends."

"You're wrong. We all want these crimes to end. Have you forgotten about the poor man who was murdered at the high school?"

He shook his head. "Unfortunate. The truth is you'd much prefer Prince Omar take his mother home and rid you of our presence. Princess Gharam is dying, and the clinical trial is her last effort to put the cancer into remission."

She believed the prince's main motive for staying was business negotiations. "I'm sorry your friend is gone, and—"

Ali raised his shoulders and tightened his jaw. She righted her body for a potential fight. The elevator signaled arrival, pushing Ali and her into duty-first mode.

She reached to her back waistband and drew her weapon. When the door opened, Kord emerged with the consul general and his bodyguards.

Kord caught her attention, and she lowered her weapon. The two moved to a private corner where they could watch the door of Princess Gharam's room and the cluster of men convened around it.

Kord quickly explained what happened in front of the hospital. "What bothers me is how the prince's decision to cancel with Consul General al-Fakeeh happened at the last minute."

She mentally reviewed the press secretary, each of the four bodyguards, and the two who'd been with the consul general. "Is the mole one of the men here?" she whispered. "But if he is, he knew the prince's schedule change. So why wasn't the plan to take out the consul general's driver canceled?"

"Maybe he couldn't get to his phone in time."

"Let's talk to every man with the prince."

"Rushing into this before I talk to the prince is—"

"Are you out of your mind?" Had Kord been entrenched in this culture too long? "We need decisive measures now."

"And have a firefight?"

"So we wait until someone else is killed? Ali and I were about to tangle before you arrived."

He glanced at the man. "You still suspect him."

"He's a hothead. This must end with an arrest soon." She pointed at Princess Gharam's doorway, where Prince Omar and the consul general waited. "They want an explanation."

Kord acknowledged the prince. "I'll be right there, Amir." He peered at her. "All right. What do you propose?"

He wanted her feedback? "While you're discussing the situation with the prince and insisting one of his men has betrayed him, I'm checking on additional history, adding Consul General al-Fakeeh's two bodyguards. We need to confiscate everyone's phones now before anything is deleted. And I want surveillance on all these hired thugs."

"Not sure my walking into a hornet's nest is the best way."

"You have the clout to speak with Prince Omar and the men as one who respects their culture." She hesitated, then added, "In a normal case, wouldn't you move forward?"

He swung to the men in question. "The guilty one will not raise his hand and admit he's guilty. He'll take precautions. If any of them has a suspect, we'd know about it—and that man would be lying in a pool of blood."

"How would they handle it if the roles were reversed? Ali claims we Americans will do nothing about Zain. I intend to prove him wrong. Better you confront them than me." She offered a slight smile. "I can shoot, call Jeff, and keep an eye on any man attempting to use his phone at the same time."

"Right."

She lifted a brow at his sarcasm. But he walked toward the cluster of men.

Monica pressed in a number while watching the bodyguards. When prompted, she gave her security code and waited for Jeff to answer.

"Is this about the consul general?" Jeff said.

"Yes. Only someone close to Prince Omar could have orchestrated this."

"We suspected it. Who and what do you need?"

"The intel I already requested, extensive backgrounds on the prince's bodyguards. Add to that more about the prince. All the recent cases where he's angered another country or person. Include additional history on Princess Gharam and the younger princesses. Another background on Consul General al-Fakeeh and his bodyguards. Get our people in Saudi Arabia to dig deeper than their precious oil."

"This will take days to sort through."

"I want it ASAP."

"Haven't heard you this demanding since—"

"Jeff, you dumped me into an operation because I can do the job."

He chuckled. "And you'll get it done."

She heard sarcasm in the compliment, but she'd take it. "Two people have triggered my alarm button—the bodyguard Ali and Prince Omar's sister Fatima. Could be distinct personalities or something more."

"What does Kord say?"

"When I can trust him, I'll open up."

"You and I have had our share of differences. One thing I know is you have trust issues."

"It's part of the job. Keeps me alive."

"Kord Davidson is not Liam Fielder."

The mention of the name was like pouring alcohol on an open wound. "What does Liam have to do with my current mission?"

"Your lack of trust could get you killed. Or is that what you want? To go down in a blaze of glory?"

A chill attacked her nape. "You have no clue what you're talking about."

"You run on facts. Do I need to alert SAC Thomas about anything concerning Kord's behavior?"

"Not yet. I'm observing."

"I'm listening."

"First off, my personal thoughts and life are off-limits. Kord and I have an okay relationship at the present. And I doubt he trusts me either."

"You're on the same team. Base your evaluation on that." He ended the call.

The memories of what Liam had done, the people he'd killed, and the betrayal stung. The one area where she'd found it impossible to forgive was herself—innocent people died because of her idiocy.

Ali walked her way with long strides. His face

a road map of lined anger. "A woman has no place here with Saudi men."

"I'm working with Kord. Deal with it. I'm here. I'm good at what I do, and I don't cower to bullies."

20

KORD SPOKE TO PRINCE OMAR away from his men while Ali blocked the doorway of Princess Gharam's room. "You believe your men are loyal, but there's no other explanation for today. What happened outside the hospital confirms what my informant said—a mole is among your trusted men." His gaze drilled into the prince's dark eyes. "I refuse to watch you die. Does the killer have your mother's death planned too? What about your sisters?"

The prince jutted his chin. "How do you propose we find this mole? Offer a reward? Replace all my men?"

"Force him into the open. Loyalty is your ally. Demand we check every man's cell phone now."

The prince stared at those who'd vowed to sacrifice their lives for him. Long moments passed.

"Someone close to you has plotted your assassination. Ignoring it has deadly implications."

"You're right," the prince said barely above a whisper. "The plan is cleverly constructed, but we are smarter. I too am concerned about my mother's and sisters' safety." He turned to the men. "Each one of you is to bring his phone to me now. You are not permitted to use them until they are checked."

Kord inwardly sighed. Prince Omar either suspected one of them or wanted to prove his men's loyalty.

"Kord," the prince began, "if the killer would attempt an abduction and possibly the life of Consul General al-Fakeeh, then he'd surely find access to others. Since he's failed with me, who's next on his list?"

"Your family's the easiest target." His sisters needed to be sent home, but the prince knew the danger.

"I understand. We will talk later."

The bodyguards laid their phones on a side table near the prince and Kord.

"Have you received intel that can help?" Kord said.

"Nothing more than what I've told you. Conduct the investigation to the best of your ability. Keep me informed of every development. Nothing is too small. Details will help us find him. My friend, you have my cooperation. Find the man and stop whoever is conspiring with him."

Kord shook Prince Omar's hand. "Thank you."

"I assume your assistant is already at work?"

"Yes, for as much as she can accomplish without interviewing each man."

Prince Omar glanced her way. "You will pose the questions."

"Yes, Amir." No need to explain the procedure to Monica.

The elevator opened and two HPD officers exited—men Kord recognized. He greeted them and conducted introductions. "These officers will escort Consul General al-Fakeeh to his office."

The consul general focused on Kord. "What about my bodyguards?"

"They'll be released once their interviews are completed," Kord said.

Further background checks would happen next. Once the officers and consul general left, Monica and Kord arranged furniture in a corner for private interviews.

"All requests have been made to my handler, and you'll receive the same report," she said.

"Good."

"Am I to be submissive?"

He stared at her and tried to hide a grin. "What do you think? But use your best judgment."

"Tell me why Inman has a scar."

"He fell as a boy."

"Are you positive of his commitment?"

Kord reserved his opinion until he saw the intel on every man there.

Prince Omar walked their way. "Is it possible someone could retrieve my cell phone from my car? I remember taking a call and leaving it on the armrest."

Monica touched Kord's arm. "Ali could get it."

"Okay." Kord made his way to Ali. "Prince Omar needs his phone. Would you and Wasi mind getting it from the limo?"

As Ali left the area, Kord sensed the prince studying him. "I'd trust those two men with my sons."

"I want to have the same conviction," Kord said. "You changed your mind about accompanying Consul General al-Fakeeh after you were notified of Dr. Carlson's request for a meeting. How were you contacted?"

"When I couldn't be reached, the doctor phoned Malik."

"The decision saved your life."

Within fifteen minutes, Ali and Wasi returned with the prince's phone and handed it to the prince. Kord saw little reason to doubt Ali, not when he had an opportunity to escape if guilty.

The prince and Dr. Carlson held a private meeting in Princess Gharam's room. In the meantime, Kord questioned each man for formalities and Monica took notes. The real intel would be revealed later on today.

All seven men were seen in the presence of others.

None of the men had witnessed anything suspicious.

Each man willingly handed over his mobile phone. No texts or calls to follow up.

The men followed Wahhabism.

157

Body language raised few questions, but those who objected to questioning did so respectfully. Except Ali.

"This is an insult," Ali said. "Loyalty is earned by service, not by ridiculous interrogation." He blew out his anger. "For the prince, I will answer you."

None of his responses caused concern, but Ali remained hostile. Kord couldn't blame Ali for grieving Zain's death. Every man handled sorrow differently. As long as his method didn't involve more deaths.

When the interviews were completed, Kord and Monica discussed their vague findings beyond earshot of others. Someone who'd been trained in deceit was among them.

"The consul general wanted to discuss another matter, but we were interrupted when his office called," Kord said.

"Call him."

He pressed in the number and then Speaker. "Consul General al-Fakeeh, has a new driver been assigned to you?"

"Yes. I'm on my way to my office. Do you have a new development?"

"No, sir. We're working through interviews. You'd mentioned another topic earlier."

"Prince Omar has a reputation for being a little reckless when it comes to his safety. He likes to take matters into his own hands. I encouraged him to cooperate explicitly with the US regarding Zain's death and to take heed for another possible assassination attempt. I also asked him to refrain from public appearances. I doubt he'll take my advice."

"Thank you." Kord well understood Prince Omar's unpredictable behavior. "I'll remind him of your precautions."

"Perhaps he'd send his sisters home."

The thought had entered Kord's mind. "I'll do my best." When the call was completed, he glanced at Monica.

"What's driving you crazy?" she said.

"Prince Omar forgets his phone, and the situation may have saved his and the consul general's life, while another man is killed."

"Picking at me too. Any of his men could have more than one phone. Coincidences are not in my vocabulary."

"Wondered where you stood with the faith thing."

"I deal in facts and solid leads. My faith is how I live my life, in obedience to God. The supernatural and chance can weave together, but I'm no expert on the subject."

He expected her to quote Scripture. Maybe he needed to put aside his stereotypical view on Christians. He'd read the Bible as well as the Quran, Hindu teachings, and Buddhism. None of it made sense. Kord took a quick look around to ensure they maintained privacy. "Why did Prince Omar leave his phone behind?"

She blinked. "Unintentional? Wanted solitude to speak with his mother? A bodyguard picked his pocket?"

"Didn't want to be interrupted."

"Interrupted from what? Kord, what are you implying?"

"Not sure, but I intend to find out. If I'm spending too many brain cells with this, I'll admit it."

"Boils down to who in his entourage wants him dead." She folded her arms in front of her. "Let's discuss this later when you reach your conclusions because I have an opinion."

"Will I want to hear it?"

"Probably not."

21

AT THE SAUD HOME, Kord requested a private meeting with Prince Omar. The past two days of chaotic events had them all sifting through facts and opinions. Until they were able to narrow the list of those with motive, the protection detail took the role of defense. He'd do whatever it took to stop the killer and stand in the way of a bullet. Not a good position for Kord or the prince and his men, especially with rising tempers and suspicions.

Prince Omar gestured for him to sit in his office beside a small table that offered coffee, fruit, and dates. Kord welcomed the caffeine to fuel his mind, but he passed on the food.

"Has the man who posed as Consul General al-Fakeeh's driver been apprehended?" Prince Omar said.

"No, Amir. A limo matching the description of the one at the hospital was found a few blocks away in a parking garage. Inside were the man's clothes and a fake beard. Doubtful we find fingerprints." He pressed his lips together to avoid audible irritation. But why hide his feelings? "Consul General al-Fakeeh and I worked with an FBI sketch artist. I don't think it will push us ahead in finding the man. Only a fool would show his real face, and we came up empty with facial recognition from the hospital's security cameras."

"I've never seen you cynical."

"And you?"

"The men you interviewed are currently attending their duties, so they're cleared?"

"For the moment."

He sighed. "My mother's treatment begins tomorrow. I wanted her shielded from this, but she's a smart woman. Quite capable of putting information together."

To be suffering from cancer and know her son was in danger had to be depressing. "I'm sorry. Were you able to calm her?"

"Dr. Carlson prescribed a sedative." Prince Omar took a drink of his coffee.

"After today, don't you think it best to send your sisters home?"

"Mother would be very upset, enough to hinder her recovery."

"How would she react if they were killed?"

Prince Omar stood and paced the room. "Fatima and Yasmine are my responsibility, and—"

"They have a father."

"He's more concerned with his younger children."

"There must be someone who'd protect them until you return."

Prince Omar stopped his pacing. "No one in

whom I'd feel confident with the current turmoil. For now, they will remain with me." He made his way to his chair and eased down. "I want to talk to you as a friend."

"What else is going on?"

"You know I'm here to arrange leases for oil reserves. It's important to the economic future of my country, and I will do everything I can to make sure the negotiations are positive. Too long the world has seen me as Prince Omar who spends money on Western indulgences and expensive race cars." He smiled. "And I do value my collection." He leaned forward. "I want my reputation changed to be Prince Omar bin Talal, the man who helped bring business prosperity to his country. It's wrong for me to pray and not follow the Quran. No more carrying the title of a playboy." He folded his hands. "I want to leave a legacy like King Abdullah. His reforms and economic policies have kept our country moving forward. The energy minister has made strides in balancing supply and demand. My desire is to offer support in every way possible. Many of my countries' leaders are working to lower the unemployment rate while adding more women to the workforce. Lessening our dependency on oil means leasing from our reserves. For me, no sacrifice is too large."

"What are your plans to make this happen other than meetings with Shell and Exxon?"

"Two additional things: I'm arranging an invitation-only press conference here at the home to make the announcement of Saudi Arabia working more closely with our American business friends. Secondly, I'm hosting an event at the rodeo with many oil and gas executives. There I'll announce the negotiations in progress to buy a US company that focuses on shale."

"Excellent news, but I'm sure the conservatives are—"

"Highly critical. That's at home. I left the opposition there. Then I walk into a snake pit."

Kord placed his cup on the table, thoughts swirling with the prince's announcement. The ideals were exemplary. But he'd heard the rumors, and many Saudi citizens were not happy to work for less money while the country built its economy. More suspects in the plot. "Who else is aware besides Malik?"

"Ali."

"Do you think they would have sabotaged your plans?"

"When happenings like today make little sense, I must look to any possible adversary. But not Ali or Malik. They'd die for me. They understand I'll give my life to make positive changes for my country."

"Why aren't the business appointments on your itinerary?"

"Malik hasn't confirmed all of them. He's

making arrangements for a press conference on Saturday afternoon to announce my goodwill, and the invitations for the rodeo event were sent an hour before leaving Riyadh. That's a week from Thursday. If the meeting with the consul general had taken place at his office, I would have made him aware of the press conference and rodeo event."

"How long have you known Malik?"

"Since he was a boy. He's dedicated to his profession."

Malik's position put him in the thick of the prince's affairs. If compromised, his relationship with the prince—the goings-on of personal, business, and social affairs—placed Prince Omar at the mercy of a killer. The nightmare repeated in Kord's mind. Two failed attempts . . . If Malik was the mole, why hadn't he succeeded? In Saudi, he'd have more of an opportunity with so many others to take the blame. Unless Malik was determined to destroy the relationship between Saudi Arabia and the US. But the prince scoured intel and background for all his bodyguards and staff. He'd have picked up on anything questionable.

What about Ali? He was at the top of Monica's list. Kord's suspicions needed to be explored.

"And when did you plan to tell your other bodyguards about the two events?" Kord said.

"When everything was in place. Remember last

May when I attended the Offshore Technology Conference? All the hours we spent talking at dinner and then later?"

Kord chuckled. "Until sunrise."

"I didn't drink."

"Right."

"Neither did you. But I've never seen you drink alcohol." Prince Omar paused. "The thought occurred to me then about how I was failing my family with my lifestyle. Since then, I've dedicated my life to being a prince who is sincere in what he says and does."

"I've never doubted your loyalty to your country and those you love."

"Others must see the new man so they will put aside my former reputation." Prince Omar raised a brow. "Have you thought more about following Allah?"

The prince had spoken to him on more than one occasion about Islam, but Kord still searched for answers. "I'm reading and thinking."

"Feeding the mind." He stretched his back—obviously tired with little time for rest. "My country's betterment is another reason why I must be seen respectfully in your city. When others see me, they see every Saudi citizen. While my mother is undergoing treatments, Malik will arrange business luncheons. Another opportunity for me to be seen without my past habits. But these will be short excursions to repair my name. Business negotiations of oil leases are vital."

"Amir, the more you are exposed, the greater the chances of a killer's success."

"Hiding is for cowards. I refuse to leave the country or stay in this house like a prisoner."

"I understand but I don't agree," Kord said. "And I promise I'll find who's behind these crimes."

"To me, it all points to Iran. How better to destroy our alliance than to assassinate a Saudi prince on US soil. Think of their position if diplomatic relations fail between our countries. Our united efforts of foreign policy are destroyed. Syria has less opposition to their policies. Yemen's rebel movement succeeds. Oil. The position of the Sunni—you know these things."

"But they must be proved with solid evidence. And they know if exposed, you'd launch all-out war."

"We cannot fail in finding the assassins." His words were filled with determination. "I'll send you any findings. Nothing more to discuss about the matter until more intel arrives."

"I need to get some work done." Kord rose to make his exit, but the prince called to him.

"Your assistant handles herself well."

"I'll tell her you complimented her."

"She's a beautiful woman."

Kord realized where the conversation was

going. "Yes, Amir. Monica is not my type. She's a crack shot, and if I ever make her mad, I'm a dead man. Too headstrong."

Prince Omar raised a finger. "I said similar words about my second wife."

22

DURING THE LATE AFTERNOON, Monica processed what had been drop-shipped into her life since Tuesday. While the household quieted for *Asr*, she walked to the window of her bedroom and admired the incredible scenery. The view was breathtaking, no matter what window of the home. Fountains sprayed like sparkling crystal, and the vibrant-green grass and shrubbery blending with spring's display of color reminded her of a painting. How such beauty in a respite could carry a sinister air wasn't unusual, just regrettable.

Dark-blue storm clouds rolled into view.

She took a moment to pray for all those within the house to see a woman who conducted herself in a respectful manner. The need for wisdom dominated her thoughts and discernment. She added thankfulness for God's presence and a plea to curb her tongue.

She wanted to forget about Liam and the damage he'd inflicted upon countless lives. Why did Jeff bring up his name and link him to Kord? Her new partner hadn't shown any of the man's traits—no charming side mixed with brooding. No lies about how he longed to make the world a better place. No feigned desire to serve God.

No promises of a future together with her. No late-night scribblings of the house they'd build together. No writing their vows. No lists of what they'd name their children.

Why couldn't she get past it?

Since Liam's betrayal, the male gender frightened her, pushed her into a corner where she doubted her abilities. Didn't help that she worked in a male-dominated career. She'd created more walls and added mortar to the existing ones. Jeff once called Liam the "unfortunate incident." He'd been more than an unfortunate incident—he'd been a gruesome degradation of a greedy man.

Her nightmares reminded her of the miserable mess and how she'd fallen prey to Liam's manipulation. Night after night she relived it in vivid color. Mostly red.

God promised to help her get past the memories, but first she had to stop punishing herself and allow Him to work.

A text landed in her secure phone, interrupting her preoccupation.

From Kord. Can u meet me on the W terrace? 3 things 2 discuss.

OMW

Attached to the text was a link to Prince Omar's informant report and another to the security footage at MD Anderson.

Monica left her scarf behind. If she ran into the prince, at least her arms and legs were covered.

Outside the home, Kord stood near potted flowers and plants. A great shot for a photographer. She caught herself and reined in the attraction that couldn't go any further than a flirtatious thought. Hadn't she just admitted the whole male population prevented her from moving forward in any relationship?

He waved and joined her. "Up for a walk?"

"Sure." They ventured toward a far corner of the property near a clump of oak trees. A white marble bench seemed to invite them.

Once seated, Kord grabbed his phone. "I sent you a file."

Monica read the intel from the prince's informant. "The man gives three names, all Iranians. I'll forward this to Jeff to check them out too."

"I doubt they are still alive."

"I'd rather know who was behind this. Adding to the body count is not my style."

"Take a look at the security footage," Kord said.

She reflected on the images of the person authorities believed was responsible for three deaths. Relaxed. Observant. Wore gloves. Most criminals worked alone, but due to the nature of international terrorism, she banked on a conspiracy. She replayed the footage outside the hospital entrance three times.

"Do you see anything unusual other than the

man knows where every camera is located, just like at the high school?" he said.

"He either knows how to utilize a disguise or the scheme has more than one player."

"My analysis too." Kord pointed to a taxi driver who'd spoken to the killer. The man was Caucasian. Six foot. Red hair. "Can you read what he said to the killer?"

"Zoom in." The footage rolled just enough for her to make out two words. "He said, 'Morning, sir.' Nothing there unless that was a code for something. Has he been questioned?"

"Yes, and released. He checked out."

She read additional investigation reports. "What's your take on the FBI interviews here in Houston? I see they've conducted four—three Iranian men and one woman from Syria who've been on our watch list."

"All had alibis for yesterday and this morning. National and international interviews are in progress. Early reports show nothing substantial. Surveillance teams are in place."

She considered the strong possibility of another attempt and a driving force propelling her to find the killer.

A cardinal fluttered into the treetops.

Monarch butterflies tasted spring flowers.

She didn't have to end this case herself, but being honest hadn't stopped the need to prove her value. Her insides burned.

"You mentioned three matters," she said. "Curiosity is getting the best of me, and patience is not part of my operating system."

"Who is in our line of work?"

She gave him a thumbs-up. "You didn't answer my question."

"I'd like for you to help me figure something out."

"If I can."

"In talking to Fatima and Yasmine, did either of them bring up my name?"

Okay, she'd play. "Does this have to do with your Romeo role?"

"I didn't tell you everything. Fatima thought I was in love with her."

Now she understood Fatima's animosity. "Are you telling me you two had an affair?" She shook her head. "That would be punishable by death."

"She mistook my interest in the family as a lifelong commitment to her. She approached me in secret and declared her love. She was only sixteen. I tried to be gracious and flattered, but she was very upset."

"You're sure Prince Omar didn't learn about it?"

"If Fatima had gone to him or their father, she'd have to admit to sneaking off to see me."

"I get it. Have you talked to her since their arrival?"

"No. The vibes are bad."

"Do you want me to bring up your name?" Monica startled at a thought. "We have everyone in this house under a microscope, but do you suspect her involvement with the murders?"

"Hope not. If she chooses to be confrontational, it would be to discredit me in her brother's eyes. I hurt her pride. She's impetuous and stubborn but not stupid. If Prince Omar believes I acted inappropriately, our friendship would be over. Due to the current mess, the situation between our two countries could go south real fast. Think about the nightmare media headlines. 'Prince Omar's friend and requested US bodyguard accused of having an affair with his sister.' I'm asking if you think I should arrange a meeting with her, both of you."

"Avoiding the subject with Fatima is the best route."

He stared into the trees. "Use your best judgment. If I need to talk to her, we can work something out. The last thing we need is her ruining my credibility."

"Yasmine told me she was upset because one of Prince Omar's friends was here. I assumed a bodyguard."

"Not exactly. I do have another matter to run past you."

She held up four fingers.

He gave her a quick nod. "Just had a private meeting with the prince." Kord revealed the prince's desire to take a better front in assisting his country's development by initiating a press conference and a rodeo event in a private suite. "Plans are to dine oil executives. Not bring up leasing of oil reserves."

"If he's determined to become a leader, why are his sisters here in the thick of danger?" She found it difficult to accept a changed man when his views about the modern world and women were archaic.

"His mother would be devastated if they left. I tried to convince him, but for now the princesses are under his eye. There's no denying Saudi Arabia's enemies will continue to press against them in every direction. Especially when the country's advancements in every arena make them stronger as a world power."

She nodded. "Our killer is organized, mobile, one step ahead of us, and hiding in plain sight. Kord, he's among us and knows every move Prince Omar makes. Why doesn't he send his bodyguards home and get a new crew?"

"What would you have him do with them once they're back in Saudi?"

"Hold them in custody until someone confesses. Their judicial system accelerates ours in the way of obtaining information. Even if I don't agree with their methods." She peered into his brown eyes. "How much do you trust the FBI?"

"How much do you trust the CIA?"

"Don't want to go there unless we have proof," she said. "But it's a no-brainer—a mole on the prince's team or ours. And someone has us scrambling."

"Tough call. Let's hope we don't have to explore it further. We have a suspicious nature, and if I had a reason to doubt either agency, trust me, I'd be overturning rocks."

Kord's use of a familiar phrase ripped open an old wound. "Do me a favor. I have an immense dislike for the phrase 'trust me.' The moment I hear it, I want to choke whoever said it."

He laughed, taking her off guard. "Thanks for the warning."

"Glad you find me amusing. Something else you should know. Our job is protection detail, but I want to be the one to bring down these bad boys."

His eyes flicked a peculiar glance her way, one she couldn't read. Had he been informed about Liam?

"What?" she said.

"I took a bullet for Prince Omar, and the scar on my back is a reminder of what happens when I begin to think I'm invincible."

Possibly she'd met her match. "When you were involved in rescuing his wife and son?"

"Another time. We were outside a restaurant in Paris when shooting broke out. Figured the bullets were for him and made sure they didn't reach the target."

"You shielded him?"

"Yep."

"Anything else I should know about your and the prince's relationship?" she said.

"No. Those are the reasons why we're friends."

"So who has the most to lose from Prince Omar continuing with economic improvements? Ali wears his anger like a plate of armor, but it appears a righteous rage. I have Jeff digging for anything on him, but so far nothing. The other bodyguards and house staff have no red flags in their backgrounds to question. Then there's Fatima and the wrath of a spurned woman."

"I'm delving into Malik, the press secretary. Having problems reading him. Too quiet for my liking. Our reports exonerate him—not sure I do."

"I'll keep my eyes open on all counts, including Fatima."

"Too bad she's not married."

Monica didn't envy his worry about Fatima destroying his friendship with Prince Omar. Neither was she apprehensive about his ability to complete the job. Taking a bullet for someone vested the relationship. What she feared was one of the Saudi men paving the way for Prince Omar's killer.

"Kord, what if a member of the household is helping the killer unwillingly?"

23

HANDS IN HIS POCKETS, Kord walked along a stone path that wound around the rear of the property leading to the patio of the Saud home. The business of arranging a meeting with Fatima rumbled through his mind, much like thunder in the distance. He believed in honesty, which meant having a long talk with Prince Omar about what didn't happen five years ago.

The other situation was how the sniper had Prince Omar's schedule. Who had access other than Malik and Ali? Who in Riyadh?

Gray clouds gathered and the scent of rain met his nostrils with a few drops of moisture. Houston's ground had hit the saturation point, and many neighborhoods were flooded. If the water level continued to rise, Prince Omar might have difficulty keeping to his plans. But if the weather prohibited his getting out to meetings, then bring on more rain.

Kord had left Monica on the bench, and if she delayed, she'd be drenched. Her final comment held logic. Someone in the household could have been forced to assist the killer. Not an impossibility. But that meant taking a strong look at Fatima and Yasmine—another reason to bring Prince Omar into the loop about what *didn't* happen—and more questioning of the bodyguards and staff. The FBI were running data on all the calls the entourage had made, and so far nothing had materialized as suspicious. The who, how, and why pierced his thoughts.

"Kord."

He turned to see Monica racing toward him. "Something wrong?"

She shook her head and made a breathless stop at his side. Her flushed face was . . . very attractive. "I have an idea," she said. "Got a few minutes?"

"We're about to get wet."

"I'd rather talk in the open."

She usually made sense, which drove him nuts. "Go for it."

"The FBI checked all the cell phones belonging to Prince Omar's men, and they were cleared. Just got the CIA report for the numbers called and received."

He yanked his phone from his pocket.

"Haven't sent it yet. Let me finish. Authorities have researched the prince's laptop and found nothing. But what about his iPad or tablet? What about his cell phone?"

"He has tight security on his devices." A bolt of adrenaline hit Kord. "He uses his iPhone for everything—e-mail, texts, notes—and has downloaded apps to help him manage business affairs."

"So his schedule is on his phone?"

"Right." His mind whirled. "No one inspected it—didn't seem necessary."

"We need to take a look. The problem could be there. What if a virus was planted on his iPhone?"

He rubbed his face and reflected on the earlier foiled plan. A near-field communication hack would allow a person to obtain Prince Omar's private information—even hear all that was being said within the phone's mic range. "At the hospital, he left his phone in the limo, and his decision to cancel the trip to the consul general's office occurred later inside."

"That aspect is why I want to investigate the possibility of a virus. It's a legitimate means for our killer to obtain information. Hacking a mobile device through wireless technology isn't rocket science."

"We need to talk to Prince Omar."

"Barging in and giving our theory could tip off the killer. We need to think this through."

"If you're right, why not set a trap?"

She grinned. "Telepathy is the first sign of an operative."

Monica was really getting under his skin, in a way he'd never imagined. When this was over, he wanted to see more of her. A lot more.

When Kord learned Prince Omar and Malik were in a meeting, he texted Ali and asked to speak with him privately in the rear yard. Monica didn't approve, but Kord observed him and saw a man loyal to Prince Omar. When he and Ali talked, he'd explain the private meeting. While he waited with Monica, Ali approached them.

"What's the secrecy?" Ali said.

"We have a possible theory to test." Kord explained Monica's idea of a phone virus. "We need your help to give him a note in privacy. No one else can be privy to the conversation." He handed Ali a slip of paper requesting Prince Omar's presence.

Ali snorted. "That would explain the how."

"He's to leave his phone and Apple Watch behind," Kord said and glanced at Monica.

"Not a word can pass between you and Prince Omar," she said.

Ali disappeared. Within three minutes he returned with the prince. Malik was nowhere around.

"Kord," Prince Omar began, "my phone and watch are on my desk. If you're right, I'll have the head of whoever is responsible."

"We all will." Kord had no doubt the fate of the killer lay in the hands of an enraged Saudi prince.

"How does this kind of thing happen?"

"The guilty man could have been standing next to you and sent a virus."

"It would have happened in Riyadh." He

clenched his fist. "Even planted by one of my men."

"Is your schedule, since the announcement about this trip, documented anywhere besides your phone?"

"Malik and Zain. Would you like Zain's phone?"

"Yes, Amir. I want to know where you've been and who was present," Kord said. "No one but the four of us can be aware of this."

"Sounds like a difficult process for a suspicion. But I'll cooperate. I want to be part of the plan to catch him."

"That could be dangerous."

"I live with those who want me dead. No argument, my friend. As your note said, a trap will catch him. I've lost Zain, and I will not lose you."

Kord had faced opposition with the prince in the past and experienced his stubbornness. "With all due respect, I prefer allowing the killer to think I'm you. You can hear the story when he's in custody. Let me do what I'm trained to do."

"I agree with Kord," Ali said. "He and Miss Alden know how to defend themselves." He raised his chin. "She does handle herself well, and I hope we can be more civil to each other. We have an important job to do."

Kord hid his surprise.

"Thank you," she said. "I agree our duties require us to be amiable."

Prince Omar drew in a breath, a common sign of his reflections. "All right. The killer and his accomplices must be apprehended." He turned to Monica. "Thank you for taking care of my sisters. I'm grateful."

"You're welcome." She respectfully avoided his gaze.

The prince focused on Kord. "What are your thoughts?"

He allowed his satisfaction to fuel the setup. "First of all. Be aware of anything you say around your phone or watch. I prefer you use new ones or put those aside until we've worked through our theory."

The prince nodded.

"In the past, you enjoyed Morton's steak house. I'll reserve the location across from the Galleria for a late-afternoon meal with a few of your bodyguards. Not just a boardroom, but the entire restaurant for safety reasons. It's fairly quiet during this time, and I'll state you desire privacy. I'll be dressed as you. With your approval, the FBI and CIA can move into action. FBI agents will act as staff to ensure no one is hurt. Monica will pose as the hostess."

"Include me," Ali said. "Someone has to keep Kord safe."

Kord chuckled. "Who's keeping you from a bullet?"

"Me," Monica said. "I'm a better shot."

"When will this occur?" the prince said.

"As soon as possible. The moment I receive your permission, arrangements will be made. The luncheon plans will need to be made in the presence of your phone and watch."

"Take care of it now. I'll pay whatever's required."

"Prince Omar, your money is not the problem, but keeping you alive is. The FBI needs to check your devices for a virus. I've put them off until after Friday afternoon. I know that's your holy day—"

"Do it."

"Okay. Until then, we play it safe."

Twenty minutes later, Kord received the go-ahead. Target was Friday afternoon at two thirty.

24

IN HER BEDROOM QUARTERS, Monica spent Wednesday evening rereading and probing the backgrounds of every person in the house for a snippet of information that could twist into something shady. All still looked squeaky clean. What about their families and past grievances? Until the killer was caught—possibly Friday afternoon—danger lingered. If she and Kord were wrong about the prince's phone, their original assumption of a mole meant every person in the home must be viewed under a microscope. And if the prince's phone had a virus, a mole could have planted it.

So many possibilities, and all had the potential to be deadly.

Rain beat against the windows in a steady downpour, while her phone alerts warned of rising water. Such was her mood. Didn't help that her throat and head weren't in the best of condition.

If someone inside the home wanted to harm Fatima or Yasmine, he'd simply enter the women's bedchambers in the middle of the night. Why wouldn't the prince send them home? Was it really his mother's peace of mind, or was he using his sisters as cover for another reason?

She rose from her comfy seat in her bedroom

and made her way to the common area, where Fatima and Yasmine sat talking. Again they were dressed in designer gowns and accessorized in pure gold. If the evening meal found her with them, she'd explore more of a friendship. Fatima might not be in such a sour mood.

"Excuse me," Monica said. "I'm concerned for both of you. Until the person who's endangered your brother is found, please lock your bedroom doors at night, and keep the door leading to the hallway locked."

"Thank you," Yasmine said, her voice sweet and her face filled with youthful light.

"Once we've arrested the killer, those precautions won't be necessary."

"When will it be?" Yasmine said. "I'm afraid for my brother. With Zain gone and the attempt on Consul General al-Fakeeh, everything's scary."

"Staying safe is a priority. I encourage you to remain inside the grounds."

"Is Mother well-guarded?"

"Prince Omar has men positioned around her at all times. No one comes near her without clearance."

Fatima lifted her chin. "If we are the next victims, locks won't keep anyone out. There are men within this home who will protect us. We don't need Americans interfering in our business."

Did she have no clue of the real world? "We're risking our lives to ensure you have yours," Monica said.

"Aren't you an assistant to a press secretary?" Fatima said. "What do you know?"

"I have solid training."

"What if you make mistakes?" Fatima said. "Whose fault is Zain's death? If we were home, he'd be alive today."

"Are you saying the tragedy is Mother's fault?" Yasmine's voice rose.

"No, Sister. I'm saying this wouldn't have occurred at home."

"I do have a license to carry a firearm, and I've taken professional instruction," Monica said. "I'm a light sleeper. If an intruder is able to sneak past the bodyguards, I assure you the rustle of gaining entry would wake me. I'm quite capable of defending you." Monica refused to mention a trained killer had methods beyond their understanding. Or that she'd really like to shake a few people in this house and open their eyes to the seriousness of the matter.

Ignorance was not bliss.

Might get a throat cut, like the poor janitor at Paramount High School.

"How did you move from serving coffee to being Kord's assistant?" Fatima's voice would freeze water. "That's a little degrading for him, don't you think? But you Western women have your ways."

Realization hit—Fatima believed Monica and Kord were together. The princess's flame burned hot and green. Kord needed to straighten out this mess with her. But how?

Monica plastered a smile on her face. No point in Princess Fatima having the satisfaction of riling her. "My job is to follow Kord's orders. So get over your animosity." She walked to the door leading to the hallway, locked it, and made her way back to Fatima. Forcing pleasantness into her voice, she stared into the woman's brooding eyes. "If you like, I'll show you the art of self-defense, how to use a knife or send a bullet into the heart of an enemy. I took those lessons too. Let me know, and I'll fit your training into my schedule."

"It's impossible for a woman to defend herself against a man," Fatima said. "It would be a waste of time."

"Just because they're bigger and stronger doesn't mean we can't overpower them."

Yasmine reached out to Monica. "I want to learn. If the offer is for me too, I'll request permission from my brother."

"By all means. Every woman, regardless of her religion or culture, needs to have the skills necessary to keep her from harm."

Fatima rose and returned to her bedroom.

"My chances of becoming her friend are zero," Monica said. "She's a beautiful woman, and from her accomplishments, she's highly intelligent." Would Yasmine open up about her sister?

"The problem is not you," Yasmine whispered. "She's very unhappy."

"I'm sorry. Is there anything I can do?"

"Nothing will make her happy but the impossible. She's been in love with Mr. Davidson for years. Seeing him here is difficult."

The prince would hear every word. Would he confront Kord about his sister's feelings?

"And since he's training me, I spend a lot of time with him." Monica kept her voice low.

"Yes. I'm sorry. She fears our brother may have arranged a marriage to a man she despises while her heart is for another."

How would Monica ever win Fatima over?

Kord sat with Prince Omar alone in his office and discussed personal times together, avoiding critical matters at hand. The prince's phone alerted him to a text. He read it and handed the phone to Kord. A photo of Princess Gharam covered in blood filled the screen. A caption read, Cancer won't kill her. I will. U 2 will soon b dead.

Taking a pad of paper, the prince wrote and pushed it Kord's way. *Your theory about a phone hack may be correct.*

Kord motioned for them to leave the office. Once the door closed, anger creased the prince's features, and rightly so. Saudi men shielded their women from evil. The threat against Princess Gharam had come as a personal blow, as though he'd failed in his responsibilities.

"It's Photoshopped," Kord said.

"True, but I'm ensuring my mother is all right. May I use your phone?" When Kord handed him the device, he selected numbers. "This is Omar. Is my mother resting comfortably?" he said in Arabic. "Tell her I called. I'm requesting another bodyguard for her detail, but keep it from her." He ended the call and phoned another number. After introducing himself, he continued. "It is imperative I speak to Consul General al-Fakeeh." A sweep of sadness crossed his face. "Yes, good evening, Nasser. I need additional protection for my mother. Can you send a trusted man to the hospital immediately?" He paused. "Thank you."

"I think the extra precautionary measures are in order," Kord said.

"I'd like for you to talk to Miss Alden. Make sure my sisters are all right. If you're correct about the theory of my phone being hacked, theirs may be too. Ask her to collect their phones per my request. No explanation need be given."

Kord contacted Monica and explained what had happened.

"Hold on while I take this in my bedroom." A

few moments later, she responded. "Yasmine and I are talking in the common area. Fatima is in her room. Please tell Prince Omar I will do as he asks."

"Thanks." Kord would have rather confiscated them, but he'd not embarrass the prince by insisting. "We'll want to run diagnostics. Can you meet me on the covered terrace in fifteen minutes? Bring the phones with you?"

"I'll be there."

"These people have no idea who they're messing with. Friday afternoon, this guy's toast." The call ended, Kord processed the now stronger possibility of a hacker planting a virus in the prince's phone.

A crack of thunder rattled the windows of the mansion.

25

WITH THE GROUNDS DRENCHED in water and dark shadows, Monica walked with Kord along the path they'd trod earlier. Unlike her initial impression of him, she was beginning to enjoy his company and respect his input to the team. Her stomach tingled. Oh, my goodness, she was attracted to him.

Strange. Frightening. And she refused to think about it.

She'd given Kord Fatima's phone, but Yasmine asked to wait until the morning because hers was charging.

The rain had let up, but the weather forecasters predicted another downpour around midnight. In the northwest part of the city, Cypress Creek had flowed from its banks and into homes. Nature's fury was no respecter of persons—the rich and the poor needed boats to navigate many of the streets.

The weather added to her wariness about the mission. She'd been threatened by big dogs before, and it always caused two responses— caution and persistence in finding the coward who tossed warnings but refused to expose himself for a head-on fight.

Kord needed to hear the latest from the CIA. "I

have news. CIA intel came in from our sources in the Middle East about thirty minutes ago. It confirmed what your informant claimed," she said. "The plot to kill Prince Omar has been in existence since his announcement to bring his mother to MD Anderson. Right now I want to know who. The motive, whether it be religion, honor, politics, or whatever, can crawl out of the woodwork later."

"My informant will be back with me as soon as he has a name. I'm thinking religious dissenters."

"Because of Wahhabi interpretation of Islamic law?" she said. "Or are you rethinking the conservatives' opposition to the leasing of oil reserves?"

"Both. But none of the prince's men are tied to those groups."

"That we know of." Her thoughts lingered on the one man who weighed in the heaviest. "If Ali is part of the scheme, Zain's death would still have made him angry."

"I was in the limo and he didn't attempt to stop Zain or me."

"I feel like my hands are tied, and I'm babysitting when I could be running down terrorist affiliations."

"You and I are action people. Our roles here can be frustrating unless we can determine if someone has betrayed him, and who."

They stared back at the mansion. The yellow

lights shining through the windows appeared to imitate the owners' gold.

"Prince Omar has people searching for the ID on a phone hacking, just like we are," he said. "The expertise of this operation scrapes some of the scum we've suspected off our shoes and zeros in on the internal picture. Which may be exactly what the killers want."

God, we need Your help before others are killed. "Who has the ability to orchestrate an operation of this size and be assured of not failing? Saudi Arabia isn't known for its leniency to lawbreakers. Will they execute before we have time to question any of their suspects?"

"What do you think?"

"Thought you might have a little clout."

"I wish. Friday can't get here fast enough. I'd like to chain the prince to his office. But he'd interpret our request as a coward's mentality. If the rumors of a mole are designed to send us in the opposite direction, we're looking at more deaths, and the repercussions could be worldwide."

Kord wasn't exaggerating. The severity of what Saudi Arabia could do in the name of revenge paved the way to massive unrest across the Middle East. "We're fools not to explore how many people are involved. At this point we have an assassin and a hacker or mole. If the motive is to crush the Saud family and cause it to implode for a new regime, we're looking at an architectural blueprint for multiple disasters."

He studied her. Was he mulling over her words or developing his own strategy?

"What are you thinking?" she said.

"The assassin has tried twice and failed. Means taking more chances." Kord shook his head.

She warmed as frustration poured into her blood. "With all of modern technology, there has to be a way to detect a virus on his phone without alerting the killer."

"Do you want to underestimate the virus's ability?"

"Not at all."

"Prince Omar believes his goals are worth any sacrifice."

"The lives of loved ones?" she said. "His pride is worth watching more deaths? Another tragedy where the US will be held responsible? The conservatives are blaming us for Zain."

"I know, Monica. We need intel and evidence now."

Long after midnight, Monica wrestled with data, faces, and names. The enemies anticipated a payoff of some kind. Who fought alongside them in the US? None of these terrorists worked alone. Ultimately the motive wove greed into the mix. It always did.

She stared at the ceiling while sleep evaded her.

A click sounded. Tossing back the blanket, she grabbed her weapon and crept to her bedroom door. In the common area, her eyes adjusted to the dark, but nothing seized her attention.

Her imagination?

Doubtful.

The door to the hallway wasn't open, so the sound had likely come from one of the princesses' bedrooms. Monica made her way to Fatima's room. She gently tried the knob. Locked. She crept to Yasmine's door. The knob turned easily. An empty bed. Where was she going this time of night? And alone?

She rushed back to the common area windows and peered out over the grounds. Prince Omar's bodyguards walked the perimeter of the property. She shoved patience into her stance. A shadowed figure stole across the area. Then movement in the oak trees captured her attention. She hurried to her bedroom and snatched her night vision goggles from her shoulder bag. Moments later, she once again observed the treed area, where she and Kord had met earlier. Two people stood within the oaks. Together. A man and woman in a definite embrace.

Where were Yasmine's brains? Who had persuaded her into meeting a man in secret?

She stuck her weapon inside her back waistband and grabbed a jacket on the way out. Down the stairs and around to the rear of the house. Once outside, she walked toward the pair hiding in the trees. Monica paused to observe the two.

"When, Malik?" Yasmine whispered.

"Soon. Your brother has business here and can't be interrupted."

"I love you."

"And I long to make you my wife."

Monica entered into their tryst. "Does Prince Omar approve of this meeting?"

Malik turned to her. "This is none of your business."

"When a killer is on the loose, yes." She pulled her phone from her pocket.

"Miss Alden, we can talk," he said. "Yasmine and I are speaking of our future."

"Shouldn't your first discussion be with her brother or father?"

"Please, Miss Alden." Yasmine's voice quivered.

Monica despised the use of strong-arm tactics on a seventeen-year-old. "You and I will go back to the house together."

"The prince will never believe you," Malik said. "You're nothing but Kord's servant."

"And you're not in Saudi Arabia. Yasmine, now, before I change my mind."

They walked in silence to the rear of the home. Yasmine knew the cost of being caught, much higher for her than for Malik. Why slip away and risk her brother's anger? Monica would wait and ask the girl those very questions.

In Yasmine's dark bedroom, she snapped on the bedside lamp, and compassion for the young woman dressed in black swept over her. Yasmine closed the door behind her and eased onto her bed while Monica took a chair.

"Yasmine, if I saw you, then others might have too. I can only imagine the seriousness of your brother learning about your careless actions. What is going on between you and Malik?"

Yasmine trembled. "I can't say anything."

"Unfortunately, if you don't tell me, I'll have to contact Prince Omar. Which is it?"

26

KORD READ FBI UPDATES on his phone, reviewing every e-mail linked with Arabic chatter regarding the Saud family. The FBI's terrorism division actively monitored enemy online conversations, and he needed to know the latest intel. US enemies commended the assassination attempts aimed at Prince Omar and offered support for those working against the West, but Kord wanted insight specifically to the plans—and why.

An update came in about an e-mail that, according to the sender's IP address, was coming from Malik al-Kazaz, the press secretary.

> Prince Omar and those like him will be crushed like the *ahle-Kitab*. Prince Omar will not leave US soil alive. Allah has given him into our hands. We know every move he makes while he stumbles into a sniper's path. He's a fool to trust the ones close to him. Many will be killed. Soon he will be under our feet.

Malik—a loyal and trusted cousin of Prince Omar? A man who had risen to his position within the last nine years? He made the detailed arrangements for all events.

The enemy didn't need to send a virus into the prince's phone when his most trusted man had betrayed him.

Uneasiness punched Kord in the gut, and he stopped his thoughts midstream. With the anonymity observed since Tuesday, why would Malik deliberately identify himself? Had the enemy set him up?

He reread Malik's background. If the man was working with anyone, only one documented item pointed to him. The man had a stellar reputation.

What better man to lead an assassination attempt?

But why put himself in a vulnerable position online?

Kord slipped his Glock inside his jacket and left his suite. He wasn't waiting for FBI confirmation before he confronted Malik. Being awakened at 2:15 a.m. might test the press secretary's quiet temperament. Why should Kord give him an opportunity to leave or carry out a plan to kill the prince?

Outside Malik's door, he rapped several times. "This is Kord. I need a word with you." He waited fifteen long seconds and repeated.

"Is Prince Omar in danger?"

"You tell me. I have questions. Face-to-face."

Silence.

"Should I find a bodyguard?"

200

The door opened, and Malik stared at him. Fully clothed. "Come in."

"Are you alone?"

"Yes, of course."

"Are you armed?"

Malik frowned. "My weapon is beside my bed."

"See that it stays there. Keep your hands where I can see them."

Once the door shut behind them, Malik ran his fingers through his hair. "I'm not shocked you've figured me out. I should have been more discreet. Does the prince know?"

Discreet? "Do you want him here? I can arrange it."

"I prefer this stay between you and me. I'd be a fool to have others learn about my actions."

"I'm surprised at your openness, considering your fate. Once we've finished with your confession, you'll be under arrest."

Malik startled. "For what? You have no jurisdiction over what I've done. Prince Omar may have my head, but not you."

"Murder on US soil. A scheme against Prince Omar. Be glad I'm making the arrest instead of one of the prince's bodyguards."

Malik stepped back and held up his palm. "I had nothing to do with the plot to kill the prince. Are you an idiot? I'm loyal. Why am I even a suspect?"

"A stupid question, don't you think? I read intercepted e-mails."

"What are you talking about?"

"The assassination attempt. An e-mail calling for Prince Omar's death came from your IP address."

He raised his shoulders. "You have the wrong man. I too have an enemy."

"Then what did you confess to?"

"Nothing you'd understand."

"Your role as the press secretary means you have more knowledge about what is happening in Prince Omar's life than anyone else."

"I'd never lower myself to betray a man I respect."

"Your background shows a trip to Mosul in January. What was the nature of the ten-day visit?"

"My cousin lives there, and I wanted to persuade him to return to Saudi Arabia as a favor to my father. Prince Omar knows this."

That could be verified. "Were you successful?"

"He moved back to Riyadh with his family."

"What's his occupation?"

"A baker. I can give you his name."

"I'd like it now."

"Rashid Dagher."

Kord typed the name into his phone.

Malik shook his head while his hands remained in full view. "We aren't speaking about the same matter. Saudi intel says the plot against the prince is internal, but that doesn't mean me."

Kord pointed to a chair. "Sit down and explain what you've done."

Malik complied. His face mirrored granite. "I've been seeing Yasmine."

Was Kord supposed to swallow this?

Malik continued. "My intentions are to ask for Yasmine's hand in marriage. I should have done so before now."

Kord didn't know whether to believe Malik or bang his head into a wall. But he wasn't a fool, and Malik had violated trust, a serious offense. "You're guilty of seeing Yasmine without a chaperone?"

He nodded. "Please keep this private. I promise you: tomorrow I'll speak to Prince Omar. He could very well beat her. You know how this will look to her family."

Kord knew of the disciplinary actions for women, an accepted practice in the Saudi culture. Wrong. Insanely wrong.

Malik glanced around. "There's no need for you to waste time with this when you have more serious items to tend to."

It wasn't wasting time. Kord's mission was to find a killer, and what choice did he have but to bring all information to the surface? "I'd like to ask her for myself."

"You have my word. She'll be upset. Besides, what else is needed?"

"In the US, we want to hear from every man

203

and woman who may be involved in a crime. If you want to discard our procedures, I can take you immediately into custody as a person of interest in the plot to assassinate Prince Omar. You choose."

"You'll overlook what you've discovered?" Malik whispered as though his secret had ears.

"Would she rather you be arrested for murder? I'll wake Monica and have her escort Yasmine to meet us in the kitchen."

Malik rubbed his face. "This is not how I planned to seek Yasmine for my wife. Prince Omar will learn of it."

"If she doesn't back up your story, you're facing a lot more than loss of a woman to warm your bed."

27

FATIMA OPENED Yasmine's bedroom door. "I heard you crying. What's wrong? Is Mother all right?" She frowned at Monica. "Did you cause this?"

Another can of worms. "Indirectly." Monica touched Yasmine's arm. "Would you like to tell your sister what I discovered?"

The younger woman shook her head. Fatima slid onto the bed beside her sister and wrapped her arm around Yasmine's waist. "You can tell me."

Several seconds passed with only the sound of Yasmine's weeping. She swallowed hard. "I've been seeing Malik alone. Tonight, Monica caught us outside."

Fatima stood abruptly from the bed. "How could you disgrace yourself to meet him without an escort? At night too? What else have you done? Been with him? Are there other men? Yasmine, are you pregnant?"

Yasmine was in Fatima's face before Monica could break them up. "How dare you ask such a horrible question? Malik would never seduce me. He's good and kind."

Monica could have argued against Malik's intentions, but she'd not interfere with two sisters quarreling unless it meant they'd waken the household. That tipping point had arrived. "Enough. You will have the prince pounding on the door and demanding an explanation."

Fatima whirled around, her back against her sister. "You're right. If our brother learns of this, the outcome could be unthinkable. He can't find out, but this can never happen again. Is this why you wanted to delay giving Omar your phone? I knew it wasn't charging."

"Yes. I . . . I needed to delete Malik's number."

"How shameful."

"He wants to marry me."

"Then let him seek permission the proper way."

A text alerted Monica. She glanced at the screen. Kord. **Bring Yasmine 2 the main kitchen ASAP.** She captured the young woman's attention. "Why would Kord need to speak to you immediately?"

The young woman's eyes widened. "Did he see me with Malik? I thought we were careful, but—"

Fatima touched her throat. "Omar must know what you've done."

Monica typed into her phone. **On our way. What's up?**

Malik may b the mole.

Monica placed her phone inside her pocket and stared into Yasmine's face. "We're to meet Kord in the kitchen now. How much do you trust Malik's allegiance?"

"He's loyal to my brother. Why? Will my brother be with Mr. Davidson?"

"I have no idea."

"I'm scared."

Yasmine had the look of innocence and young love. Monica had been there, and she wanted to shield her from heartache. "Take a deep breath. First we need to find out why Kord has questions for you."

"What am I supposed to say?"

"Simply answer him. The truth has no competitor."

"I'm going with you." Fatima moved to the doorway of Yasmine's bedroom. "I'll grab my *hijab*. My sister deserves my support."

Monica blinked. "What brought on the change of heart?"

"Yasmine and I will discuss her indiscretions later. Right now she needs me."

Monica had grown up with brothers, and her best friend—as close as she could get to a friend—was Lori. This love-hate relationship between Fatima and Yasmine seemed as foreign as their mannerisms.

What had Kord discovered? Before they reached the suite door leading to the hallway, Monica stopped and stared at Yasmine. "I need to know now. Do you have information about Zain's murder or the assassination plot against Prince Omar?"

Yasmine sobbed. "No. I promise you. I love my brother."

Monica understood how a woman could love a man and have him manipulate her for his own self-serving purposes. The three crept down the winding staircase and on to the kitchen. A single light shone in the cooking area, where Kord stood with Malik. The Saudi press secretary arched his shoulders the moment she and the other two women entered the area. Fatima wrapped her arm around her sister in a vise grip hold.

"That was fast," Kord said.

"We were talking when you texted me." She glanced at Malik. His eye twitched.

Kord leaned against the marble counter. His typical serious mode and more. "I need to ask Yasmine a few questions."

"About what?" Fatima said, anger simmering with each word like a slow boil.

Monica sent a silent message to the woman: *Leave your personal feelings out of this.*

"My job is to keep your brother alive. Zain is dead. Two other innocent men are dead. Unless you can give me a name of who's responsible, I suggest you listen while I do my job."

Fatima's face reddened, but she said nothing.

"Yasmine, how many times have you met Malik alone?" Kord said.

She trembled. "Twice here."

"And at home?"

"Not sure."

"Yasmine?"

"Several times."

"Why have you broken your culture's laws, dishonored yourself, and shamed your family?"

Yasmine wept against her sister's shoulder. Monica wished Kord would take the young woman's age into consideration.

"Yasmine, this is serious." His voice gave no hint of sympathy.

"Why is Yasmine your concern?" Fatima said.

Kord glared at Fatima with a look that could have cracked concrete. "Yasmine, I need an answer."

The young woman broke away from Fatima as though finding strength. "I thought only of being with Malik."

Probably not the best response.

"What did you talk about?"

She paled but kept her stance. "Our love and our future together."

"Does Malik have plans to eliminate Prince Omar?"

Yasmine inhaled sharply. "Never. He loves him like a brother. Respects him."

"I differ with your assessment since he's broken laws regarding you."

"That will soon change," she said. "He will take care of—"

Malik stepped in front of Kord. "Yes, I assure

209

you the matter will be handled as soon as we are finished here."

Kord intercepted the man and shoved him back. "I'm talking to Yasmine. Has he spoken against Prince Omar?"

"No. Aren't you listening to me?"

"Has he talked to your brother about marrying you? Has the prince refused to speak to your father?"

Yasmine flashed a bewildered look at Malik. "I don't think so."

"I'm loyal to the Saud family," Malik said. "Look at my record."

"He'd never hurt my brother."

"But he'd entice you to meet him in secret," Kord said. "To break rules and risk damaging your reputation."

A second light flipped on. Monica whirled to see Prince Omar already in all his regalia for so early in the morning. How long had he been listening?

"Malik, are you guilty of murder?" The prince's voice rumbled low.

"No, Amir. I'm loyal to you at all costs."

"Yet you tempted and succeeded in having my sister meet you in secret."

"Yes. I'm guilty of dishonoring her, and I regret my actions."

Prince Omar nodded at Ali, who stood behind him. "You will assume Malik's duties. The first one is to arrange a commercial flight home for him tomorrow." He turned to Yasmine. "You are to remain in this house under Fatima's care. You will visit our mother and resume your studies. You are not to mention this to our mother. This matter will be resolved when we return home. Until Malik leaves, you are to remain in your quarters."

"Yes, Brother." Yasmine shook.

"Your phone. Now."

She pulled it from a pocket and gave it to him.

"Fatima, take your sister upstairs."

The princesses left the room.

Monica stayed and slid a look at Kord. His dark eyes captured hers. Had he detected disapproval from the prince for her presence in the kitchen? Not that his approval mattered. She had a job to do. But Kord's slight upturned lip gave her a bit of a lift before he looked to the prince.

"I read encrypted e-mail messages in which the IP address led back to Malik. A plot—"

"The words."

Kord lifted his phone and scrolled through it. "These were traced to Malik's IP address. 'Prince Omar and those like him will be crushed like the *ahle-Kitab*. Prince Omar will not leave US soil alive. Allah has given him into our hands. We know every move he makes while he stumbles into a sniper's path. He's a fool to trust the ones close to him. Many will be killed. Soon he will be under our feet.' "

Monica studied Malik for his reaction.

Ali pulled a knife from inside his *thobe* and lunged at Malik. Kord slammed his fist onto Ali's arm. The knife hit the floor, its pearl handle glittering in the light. The two men struggled. Kord twisted Ali's arm behind his back.

"Listen to me," Kord said. "If Malik is guilty, why would he allow his IP address to be exposed?"

Ali fought against him. "He made a fool's mistake."

Monica could step in, but this was Kord's battle.

"Let me get to the truth," Kord said. "No need for another killing."

"Ali, stand down," Prince Omar said. "Kord has a solid argument."

Ali relaxed and Kord released him, then proceeded to cuff Malik. "Prince Omar, I need to take this man to the FBI office for questioning. With three murders, this is not an issue of diplomatic immunity."

"I waive immunity," Malik said.

"You can't. Not up to you." Kord had the authority to apprehend him, but having the prince's approval would ease the tension.

"Prince Omar—" Malik's voice was firm—"I welcome the questioning. The killer must be found, but I'm innocent of being part of a conspiracy or having any knowledge of the murders."

A flash of regret crossed the prince's face. "It's hard for me to say *killer* and *Malik* in the same breath. But do we ever really know those whom we trust?"

Yasmine's actions had hurt him.

"Omar. I'm your friend," Kord said. "I'm going to find who has committed these crimes. I don't care who's responsible."

"This is disappointing, and I'm angry. I was aware of his interest in Yasmine, but to bring disgrace on her is unforgivable."

"I'd like to leave now. Whether Malik's guilty or innocent, we'll find out."

"All right. I'm coming with you. If he confesses to these crimes, I want to hear it."

"What if an assassin is waiting outside the gates?" Kord said.

"You know I will not cower to fear."

Monica took a deep breath and prayed for respectful words. "Prince Omar, I'm a novice with your culture, but I'm learning. Yasmine is a child. I beg you to remember her naiveté."

Lines creased his face. "Yes, she is young, but she's been versed in our ways. Her actions are inexcusable. Thank you. Your concern is appreciated. Will you remain with my sisters while I'm away?"

Was Prince Omar asking her to probe for

information? No need. If Fatima or Yasmine knew anything, she'd find out. "Of course. Is there anything else?"

"No. Two of my men will guard the home—Karim and Fares. You're free to go."

She hid a smile.

"Monica, I'll text you with updates of Malik's and my conversation before you arrived," Kord said. "And will you tell us why you and the princesses were up so late?"

Such formality. "I hesitate to mention this with the cultural variances between our countries. But I heard Yasmine leave tonight. Saw her and Malik in the garden area. I followed and questioned them."

The heavy sound of Prince Omar's sigh echoed around the room.

28

FOUR THIRTY THURSDAY MORNING, and Monica saw little hope for sleep. She sat with the two sisters in the common area sipping fresh coffee. Monica must prove her sincerity to Fatima and Yasmine and search for the truth. If they knew anything about the betrayal in this house, it would not surface easily, and certainly not to a woman outside their culture. Their differences demanded an assurance Monica was on their side. Being straightforward was the best approach.

"I want to be your friend," Monica said. "What I'm about to say cannot be told to your mother. She has enough concerns. On the surface, my job is an assistant to Kord. In truth, I've been assigned to help him protect this family and use every means to find who's responsible for the tragedies. You two are in as much danger as Prince Omar. The text sent to your brother's phone proved it. The killer has an agenda, and he has no thoughts of mercy. A conspiracy of this size means more are working against your family. They will kill again unless they're stopped."

"I have a question." Fatima arched her back like an irritated cat. "Are you an FBI agent too?"

"Does it really matter?"

"You are the one who said 'truth has no competitor.' "

Touché. "I've received similar training."

Disdain passed over Fatima's face. "Why send a woman?"

Yasmine huffed. "To protect us. Even I can see that."

"A bodyguard could be positioned outside our door. How long have you known Mr. Davidson?"

The source of Fatima's irritation. "Since Tuesday. Why?"

"Curious. Did he request you?"

"Our superiors made the arrangement. We're a team. I don't know him very well. Any other questions?"

"Not right now."

"And I have nothing to help you find the assassin," Yasmine said. "Malik and I have talked of marriage for the past several months. I'm a modern woman, and the treatment and restrictions for women in my country are deplorable, archaic."

"Has he asked you to lie or has he said anything inappropriate about the Saud family?"

She stared into the coffee cup in her hands. "The only thing he's done is suggest I sneak away to see him. Nothing else."

"I sense there's more." Monica waited, allowing silence to strengthen her words.

When Yasmine failed to speak, Fatima touched

her sister's arm. "If Malik is an enemy, he's thrown your love away. If you think his love is true, would he request such a thing? Do you want a man who urges you to break our traditions? Dishonor our family?"

Yasmine laid her cup on the table and buried her face in her hands. Fatima drew her into an embrace.

Time for Monica to be transparent. "I loved a man who used me to destroy hundreds of innocent people in Africa. All for money. When I discovered his treachery, I had to help others find him."

Fatima stared at her wide-eyed. "Were you able to help?"

"I was placed in a situation where if I didn't kill him, he'd kill me and others. I pulled the trigger on a man I thought loved me as much as I loved him." Monica moistened her lips. She'd not uttered the story aloud to anyone but Jeff, and even then, her words were cold. Facts. "I will never forget the heartache, the intense grief, as though I'd died with him. Even worse was the betrayal. I often dream about the men, women, and children who died because of him."

"How did you survive?" Tears formed in Fatima's eyes. Was her sorrow for her sister or her feelings for Kord?

"God gave me strength to work through the

agony and live with purpose. He urges me to forgive myself, but that is the hardest task. I haven't been able to conquer the unforgiveness, but I will. His Spirit is with me." The prince might not approve of her words. But what good was her faith if she didn't stand for it?

"My brother said you were a follower of Jesus," Fatima said.

"I am." Jesus was not a stranger to the Muslims.

Fatima nodded. "Thank you for sharing your story. I've been rude, and I apologize. Is there someone special now?"

"No. When the right man comes along, God will tear down my self-imposed walls." The conversation had gone in a direction Monica hadn't anticipated. "Because I've experienced the same kind of hurt, I want Yasmine to understand she's not alone. Doing what's right is seldom easy. We women must be courageous, despite tender feelings."

Yasmine raised her head, and Monica used her fingertips to wipe away the young woman's tears. "I will tell you all I can remember."

"I'm here with you," Fatima whispered.

"When I was almost fifteen, Malik began working for my brother as his press secretary. Once he smiled at me, and I believed he was the most handsome man I'd ever seen. From then on, I stole glimpses of him whenever I could. A few months later, he saw me alone in the garden, and we spoke." She looked at Fatima and took her sister's hand. "I'd stolen away after our father scolded me about poor grades. Seeing Malik softened my anger. I thought it was innocent enough. He asked me about my music and told me to work hard and bring honor to my family. Nothing inappropriate was ever said. We were friends."

Monica saw the young girl's infatuation and how easily she had been tricked by a man who was fifteen years older. "How did your relationship change?"

"He talked about my plans for higher education, and I shared with him my desire to raise the status of Saudi women. He asked if he could be a part of my future."

Full-blown manipulation.

"Don't you see how wrong his words and meeting with you were?" Fatima's question didn't carry the harshness as before. "Never mind. I see you're thoroughly ignorant of his faults. What else happened, Sister? We must be honest with each other."

"Malik has kissed me. That's all. Tonight he promised to speak to Omar and our father about marriage very soon."

Promises to secure her cooperation? "Has Malik asked you to do anything strange or unusual?"

"Only to keep our meetings secret."

"Has he talked to you about his work for Prince Omar?"

"He enjoys his position as press secretary."

"Any dislikes or what he'd like to see different in politics or specific reforms?"

Yasmine straightened. "He agrees with me that women need more rights."

Again to draw her into his confidence? "Has he shared with you about his day-to-day duties?"

"I've heard one-sided conversations on his mobile phone. I found them fascinating. Just listening to Malik detail and arrange my brother's schedule built my pride and love for him."

"Give me an example," Monica said.

Yasmine tilted her head. "Arranging speeches at home, times and such. Nothing about this trip."

"Have you heard anything forbidden or frightening?"

"Not about Omar. In January, he traveled to Mosul in Iraq as a favor to his aging father. A distant cousin lived there and Malik was to persuade him and his family to return home. I feared for him. Too many enemies there. He was gone for ten days."

"Why did the cousin live in Iraq?"

"I asked Malik the same thing. He told me his cousin had married an Iraqi woman, and his father forbade him to return home. Then his father died, and the family wanted him in Saudi Arabia."

"Did he contact you during this time?"

"A few texts. Too risky for someone to intercept the call. But he was successful in bringing his cousin and his family to Riyadh."

Yasmine's story matched what Kord had texted her. "What do you know about the family?"

"The cousin's name is Rashid Dagher, and he's a baker. He has an Iraqi wife, three daughters, and one son. All living in Riyadh."

One thing about Malik sounded amiss—his lack of discretion. Both gave her spirit caution. Monica wanted everything available about the cousin, a man who had lived outside his country where it was potentially dangerous.

She stood and walked to a window. When assured no cameras were in sight, she typed into a secure site and requested a background and photos for Rashid Dagher and his family.

29

FROM THE FRONT PASSENGER SEAT of the limo, Kord stretched to see the shadowed, empty street ahead through the blinding rain. Wasi drove with the same frown he wore every day. At the moment, his look fit. Rain attacked the windshield while the wipers swiped back and forth at lightning speed. The gush of tires moving forward through high water had the six men in Prince Omar's limo quiet. Or maybe it was the seriousness of taking Malik in for questioning. If any doubt of Malik's innocence surfaced, the bodyguards would slit his throat.

They'd barely driven to Paramount High School, and memories of watching Zain die played out in Kord's mind. He assumed the crime replayed in the other men's too.

Kord reached inside his jacket pocket and pulled out his weapon. If they were being followed in the torrential rain, the outcome could be ugly. The windows were bulletproof but not bomb resistant.

"I want to know about anything suspicious," he said. "Hard to see a tail in the rain."

Prince Omar no longer used his original cell phone, so if attacked, the theory about his phone being infected with a virus might not hold ground, or in this case water.

Kord caught sight of a barricade ahead. Lights flashed, and two emergency trucks were parked to aid those stranded. "Don't attempt to go through."

Wasi stopped the vehicle. Even so, the water outside was nearly knee-deep. He placed the limo in reverse and slowly made it back to higher ground. Still the water rose steadily, and none of the streets looked any better. Kord pulled up his phone for weather info, and the dismal report cast doubts of making it to the FBI building on Highway 290. No signs of rain ending and flash flood warnings in low-lying areas.

Kord phoned SAC Thomas and explained the problem.

"The streets are impassable from that part of town," the SAC said. "Hold on to your man for a few hours."

If Malik survived until then. "There's a helicopter pad at the property."

"We're using everything the city has, including trucks, to evacuate civilians. Just get back to the house and sit tight."

"Keep me updated." Kord relayed the instruction.

The limo stalled. Wasi's attempts to restart failed.

"We've got to walk," Kord said. "Keep your eyes open."

Malik remained cuffed. The prince knew the

immunity law and termed Malik as a potential serious threat. The men in the rear would shoot him if he gave the slightest indication of running.

"Grab flashlights, but don't use them unless I give you the go-ahead. Leave the umbrellas. Hides our view. Avoid streetlights if possible." He turned to the prince. "Prince Omar, I know you'll be drenched, but . . ."

"I agree. Inform those at home to stay inside. No point in anyone attempting to rescue us while we're waiting in rising water. We can walk."

He opened the car door and water rushed into the vehicle and onto them. Instantly they were soaked. Everyone exited onto the empty lakelike street. Wasi released the trunk and retrieved flashlights for himself, Ali, Saad, and Prince Omar. Kord had his Glock in one hand and a small personal flashlight in the other. The men formed a circle around Prince Omar. Kord assigned Saad to Malik detail and then took that bodyguard's place. Street and business lights flickered in the heavy rain, making Kord question their reliability. In the open, they were like flies ready to be swatted. Add to that the blinding rain. He swung to anything stirring. For sure Prince Omar thought sand was easier to navigate than fast-moving water.

He phoned Monica with an update. "No one is to leave the house. We're not far."

Again they walked toward the River Oaks estate.

Ali walked beside Saad. "Faster," he said to Malik.

"Take these cuffs off, and I will."

"Not happening," Kord said. Street and business lights silently disappeared, indicating loss of power. Relieved, Kord waded on. He preferred a shield of darkness. They needed the flashlights, and yet an assassin could mow them down.

He glanced back at Malik stumbling through the water. He fell face-first. Ali held Malik down.

"Don't let him drown," Kord said. "We need his intel." He hoped the order would keep Malik alive.

Ali continued to hold him beneath the water.

"Ali, let him up." Kord pulled his Glock and moved to where Malik was flailing in the water. "What if you're drowning an innocent man?"

"He's guilty."

"Now, or I'll pull the trigger."

"Ali, release him." Prince Omar emerged from the circle of bodyguards. "He's Saad's responsibility. This man will not die tonight."

Ali jerked Malik up and shoved him toward Saad. Malik coughed and sputtered.

If they made it back to the house without being killed, who'd prevent the bodyguards from carrying out their own justice?

30

KORD AND THOSE WHO'D BEEN in the limo arrived at the wrought-iron gate of the Saud home. Security hadn't been hampered by the inclement weather and allowed them access. They plodded up the driveway in wet clothes and waterlogged shoes to the home lit by generators, as were many of the residences in the area. Karim and Fares ushered them inside the front entrance and provided them with towels and a change of clothing.

Prince Omar raised his shoulders. Kord knew the prince would not complain of the wet and cold. Not his style. "Saad, lock Malik in the safe room until he can be transported. He won't be able to hear a word there."

"Amir," Malik said, "I'm innocent—"

Prince Omar whirled and did a nose-to-nose in Malik's face. "Be glad the FBI will be questioning you. If you have information, you'd better tell all. Every moment lost to the FBI's questioning infuriates me. Don't make me wish I hadn't stopped Ali. One more word, and I'm walking away."

Nothing else was said. Kord would need to stay close to the safe room or Malik wouldn't survive the day.

• • •

Monica heard the men enter the house, and she could only imagine the tempers flaring. Angry bodyguards with blood on their minds? Plus they'd dealt with rain pouring buckets on the terrain with no sign of easing up. She counted ten minutes and texted Kord.

Malik alive?

In safe room.

Who's guarding him?

Me.

She left the women's area and walked down the stairs. Karim and Fares nodded her direction. No eye contact, but that was a better reception than she'd received in the past.

Her pattern of investigation and protection since Tuesday hadn't deviated from watchful mode, and she despised it. At times, she wondered if Liam's heinous crimes stalked her like a demon.

She made her way to where Kord sat on a tufted bench, peering at his phone's screen as though a massive glob of superglue held him in place. Dressed in jeans and a T-shirt, he looked rather pitiful.

"Greetings from the dungeon," he said.

She pointed to his bare feet. "Shoes destroyed?"

"That's the least of my worries. Ali nearly drowned Malik. My guess is he'll try to finish what he started."

"Why not get some sleep? I'll stay alert."

He shook his head. "I could ask the same of you."

"We're partners."

He gave her a slight smile. "If this blasted rain would stop, the FBI could arrange to get Malik out of here."

"I have a whole list of what I'd like to see happen."

He studied her, and uneasiness crept over her. "What were some of your past assignments?"

Not going there. "Boring compared to yours."

"Your résumé skims what I know is an outstanding operative."

"Off-limits."

"Only making conversation. But I get it."

She eased down beside him and met his gaze. His eyes told her more had crept into his mind than their mission.

"Strange," he said.

"What?"

"If we were sitting here and not working, I'd take your hand."

"Oh, really." She kept her words flat.

"Then I might kiss you."

She tingled. "Only if I let you."

He laughed, allowing the tension between them to fade. So Kord felt the same attraction.

"You're blushing."

"I'm a pale blonde. We do that."

"Oh, really." He mocked her previous tone.

"But you'd have the unequally yoked thing going."

"That's from the Bible."

"Yep. I've read it."

"And?"

"I'm still searching. Prince Omar urges me to accept Islam, and I see similarities with the Bible." He paused. "But I see the differences, too."

"Take a look at archaeology," she said. "The Dead Sea Scrolls, the writings of Josephus."

"Have been. A discussion for another time."

She pressed on with her own agenda before he attempted to kiss her and she let him. Great, she should be praying for his soul, not contemplating a kiss. "Prince Omar had Fares deliver new phones to Fatima and Yasmine right away. They voiced their displeasure about not having their previous contact information, which I assume the prince heard. Not sure why those two haven't figured out their brother hears everything. Or maybe they have and don't care. A few moments later, they were both on the balcony texting. Could be innocent, or it could be treacherous."

"What are you thinking?"

"Looking for an opportunity to see for myself. And I'm certain to have Prince Omar's support."

"He may confiscate their phones again for the same reason."

"If I'm caught, I lose their trust. Tough call.

I believe transparency is my key to either exonerating the princesses or proving one or both of them is guilty. I hope not the latter. Malik hasn't left the witness stand for me. Yasmine is in love with him. But if she's hiding anything, then she's a master at lying." She lowered her voice. "Of course her sister has the same broken heart issue."

"Thanks for the reminder." His phone buzzed with an incoming call. "Great timing." He answered. "Nasim. I'd like for my partner to hear our conversation. She's CIA." Kord listened and nodded. "Thank you." He motioned for her to lean in to the phone. "What's happening?"

His voice cracked. "My wife and sons are dead. They took my daughter."

"Who?"

"I never saw them. They broke into my home while I was at work. I blame those who found out what I learned about Prince Omar."

"I'm sorry. Let me help you escape. Where are you now?"

"At my brother's house, but I can't stay here."

"The safe house is eleven miles from your village. Head north. I'll alert them."

"No car. Will call later."

"Get help before you go after your daughter."

The call ended, and Kord pressed in another number. The man would not survive unless he followed Kord's instructions. "Nasim is walking your direction. Family killed. Daughter taken. No positive ID on who's responsible. I'll get back to you ASAP." He pressed in another number and explained to Prince Omar what had happened.

When the calls ended, she secured his attention with a whisper. "Nasim al-Bazzi?"

He nodded.

"One of ours too." She texted Jeff, the third message tonight. She prayed that between the CIA and FBI, Nasim would escape death.

"Problem is," Kord said, "I bet he goes after his daughter."

She moaned. "Can't blame him."

"I'd do the same. She's probably dead, and he's walking into a trap."

"I'm staying here until we have intel about Nasim and a plan forward with Malik. The princesses are busy, and I can keep you company. Or help take out Ali."

"Ali's not a bad guy. Just thinks differently than you or me." He leaned his head back. "If the mole is here and giving the enemy our every move, then those of us caught in the rain would be dead."

"Depends. If all of you were dead but one man, the authorities would have the name."

"Are you the voice of reason?"

She wished. "Just trying to think like those who want us out of the picture."

"I'm banking on the prince's sporadic use of his

cell phone to keep the killer baited. I asked him to use it for a call to Riyadh regarding Malik's arrest. Should ease the killer's mind."

She shook her head. "Unless Malik is guilty. Then he has reasons to be afraid."

They talked until 6:55, when SAC Thomas alerted Kord that a helicopter would be landing at the Saud home to pick up Malik, Kord, Prince Omar, and Ali.

Monica longed to be a part of the interrogation detail, wanted to hear Malik confess to the killings and end the tragedies. Instead she was stuck at the home in a Saudi man's world. "I never enjoyed inaction."

"Sorry. I'll tell you everything."

"Not the same, partner."

31

A FEW MINUTES BEFORE NOON on Thursday, SAC Thomas walked into his office at the FBI and shut the door. "Kord, we have nothing on Malik al-Kazaz to hold him. Forty-eight hours, and he's out of here unless we find proof of his involvement." Frustration scraped every word. "The only suspicious activity is the IP address linking him to Arabic chatter. But the time stamp on the e-mail was when he and Princess Yasmine were having their little tryst. We're waiting for evidence to prove an e-mail hack because this may be a setup."

"I heard the interview, and I see the holes. Did he give you a name when he asked to speak to you privately?"

The SAC slumped into his chair. "No. Malik's afraid you'll assist in his death. His story about the trip to Iraq for his father checked out. We ran a background on Rashid Dagher, and he's not affiliated with any terrorist groups or those opposing the Saud family."

Kord could have guessed that, but he wasn't about to say so.

"There's a twenty-one-year-old son, Youssof, who cleared too."

"Can't we keep him until we have arrests? The

diplomatic immunity went by the wayside with suspected murder." He heard near exhaustion in his own voice and forced strength into his words. "At least until you verify the link to Arabic chatter."

SAC Thomas uttered a familiar phrase about Kord's smart mouth, the curses rattling the small room. "Do you need a reminder of the critical nature of this case? You're wasting your time with an innocent man."

"I brought Malik in this morning with suspected ties to a murder. My job. What more do you want?"

The SAC rubbed his face. "If nothing surfaces, I'll have him escorted on a flight back to Saudi Arabia. Let the royal family handle him."

"Three men are dead."

"I don't need a reminder. The man in custody was with the prince during the three killings."

"Has he contacted Consul General al-Fakeeh for legal representation?"

"No mention of it."

"Has the FBI informed him?"

"Yes."

The conversation was getting nowhere, and the air-conditioning inside the SAC's office ran as cold as their differences of opinion. "So I accompany the prince and his men to River Oaks? Tell them if the FBI concludes Malik's innocent, he's expelled home? The man will be dead five minutes after the plane lands in Riyadh, and we won't know a thing more than right now. You must have dug up something since Tuesday."

"We've questioned him for over four hours, and he hasn't budged from his story. You heard me offer him a deal if he'd give the names involved with the murders."

Kord listened. No point in fueling the chilling temps unless he needed to make another point.

"I could care less about him meeting with a princess minus a chaperone. That doesn't add up to murder."

"Sir, I agree. Nothing in the interview or his body language indicated a conspiracy. But the Saudis are looking for someone to blame." Malik had lost credibility with the prince, and Kord wished there was something to keep the man in custody longer than forty-eight hours.

SAC Thomas held up a finger. "The mole is in that fancy house, eating the best food and planning murder. No doubt in my mind. But it's not Malik. Don't ever question my authority again, understand? Every minute ticking by increases the chances of another American's murder or Prince Omar's death on American soil."

"The man is like a brother to me. When have you ever seen me use poor judgment, emotion or not?"

"Our careers are finished if the plot is successful.

More innocent Americans may be at risk. The conservatives in Saudi Arabia are dragging us to the gallows with the death of one of their own citizens."

Kord swallowed his ire. "I am well aware of the potential repercussions. The consul general's security is also a concern. What's being done there?"

SAC Thomas drew in a breath. "Everything possible. Heavily guarded. Surveillance teams."

"Doesn't mean he won't be a target."

"We'll work our end. You work yours." He looked at his watch. "When will Prince Omar and his bodyguards be done with prayers?"

"About ten minutes."

"I'm due in a meeting, which means I'll miss them. Give my regards and contact me later. You want to prove Malik's knee-deep in this? You have forty-eight hours. We all have the same amount of time. No one wants this settled more than I do. Don't disappoint me."

"Yes, sir."

SAC Thomas frowned and left the room. Kord understood the pressure the FBI and the CIA were under to keep the prince alive. But neither of the men had more at stake than Kord. Nothing in his growing-up years slid close to the level of commitment he had with Prince Omar.

He texted Monica.

Holding Malik 48 hrs.

If he'd lure Yasmine 2 lie & break culture, he can't b trusted. What about trip 2 Iraq?

Same story as yours. Anything on ur end?

Youssof Dagher returned 2 Iraq.

Why?

Don't know. Working on finding him.

News from princesses?

No. I don't trust Malik.

Jury's out here.

Why had Youssof returned to Iraq? The other matter that wouldn't leave Kord alone was Nasim. Why hadn't he called?

32

SHORTLY AFTER 1 P.M., THE FBI arranged transportation for Prince Omar, Ali, and Kord to the Saud home. The rain had ceased and receding waters made driving easier.

"Ali, contact the men at the house. I want all of you to hear this," Prince Omar said once in the vehicle. When the three bodyguards were in listening mode, the prince began again. Obviously not concerned about the FBI agent driving the car hearing every word. "Authorities have enough cause to keep Malik in custody forty-eight hours while they investigate his story and a possible connection to the assassination plot. According to US law, they need evidence to incarcerate him any longer. In my opinion, he's not being held long enough to verify his statements. But if released, he will be sent home for us to deal with. He's lucky to have his life."

No mention of Yasmine.

"Do any of you have reason—and proof—to distrust Malik?" His voice was shrouded in anger.

None of them expressed doubts.

If a thirty-two-year-old man had been sneaking around seeing Kord's teenage sister, which he didn't have, Malik might have a few broken bones. The one consolation was Ali acting as press secretary. A fine man in Kord's opinion. Hot-tempered and highly intelligent. Although Monica distrusted him. Kord could be closer to Ali and the prince, a strong team. And if Malik was at fault, his treachery ended now.

The vehicle pulled up to the gate, but it was open.

"Why is the gate unlocked?" Kord strained to see any vehicles.

"Food delivery." Ali rubbed his face, no doubt worn-out like the rest of them. "The driver is prompt every afternoon."

"Who do you use?"

"A service on Wilcrest."

Working without sleep had hit Kord hard this morning, and at times it clouded his judgment. He blinked and studied the van parked in the rear. The food delivery service had an impeccable reputation, but something wasn't sitting right with him.

"Ali, once we've parked, let's talk to the driver," he said.

"I've met him, and he's trustworthy. I made sure he passed security clearance."

"The one you've spoken to could be a great guy, but I'd like to talk—"

"Makes sense."

Once Prince Omar was escorted inside the home, Ali and Kord made their way to the kitchen

239

pantry, where fresh food was being stacked on a counter.

"You're a different driver from yesterday," Ali said in Arabic.

A short, round man with olive skin and dark hair sized up Ali before responding. "This is his day off." He answered in English, his voice holding no hint of an accent.

"I'd like to see your identification." Ali's size alone spoke of intimidation. Possible face-off? Kord might recruit him for the FBI.

"I left it in the van." He added a small box of bananas to the counter, and the cook examined them.

Ali glared down his nose at the driver. "We'll retrieve it together."

"I don't understand what's going on."

Ali crossed his arms over his massive chest. "We're doing our job for Prince Omar. Ensuring his family's safety is our priority."

"I'll join you," Kord said. Ali nodded and he followed.

Outside, the spring weather held a hefty breeze. Typical March. The closer they walked to the white food-service van, the more the driver sped up his pace.

"Are you new to the food industry?" Kord kept stride beside him.

"I've been driving this van for eight years."

Kord touched his Glock inside his jacket. "The

owners have been in business for six years."

The man chuckled. "Seems like eight." He opened the driver's side of the van. "I thought I'd left my wallet on the rear seat."

Kord and Ali waited.

"Maybe I dropped it." He entered the van and the door slid shut. The lock clicked.

Kord reached for the driver's door at the same time Ali grabbed the passenger door. Both locked.

The engine roared to life. The driver slammed the van into reverse, knocking Kord and Ali backward. The tires squealed in protest, and the van whirled around, heading straight for the gate. The driver lowered his window and fired their direction.

"The gate controls." Ali rushed toward the manual panel in the garage with his phone to his ear.

Kord fired repeatedly at the moving target while racing after it. Bullets flew through a passenger side window. The van swerved as though Kord had hit the target. Bullets soared into the metal and one hit a tire. The van pushed through the gate on three wheels.

Yanking his phone from his jacket, Kord pressed in the secure line that fed to HPD, giving the driver and van description along with license plate numbers. Second call went to SAC Thomas while Kord hurried back to Ali.

"Are you all right?" Ali said.

Kord nodded. "Made the calls. I got his license plate, and the security camera at the gate will have it too." He pointed to the rear entrance leading to the pantry. "The food's probably poisoned." Alarm jarred his senses.

While bolting through the door, he remembered the four boxes of fresh produce and the ability to hide an explosive device.

"Get those boxes out of the house." Kord's arm stung, and a quick look showed blood had seeped through his left jacket sleeve. Ali's question made sense. Grabbing two boxes, he pushed through the pain to carry them to the far corner of the property. Ali was right behind him with the other two. Near the rear west corner, they carefully laid them on the water-soaked grass.

"Get on back to the house," Kord said. "If a bomb's here, you'll be blown with it. Don't think you'd do well as vegetable soup." He lifted produce from a box, listening and looking.

Ali did the same. "My loyalty is to the amir." He snorted. "Here it is. Five minutes and counting. Have you ever disarmed a bomb?"

"Only a trip-wired device in your neck of the woods. Anything else is . . . Monica. She can do it."

Ali tore across the grounds to the house, his phone in hand. Kord called her. Didn't matter who got to her first.

When she answered, he said, "Bomb on west side of grounds." He pressed End and dropped the phone on the grass.

Staring at the bomb, he noted, in addition to the timer, a cell phone was attached and could also serve as a trigger for the explosive device. Anyone with that phone's number could initiate a remote detonation at any moment.

The sophistication of the bomb was a long way from a wire across a dirt road in a third-world country. Seconds ticked away as he kept one eye on the timer and the other on the rear of the house, as if his concentration could hurry her or delay the driver from remotely triggering the explosive.

Monica raced toward him.

Three minutes, eleven seconds.

Not sure how those short legs pumped her body so fast. Ali hurried behind her carrying what looked like a small tool belt. Smart man. She'd need it. Once she was beside Kord, she knelt with her focus on the device. "The last time I did this was in the downtown underground tunnels," she whispered, not once looking his way. "Then I had a coverage suit, Kevlar vest, a mask, and a pair of Nomex gloves. But I can work without them. First off, I need wire clippers before some jerk detonates this baby."

Ali handed her the tool.

Kord didn't respond. From experience, he

understood she needed to concentrate on each step, and talking must put her in the right zone.

Two minutes, forty-seven seconds.

In the distance, sirens grew closer. His phone vibrated.

"Answer it, Kord," she said with the voice of an angel. "I have this."

"It can wait."

"Unless you're praying, you aren't a help."

One minute, fifty-one seconds. He turned his phone off.

She explored the device.

One minute, eleven seconds.

If her God was watching, they all could use the help.

Fifty-eight seconds.

Monica peered at the wires and clipped. "Not yet," she said. "There's another wire."

Twenty-three seconds.

"Where are you?" She smiled and clipped a second wire. "We're good."

Seven seconds remaining.

33

MONICA PICKED UP a box of veggies and walked toward an FBI SUV. The agents would transfer the food to a lab for testing. Perspiration beaded her face while adrenaline continued to flow. Inside, she trembled like a leaf blown by the wind.

Thank You. Every inch of me shivered. You know I'd never seen that type of bomb before.

"You can have my back anytime." Kord attempted to take the box from her arms.

She hadn't noted him approaching her. Where were her operative skills? "I still have this. You're bleeding, by the way, and I'm not a nurse."

"I can plaster on a Band-Aid."

Ali took the load with the toolbox in the other hand, and she laughed. "Thanks."

"Miss Alden. I have never seen a woman with your skills. I'm impressed."

"I grew up in a family of boys, climbed trees, fished, played baseball, and hunted instead of learning girl things."

"You don't cook?"

She laughed again, one way she relieved stress. "I can roast and brew a mean cup of coffee, and I can bake, but not cook." She noted Kord's blood-soaked jacket sleeve. "You need that tended to ASAP. Infection can set in real fast."

"I requested an ambulance," Ali said. The man had spoken more in the last thirty minutes than the entire time she'd been there. "Kord has a reputation for not seeking medical attention."

"Do you have firsthand knowledge of some of his exploits?"

"Zain told me plenty."

She softened her tone. "I'd like to hear them."

"Ask Kord. I'm sure he'd play the hero."

"I'm right beside you," Kord said. "My hearing's just fine."

"I remember you running barefoot after a man who attempted to assault the prince," Ali said.

"In Saudi?" she said. "Why was he barefoot?"

"Actually, he'd just stepped out of the—"

"Never mind, Ali. Monica doesn't need to hear that story. Are you getting all Western on us?"

"I think so."

The bantering between the two men relieved the apprehension she'd once had for Ali's reasons for protecting the prince. Ali's staying close while she disarmed the bomb had garnered a huge load of respect for him.

"Kord, who called you when we were back there?"

"SAC Thomas. Left a voice mail."

Curiosity about Special Agent Kord Davidson swirled warm through her. The more she discovered about him, the more she admired. At the outset, he'd been against her as his partner.

And when she learned he and Prince Omar were friends, she understood he felt responsible for what had happened, although it wasn't his negligence but the work of a killer. Yet he'd demonstrated courage and wisdom with his priority as a federal agent in a case that had the potential of serious implications. A twinge of undeniable attraction had crept into her heart. Memories of Liam slammed into her brain, and she swept personal thoughts about Kord under a rug called "detonated dreams."

A paramedic treated his left arm. Thankfully, the bullet had taken a hunk of flesh but not embedded. He refused a ride to the hospital and requested they bandage him up.

"He needs a tetanus shot," she said. His type usually let precaution slide. She should know.

"You're in luck. We have one." A young paramedic turned to Kord. "When's the last time you had a tetanus shot?"

"Don't remember."

"Kord?" Monica felt as though she were talking to one of her burly brothers. "I saved your rear. Take the shot."

And he did.

After the boxes of food were loaded and the agents drove away, Prince Omar approached them on the terrace with Saad, Wasi, and four police officers. Even with a bomb nearly sending him to pieces, the prince walked proudly. Sort of reminding her of a lion. Kord explained what happened and his role of alerting law enforcement and contacting the security company that allowed the van to enter and exit the property.

Kord nodded at the officers. "Has the driver been arrested?"

"HPD and the FBI have men on it," an officer said. "The original driver was found unconscious by a Dumpster at the food distribution center, and the van had been abandoned in a downtown alley. The FBI has sent a team to sweep it."

Monica bit her tongue. The intricately designed scheme had *well-plotted* stamped on it—and Middle Eastern money, in her opinion.

"The driver spoke English when Ali questioned him in Arabic," Kord said.

Reality swirled in her stomach. Today had come dangerously close to the enemy claiming victory. The driver had failed but for certain he had plans B and C with every detail covered.

"How was the original driver injured? A blow to the head?" she said.

"No, ma'am. I've been told a medically induced coma."

"Probably a barbiturate." She'd contact Jeff at the next possible moment. Her handler had a way of pulling facts from thin air.

Ali interrupted her thoughts with his announcement of her heroism. "Miss Alden disarmed the bomb or we'd all be dead."

She sensed Prince Omar's gaze. Dare she be Western and give him eye contact, or should she avoid those dark pools of power and age-old culture? She chose the latter, feeling God wanted her testimony to be respectful.

"Miss Alden, I sincerely appreciate your contribution to saving lives today. My family is indebted to you," he said. "Later, we should discuss other matters."

A nudging in her spirit told her two things— she'd succeeded in gaining his favor, and he'd overheard the earlier conversation with Fatima and Yasmine. The prince would have questions, and she hoped none of them dealt with Liam.

Within the hour, Monica had identified the coma-inducing drug used against the food-service driver—injected pentobarbital. The original driver was a naturalized Iranian, been in the US for sixteen years. No priors or ties to terrorists. She wanted to talk to him, but her duties stayed intact at the Saud home.

Jeff offered to patch her and Kord into an FBI interview with the driver at the hospital. She connected to the video feed while Kord watched the interview with Prince Omar in the prince's office.

"While I was leaving the warehouse parking lot, a car pulled in front of me so I couldn't move. A short, round man wearing a ball cap and sunglasses exited and approached me. Beard too. He smiled and waved. He said he needed directions and had a hearing problem. That's when I saw his car, a Honda."

"Did he speak English?"

"Farsi."

Was the man they were seeking Iranian?

"Did you see the license plate?"

"No, sir. But I do remember a huge dent on the passenger side of his car." He paused as though trying to recall any details. "I got out of my van. It happened so fast. He stuck a needle into my neck. That's all I remember until I woke up here."

"Had you seen the man before?" a female FBI agent said.

"No, ma'am." Tight facial muscles.

"Can you give us more of a description?"

"He was Iranian like me."

"Could you identify the man in a lineup?"

"Not sure. But I'd try. Don't you have people who can draw a picture of what I remember?"

"We do, and we value your help."

When the interview ended, Monica closed her eyes. She'd not seen the potential bomber to recall his identity, her one trait that had raised her status for this mission. The Iranian driver could have been victim number four. Her phone rang, and as she expected, it was Kord.

"Not much to go on, but the assailant's description is similar to the man who posed as the consul general's limo driver outside MD Anderson."

"Kord, the two men have different body shapes, but I agree he can't conceal his height unless he wears platform shoes. Is the driver alive because of his nationality or is he lying?"

"I requested a surveillance team."

"And I'll see if there's anything hiding in his background." She saw the hour approached 3:30. "I'll be downstairs in a few minutes. Has SAC Thomas questioned Malik about the bomb?"

"Going on now. Might have an update when we talk."

"We need more of a break than two men who share the same height."

"Right. You were amazing today. I'm a lucky guy to have you as my partner."

His words touched her in a forbidden place. *Change the subject, Monica.* "You'd have done the same thing. I have a topic to discuss with you. The prince sent me to join his sisters after the episode with Malik and Yasmine. We talked in the common area. I assume he's listened to every word."

"Bank on it."

"Would he share that with you?"

"Possibly, if Yasmine admitted something. Is there a problem?"

She wished for the umpteenth time that she hadn't mentioned Liam. Telling Fatima and

Yasmine came far too easily. The truth flowed from her lips despite that others would learn about her regrettable past. Not her normal mode of operation. Small comfort if the prince or Kord had done a thorough history—they already knew. "This house is filled with cameras and listening devices. Makes me uncomfortable. But in his position, I'd do the same to protect my loved ones."

"We have nothing to hide."

Privacy was essential in their mission, but she'd not speak of needing it inside the home and neither would Kord. Ali . . . maybe he wasn't a part of the prince's betrayal. He'd risked his life today.

Malik was in a cell when the bomb was brought to the house. But she believed Malik had not worked alone.

The undeniable fact repeatedly surfaced. They had no clue who wanted Prince Omar dead. And she felt incredibly inept. Why hadn't Jeff given her the mission of finding who was responsible for the murders instead of . . . this?

34

SHORTLY AFTER 4 P.M., KORD LEARNED the Honda driven by the suspect was found at a used car lot.

The owner of the dealership became suspicious when the news indicated a potential killer was on the loose in a car matching one he'd just taken as a trade-in. A Hispanic man with an accent had paid cash for a red Chevy pickup truck. He wore jeans, a T-shirt that said *Anything for Selenas*, a tattered cowboy hat, and dirt-covered boots. Went by the name of Jose Alvarez. Upon further questioning, the dealer claimed Alvarez was of slight build and had no mustache.

They assumed at least two men were involved in the assassination attempts, but that speculation needed verification.

HPD verified the Honda had been reported stolen the day before, and the owner of the used car lot had been given a false title. Kord relived the frustration he'd seen in Monica's face earlier.

Nasim hadn't called, and Kord feared the worst. Others inside Iraq could provide valuable intel, but this man was a friend. Took risks to bring positive changes to his country and the Middle East. The tragedy in Nasim's life made Kord question why he considered the existence of God, why the matter pressed against his mind.

Only his desire to find a superior being who made more sense than the failings of mankind kept him looking, exploring.

He'd become way too philosophical.

Kord walked to the natatorium, reaching deep and searching for who and what motivated the relentless assault. Two and a half days with Prince Omar, and he knew little more than on Tuesday morning when he'd met his friend at the airport.

Prince Omar entered the area and the two men ventured outside onto the grounds, warm with the western sun. "Kord, you would tell me if the plot is from the Americans?"

The somber look on his old friend's face clouded the truth of who Kord was and his ideals. "I assure you the US government is not behind this. Why would SAC Thomas and the CIA be supporting you to end the killings and crimes?"

"The perfect American cover-up?"

"No, Amir. In this instance you're wrong. I understand your doubt, the distrust, but the US government is on your side. Are you thinking Malik is innocent?"

"Looking at all the possibilities. I've spent hours thinking through every person in this house and at home, even my sisters. Kord, I have no suspects."

"Malik is no longer here, but he could have easily given your schedule to the media, or an accomplice, before arriving in the US. He could also have arranged for the bomb to be planted in the food delivery. If he isn't the one who betrayed you, we'll soon find out."

"What course of action do you recommend? Because the waiting is making me short-tempered."

"I suggest rearranging every item—again. Better yet, don't go anywhere."

The prince smiled despite the bleak circumstances. "That won't happen. Once dinner is over, we'll retire to my office and reschedule everything. It may be a problem with some appointments, especially those regarding my mother. For example it's impossible to change her surgery date and time. We'll need extra men with us to cover it."

"For the after-dinner meeting, shall I include Monica?" Kord wanted her input rather than giving info to her secondhand.

"I prefer she keep company with my sisters."

"What have you heard from their conversations?"

He gave a slight nod. "Come with me, and you'll see the burden I have with my sisters."

The two returned to the house and entered Prince Omar's office. He closed the door. The prince inserted a flash drive into his laptop. Once the recordings were downloaded, Kord listened to Yasmine's confession about her relationship with Malik. Fatima's voice came through as well as Monica's with comments and questions. But the confession of what Monica experienced two years ago came as a surprise. Kord knew she'd killed an operative when he used biological weapons on a village in Africa. But he didn't know the extent of her involvement with the man. Now he understood why she followed up on his every move. Her lack of trust came into play. She blamed herself and couldn't get past it.

Prince Omar ejected the flash drive and tossed it in his hand. "Miss Alden is fearless, although she blames herself for the tragedy in Africa."

"Why did you want me to hear the recording?"

"To commend you on your partner's sensitivity to a young woman's feelings in the midst of her pain. And . . ."

"What?"

"Fatima still has feelings for you. When she learned you were assigned to me, she was upset. Yasmine told me about her foolishness."

Kord valued the word *foolishness*. A sense of what Malik went through crept into his mind. "I never led her to believe I had interest."

"You talked with her as a friend on two occasions, and on the second, you reminded her that your meeting was forbidden, and it could not happen again."

"I should have told you myself, and I apologize." The idea of Fatima still hurting unsettled him.

The prince waved away Kord's comment. "She will have a husband soon. A favorable match for both families, and he has no other wives. She's not aware. I intend to tell her before dinner."

Marrying a man she didn't love wasn't the solution, not in Western culture anyway.

"Fatima is a woman weak with emotion, like her younger sister. Once she's busy with a husband and family, she'll be happy.

"If Malik attempts to contact Yasmine, I must be informed immediately. His life is thin right now. Both Yasmine and Fatima have mobile phones with international accessibility. I blocked his number, but he could find the means to contact either of them."

"I'd want to believe they would tell you."

"Who is behind this? It's as though another person lives in my mind and is transmitting my life to the enemy." He sighed. "The source must be my original cell phone, like you suspect."

"The security company was cleared. Are you confident in their discretion?"

"So far. I'd like to face this man and end it on my terms. As you say, playing defense isn't my game."

If only they could attach a name to the man instead of a faceless executioner. Kord took a look at his watch. "We have time to go over your itinerary, before I notify SAC Thomas and the CIA that we've taken measures to rearrange your schedule. We want to make sure tomorrow's luncheon is leaked to the media."

The prince's new cell phone rang. He took the call while facing Kord. "What have you learned?" he said in Arabic. Prince Omar lifted a brow and thanked the caller. He ended the conversation. "We have answers. Someone within my country has paid an Iranian to carry out the assassination here in Houston. No names. My people are investigating the possibility of the Iranian government backing the plot. They may have nuclear weapons, but we'd blow them off the map first."

"Neither is necessary."

"Men take risks when the stakes are high."

Kord snatched his own cell phone, called SAC Thomas, and revealed the recent findings. "The killer could have gotten access through Mexico, or he could be a naturalized citizen."

"I'm working with a cartel informant," SAC Thomas said. "He claims no hit contracts have come through. Send me the updated itinerary once you've finished it. I'll have Malik questioned again. See if he's ready to change his story."

"Word about Nasim on your end?"

"Waiting."

Kord hung up and relayed the SAC's response to Prince Omar.

"Answers lead to arrests," Prince Omar said. "Now to figure out who in my country seeks to betray me and why."

"Have the conservatives followed through on any of their threats?"

"Only talk. But three men are dead."

They needed so much more intel.

35

AT THE PRINCE'S REQUEST, Monica prepared to enter the common area with the princesses and share dinner with them. If given a choice, she'd eat in her bedroom and sort through the day's intel and happenings. What a day . . .

The bomb.

Kord's flesh wound.

Nasim's plight.

Malik's fate.

Another confirmation of a plot inside Saudi Arabia against Prince Omar.

And tomorrow the trap for the alleged killer. Add to all of it the rising floodwaters devastating much of Houston.

Shaking off the load of work, she opened her bedroom door to greet Fatima and Yasmine. The aroma of fresh bread and vegetables caused her stomach to rumble. The sisters stared out the same window where she'd stood observing Yasmine with Malik. The younger sister had her arm around the older. Kord had texted her that Prince Omar had requested a meeting with Fatima. Could this be bad news?

"Dinner smells wonderful," Monica said.

Yasmine gave a sad smile.

"Is everything okay?"

Fatima shook her head and faced Monica with tears streaming down her face. "My brother and father have arranged marriage."

Dare Monica apologize, soothe, or listen? "I'm sure he has your best interests at heart."

"He thinks so. Plans are being made."

Monica had more than once been grateful for living in the US. "I hope you find happiness."

Fatima sighed. "I will do my best. I've known the man since we were children." She lifted her chin as Monica had seen before. "He's kind."

"Sister, your dreams of children will come true," Yasmine said. "You'll be a wonderful mother."

"I'll try to think of those things."

"We can begin by having a celebratory dinner," Yasmine said. "Mother will be pleased."

"My appetite has vanished." She took a glance out the window. "Yes, we will eat and chat and laugh. Omar would not have agreed to the arrangement if he did not think the marriage would be good."

When the meal was over, Monica addressed the sisters. "I need to ask something that's important to you and your brother's protection. Both of you have new phones. If the prince requested to see the numbers you've called, would there be a problem?"

Fatima rose and walked to her room. Yasmine

did the same. Both returned and handed their devices to Monica.

"All female family members, including Mother," Fatima said.

"So are my contacts and calls," Yasmine said.

"Yes," Fatima said. "Above all things we are loyal to our beloved brother."

Monica slipped into bed before 9:00 p.m. Tomorrow's demands left no room for error or an exhausted body. She fell asleep and prayed the nightmares about Liam were over.

An incoming text woke her. She reached for her phone on the nightstand and glanced at the time: 1:45. It was Jeff.

Nasim al-Bazzi found shot dead.

Who killed him?

No one's talking.

Where?

Near his village.

Have u informed the FBI?

Yes. Will update u later.

Monica leaned back against the pillow. Wide-awake. She hadn't met Nasim, just knew he was a valuable informant who desperately wanted to get to the US with his family. He'd infiltrated many areas of the Middle East to keep the world safe. And he was Kord's friend.

Liam had stalked her sleeping hours, and terrorists plagued her waking ones. Now another victim. She texted Kord with the news and closed her eyes while waiting for his reply. He called instead.

"Another honorable man down," Kord said.

"How did you meet him?"

"He tried to take me out while I was on a manhunt. He thought I meant him harm. Convinced him to work for the good guys."

"I'm sorry." Kord had lost two friends in less than three days.

"His father lives in Seattle. They were looking forward to a reunion. I want whoever's behind this prosecuted."

She'd been on a similar mission like this in Tanzania . . . with Liam. "We need to find them alive."

"It's set for tomorrow at two thirty."

"Anything you can do for Nasim?"

"Need to call his father and relay the tragedy."

"I'm sorry." She said good-bye and laid her phone on the nightstand. She prayed for Nasim's daughter in hopes she escaped her kidnappers alive.

But what if she and Kord were wrong? What if the cell phone virus was an incorrect hunch? All they had was an internal plot against Prince Omar, one in which the Iranians were involved. Nasim had proven himself many times before his death, and she believed he'd died for learning the truth.

36

FRIDAY AFTERNOON Monica took her place inside Morton's steak house as a hostess. CIA operatives and FBI agents, dressed as staff, monitored their posts. She walked to the glass door. Snipers were in position across the street at her 10:00 and at her 3:00. The parking lot held a mix of law enforcement, and the city's cameras had every foot covered. Soon Kord would arrive in the limo. Ali insisted upon being part of the operation, as well as Saad and Wasi.

She prayed to be alert and filled with wisdom. Kord had put himself in far too much danger. She'd do the same thing. But in a few short days, Kord had touched a part of her that she hadn't believed possible. Neither was she sure she wanted, needed, or deserved that.

At 2:29 p.m., the Mercedes limo stopped in front of the restaurant. The bodyguards, dressed in suits, emerged and scanned the area before Ali opened the door for Kord, disguised as Prince Omar. Two agents in the hostess area opened the restaurant doors to greet the arrivals. Monica held her breath as Kord left the limo. Zain had been killed by a sniper in a similar situation.

The small group walked inside with all the flair of royalty and no incidents.

Two operatives escorted the entourage to a private dining area. The restaurant doors remained unlocked. How easy could this be for the killer?

Now the wait.

The prince, like others in his country, supported moving beyond a dependence on oil. Those goals and ambitions for a country to stay afloat in a yacht instead of a rowboat meant acquiring allies to make it all happen. A worthy project, and she commended Prince Omar for his dedication. He simply needed to live through whatever was planned against him.

She'd gained respect for the prince.

A couple entered the restaurant, and she explained they were closed for a private party. They made reservations for dinner.

Two men in business attire requested the bar, and she repeated the same. Their disappointment came through in language she preferred not to hear.

An impeccably dressed man entered, Hispanic, three-piece gray suit, conservative silk tie, and jet-black hair worn above his collar. Slender. An attitude and expensive shades. He smiled at her and she returned the gesture.

"Good afternoon." His accent indicated Spanish, but a little high-pitched.

"Sir, we're closed until four thirty for a private party." Her words sounded into the ears of agents and operatives.

"All I need is a table for one."

"I'm sorry. Perhaps I can make reservations for later on this afternoon?"

He reached inside his suit coat. She tensed, then slowly relaxed. A wallet. He presented her with a bill. Benjamin Franklin smiled at her. "Will this help?"

"I'm afraid not. I must ask you to leave."

He swore in Spanish, then stiffened. "The door's unlocked for anyone to enter. Which means open for business."

"I'll take care of the oversight once you've left."

"Allow me to speak to your manager."

"He's with the private party."

"I'd like to use your men's room."

"I'm sorry. Do I need to call someone to escort you out?"

"Your rudeness will cost your job. I'll stay until I can speak to the manager."

"That won't be necessary. I'm calling security." Monica touched her weapon with her left hand, habit.

The man whipped out a firearm and aimed it at her face. "I know Prince Omar is here. Take me to him now."

"Stop." A male agent moved into the hostess area.

The intruder swung his attention to the agent, and Monica drew her weapon.

"Don't move," the intruder said. "Drop your weapons, or one of you is dead."

"We're not budging," she said.

He felt for the door behind him and backed through. A woman with two teenage girls stood outside the restaurant doors, crowding the entrance and limiting a potential rooftop shot.

The man took off running toward the mall area, and Monica chased after him with the agent on her heels. The intruder dashed around a few pedestrians crossing the street.

Not a clear shot for her or anyone.

She sprinted after him as he whipped down the street and into a parking area. Her warnings didn't deter him. She itched to take a shot but not with the mass of people.

He pushed through some teens and ducked behind a car, then aimed his firearm her way. She knelt beside a car, and his shot went wild. Kids screamed.

She had a clear shot and fired as he twisted around a pickup truck. She followed to where the man lay facedown on the pavement, a puddle of red gathering from the right side of his head.

The agent hurried toward her.

"Call 911," she said and bent to feel for a pulse. "He's alive."

The shot had knocked a wig askew.

Monica reached for the hairpiece.

The killer was a woman.

37

IN THE ER WAITING ROOM of Memorial Hermann–Texas Medical Center, Monica texted an update to Kord. I have the woman's phone. Jeff is aware. FBI will arrange 4 an agent 2 pick it up.

Before HPD had arrived on the crime scene, Monica had slipped into a pair of latex gloves and confiscated the woman's phone. It was safe inside her bag.

She'd ridden to the hospital with the agent who'd assisted her, and Kord and Ali were within minutes of coming through the door. Saad and Wasi had returned to the Saud home while the nameless woman lay in critical condition. Monica's reasons for the woman to live were selfish—the investigation needed answers.

HPD officers swarmed the area, and FBI agents were posted near the woman.

A message flew into her phone. She expected it to be Kord, but it was an FBI report. The woman had been identified as Parvin Shah. Authorities were en route to her apartment.

The moment Monica received her name, she eased into a chair and entered the CIA secure site to gather intel. Parvin Shah had arrived in Houston from Iran in February 2011. Birth date: August 10, 1989. Address in the Montrose area.

Parents deceased. Granted citizenship in 2017. Worked at Macy's. No known terrorist affiliation. But the investigation pointed to an Iranian hired to carry out the assassination.

Monica watched Kord and Ali walk through the ER doors. Kord no longer wore the *thobe* and *ghutra* but jeans and a black T-shirt. She greeted both men.

"Is she alive?" Kord said.

"Critical head wound. Hasn't regained consciousness."

Kord glanced around. No one stood close enough to listen. "The agents inside the restaurant gave me the story."

"Never had a clue our killer was a woman."

"But she was stopped," Ali said, his voice low. "Thanks to you. I didn't detect the driver of the food delivery truck was female."

She hadn't expected gratitude. "My concern is someone taking her place or if she's working with a partner. Unless authorities find evidence at her apartment, we have unresolved questions."

"Remember Agent Richardson from the Frozen Rock?" Kord said. When she nodded, he continued. "He and a team are at Shah's apartment and will call with updates."

Impatience stamped onto her mind. She wanted the findings now.

The TV in the seating area flashed with local news and captured her attention. A male reporter sat behind a desk. "We've learned a shooting at the Galleria has prevented the would-be assassination of Saudi Prince Omar bin Talal. The FBI has been working with the Saudi security detail since a bodyguard was shot and killed on Tuesday morning. An unidentified woman lies in critical condition at Memorial Hermann–Texas Medical Center, shot by an FBI agent. We have an unconfirmed report the woman is an Iranian national. No other details at this time."

"What are you thinking?" Kord said to her.

"I want to be here and at her apartment."

"Qualified men are on it."

She smiled. "They aren't me, and I have a perfectionist streak that would go around the world. Twice."

"Right there with you." His phone alerted him to an incoming text. He read and glanced up. "Richardson wants to talk." He turned to Ali. "I need to take this call with Monica. Would you get us if there's any news about Shah?"

"Of course."

Kord and Monica made their way to a secluded corner, leaving the Saudi bodyguard alone near the nurses' station. She felt sorry for the women dealing with him.

Kord pressed in a number and then Speaker. A man responded on the first ring. "What do you have?" Kord said.

"Looks like Parvin Shah worked alone. At least

that's what her apartment indicates. We found the makings for a bomb and a suicide vest."

The potential nightmare swept over Monica in an icy chill. "One bomb or more?"

"Three. I'm also looking at photos of Prince Omar, his sisters, and his mother attached to Shah's living room wall. Arabic words in black marker written across them. No idea what it says, but I can pull up my phone and translate."

"No need. We'll handle it when we get there," Kord said.

"On a table is a printout titled 'Prince Omar's schedule.' Where did she get it? I've already checked and it's inaccurate. Men's clothing and various disguises in the closet. And—"

"Hold off bagging evidence as long as possible until Agent Alden and I get there. We're waiting to hear about Shah's condition. Shouldn't be long."

"We're good. It'll take a while here."

Kord ended the call.

The photos sailed in with a text, as vivid as Agent Richardson described. How unusual and yet a smart move to enlist a woman to carry out the death sentences.

Monica looked at the ER door facing the street. Could the woman have acted alone here in the US while taking orders from someone in Saudi or Iran?

Prince Omar arrived. What was the prince

271

thinking? Saad and Wasi were on both sides of him. The prince wore designer jeans and a button-down shirt. A good choice since his face and Saudi dress had been flashed all over the media. But with the shooting, the place would soon be swarming with reporters—who'd recognize him. She wanted to shake him until his teeth rattled.

Prince Omar marched to Kord and Monica like a general in command of his troops. He turned to Kord. "Wasi drove your car here."

"Thanks. I'll need it."

"Has the woman spoken?"

"Still unconscious," Kord said.

"What do you know about her?"

Kord confirmed what the news had claimed and described the incriminating evidence at her apartment.

"Suicide bomber. Photos of me and my family," the prince said. "I suppose she could have downloaded those of me, but my mother and sisters would be more difficult. When can we talk to this Iranian?"

"Prince Omar, the woman may not live."

He pressed his lips together with a hint of a smile. "The killer has been apprehended, perhaps forever, thanks to Miss Alden."

She stifled a smile with the prince's compliment—said to Kord, not to her.

"Prince Omar, with all due respect, would you

let Saad and Wasi drive you home?" Kord said.

"I'm staying. I'm tired of others risking their lives. It's imperative for me to assist with the investigation."

"You'd end up as target practice and most likely a few others as well."

"I'm an excellent shot. And I want you gathering evidence on this woman. We'll work together."

"How can I do that and protect you at the same time?" Kord said.

Monica heard a bit of frustration in Kord's voice. She'd felt the same, often. At times the prince seemed to grasp the seriousness of endangering others, and other times he took on his "gotta be in control" status.

"Prince Omar," Ali said with the same quiet firmness she'd come to recognize as his caring trademark. "Kord is making an appropriate assessment of the situation."

She breathed a thank-you.

The prince stiffened. "I'll remain at the hospital until I have word from the doctor. If she's alive, I will talk to her. If she dies, I'll have my men take me back to my sisters." He snorted. "But I won't like it."

"I'll make sure there are FBI agents at the home until we return," Kord said.

The prince reached into his pocket and handed him his original cell phone. "I removed the battery once I heard about the shooting. Your people need to figure this out."

Kord appreciated Ali running interference with Prince Omar. Although the prince had made himself less conspicuous in his dress, he wasn't safe and would never be as long as he held the title of royalty—with a price on his head.

They'd waited over thirty minutes for the doctor. Updates poured into his and Monica's phones with the national and international reporting on the shooting.

The BBC stated the assassination attempt was only temporarily thwarted.

The *New York Times* showed a photo of Parvin Shah upon entrance to the US.

CNN claimed Parvin Shah could not have worked alone.

Arab News reported arrests had been made in the US and Saudi Arabia. The report was somewhat true for the US, but he had no indications of arrests made in Saudi Arabia.

Thoughts lingered on about Nasim and his regrettable death. His father had wept with the news. Kord felt the same sorrow, and he hoped there was a God who rewarded the sacrifices of good people. Prince Omar believed in Allah. Monica clung to the Christian God. Kord's problem with both centered on the innocent suffering at the hands of evil men. And Kord wanted proof of anything or anyone in control of this screwed-up world.

An elderly doctor walked through the ER doors. "Monica Alden?"

She rose and those seated around her followed. "Yes, sir. You have word on Parvin Shah's condition?"

"Yes, ma'am. I'm sorry. She didn't make it. Nor did she regain consciousness."

Monica thanked him. "I appreciate your efforts to try to save her."

"I know you're FBI. Is there family to contact?"

"Not to our knowledge."

Kord thanked the doctor and introduced himself. "We'd like to sign for her personal belongings."

"I'll have a nurse bring the paperwork and the items."

When the doctor left, Kord persuaded Prince Omar to return to the Saud home. The prince agreed with one condition—Ali would accompany Kord and Monica.

In Kord's Charger, with Ali in the front seat, he pushed ahead with a critical matter.

"Monica," Kord said. "Would you pull out Shah's phone?"

"It's in my hand."

"What have you learned?"

"Filled with contacts regarding the Saud family. E-mails. Texts. Looks like it mirrors Prince Omar's phone before we suspected the virus."

"As we expected. I'm dropping it off at the FBI office before we continue."

"How did this woman get the prince's information?" Ali said. "I know you said a virus, but it had to be planted by someone close to him, then transmitted to her."

"Everywhere he goes, the prince is surrounded by bodyguards, which makes nailing the mole difficult," Kord said. "The person in Saudi would have been in near proximity to gain access. How many people are involved?"

"Malik's hand is all over this," Ali said. "He had the ability to plant a recording device in Prince Omar's phone and pass information on to Parvin Shah or anyone else."

"Monica?" Kord said. "Have you changed your mind about Malik's potential guilt?"

"Need more evidence. He convinced Princess Yasmine to lie. Why not another woman? Shah was recruited by someone."

Ali turned to the backseat. "Miss Alden, I like the way you process information."

Kord inwardly startled. Ali had given her a compliment.

"Does he have many friends or anyone close to his family?" she said.

Ali shook his head. "Never saw him with anyone but Prince Omar. His mother was murdered some years ago, and I thought the trip to Iraq for his father was more of a duty."

"Brothers or sisters?"

"None."

Ali still faced her. What had changed his mind about Monica?

"Thanks," she said. "Investigators are searching the same info, but this helps us determine if Malik and Parvin Shah are connected."

"Shah concealed her identity today and likely other times too," Kord said. "But we have no idea why or who's calling the shots. Except she has evidence in her apartment."

"Can't get there fast enough," she said.

Kord drove on to the FBI office. They'd learn more about Parvin Shah's phone in a few hours. Until then they had work to do at her apartment in the Montrose area. "The bottom line is the betrayal happened while the prince was in Saudi Arabia."

38

MONICA WOULD NEVER get used to the boys' club game. While Kord was inside the FBI office delivering Parvin Shah's cell phone, Ali asked Monica about her family and the coffee business. One of the two times she'd seen or heard a light side of him. Odd. And she felt uncomfortable. Could be the persistent headache.

Within fifteen minutes, Kord returned and drove to Parvin Shah's apartment building.

"Monica, where are you on this?" Kord said.

"I want to visit with her neighbors. I've requested her work record at Macy's. And we need to know names of friends and how she related to others."

"Have you requested footage in and around her apartment?"

"The request was made while I was at the hospital."

Ali chuckled.

Kord parked outside the apartment building, and the three walked to Shah's door on the second floor. Two HPD officers were posted outside. After Agent Richardson vouched for Monica, Kord, and Ali, they stepped inside with those working the investigation.

"How's the suspect?" Richardson said.

"Didn't make it," Kord said. "Looking for the sweep to give us answers."

Monica studied the assortment of nefarious photos covering the living room walls, just as the texts had indicated. Not just one each of Prince Omar, Fatima, Yasmine, and Princess Gharam, but several, often with familiar bodyguards. Even Malik. She snapped pics. Prince Omar could offer additional info on where they were taken.

"Kord, figured you or Ali could read this," Richardson said.

Kord pointed to each image and the Arabic words. " 'Kill, destroy, murder.' The woman had a definite agenda."

"Take a look at the kitchen wall," Richardson said.

Monica stood closest to the small area and turned to view a three-by-three-foot calendar held in place with red pushpins. Prince Omar's arrival was noted and circled as well as dates, times, and addresses that matched the prince's original schedule for his time here. Even Princess Gharam's room number and the names, as well as contact info, of her doctors in Riyadh and at MD Anderson. Each piece of evidence seemed to confirm the phone being infected with a virus or an insider's betrayal.

Monica walked into the bedroom, where bombs were laid out on a desk: toggle switches, 9-volt batteries, ball bearings with nuts, a spool of wire, soldering iron, black electrical tape. All neatly arranged.

She stared around the room. Nothing feminine about where the woman lived—or rather, existed. Drab gray. A single bed. A chair. Nothing on the walls. Her artwork had been handled in the living room. How did one decorate an apartment with hate?

Kord stood in the doorway. "They've gone through every inch, but not the—"

"Baseboards, plumbing."

"And light fixtures."

She smiled, but the sadness for a woman ready to blow herself up was still there. "Don't you think the layout of the bomb parts is peculiar? All the FBI needs to do is tag and bag."

"Fastidious, or she was set up."

"Looks that way to me too." She took a couple more pics. "Unless she's OCD, this doesn't follow a terrorist's pattern. Have you conducted an investigation like this one before?"

"Each one's different."

"We'll learn more as we study her personality and work habits."

"I'm ready to end this case."

"Some cases are worse."

His brown eyes peered into hers. "I'm sorry."

How much had he learned about her past failures? "I'm ready to knock on a few doors, see what the neighbors have to say."

"With or without Ali?"

"Now who has the sense of humor?"

"I'm a bodyguard, not deaf," Ali called. "I'll help Agent Richardson and his men remove a few baseboards."

The man might be human after all.

39

AT APARTMENT NUMBER FOUR, Monica greeted a young mother who had identical twin girls clinging to each leg and crying. "We're from the FBI." She displayed her ID. "We're talking to your neighbors about Parvin Shah. What can you tell us about her?"

The woman took a cursory look at their creds. "Miss Shah never spoke to anyone. I'd smile and say hi. But she had this rock-face thing going." She touched the toddlers with each hand and quieted them. "I saw men come and go from her apartment. Made me wonder . . . you know."

"What?"

She shrugged. "One man at a time."

"Did she accompany them?"

"They were alone."

"The same ones?"

"Pretty much."

Monica thanked the woman. She and Kord moved on to the fifth apartment. Those they'd talked to previously reported the same thing: Parvin Shah was a loner, except for the men seen coming and going from her apartment.

Kord knocked on the door of apartment number five. An older man with a cane responded. After they showed their IDs, Monica asked about Shah.

He moved into the hall. "You folks alone?"

"Yes, sir. The police are at her apartment," Kord said. "Is there something you'd like to tell us?"

"She must have been a prostitute 'cause I saw a lot of men comin' and goin' from her apartment."

"Why do you think that?" Kord said.

"She wasn't ever with 'em."

"What did they look like?"

"About her height. She must've liked short men."

Shah knew how to play the role of a man . . . or were there more involved? "Would you be able to pick out one of those men in a lineup?" Kord said.

"I'd try. Is she in trouble?"

Kord nodded. "She's dead."

His eyes widened. "Do you think one of them men did it?"

"We know who killed her."

"Have you seen the manager?"

Kord smiled. "He's on the first floor."

"Right." He grinned at Monica, revealing a mouthful of missing teeth. "Miss, I hope this man here appreciates his pretty partner."

She wanted to laugh, but he was serious. "I'm sure he does."

"You come back by yourself when you're done, and I'll brew us some coffee."

"Thanks." Again she swallowed her humor.

Kord took the man's name and phone number,

283

and the two took the stairs to the first floor, where the manager, J. D. George, lived and worked.

"You were being hit on," Kord said.

"He simply appreciates the female gender."

"I'm jealous."

"You'll get over it."

"My heart's breaking."

"Superglue is amazing."

"Do you talk like this to all your partners?"

"Just my current one." Flirting was for kids, in her opinion, and here she was jumping in with both feet.

George's office was in the front of the building, and the door stood open.

"Can I help you?" A balding man whirled around on a squeaky chair. "This must have something to do with the HPD and FBI investigation upstairs."

"Yes, sir." Monica's turn to take the lead on this one. "We have a few questions."

"Gave my statement to the officers."

"We're not HPD." Kord whipped out his FBI ID.

George rubbed the back of his head. "I want to cooperate." He pressed his computer to life and typed, bringing up Parvin Shah's file. He stood and pointed to his chair for Monica. "Take a look. I have a spreadsheet with my renters' payment records and how they paid. Hers was cash on the day due."

Monica slid into the chair. Shah's rental application had been completed in June 2011. But her entrance into Houston was February. Where had she lived during that time? The information was basic with nothing verified except her employment at Macy's and proof of citizenship.

"She doesn't list a previous address," Monica said. "And it wasn't an issue?"

"Told me she'd stayed at a Motel 6 until she found this apartment. Paid three months' cash in advance, then cash on the day due like I already said." He swore. "I neglected to check it out."

Money talked. "She listed her supervisor at Macy's as an emergency contact."

"Claimed to have no family or friends in the US." George's face flushed. "Not smart in hindsight."

"Did you ever see her with anyone?"

"My renters have rights, and unless I suspect one of them breaking the law, their activities are private."

Monica gave him a smile. "But you have eyes. What did you see?"

"She had men friends. No women."

Kord cleared his throat to take over the interview. "We'd like to see your security cameras."

George nodded. "I have the footage already. When the police arrived and informed me she'd been shot in a takedown, I got nervous. It's on the computer."

Monica pulled it up. "How far does this go back?"

"I have the last three days pulled up here. Thought it would be easier for investigators."

Kord peered over her shoulder. His breath tickled her neck. Whoa. No need for him to be so close.

"At 1:03 this afternoon, a man left her apartment and took a taxi," George said.

The same person she'd shot and killed. She zoomed in on a camera positioned outside the apartment building and memorized the taxi's license plate.

"Handling that now," Kord said, again incredibly close to her neck. "Will check to see if she used the company or same driver regularly."

As in the footage from Paramount High School, the person dodged the cameras.

"George, can we copy this footage and her payment records?" Kord said.

"Sure thing. Forget the legal paperwork stuff. If I had a terrorist in my building, I want it on my record about my cooperation."

"We'll get back to you about footage going back farther. The FBI will want to image your records."

Monica reached into her pocket for a flash drive and copied Shah's records and clips from the security footage. Moments later they thanked George and took the stairs to Shah's apartment.

"Do you always carry a flash drive?"

"Like lipstick." She paused and sent a text to the CIA for updates. "I wanted to review the footage over the last few hours before giving it to the big guys."

"If we can get a facial on every disguise, then we can figure out where she fit."

"Really?"

He chuckled. "Wishful thinking."

Agent Richardson was speaking with Ali in the hallway of Shah's apartment. Richardson waved at Kord and Monica.

"Find anything?" Kord said.

"Ali found another passport. Hidden behind the bathroom mirror."

"Good one." Monica smiled at the bodyguard before realizing it wasn't appropriate. Strangely enough, he handed her the passport instead of Kord. Issued by the US. She opened it and memorized the contents. The photo of Parvin Shah stared back at her with glasses and longer hair. Name: Miriam Hosseini. US citizen. Birth date: September 3, 1983. Born in Michigan. Issued January 7, 2014. Expired January 2024. No date or country stamps to indicate usage.

"Already checked," Richardson said. "Fake."

Monica retrieved her phone and clicked a pic of the signature and the number.

"One more thing," Richardson said. "We found three unactivated burner phones."

Who was Parvin Shah?

How much info would the sweep reveal?

Would the taxi driver offer more insight?

Who hired her to kill?

40

OUTSIDE THE APARTMENT BUILDING, Kord talked to Ali while Monica took a call about thirty feet away.

"I understand your argument against giving Agent Richardson Shah's phone and fake passport," Kord said. "But it's the way law enforcement works. Monica snapped a pic of the passport, and she pulled the SIM card and copied the phone's info before handing them over."

"Should have known she'd be ahead of their thinking. What about the apartment management records? Her rental application?"

"Copied. The manager was glad to help. Agreed to let the FBI image all his records."

The two men walked the sidewalk leading to Kord's Charger. The temps were nearing sixty-five, comfortable until they soared into the heat of late spring and summer. The rain had stopped for today. He'd take a little sunshine and hope Parvin Shah's death and investigation meant time for the FBI to find those behind the plot while the masterminds scrambled to regroup.

"Miss Alden handles herself well. Fearless and beautiful." Ali kept his gaze straight ahead.

Unusual comment from Saudi culture. "Her record's outstanding."

"I've read it. Like you, she values others more than herself."

"The reason we're teamed up."

"I watched her chase the killer from the restaurant. Impressive."

"I missed it."

"Is she unmarried?"

Kord understood exactly where Ali was headed. "Yes."

"Spoken for?"

Monica was in for a huge surprise. "I have no idea." Kord wanted to laugh considering she suspected Ali as aligning himself with the enemy. "She'd be a tough woman to tame."

No emotion creased Ali's face. "I think she'd be worth the trouble."

Kord glanced away to hide his grin. "I thought you two didn't get along?"

"Controversy makes life interesting."

"Your temper might get you killed."

"I might enjoy it."

"She's a Christian."

He shrugged. "I like a challenge."

Before he could discourage Ali any more, Monica walked their way. "I have the report from Macy's. Shah quit two months ago. Excellent work record. Detail oriented. No absenteeism. No friends. Disconnected phone number."

"Another dead end—" His phone rang. FBI tech division.

"Found a library card for the downtown branch in the taxi Parvin Shah used today."

"Find out what she's been reading."

41

ONCE MONICA AND KORD returned to the Saud home and shared dinner, he with his boys' club and she with the girls' club, the two met in the natatorium with their laptops. They chose two chairs by the pool's edge. She hoped the bubbling waterfall distorted their conversation. No one else was around, but ears were always listening. Sheer stubbornness and an intense desire for privacy caused her to hide her words and thoughts. If she wanted the prince to hear a remark, she'd make sure he heard it.

"Do you have the taxi driver's interview?" she said. "If not, I'll send mine."

"Got it."

Sitting next to him made her nervous. This mission deserved her 100 percent focus, but between an attractive agent and a persistent headache, she was scattered.

They pulled up the feed. The driver, a Caucasian, gave his name and address to a pair of agents. His background checked out— Houstonian. Father of two teens. Lived in the southwest part of town. Worked for Yellow Cab fifteen years. A team of agents was working on the taxi and interviewing personnel.

Kord and Monica played the interview on his laptop.

"Was today the first time you've picked up Parvin Shah?" an agent said.

"I picked up men, not a woman. But I've been called to the address three other times. It's in the company's log."

Kord paused the video. "Two of those dates match up with the prince's arrival and the following day at MD Anderson." He allowed it to continue.

"You say this address," the agent said. "You mean the apartment building."

"Yes, sir."

"According to your log, the calls were made from the same phone."

"Each time the caller requested me specifically."

That could have been to eliminate him when she finished her assignment.

"Can you describe the men?"

He tilted his head. "Today was a Hispanic businessman. Before Middle Eastern, I guess. Maybe Indian or Pakistani."

"How were you paid?"

"Cash."

"Where did you take these men?"

"First time was a Westheimer address. Second at the front of the family court building. The third, today, was the Barnes & Noble near the

Galleria." He pointed to a file in front of the agent. "I'm sure you have the dates and times right there."

"We do, and two of the pickups correspond to crimes."

Monica held up a finger, and Kord paused the video again. "Everything points to Parvin Shah. We need to dig deeper for bank records, alias names, city surveillance cam reports." She shook her head. "We needed her alive. What about her library card?"

"History and current writings about Iran and Saudi Arabia. And before you ask, techs are working on security camera footage corresponding to when she checked out books." He resumed the video with the taxi driver.

"Did you have a conversation with the men?" the agent said.

"Just where they wanted to go."

"Anything more you can tell me?"

"Today the man seemed angry, agitated."

"How so?"

"Slammed the door when he got in. When I greeted him, he didn't nod. Before the car stopped, he tossed me a twenty and left."

The interview ended. Monica waited for Kord to offer feedback.

"Had Shah been nervous with what she'd planned?" he said. "She'd killed before. If she failed, what were the repercussions?" He studied her. "Thoughts?"

"She had less than a thousand dollars in the bank and no cash in her apartment, which says overseas account and a labyrinth of names. Her agitation could be because the prince's phone had been silent and then the luncheon scheduled."

Their phones alerted them to an update. The FIG—Field Intelligence Group—had run footage from the high school, Saud home, restaurant, and hospital through facial recognition software to compare images. Analysis confirmed Parvin Shah had been the driver of the food delivery truck, but nothing else matched.

"It's one checkmark," he said. "We have the instrument of one of those involved, but I doubt Parvin Shah is the one who ordered the hits."

Using a secure program, Monica typed criteria to narrow the list of known Middle Eastern female terrorists: sniper skills, disguise master, around five foot six, conversant in Spanish. With the ongoing training of extreme Islamic terrorists around the world, the number of females involved had increased to roughly 20 percent. The woman she'd killed today wasn't among the names or photos.

She deliberated the rising use and growing force of female terrorists, especially when the average person believed men were the real foes. A female easily gained access to public places where they looked harmless. Females were less likely to be suspected of killing others, allowing them to sneak in and out of targeted areas and resume a normal life. When working in Africa, Monica watched a female terrorist feeding a toddler ice cream, and then an hour later, she blew up a café. Women were known to be more radical than men, and they were drawn into a cause and adventure just like men, enforcing radical doctrine on other women while recruiting them for suicide bombings. Reasons for their enlistment varied. Some European women joined the fight simply because their dress was criticized. So many reports and facts swarmed in Monica's head, but it was difficult to nail Parvin Shah—Iranian and probably paid by a Saudi to assassinate Prince Omar.

Investigators were on it, but she wanted answers now. Nothing new there.

"Where are you?" Kord said.

She glanced up from her laptop. "Thinking about female terrorists and their growing numbers. Parvin Shah fits the mold. The male clothes and accessories in her closet point to a single conspiracy, but that's ludicrous. Track with me a moment. Let's assume a man enlisted her, a man whom she was emotionally tied to—a lover or husband. He saw to her training and convinced her to carry out an assassination against Prince Omar. So who is the man? The scheme is too high level, and as you indicated, we only have a checkmark in a playbook."

He studied her. "Ali said the mirror was secure to the wall. He started to give up, thinking nothing was there. He persisted and found the passport. I'm going with the idea she intended to use it when she completed the kill."

"And today's date was not marked on her calendar or on the original schedule. She could have been apprehensive about moving forward."

Kord left his laptop on the chair and walked a few feet to the pool. "She was Iranian, an enemy of Saudi Arabia." He shoved his hands into his pant pockets and looked out over the water.

"Now where are you?" she said.

He swung her way, his gaze on her but his attention elsewhere. "The list of questions with no answers. Malik's denial of his involvement, but he's been implicated. Was it to throw off the real mole? He'll be released tomorrow. Prince Omar has made arrangements for him to fly home commercially."

"Do you think Malik's hiding something?"

"Why? He knows what he's facing in Riyadh."

"My point," Monica said. "Would he rather face death than tell the truth?"

"Depends if he's protecting someone or a cause. His story hasn't changed."

"Yasmine is a pitiful mess. I may need to

rethink my approach with her to see if she's concealing anything, either knowingly or not."

"Do it. Any comments he made to her are useful."

Monica smiled. "How is Prince Omar handling this?"

"He's no fool, and he's been on the phone constantly to his people."

Her cell rang and she recognized Ali's number. "Hi, Ali. Is there a problem?"

"Are you available for a walk in thirty minutes?"

"That's fine. Will Kord be joining us?"

"He has a meeting with Prince Omar."

What was this about? "Where will I find you?"

"Where you disarmed the bomb."

"All right. See you then."

Ali ended the call. His request tapped at her curiosity. Why her and not her partner? She looked at Kord, who grinned back. "What did you and Ali cook up?"

He lifted a brow. "I'm innocent."

"I think you have some explaining to do."

"What did he say?"

"Asked me to join him for a walk."

Kord laughed—far too long and hard. A joke? "What's so funny?"

"He told me this afternoon he's interested in you as potential wife material."

How did this happen? "Why didn't you tell him

298

I had a boyfriend or something?" she whispered. "We nearly killed each other at the hospital."

The grin stayed intact. "I thought you might be flattered. Think of the press. The wedding would have international coverage."

"When I'm not with the CIA, I'm a woman. I get my nails done, enjoy bubble baths, get my hair cut. I have more shoes than I'll ever wear. I bake and give it away. I decorate. I weigh myself every day and count calories. But I'm not looking for a husband." Now why had she made such a fuss?

"You've broken my heart and now you'll break his. Might damage US relations."

His teasing caused her to groan. An international incident because she refused marriage to a Saudi bodyguard? "The culture is killing my operative skills."

"He welcomes you as a challenge. Claims you're fearless and beautiful."

A slow rise of heat crept up her face. "Couldn't you have said something to his inquiry?"

"I did. Told him you'd be hard to tame. And you were a Christian."

How had she encouraged Ali? "Thanks for the warning. Does he want my father's name for the bride price?"

"Never know. Look, Monica, he might pop the question tonight. You're lucky because he's not married. You'd be number one wife."

"And the FBI is about to lose one of its prize agents."

"I forgot you're a crack shot." Still he made her wait for nearly a minute. "Okay, I'll help you out with this. *Knqdr walakin ma'yimkinlish.*"

" 'I am able but it is not possible for me.' " She laughed at the translation. "Like, 'No thanks, I could iron your shirts but it ain't gonna happen'?"

"Exactly."

"All right. I need to meet with him and get this handled." Actually, she felt sorry for Ali. She closed her laptop. "I'll take this to my room before the meeting."

"Enjoy your stroll," he said.

"I'm sure it will be memorable."

"Where will this happen?"

"The spot where I defused the bomb."

"I bet he lost his heart when you cut the final wire."

She wanted to smack away his smirk.

Once she'd secured her laptop upstairs, she made her way to the designated meeting spot. The sound of insects greeted her, and a dog barked in the distance. The earthy smell of evening teased her nostrils. Too bad she couldn't enjoy it. Ali's huge frame towered over the plot of ground that had nearly been their final resting place. She waved and walked his way.

"Hope I haven't caused you to wait," she said.

"Not at all."

"Curiosity has gotten the best of me. Is there an update on the assassin attempt? New info? Something I can help you with?"

"Walk with me."

"Sure." Her heart thudded as fiercely as if he'd held a weapon on her. She'd prefer the gun. She joined him and prayed for a text, a call, the Second Coming—anything to interrupt them.

A soft breeze of optimism blew her way. Kord could be wrong in his assumption. They stopped in front of the white marble bench where she and Kord had discussed the case.

"Would you like to sit?" he said.

Get it done. "I can."

He eased onto one end, and she slid as far to the opposite side as possible.

"Miss Alden, I've enjoyed getting to know you. Although initially I was skeptical of your abilities—"

And gender, but she'd not say it.

"—since then, I've seen you act boldly with no thought of danger. Your skills are exemplary. And I've also come to appreciate your beauty."

"Thank you. I value you as a friend too."

"Are you engaged to be married?"

She faced him head-on but without eye contact. "No."

His shoulders settled. "I'm pleased with the news."

"Ali, I'm not looking for a husband."

"Why? I don't understand."

Manufacturing an excuse would lead her down a path of trouble. "Not so long ago, I was engaged. I'm being honest with you. He lied to me, a horrible betrayal. Not sure I can ever trust again, so I'm waiting for God to heal my heart. And I'm a follower of Jesus."

"A great prophet."

"But I believe He is the Son of God."

He looked at her with a tilt of his head. "What will change your mind about me?"

"Nothing. Sometimes I think I will be single for the rest of my life. It's useless to give me any more thought."

"There must be something I can do."

"I've acquired an expression in Arabic: *Knqdr walakin ma'yimkinlish.*"

"I'm not easily shaken. How do I win you?"

"Can we be friends? Or is this not permitted?"

"We are bodyguards for Prince Omar. We must have respect for each other, and friendship is valuable."

She smiled in the shadows. "Ali, I'm honored. You have so many beautiful and talented women in your country."

"But they aren't you. I'm quite wealthy and you'd not want for anything." He paused for a moment. "My home is empty. If you change your mind, I'll still be interested."

His phone vibrated, and he answered. "Yes,

Amir." Ali was an imposing figure for sure, and a handsome man for another woman.

"I'll escort her." He slipped the phone back into his pocket.

Now what?

"Miss Alden, Prince Omar is summoning you."

42

MONICA RESPONDED to Ali's statement by standing from the bench. Most likely Prince Omar had questions about what he'd overheard in her conversation with Fatima and Yasmine. Or the natatorium. "I'm ready."

"And you will consider my offer of marriage?"

"I promise you I value our friendship."

They walked toward the house. "How long have you worked with the FBI?" Ali said.

"Not long."

"The prince told me you're CIA."

She sighed. Was nothing secret?

"It's all right. I understand the secrecy and undercover work for a government."

"Were you testing my honesty?"

He chuckled. "I was testing your loyalty to the US."

Once inside Prince Omar's office, Ali stood near the door, and she waited in a chair that resembled a museum piece. As expected, he offered both of them coffee, and she accepted the hospitality.

"The rain has stopped," he said.

Pleasantries. "Giving people an opportunity to begin cleaning up their homes and businesses."

"Have you ever been caught in rising water?"

Was he posing a trick question? "I've assisted those who were in need."

"A wise woman. Miss Alden, thank you for your kindness to my sisters."

"I'm sincere. They are fine women."

"As you are aware, conversations are available to me."

Great way to put eavesdropping into perspective.

"If you'd like to instruct my sisters in the art of self-defense, I approve on the condition I be apprised of what is being taught and their progress." He waved his hand. "Specifically, an evaluation of their skills."

"I'll complete one for each of them." She avoided his face.

"As a courtesy to me, please continue to encourage Fatima and Yasmine to be strong. Our mother is not well. I've seen the test results, and my sisters must be able to handle the grief."

"Most certainly." Would he address his sisters' broken hearts over lost love?

"Thank you for saving the lives of my family and friends. Before the evening is over, I will speak to Fatima and Yasmine, let them know they can relax. With Parvin Shah's death, we can carry on."

She moistened her lips. "I respectfully disagree, Prince Omar. We have no idea how many others are working against you."

"Our responsibilities take us many places. I don't want them to be worried about me. Your country and mine will not let this rest until the murderers are found." He took a sip of coffee. "What is your professional view of Parvin Shah?"

"She didn't have the typical characteristics of most terrorists. Extremely neat. Her behavior patterns followed the same order with attention to detail in the killings. Whoever recruited Shah approached her with a logical reason to kill. Intel claims money. The person would have known her background and provided something of value."

"Has your ability to remember the things you've seen given you any additional insights?"

"The MO of female terrorists. They're in the minority, but their involvement has killed hundreds of innocent people. She may be dead, but we don't know who was giving her orders. Or who trained her. It's unlikely she saved enough money at her job to live on for two months, and her financials are minimal."

He steepled his fingers. "Do you have a name of who could have taken her place?"

Another test of her loyalty to the US, like Ali. "If I had a suspect, that person would be in custody. Between both countries, we will make arrests and destroy this plot. We just don't know how soon."

"Kord said the same."

Her phone sounded with a text.

"Take it," the prince said.

She read the message from the CIA. Kord would have received the same intel from the FBI. "Prince Omar, your phone was infected with a virus that copied all your contact information. Everything available on your phone. A recording device too."

He muttered a phrase in Arabic, one she recognized. "This explains Zain's death and those that followed." He tapped his hand on his knee.

"Malik is still a suspect, but I could be wrong," she said. "I know you've been retracing your steps there to help determine when and where."

Prince Omar turned to Ali. "Make sure Kord and Miss Alden have all they need. Also, what's the status of Malik's cousin Rashid Dagher, regarding his son, Youssof?"

"Rashid hasn't heard from him since he left for Iraq and fears he's dead."

"Why?"

"The father could be giving an excuse to avoid further questioning. Stating his son is a good man and he fears his death sounds better than betrayal. Amir, we have the father in custody."

Prince Omar huffed. "Miss Alden, do you have intel about either man?"

"We haven't located Youssof either." At the first opportunity, she wanted to recheck for a link between Parvin Shah and the Daghers and Malik al-Kazaz.

Prince Omar lifted his chin as though thinking. "If one of them is guilty, then the plot could spread to Iraq. But if they have chosen Iran over Saudi Arabia, that paves the way for violence. We need information now." He turned to Monica. "I want to speak to Kord again tonight. You are free to leave." Before Monica could stand, he spoke again. "One more thing. Have you accepted Ali's proposal?"

Heat raced up her neck, the second time this evening. Ali stood within feet of her. "I'm honored, but I declined."

"Understandable with what happened to you in the past. You are a spirited woman, and Ali recognizes the quality." He smiled. "So does Kord."

For once since she stepped into this mission, she was grateful not to look a man in the eye.

Back in her room, Monica flipped on her laptop and shook off Ali's proposal and Prince Omar's final words. No way would anyone pick out a husband for her except God, and she was sure neither Ali nor Kord was on His list for a lifelong companion. Besides, she wasn't looking.

How much did Prince Omar know about Liam? She shuddered at the thought of Kord knowing the ink stain on her career . . . and heart. Of course he'd seen the documented portion about how she'd killed an agent who'd used biological warfare in Africa. But she'd said far too much to Fatima and Yasmine knowing the prince would hear. She hoped her transparency worked positively for the case.

Digging her fingers into her palms, she longed to understand why God allowed her to feel such hurt and shame. Would she ever be able to deal with the past? Tuck it away? No matter how much prayer or Scripture hit her senses, she'd never see good from such evil this side of heaven.

Get over it, Monica. If you weren't capable, you wouldn't be on the mission.

She sent a request for more intel regarding the four persons with questionable backgrounds. Who else ran the streets with a weapon aimed at Prince Omar and his family? In the morning, he planned to visit his mother with Fatima and Yasmine. If only the man would stay put.

Ali, as the new press secretary, announced the prince refused to make a statement about Parvin Shah until there was more information. To ease the media's onslaught of questions, Ali scheduled a private press conference at two tomorrow at the Saud home. That would allow the prince to speak about his goal of forging a better relationship between Saudi Arabia and the US.

Monica had no illusions about assassination plots. Failure only increased determination. Terrorists didn't burn brain cells worrying about the body count for either side. They'd march forward until permanently stopped.

She closed her eyes and relived today for anything she might have missed. Shah had worn an expensive men's suit. Monica swiped across her phone to see the pics snapped before HPD and the ambulance arrived. She couldn't make out the suit brand, but it dripped with money. Unlikely Macy's carried it. She texted Jeff and copied Kord.

Shah wore hi $ suit. Find brand. Probably bought in last 3-4 months.

On it

And list of Houston retailers who sell the brand.

By normal calculations, she should be craving sleep. Instead her mind repeated facts and questions about who had designs to kill.

43

WHEN THIS CASE ENDED, Monica intended to take a vacation to Yellowstone National Park. Rent a cabin, hike, take pics of buffalo, create memes for no one but herself, marvel at Old Faithful, fly-fish, and find time to sleep for a week. Or venture home and relax in the slower pace of rural Ohio. Until then, she'd catch a few hours' rest at a time. At 3:00 a.m. Saturday, her head hit the pillow with a soft thud, only to be jarred upright again at 6:15 when her personal cell phone rang to the old tune of "Bad Boys." Stumbling out of bed, she snatched it from inside her purse. Lori.

"Are you okay?"

"The question is you."

"Why?"

"A man walked in right after we opened. Wanted to know about the short blonde. Said you and he'd been talking. When I told him you weren't here, he asked for your number. I told him I couldn't give it without your permission. Wanted to know when you'd be working. Told him you were on vacation. He said I was lying. Wanted to know how to find you. Again, I refused. He said to tell you he wasn't stupid. You would pay. I called the police, but he left before they arrived."

"I'm sure it was nothing. Maybe an admirer."

"Doubt it."

"Take a deep breath. Don't worry about the guy unless he comes back. Had you seen him before?"

"No. Hope never again. He did write his number on a napkin, but I was nervous and forgot to give it to the police."

The café camera would have his pic, but she needed the number. "Would you hold on to it for me?"

"Sure. Don't you think I should give it to the police?"

"Not unless he returns. Why not stick it in the safe?"

"Good idea. Are you in town?"

"In and out."

"I'm sorry to bother you. Afraid for your safety. The guy was freaky."

"I'm fine, but I have no clue about him. You gave his description to the police?"

"Down to his bushy eyebrows."

"An old man?"

"Our age, maybe. Dark-skinned. Medium height. I'll let you go. Take care, sweet friend. Praying for you."

"Thanks. I'll be in touch."

Monica texted Jeff for the police report. She also wanted the camera footage inside Coffee Gone Dark. Was it just a coffee drinker who had a crush on a blonde? Or could the wrong person have figured out her cover? She'd be a fool to discount it, especially after Parvin Shah's death.

Fully awake, Monica needed to sleep for a little while or she'd be worthless the rest of the day. She forced her mind into submission.

Her cell phone rang. Kord.

"How about a stroll in the garden?" he said. "I'm too wired to think about sleeping."

"Looks like we'll both survive on coffee today."

"Meet you in the kitchen."

After slipping into jeans and a sweatshirt, and tucking her weapon into her waistband along with a scarf in case they ran into bodyguards, she walked to the lower level and found Kord downing a bottle of water. They stepped out into the chilly early morning air. For once it wasn't raining.

"Want to race to the gate?" she said.

"Nope. I want to clear my head, not lose to a girl."

"So sad. Kord, the enemy is no longer ahead of us. They're working on old information that ended with Shah's death."

"With all HPD, the FBI, and the CIA are doing, why haven't we nailed this?" He ran his fingers through his hair. "I asked Ali to reroute the limos for every excursion. And to arrange new bulletproof vehicles for each time we leave here.

He's sending the FBI any security footage of Prince Omar in Riyadh since the announcement was made of his trip to Houston."

"What about his plans to lease oil reserves?"

He nodded. "I'll add to it and include all those who were present when discussions were held. Saudi security is tight, so they should have it ready shortly."

"I want to be walking the streets," she said. "We're both hands-on types."

"Another reason why I wanted to talk."

"Am I being interrogated?"

"I have a new mission."

"Which is?"

"To haul you down off the ledge."

Her heart thudded. "I'm on solid ground."

"Not every mission works the way we intend," Kord said.

"I've had my share of failures. Perfectionism is in my blood."

"Try a transfusion. We aren't 100 percent successful or right every time. The truth is, Liam Fielder played you from the start, and you didn't lose that round. You won."

So he had the complete file. "Really? How many innocent people were killed before he was brought down? I counted each man, woman, and child in that village, looked into their blank faces. None of them deserved the excruciating death."

"Monica, that was his doing." He'd used that same gentle tone with Princess Gharam.

"Still my fault for not seeing through his lies. When were you going to tell me you'd been briefed about that business? Or is this a result of overhearing me talking to Fatima and Yasmine?"

"Do you trust me?"

"Answer my question first."

"I asked SAC Thomas for your file after Prince Omar mentioned it."

Her face grew hot. "Do you still want to work with me?"

"Photographic memory. Three missions in the Middle East. Reads lips. Real kissable. Hot too. Sharpshooter. Brought down an arms deal here in Houston. Stopped bioterrorism in Tanzania and led the CIA to Liam Fielder. Impressive. I understand why you blame yourself for the victims, but if you hadn't figured it out, how many others would have died?"

Jeff had told her to suck it up, get over it.

God offered peace while pinching her heart to forgive. Kord candy-coated the gruesome thing as though her nightmares would end with the snap of her fingers. She wanted to forgive Liam and herself, but discarding the truth seemed wrong.

"Kord, you weren't there."

"But I've experienced the horror of death. Back to my question. Do you trust me?"

She still cringed at the "trust me" request. But honesty prevailed—always. "I'm trying."

"Good. I expect no less. Only a select few fall under the title of agent or operative. I can't tell family members or friends about my job, and you live the same way—more so."

"My family regrets I'm not a math professor at Stanford. Married to a political figure with one child and a dog of the opposite gender."

"So they think you're deprived?"

She laughed and sensed relaxation trickling through her.

"No, they're Ohio farmers. Big-time growers of corn, wheat, and soybeans with an organic vegetable business. They feel sorry for my lack of success and coffee obsession. Dad would invest in a café in Ohio if I'd let him. But the important thing is we love each other unconditionally."

"Siblings?"

"Four older brothers, all within the area—one farmer, one dentist, one accountant, and one high school football coach."

"How were you recruited?"

Dare she reveal so much? "What's the interest?"

"Collecting data."

"Okay. Although the youngest, spoiled, and the recipient of beauty contest awards—" She gave him a feigned scowl. "Don't even go there. Anyway, I also had an interest in economics, world politics, US security. Earned a scholarship at Ohio State, and I'm officially a loyal Buckeye fan. Upon graduation, a CIA recruiter approached me. After praying through the opportunity, I accepted."

"What did you tell your family?"

"Needed to find myself, which took care of my stint in DC. When asked to work in Houston on a few assignments, I told my family about a desire to learn the coffee business."

"How long will you be here?"

"Didn't think I'd be in Houston this long. The city's diversity, the shipping channel, Mexico, and continued growth makes it a hotbed of activity. But it could change at any time."

"Ever thought of resigning?"

Liam sandblasted her mind. They'd planned to open a coffeehouse in Paris to ensure their cover. "Despite what happened, it's the only thing I know. I suppose I'll quit when I'm too old to keep the pace."

"Does the secrecy bother you?"

She allowed a hint of her to slip. "Sometimes. But it's where I'm supposed to be."

"It still can be lonely," he said.

Where was he going with this? "It's a choice we make."

"The God factor is the hardest for me to understand," he said. "I'm trying there too."

"Searching?"

He chuckled. "Let's say hoping a God is real.

Whenever humans are in charge, greed takes over."

"I think for take-charge people like us, admitting faith in something we can't see is the hardest decision we can make. But we're not invisible to God."

"Why are you a believer?"

How could she explain God when at times she had her own doubts? "I felt an unexplainable tug to follow Him. Deep. Personal. Intimate. Undeniable." She struggled for words. "Kord, ask God to show Himself to you."

"I have to believe to ask."

"Think about it."

He shrugged.

"Tell me, what about your family?"

"We were raised to be independent. Once we left home for college, that was it. Mom and Dad travel. And I have a brother."

Sounded cold. "Are you close to them?"

"Talk to my brother quarterly. Have a calendar reminder to buzz me when it's time. Haven't seen him in over a year."

"Someone special?"

In the shadows, she saw a grin. "Are you asking for yourself?"

"No thanks. I have Ali if I choose to go that route."

"Right now my attention is on a mission, but I really like my partner."

"So glad. Whom do you trust?"

"I learned from experience the time comes when we have to trust someone. Prince Omar and Zain took the role of family for me."

"The company shrink encourages me to unleash my emotions."

"I'm getting there. Is your handler a friend?"

She laughed. "Not hardly. Jeff and I barely tolerate each other."

He stopped and turned her to face him. "I'm not Liam Fielder. I'm not out to get you, to set you up for a kill, to lie, or to betray our mission. Trust that we're on the same side."

Jeff had made the same statement. Had the two been comparing notes? "It's difficult."

"Isn't God supposed to help with those things?"

She breathed in and out. "Kord, I have your back. Count on it. If I thought for one minute you shared any of Liam's traits, I'd blow a hole through you."

44

BREAKFAST WITH FATIMA AND YASMINE had become a routine. The fruit and breads were delish and the coffee amazing, yet growing closer to the sisters gave Monica an opportunity to be a real friend. She walked into the common area. Fatima greeted her, but Yasmine avoided eye contact.

At noon the FBI would release Malik and escort him to Hobby Airport to board a commercial flight. He had no future in Saudi Arabia. No future anywhere.

Yasmine needed to find strength.

"We're leaving at eight this morning for the hospital." Monica poured a cup of coffee. "I'm sure your mother will be happy to see you. You both look lovely."

"I miss her." Fatima filled a plate with dates and bread.

"This will be a special time," Monica said. "When I'm with my mother, I feel like a little girl again. She wants to cook and fatten me up. We garden together and spend long hours talking about life."

"Ours is wonderful too. Her love and wisdom will stay with me forever."

"Precious memories."

"I hope there are more."

"I wish the same for you." Monica set her plate on the small table before them. "After Prince Omar's press conference, and providing Kord doesn't have something that requires my attention, we can start the self-defense classes."

"I'm not interested." Yasmine walked to the window, weeping softly.

Enough of this weakness from a princess. "Yasmine, you have a decision to make." Monica joined her and resisted the urge to shake the princess like someone should have done to her when Liam's treachery hit the forefront. "It's time to face the facts. You broke the rules. You knew better. You played a risky game with Malik. Both of you were caught and faced discipline. Did Malik ever request your hand in marriage? Why didn't he offer to marry you in the kitchen the night of his arrest?"

Yasmine touched her lips and paled.

"Instead of facing your consequences like a strong woman of royalty, you cry as though your tears will erase what you and Malik have done. Rather selfish, don't you think? Face the truth. Time to return to your studies. Bring honor to your family. Choose now to put the past behind you and learn from your mistakes."

The room grew quiet.

"You're unfair," Yasmine said. "You have no idea what it's like for women in my country."

"You're right. But it's how you've grown up. If your goal is to help bring more reforms to women, then expand your education and seek advances in an appropriate way."

"But I'll never see Malik again."

"That could be a blessing. The man encouraged you to lie. He's been accused of betraying your brother." Monica softened her tone. "You have the rest of your life to find purpose and meaning."

Yasmine rushed to her room, the manner in which the two princesses handled their emotions. Monica returned to her coffee and looked at Fatima. "Guess I was too harsh."

Fatima blinked. "Not at all. I've been mothering her, and my efforts haven't improved her attitude."

Monica sighed. "Never had a sister to understand all the girlie-mood stuff."

"We can be strange."

Monica laughed. "Good way to put it."

"I was determined to dislike you, but instead I've found admiration and respect. Our lives are so different, but getting to know you helps me see how the Western world lives."

"And I've learned so much more about your culture."

"I've watched you. Always alert. Your habits are teaching me to look for danger. I've seen how you get up in the night and stare out the window.

Check the outer door to make sure it's locked. Even tiptoe to our rooms. I'd like to learn self-defense."

Monica's eyes pooled. Such a rare girl moment. She'd sensed Fatima was awake during those times she rose to ensure all was well. Monica took steps forward and hugged Fatima, and the young woman embraced her.

"Women must stick together to take our place in the world of men," Fatima said. "Thank you for taking the time with me and my sister to offer friendship."

Monica nodded. "If we don't have our breakfast, it will be cold."

"And all we'll have are our tears."

"Sometimes those are the most satisfying."

Yasmine stayed within the walls of her bedroom. Perhaps she'd think about Monica's words and make a positive decision. Most of what she'd said to the young woman was what she kept telling herself about Liam.

45

MONICA STARED AT THE SUPERSTRUCTURES of the medical center jutting up against the sky as if reaching for God to notice them. Castles with fountains, blooming flowers, and expertly maintained landscaping. Those in the business of healing weren't the only ones who needed wisdom.

The limos waited to turn into the hospital entrance. A car with two FBI agents followed close behind, and four HPD motorcycles flanked them. Monica wore an earbud to remain in contact with Kord and Ali. The morning looked fresh and typical, obscuring the reality of why she carried a weapon.

Medical personnel of all nationalities hurried inside the hospital, some wearing white jackets and others in scrubs. Plain-clothed people made their entrance too, and they received Monica's inspection. She scrutinized everyone. Those who donned sunglasses, were alone, or looked Middle Eastern or Hispanic took double notice.

With armed guards on every side of the limo, only an idiot would open fire. But a suicide bomber could step onto the scene and nothing would be left of the royal family and other innocent bystanders. The killer had already proven her daring. How soon before her successor took over?

The Mercedes limos parked in front of MD Anderson, and the prince exited in full Saudi dress. Kord had requested him to avoid the regalia, but the prince refused and wore his culture's clothing as a symbol of pride—setting himself up as a target. As long as the pride didn't get all of them killed. Prince Omar repeatedly put himself, his family, and those around him in danger. Monica couldn't seem to wrap her head around that concept when it looked selfish. Self-sacrifice she understood.

Behind a fence of police officers, reporters snapped pics and shouted questions. She assumed they'd be missing out on the private, invitation-only press conference scheduled for later this afternoon.

Once inside the hospital, they waited for an elevator large enough to hold the entire group. She tapped her foot, watching. Always watching. Kord and Ali bored their gazes into every passerby.

"Miss Alden," Prince Omar said, "would you pick up flowers for my mother? They're at the Park Flower and Gift Shop. Ali arranged it, and his name is on the order." Lines deepened across the prince's forehead. His mother's health must weigh heavily on his mind.

She breathed a silent prayer for him and his

sisters. "Of course. Do you need anything else?"

"Not at this time." Formal. Monotone.

"I'll escort her," Ali said. "It's a large arrangement."

No point in arguing. The elevator door opened and the group entered, except for Ali and Monica. They walked to the second floor of the main building.

"You look lovely," Ali said.

She was wearing black pants, a high-necked blouse, and a black jacket. "Thank you."

If Kord were in the elevator alone with Prince Omar, he'd sympathize with the prince's apparent worry over his mother. Perhaps later when they were alone.

The elevator dinged at their floor. Prince Omar clenched his jaw, the anxiety of his mother's deteriorating health combined with the crimes of late showing on his face.

"Fatima, can I use your phone?" Prince Omar said. "I left mine in the limo." She handed him her phone. "I need to glue it to my clothes." He laughed nervously.

"Amir, would you like me to retrieve it?" Wasi said.

"Yes." The elevator door opened and Wasi remained.

Prince Omar's forgetfulness of his phone had saved his life previously. Not a habit in the past, but his mother hadn't been facing a terminal illness, and he didn't have an assassin wanting him dead either.

Kord hated the emotional turmoil for his friend. Omar loved his family, while Kord grew up in a house that aligned with a sterile environment. No love. No hate. Tears forbidden. Laughter at a minimum. No praise. Overload on criticism. If Kord's mother were the one suffering, he'd be grieving what he'd missed. Why think about it when he'd long since grown into a man?

Fate was such an unstable foe. And this wasn't about him. Never was.

Dr. Carlson emerged from Princess Gharam's room. He approached the group, his shoulders slightly slumped, and focused on the prince. "Good morning, Prince Omar. May I have a word with you?"

"Most assuredly." He turned to Kord. "Would you join me?"

Wordlessly, the three men assumed a secluded seating area. Did the prince fear the worst?

"Prince Omar," Dr. Carlson began, "unfortunately your mother is not responding to treatment. She's weakening. I'm not confident of her ability to survive surgery on Monday."

"How much does she know?" The prince's expression was stoic as expected.

"I've told her the procedure has been postponed until she's stronger. But she's insistent upon it,"

Dr. Carlson said. "She wants to speak to you. Per your instructions, she is not aware of the critical nature. I've canceled the surgery until her body can withstand the stress."

"When do you think that will be?"

"Prince Omar, I'm afraid we're at the point where all we can do is make her comfortable."

"How long?"

"I don't give time. I believe a patient chooses to surrender life."

"Is pain medication being administered?"

"According to the nurses, she takes the meds when she knows you aren't scheduled to visit. She wants to be awake when you and her daughters are there."

"Thank you, Dr. Carlson. I will encourage her to fight and cooperate with the medical staff."

"I'll be in your mother's room completing my examination."

When the conversation ended and the doctor disappeared into Princess Gharam's room, the prince inhaled deeply. "I'm not ready to tell my sisters unless they ask. Excuse me while I phone my father and report the doctor's conclusion."

Kord returned to the group until Prince Omar completed his call and walked back to those waiting. He offered a diplomatic smile.

"Wait here while I talk to my mother alone." Prince Omar took the several feet to her room as though it were the last time he'd see her.

46

MONICA KEPT PACE with Ali's huge strides to the gift shop. The sadness on Prince Omar's face stuck in her mind. Such a complicated man.

"Prince Omar's trip here has been anything but positive," she said.

"He won't give up until she breathes her last."

"His sisters need to be told. They need to be prepared for the inevitable. The shock of what they've already experienced coupled with losing their mother is tragic to say the least."

"Your caring for others is one of the traits I admire about you."

Uneasiness crept up her spine. "I'm assuming there are women back home who will comfort them." Princess Gharam wasn't the favored wife, but did that mean the other women shunned her? Unfortunately she couldn't ask Ali.

He nodded, his bearing impressive, and no wonder, with his huge frame and designer suit, tie, and gold cuff links.

She'd much prefer being with Kord. Realization made her inwardly curb her thoughts. She should concentrate on the task force and not her confusing attraction to Kord. If she forced honesty into her emotions, she thought about him more than she wanted to admit. But memories of Liam refused to let her linger long.

Ali and Monica entered the gift shop. Her eye caught the fanciful artwork of the many children treated at the facility. She'd purchased gifts here at Christmas for her mother and sisters-in-law, all painted by children.

"Do you want a family someday?" Ali said.

Oh, please. "Yes. A houseful, and adopted children too."

"A lucky man is in your future."

What man wanted a killer for a wife? And how would her children view her past work in the CIA? She and Ali moved to the counter, and he requested the order. The clerk showed him a bouquet of three dozen red roses and baby's breath arranged in a crystal vase.

"Those are beautiful," she whispered, the delicate fragrance swirling around her.

"Monica?"

A familiar voice caught her off guard. She plastered on a smile and faced Lori. "Hi. What brings you here?" Monica hugged her.

"My cousin's having surgery this morning, and I wanted to get her a little something." Lori's brown eyes cast an apprehensive glance. Ali's bodyguard demeanor most likely.

"How's the coffee shop?"

"Busy. My niece is there." Confusion emanated from her eyes. "I'm surprised to see you."

Ali's cell phone sounded a text.

Monica held her breath. "Are you sure you shouldn't replace me? I have no idea when I can return."

"I want you back. The café is not the same place without you."

"Thanks. I miss it too."

"Miss Alden, we are needed." He picked up the huge bouquet.

"Lori, I need to go."

She took a step back, her eyes wide. "Monica, who are you? Why are you here with this man?"

"I'm your friend."

"Friends don't keep secrets."

"I'm assisting this gentleman here." She introduced the two with first names only.

Lori glared.

Ali offered a formal greeting.

"Where are you from?" Lori said.

"Saudi Arabia."

Lori startled. "Your country is in the news with Prince Omar's controversial visit."

"I'll call later." Monica had to walk away. The longer she stayed, the worse the confrontation. She left Lori, her best friend, in the gift shop.

In the hallway, Ali carried the flowers beside Monica. "I'm sorry about your friend."

"It was only a matter of time. I hate it."

"A good friend?"

"Like a sister. She also owns Coffee Gone

Dark, where I work when not on the road. We attend church together."

"You must protect your cover."

"Which means I've most likely destroyed a friendship."

"Zain and I were friends, as well as cousins. I miss him."

The anger she'd seen in Ali reared up again. Grief. Sorrow. "Does he have a family?"

"A wife and two sons."

Her cell, more like an appendage, summoned her to an update. She read it and forwarded the report to Kord.

"Can you give me the contents?" Ali said.

"Parvin Shah wore a custom tailored suit. Came from Balani here in Houston. A bit extravagant for a woman to pose as a man. What terrorist group funds that kind of prop?"

"One with plenty of resources."

"We have more and strong allies," she said.

"They believe the same."

47

KORD ENTERED PRINCESS GHARAM'S ROOM upon Prince Omar's request. The solemn looks on Dr. Carlson's and the nurse's faces confirmed the grim news. Princess Gharam's eyes were closed, and her face held the death shade of gray.

"She needs to be in intensive care," the doctor said. "Her blood pressure has dipped seriously low. I'd like to make the necessary arrangements now."

"No," the woman uttered with her eyes still closed. "This room brings me comfort. If the end is coming, then I want to be here." She cried out weakly as pain appeared to rush through her body.

Dr. Carlson bent over her. "There's no need for you to suffer. And the end is not here if you'll let me help you. We can lengthen your life."

The prince took her hand. "Mother, please listen to the doctor. Take the pain medication so your body can fight the cancer."

"Omar, I'm trying to be strong. But I'm so tired. All I want is to be with you and my daughters."

"I'd like for you to be moved to intensive care and follow Dr. Carlson's orders."

Tears slipped over her cheeks. "If you think it's best."

He drew in a breath. "Is it wrong for me to want you awhile longer?"

She opened her eyes. "Son, I will do this for you."

"I'll get my sisters, and we'll talk briefly, but then you must rest. I urge you to take the pain medication."

She gave him a frail smile. "Not enough to put me to sleep."

"A small dose?"

"Yes." Her whisper came as an onslaught of agony sped through her.

"And you will find courage to fight the cancer? I want to take you home and watch you walk among the gardens. Tell my family stories of when we were children."

"I will."

"Promise?" When she nodded, he gently placed her hand back on the bed. "I spoke to Father earlier, and he'd like a word with you." He lifted Fatima's phone from his pocket.

"We haven't spoken in a long time."

The prince pressed in a number. "Yes, Father. Mother has given her word to obey the doctor." He handed the phone to her.

The prince and Kord exited the room with Dr. Carlson.

"I need to speak to my sisters before they see her. To tell them the truth about her condition," the prince said. "But first, Doctor, I have questions. In the medication that you prescribed for my mother, is there an antidepressant? I believe it would help."

"She's receiving a small dose, but I can increase it."

"Is the pain medication administered intravenously?" the prince said.

"Yes. Would you like for her to have it now?"

"I can't bear to see her suffer. Please, the full strength."

"I'll order it." The doctor glanced at his watch. "She can be transported to ICU in about twenty minutes or so."

Monica and Ali arrived, with Ali carrying a magnificent display of roses. Kord hoped Princess Gharam was coherent enough to enjoy them. He glanced at Monica, so glad she was here to help the sisters through what lay ahead. She had a way of lifting his spirits, as though challenging him in a single look to be a better man. Prince Omar left Kord with the doctor and approached Fatima and Yasmine.

"Do you speak English?" Dr. Carlson said to Kord.

"How can I help?" Wasn't the first time he'd been mistaken for Middle Eastern.

"The prince needs to understand his mother's deteriorating health. Boosting her morale is commendable, but it will take a miracle to put the cancer into remission."

"Yes, sir. We're here to support him."

"Thank you. Your English is excellent."

The sound of soft weeping indicated Fatima and Yasmine were aware of their mother's condition.

A few minutes later, Prince Omar left his sisters in Monica's care and approached Kord.

"I saw you with the doctor in my absence," Prince Omar said. "What else did he have to say?" His words held the same sadness as when his wife and son were kidnapped—the same grief and the same refusal of acceptance.

"To help you through this. Prince Omar, I believe no one has the right to take away a fighting spirit. Princess Gharam is a strong woman."

"I'll give her your message." He summoned Ali and lifted the flowers from his hands, then gestured to Fatima and Yasmine. "Come, let's see our mother."

48

MONICA STROLLED to a remote corner of the waiting area. To think. To process. Her priorities were vested in the mission with Prince Omar and his sisters. They were hurting, and her compassionate side wanted to fix it. Impossible. The regrettable decline of Princess Gharam implied she'd never leave the hospital.

The bodyguards and staff at the Saud home supported the prince. She could see it in their eyes and their resigned faces. They mourned the unfortunate diagnosis too.

Monica feared whoever had taken Parvin Shah's place might take advantage of preoccupied bodyguards and strike again.

She must stay alert, not be distracted. Seeing Lori distressed her, but mending their friendship had to wait.

Kord took a seat beside her. "The prince has been hit with too many tragedies this week."

"I respect Prince Omar and see him as a man with many burdens." She paused. "Although I don't understand his willingness to put people in danger. Fatima and Yasmine have their own dreams and problems, and I care about them." She looked into his eyes and a chill raced up her arms. Please, she didn't need to fall for a man again. Except she was cratering.

"Princess Gharam will do whatever her son asks," Kord said.

"Because she loves him, or is it the male dominance thing?" She drew in a quick breath. "I'm sorry. Doesn't matter."

"It's okay. She loves him and her daughters."

The frightening chill of attraction again. "Is Malik on schedule to head home?"

"He is. Never budged from his story."

"Guilty or protecting someone?"

"Maybe both."

"What does this mean for Yasmine?" she said.

"She'll return to her studies and life in Riyadh. Luckily few know about her and Malik, and the prince will make sure the story isn't retold."

"Glad to hear it. Fatima and I are having our first self-defense class this afternoon." She remembered. "Unless she's needed here."

"All depends on her mother's resolve."

"Why isn't her husband here? Does it have anything to do with not being the favored wife?" Monica said.

"She and her husband haven't gotten along for years. Probably happier apart, and she's well taken care of in Saudi. Her life centers around her children and grandchildren."

"A curious culture. Actually it's much like couples who are married in name only."

He rubbed the back of his neck. "In Princess Gharam's situation, I'm not sure what road I'd take with terminal cancer. I wouldn't want others to see me struggle."

"Sounds like you've thought about it."

"You and I have seen far too many suffering people."

"The difference is I have hope for heaven."

"You've told me."

"I can share more when you're ready."

"I'm looking." He held up his hand. "End of discussion."

Their phones alerted them to an incoming text. Monica read the DNA report gathered on the roof of Paramount High School when Zain was killed. "I loathe the word *inconclusive*," she said.

"Nothing we can do about it."

She scrolled through her phone for anything she might have missed.

"What's your next assignment?" Kord said.

"Back to the coffeehouse until further orders." The reminder of seeing Lori earlier brought a surge of remorse. Monica couldn't blame her friend for eliminating her job, and it might be easier in the long term when she'd need to move on to another assignment. But Monica treasured her friendship with Lori and hated to see it end badly. "My cover might have been blown."

"How?"

"Saw my friend and boss in the gift shop

with Ali. She heard enough to guess I could be connected to the royal family."

"She's visiting here?"

"Yes. I'm debating whether to let it ride or text her."

"Would she tell anyone?"

Monica blew out her angst. "She's close to her mom and sister. Guess that answers it. I'd better take care of this now." Reaching for her shoulder bag, she pulled out her personal cell and texted Lori. R u ok? She could be too upset to respond.

"Is this the first time she's suspected anything?"

Monica told him about the man who'd asked for her at the coffee shop. "Lori said he was dark-skinned and had an accent."

His eyes flared. "When were you going to tell me this?"

"I'm sorry. I agreed to the trust thing and didn't follow through. So I'd planned to go over it with you after I viewed the camera footage from the coffee shop."

"When?" Kord's tone indicated his anger, and she couldn't blame him.

"Tonight. I have a key if you want to join me."

"Glad we had the discussion about trust."

"You made your point. Are you going or not?"

"What do you think?"

Her phone alerted her to a text, and she read aloud. "It's from Lori. 'Should I be okay?' "

Kord peered into her face. "See if she's available now. You can't let this slide."

Can we talk? R u still here?

Yes

Outside gift shop in 5?

OK

Monica stood. "If you need me, text."

"The doctor said twenty minutes if the estimate's accurate. May need to reschedule the press conference."

On the elevator, she prayed for wisdom. Strength to lie? That sounded real biblical.

She made her way to the gift shop and Lori—who stood with her arms crossed. Monica formed a semblance of a smile with little clue how to lie and not lie. Both mattered, but one always held priority.

"Shall we find a quiet place?" Monica said.

"I'd rather stay right here. Where's your friend?"

"Busy."

"Is he a bodyguard for the Saudi prince or the press secretary? Or both?"

"You're upset, and I'm sorry."

"Sorry enough to tell me the truth?"

Monica studied Lori's fury and fear. This was her sister-friend, but she could not and would not give away her role with the CIA.

"Monica?"

"I can't."

"Can't or won't?"

"They're the same."

"Afraid that would be your answer. Are you in trouble with the wrong people?"

"No."

"Are you wanted by the law?"

"Absolutely not."

"Family issues?"

Monica shook her head.

"Does it have anything to do with the man asking for you?"

"I have no idea."

"Pretty serious stuff?"

Monica stared. No lame excuses. "Trust me?"

"I want to, but this is surreal."

Monica kept her composure.

"The guy you were with is a bodyguard. I saw his photo online. Anything else you can tell me?"

Awkward.

"Is Monica Alden your real name?"

"Does it matter? Aren't we friends? Think about the times we've laughed, cried, worked alongside each other. Prayed?"

"When you put it in those terms, I have to support you."

"You're the best friend I've ever had."

"Will you ever be able to tell me what's going on?"

"No."

Lori breathed in and swiped beneath her eye. "More to pray about. What can I do?"

"Never breathe a word of your suspicions. Never bring up the subject, no matter how private the setting. When we're together, I have your back. Always have. Always will."

"I promise."

"I need to get back."

"No more questions," Lori said. "Call when you can."

Monica hugged her. "Love you, sweet friend."

"Get some rest. You look tired."

"For the record, my name is Monica Alden."

She walked to the elevator and texted Kord. OMW. All ok.

The 3 r still busy

Monica shook off her cover at Coffee Gone Dark. This was her reality.

49

BY NOON, Princess Gharam was resting comfortably in intensive care. Her vitals had improved, and she assured her family she'd not give up. Prince Omar confided in Kord that his father had encouraged her to hurry home.

"Father knows she won't survive the hospital," Prince Omar said. "I respect his supporting her."

"Do me a favor?" Kord said.

"Depends."

"Change clothes with me for the ride back."

"Have you been notified of danger?"

"It stalks you."

He breathed out a ragged sigh. "I suppose."

"And take the second limo."

He raised a brow. "You ask much, my friend."

"As I said, danger stalks you."

The prince agreed and rode in the limo with Monica.

The press conference at the Saud home would take place at two o'clock. Security bounded the grounds like a linked fence.

Shortly before the hour, hand-selected reporters arrived and were led to the natatorium, where a catered display of exquisite Middle Eastern food awaited them. Prince Omar arrived at the appointed time, smiling and shaking hands while

Kord zeroed in on every person in the crowd. The other bodyguards took their stances in strategic spots, doing what they did best. A quick glance across the room showed Monica entrenched in her job. He'd seen something earlier in her eyes, an interest that he'd felt more than once. His attraction was serious, and it gave him a jolt of fear. Never believed he'd think seriously about the future with a woman, and in a few days, he'd done exactly what he claimed would not happen. At the end of this assignment, if she was willing, he wanted to spend time finding what made Operative Monica Alden choose a covert role while swearing allegiance to God.

Why kid himself? He had lots of questions for and about her.

The prince made his way to a seating area for a brief speech followed by a Q&A. Cameras videoed for the early evening news, and reporters snapped pics. Prince Omar welcomed the press and thanked them for their attendance.

"Saudi Arabia is on a sixteen-year plan to economically change our country to rely less on crude oil. We are striving to enhance our culture, attract tourists, develop more educational opportunities, and increase the power of the military.

"Our universities are seeing more Saudi Arabian females graduating, and we're in turn adding women to our workforce. My goal is to broaden relations between our countries by proposing programs that add growth to our economies."

A reporter stood to pose a question. "Over a year ago, Dennis Rose wrote in the *Washington Post*, 'Skeptics have questioned whether Saudi Arabia can fulfill these goals, either because of a traditional culture that limits women too much, a workforce lacking key educational skills, or resistance from the conservative religious establishment.' What are your thoughts?"

"I am committed to improving our country's position in the world."

Another reporter secured the prince's attention. "What does this mean for the oil and gas industry?"

"Saudi Arabia is not an enemy of the US oil and gas industry. We strive for higher oil prices that stimulate enough investment to keep up with the oil demand. We will continue to work together to raise our economies and meet the needs of all our people."

"Does your policy mean Saudi Arabia is abandoning its current market share in regards to oil?"

"We've always said we are willing to cooperate with other producers, but we won't do it alone. We need the cooperation of strong allies."

A third reporter stood and tucked her hair behind her ears. "What practical steps is your country taking in regards to curbing violent extremism and radical Islamic terrorism?"

"We are working with the US and other allies in doing all we can to combat terrorism, perhaps most importantly state-sponsored terrorism."

The reporter thanked him and another indicated readiness to ask a question. "Since you've arrived, an assassination attempt against you was foiled, and a bodyguard as well as Americans have been killed. What can you tell us about these incidents?"

"My American friends have successfully thwarted my assassination attempt while working to solve the other two deaths. We have determined the origin, and I'm confident in the security provided by US authorities."

"So the killers are in custody?"

Prince Omar nodded as though pleased. "In addition, our enemies are globally being questioned."

Kord swallowed at the thought of how the prince's response would be interpreted by the media.

The press conference continued for an additional thirty minutes. A reporter asked about Princess Gharam's condition, and the prince said MD Anderson had provided excellent accommodations and treatments. He concluded with an announcement of his returning to Houston for the Offshore Technology Conference in May. "I'm looking forward to sharing knowledge for offshore resources and learning how to improve environmental matters."

In Kord's opinion, the press conference was a sound beginning for Prince Omar to show his sincerity in contributing to his country's growth and interest in world affairs. He'd spoken from his heart, just as he'd done the evening in his office when he expressed how he wanted to contribute to the success of Saudi Arabia. Fortunately today, he hadn't mentioned the leasing of Saudi oil reserves.

Investigators hadn't found a connection between Parvin Shah and the core terrorist group targeting Prince Omar. Who'd recruited and trained her? Who'd funded the attempts? Like Monica, Kord longed to be in the thick of the investigation.

The uncertainty wasn't over, and all Prince Omar's goodwill intentions meant nothing if he was killed on American soil.

50

AN HOUR BEFORE DINNER and after prayers, Fatima entered the common area wearing a dark-green jumpsuit that would give her mobility for the self-defense instructions. Good choice of clothes, and Monica told her so.

Yasmine's bedroom door was open. If she'd toss off her stubborn mode and listen and watch, she'd learn how to rely less on men. Especially those who manipulated unsuspecting women. Self-defense was as much about mental skills as physical.

"Are you ready?" Monica said to Fatima. "You may be sore tomorrow."

"I can handle whatever you bring my way."

Monica laughed. "Wonderful, because we're going to be working hard. I'm going to start with an easy technique. We'll not move on until you've mastered it. I want you to feel comfortable while building your skills. The most important part of learning self-defense is confidence. You can defend yourself if placed in a precarious situation." She positioned herself directly in front of Fatima. "Put your arms at your sides as though you have no idea a man or woman intends to harm you."

Fatima obliged. "For sure a man."

"Both. A woman can catch you off guard quicker than a man."

Fatima seemed to ponder the idea. "Perhaps so. I wouldn't expect a woman to do me harm. But Parvin Shah was a killer."

"The good and the bad believe their actions are justified."

"I will think about that, remember it. With my upcoming marriage, I choose to be happy and a good wife. While my brother's enemy chooses to do all he or she can to kill him. A difficult concept, but I see the truth in it."

Still facing Fatima, Monica quickly grabbed her arm, stepped behind Fatima, and positioned her arm behind the young woman's back.

"I understand. I must think fast and memorize what to do next."

Monica smiled, and the two faced each other again. "For practical purposes, you will be the attacker. Step into my personal space and grab my right arm, pushing it away from my body." Fatima followed instructions. "This leaves me defenseless, or so you think. I will counteract with a move called a wrist sweep. I'll bring my elbow to the center line." Monica demonstrated. "Then I'll twist out, which allows me to break free and punch you in a vulnerable area."

"Twist inside or outside?"

"Doesn't matter. It's the elbow's action that's important against the would-be assailant's grip."

Fatima practiced a few more times until she had the technique perfected.

"See how easy? Ready for another one?"

"As you Westerners say, absolutely." Fatima faced Monica.

"Sometimes a person will try to touch you. So put your hand on my shoulder."

"Which side?"

"Either one."

Fatima placed her hand on Monica's right shoulder. In turn she gripped Fatima's hand and thumb, lifted up and inside, forcing Fatima down, which allowed Monica to add pressure above her elbow and gain control.

"Ouch." Fatima rubbed her hand.

"Sorry. Didn't mean to hurt you."

"Have you used these movements before?"

"Absolutely." They both laughed.

Yasmine ventured into the room.

"Would you like to try?" Monica said to her.

"It's interesting." Yasmine eased onto a chair.

Monica bent beside her. "I hope neither of you are ever in a setting that calls for self-defense. But we never know what the future brings. The best we can do is be prepared. As your friend, I want to share what it takes to avoid being hurt."

"I need to learn too," Yasmine said. "First I want to say something. Your words about forgetting Malik made me angry. I hated you for them. Then I thought about my desire for women in our country to gain more independence." She took a deep breath. "By breaking rules with Malik, I did more harm for women than if I'd been obedient. I should have insisted he talk to my father or brother. I think Malik didn't value me as an equal like he said, but something he could own." Tears filled her eyes. "If I'm honest with myself, then I know he lied about his love. I will learn how to have wisdom and knowledge—not to be better than a man but to show I have value."

Monica drew Yasmine into her arms as she'd done in the past. She'd grown incredibly fond of the sisters. "You're on your way to becoming a courageous and strong woman. Respect for ourselves and others is the beginning."

"Malik is on his way home. I hope to one day look at him as a lesson learned and not a broken heart." She swallowed. "I'm changing clothes so I can join you."

In less than ten minutes, Yasmine stood beside her sister dressed in Western workout clothes. Monica repeated the same instructions she'd given Fatima. Soon Yasmine mastered the techniques too. "One thing I want to point out is every person, no matter how strong, has weak areas. Those are the eyes, ears, mouth, nose, throat, fingers, toes, and the groin. Memorize them."

"You mean hit the attacker there?" Yasmine said.

"Exactly. For example in the eyes, use your thumbs, or aim straight at the person with your fingers. By remembering the vulnerable areas, you can use what you have and not be concerned about the absence of a weapon." She lifted her chin. "Pray you never have to use these techniques."

"Has it been hard for you?" Yasmine said.

"Easy when someone meant me harm. Self-defense is about preparedness. If a bodyguard has been hurt or is not around, you can be confident of doing your best to protect yourself and others."

51

SHORTLY BEFORE MIDNIGHT, Kord met with
Monica in the foyer for the drive to Coffee Gone
Dark. Prince Omar and Ali knew of their plans,
and two FBI agents stood at the front door to
handle the prince's protection duty. No way was
she making the trip by herself, and he had two
reasons.

1. She'd been working on nailing the Nigerians
   involved in a weapons case before this
   assignment. If she'd arranged to meet a
   contact at the café, she needed Kord to
   watch her back. Whether the man who'd
   alarmed Monica's friend Lori was Middle
   Eastern or Nigerian or just an admirer, the
   jaunt was too dangerous for her to take
   alone.

2. Yesterday, she'd acquired a cough. Her face
   was flushed, indicating a possible fever.
   She could be off her game and need his
   assistance.

"I'm capable of doing this myself," she said to
Kord.
"Discussion closed, and I'm driving."

"Text me with whatever you find," Ali said. "Better yet, call. If this concerns the prince's assassination attempt, I want to be informed."

"Will do," Kord said. "Shouldn't take long."

"Ali," Monica said, "I want to see the face of whoever asked for me at the coffee shop. No matter if he's related to this case or a previous one, the idea of someone frightening my friend doesn't sit well."

"If you feel this is too dangerous for the two of you, I can come along."

"Thank you, but that leaves us a bodyguard short here," she said.

Kord had a problem with the way Ali looked at her. The tenderness thing made him . . . uneasy. She'd claimed disinterest, and Kord believed her, but Ali could be persuasive.

Kord pulled his keys from his pant pocket. "Ready?"

"Let's go."

They left the house in his Charger and headed downtown. The familiar restlessness nipped at his mind. The sooner they saw the Coffee Gone Dark footage, the better.

Kord flipped on his windshield wipers to clear the rain. The streets glistened with a light mist, and more rain was predicted within the hour. He'd been caught in rising waters a few days ago and didn't want to be there again. Ali's attitude toward Monica had gotten to him.

Focus, Davidson. End this case and then see whom she prefers.

"Are you okay?" she said. "Did I miss something at the press conference?"

"Just thinking about flooding streets."

"I can swim." Monica grinned at him, then pulled out her phone. "This is a good time to call Lori. She'll be in bed, but I was concerned she'd insist on meeting us there." She pressed in a number. "Hi, Lori, it's Monica. Sorry about the hour. Wanted to let you know I'll be at the café in a few minutes." She paused. "I'm good, and I'm not alone. I'll disarm the system and arm it when we're finished. I didn't want you to find out about it without forewarning." Ending the call, she leaned her head back.

"I'm not an idiot, Monica. You could have hacked into the coffeehouse's security system. We're going fishing, but for whom or what? Or should I ask which case?"

She frowned. "This is a no-brainer. The man who asked for me left his number on a napkin, and Lori placed it in the café's safe. I want to retrieve it before she chooses to give it to the police."

"And?"

"Figure out if the man is someone I need to talk to."

"I? Not we? This case or your previous one? Are you going all Jason Bourne on me?"

"I wish. Tired of playing housemaid."

"So you've said." Kord understood her frustration. "I get it. We're used to being in the thick of things. For the record, if anyone tailed us from the mansion, I haven't detected anything."

"Doesn't mean there isn't one. By the way, have you mentioned again about sending Fatima and Yasmine home?"

He nodded. "Prince Omar is considering it."

"Why would he want them to be in danger?"

"Because of a personal issue there. He feels he can better protect them here."

"Okay. Can we talk about Parvin Shah?"

"Go for it."

"She was prepared to use a suicide vest or at least had it in her possession. If she'd been successful, we'd never know who inside Saudi or Iran is responsible. Never mind the factions who are claiming responsibility. It's glory day for those who want Saudi Arabia and the US to break ally relations." She stopped. "I ramble on when I'm tired."

He laughed. "I like hearing your thought process. Pushes the pieces closer together. Once we've figured out who's behind this, Saudi will take extreme measures against them. Hard to say how the US will respond. The ludicrous risks Iran is taking could kill thousands."

"Who is stupid enough to risk getting blown off the map unless they have a strategic plan? Who else is backing them?" She straightened.

"What is it?"

"Techs are working on linking Shah with father and son Dagher or Malik. We're hoping to find who worked with her, and tonight we'll learn who came looking for me at the café. If this is regarding our case, why look me up at Coffee Gone Dark and not you?"

"Who knew you worked there before the prince's arrival to the US?" Kord said.

"My point. I'm not the biggest threat—you are because of your close alliance with Prince Omar. It doesn't make sense."

Kord recalled what SAC Thomas had said about his friendship with Prince Omar. "Not necessarily. You came into the task force with a superior skill set."

She turned to him. "As though you'd overlook what might be happening?"

"*Blind* was the word used."

"What's SAC Thomas's position?"

"Prince Omar insisted on having me as part of the security detail. We're the team, and we've both inflicted damage in the Middle East. We're in the top ten of that region's kill list. But you're the one who has the spotlight. That has me baffled too."

"If someone was watching when I chased Shah, she hit the pavement and fell between two cars. I spent a few seconds checking vitals. Could our bad guy be worried she gave me info? But if so, he'd be under arrest."

"If the enemy believes you have an ID, you're not in a good spot. The other factor is your ability to read lips. Two reasons to see you out of the picture."

"I think Malik is working with the enemy," she said with concrete firmness. "Use your influence to keep him alive until this is over."

"Why?"

"Call it intuition while I find the evidence."

"Yes, ma'am."

"Are you making fun of me?"

"I'd be a fool to admit that to an operative."

"Oh yes, keep my fearsome reputation in check."

He turned toward the area of the court buildings and down the street where Coffee Gone Dark thrived during the day. He parked a block away. They exited and walked in silence to the café. The few people on the street appeared harmless.

Monica and Kord stood in front of the store. She unlocked the door and trotted back to silence the alarm. "It will lock behind you," she called over her shoulder.

Kord yanked on the door to be sure and followed her to the rear. An overhead light showed a neat and upscale business, glistening stainless steel equipment, and a coffee mug selection featuring Houston sports. A wall held signed photos of featured players.

In a small, messy, and very coffee-smelling

office, Monica sat behind an industrial-style desk and brought the computer monitor to life. He peered over her shoulder as she pulled up camera footage. Stopping at a frame and time stamp, she studied the man talking to a young woman.

"Do you know him?" Kord said.

"Yep." She scooted back the chair and bent beside the desk to a small safe. After tapping in several numbers, it opened, and she eased out a napkin.

"He wrote his number on a napkin?"

"It's not his phone number."

"Must be CIA code stuff."

She didn't acknowledge him but typed something into her phone. The *whisk* sound told him it was a text message. She glanced up and smiled. How could one woman look so beautiful in the middle of a no-sleep, dangerous assignment?

"This has nothing to do with Prince Omar. I'm finished here unless you want coffee," she said.

"When this is over, I'll drink my weight. Be here every morning at six. Drive you crazy."

He observed the red rising in her face, the emotional color of blondes. "Monica, how long are you going to deny us?"

"It's not that easy. You know about Liam. I'm a mess. Then there's the faith—"

He bent and brushed a kiss against her lips, soft

360

and warm. "I'm calling in a favor." He touched her lips again.

She broke away. "What favor?"

"I'm sure you owe me for something. In case you haven't figured it out, Ali has competition," he whispered.

"Can we table this until the mission is over?"

"I keep trying, but you're irresistible."

She stared at the computer screen. "You and Ali are full of yourselves."

He grinned. "We'll see. Want another kiss?"

"Put it in my bank." Rain beat against the roof, and she groaned. "The ground is saturated. We'll need to trade in our cars for boats."

"You're an expert on changing the subject. Shall we get back to the mansion?"

She coughed into the crook of her arm and rose from the chair.

"That sounded like it came from your toes."

"And by kissing me, you'll get it too."

"I have a great immune system."

She bit into her lip, but he saw another smile.

After she texted Lori about leaving the café, Monica reset the alarm, and they made their way to the front door. Rain fell in a splashing deluge. Kord noted movement to the right side of the storefront window.

"Unlock the door. I saw someone out there," he said, grasping his weapon.

She quickly obliged. "I'm going with you."

Outside, he couldn't hear a thing but water beating against the pavement. A bullet whizzed over his head and shattered the café's glass window, sending the alarm into a screech. Gunfire erupted around them.

52

KORD GRABBED MONICA and together they knelt back-to-back on the concrete and fired in the direction of the shooters—at least two from opposite directions.

Sheets of rain distorted their vision, but it also was a disadvantage to whoever wanted them dead. A chain of expletives exploded in his mind. This was why he refused to believe in a God. They were the good guys. He yanked out his phone and called for backup.

Monica took out a streetlight, then another, in the fog-like rain.

One tiny lady with lots of guts. "We've got to get out of here." Kord twisted and destroyed a light inside the café.

They moved toward a parked car hugging the curb and crouched behind the wheels. Bullets flew around them.

"Backup can't get here soon enough," she said in the mass of nature's noise and gunfire.

"We can take these guys."

"Keep telling yourself that."

Sirens grew closer. Gunfire exploded against their car cover. The sound of a vehicle peeling out met his ears before HPD arrived. She crept around the car. Another spray of bullets indicated a shooter still had them in his sights.

"Stay down, Monica. A hero's plaque on the CIA's Memorial Wall doesn't do you any good. Nor will I get any more kisses."

Three HPD cars whirled onto the street, and when the shooting stopped and a second vehicle sped off, one of the squad cars took off after it.

"We're not letting that guy get away." She raced to Kord's Charger.

He bolted to the car first and had the engine roaring before she slammed her door.

Kord trailed behind the HPD vehicle down Franklin, the wheels sloshing through the flooded streets. The suspect's car faced the same slow progress and then picked up speed when it turned and hit the on-ramp for Highway 59 north.

The suspect raced ahead on the highway where the road lay slick. "The last thing we need is for him to kill himself."

"No answers from a dead man," she said. "I want names."

"Sure would hate to make you mad."

"That goes both ways."

He chuckled despite the situation and passed the HPD vehicle with its glaring lights and siren. "He's traveling 90 miles an hour."

The suspect's car hit a patch of water and hydroplaned. Flipped twice, landed upside down in the middle of the road. Exploded. Burst into flames.

• • •

In the diluted haze of lights and destruction, Kord and Monica assisted two HPD officers in freeing the man trapped inside the burning car. They battled hot, rising flames, shielding their faces while moments ticked by on the life of the man pinned inside. His screams in Arabic pierced through their attempts to free him. Kord ripped off his shirt to protect his hands from the hot metal. Monica did the same with her jacket. They struggled together with the officers to yank open the searing driver's door. Kord reached across the man to release his seat belt.

"Monica, you won't believe this, but it's Youssof Dagher," he said, knowing only she would comprehend the significance.

Kord pulled him by his shoulders from the burning wreckage. The officers helped move him onto the side of the highway. Dagher's body was twisted in a mass of raw flesh, his cries pushing him to unconsciousness. In the distance the call of an ambulance sounded closer.

Monica bent to the man's side, the rain increasing in intensity. "Youssof, I can't imagine your pain. But help is coming. Hold on. Be strong."

At that moment, Kord saw a woman who cared more about a criminal's physical pain than his lousy choices. Kord accepted his growing feelings for her, not knowing where it might take him.

Paramedics lifted Dagher onto a stretcher and into the ambulance. The four stood wordlessly watching the vehicle disappear in the same haze of light that had brought them here.

"Choices," she said.

He turned to her.

"They define us." She swiped beneath her eyes, but he couldn't tell if it was the rain or a tear.

"We have questions," one of the officers said.

"We're FBI on assignment."

"Figured so. What do you say about getting into our car and out of this rain?"

Kord and Monica obliged and dripped water over the rear seat of the police vehicle. They displayed their FBI creds.

The officer who'd spoken to them sat on the front passenger side. He handed their IDs to the driver before giving Kord and Monica his attention. "What happened?"

"I suggest you contact SAC Thomas at the FBI office." He gave his supervisor's cell phone number. The call wouldn't be a surprise.

"Got to verify you two first."

Kord couldn't blame the men. HPD's role in protecting the city meant confirming information. The idea of Youssof Dagher dying before answering questions played on his mind.

Monica coughed, raspy, rattling.

"You running a fever?" Her lips had been a bit too warm when he kissed her.

"I'm never sick."

Within five minutes, the police officer and Kord had talked to SAC Thomas and the two were free and ordered to return to the Saud home. They hurried to his Charger and back into town. On the way, he phoned Ali and relayed the details of the shooting.

Monica coughed again.

"Is that her?" Ali said.

"Yep. Claims she never gets sick, but she's been trained in the art of deceit."

"From now on, remind her to take better care of herself."

"I imagine she'll remember on her own." Kord rubbed his face. "I'll notify Jeff. You'll update Prince Omar?"

"On my way to wake him. See you in a few minutes."

Kord reached over and touched her forehead. "You're burning up."

"And since when is an FBI agent a medical authority?"

"Don't need fancy letters after my name to see a doctor is in your future." The woman beside him, the CIA operative who worked harder than any man, required help that he couldn't provide.

"A glass of orange juice and a couple of Tylenol, and I'll be fine. Both are at the Saud home."

53

IN KORD'S CAR, Monica fought sleep when normally adrenaline raced sky-high. In the shadows, she felt her forehead. Rats. She did have a fever, and the throb in her head, along with the sore throat and pain when she breathed, indicated a cold on steroids. She'd tried to push aside the symptoms for nearly a week.

"Can't we follow up on Dagher at the hospital?" she said. "Forget what SAC Thomas said?"

"Our role is protection. One look at you, and the nurses would have a bed ready."

She moaned, couldn't help herself. The cloud in her head messed up her thinking.

"Shall we visit the ER?" Kord said.

"Now you're talking. I want to talk to—"

"Not Youssof Dagher, but you."

"I'm not sick."

"Right. I'll see about an FBI doctor meeting us at the Saud home."

"There's no cure for the common cold."

"Let the doctor decide that."

Best change the subject. "I hate what happened to Lori's shop."

"She has insurance, right?"

"Yes. But she's going to lose business for a few

days. I'll make sure she receives a cash deposit into her bank account."

"You're such a clandestine operative."

Closing her eyes for just a moment, she drifted off to sleep.

Kord requested a doctor for Monica and alerted Ali to what he feared was bronchitis or worse. "Her whole body shakes when she coughs."

"Should she be in the hospital?"

"She'd shoot both of us."

He rumbled his laughter. "I'll be on the lookout for the doctor and meet you at the back."

Kord and Ali had it bad for the same woman. Nearing the mansion, he received a call from HPD with an update on the first vehicle that had left the scene.

"A security cam picked up license plates of a car leaving the area shortly before officers arrived," the HPD officer said. "We're on it now."

When Kord turned off the engine at the rear of the home, she didn't move. Ali hurried from the garage with an umbrella and met him on the passenger side of the car. Kord opened the door. "Monica, we're here."

Not a sound.

He scooped up her body, feeling the heat radiating through her wet clothes. Ali held the umbrella over her, and they rushed inside.

"What are you doing?" she mumbled.

"Putting you to bed," Kord said.

"Bad pickup line."

"Miss Alden," Ali said, "the prince has informed his sisters of your arrival."

She didn't seem to hear.

Kord carried her through the rear of the home and up the stairs to her room. Blonde hair lay across his arms, tickling him. He wanted to stare into her face but chose against it considering Ali walked with him. When he thought about how the two had nearly been killed tonight, how they were perfect targets inside the lit café, yet neither of them had been wounded . . . what a coincidence.

Could it have been God? But He hadn't helped her see Liam's deception.

At the door leading into the women's quarters, Ali knocked and the prince opened it. Fatima and Yasmine were nowhere to be seen, most likely in their rooms until the men left.

Prince Omar pointed to a room where Kord laid her on a bed.

"My sisters will sit with her," the prince said.

"Good." They left the room and learned FBI medical help had arrived.

While the doctor tended to Monica, Ali and Kord sat with Prince Omar in his office.

"Before we discuss what happened tonight," the prince said, "I'm thinking about sending my sisters home. This is far too dangerous for them."

Kord inwardly sighed relief. "Good."

"I'll not make arrangements until I think this through and we have more details. My father has assured me he'll protect them. It's telling our mother that concerns me. I'm afraid she'll give up." He paused before speaking again. "Tell me what you found at the coffee shop and about the attack."

Kord shared what they'd seen on the Coffee Gone Dark footage and what happened when Youssof Dagher opened fire on them outside the café. He also relayed what he had learned about how Dagher had entered the US. "The FBI is digging into how he gained access here, possibly through Mexico or under an assumed name."

"Do you want to know how Saudi Arabia would handle a border problem?"

"I already know."

"Is Dagher alive?" the prince said.

"Critical. He suffered third-degree burns over 50 percent of his body. I'll be notified of any changes in his condition."

"He didn't suffer enough. Rashid Dagher is in custody and being questioned. Do you know where he was staying?"

"No, Amir. We haven't learned that yet."

"How long will it take?"

"A few hours. We want answers too, and my patience is wearing thin."

Prince Omar released a deep sigh. "This has all of us short-tempered."

"In addition to the Dagher men's family ties to Malik, Monica and I are working on a separate link tying them all to Parvin Shah. Intel is scouring for footage all over the world as well as reaching out to informants while monitoring online presences."

"Earlier, I sent word to have Malik questioned again. The people around me always meet with rigid security, but that doesn't mean one or more of them isn't an enemy."

Kord received a call from the FBI doctor and tapped Speaker.

"Agent Davidson, Miss Alden has double pneumonia. She claimed to have had cold-like symptoms for the last week, and being exposed to the recent weather hasn't helped. I recommended hospitalization, but she opposed it. I've prescribed antibiotics. With Prince Omar's permission, I'd like to have some IV equipment and meds delivered with instructions on how to change the bag. ASAP."

"Fatima could do this," the prince said.

"I'll need to report her condition to SAC Thomas."

The prince held up his hand to signal Kord. "She stays here, and she doesn't need to be replaced."

"If she doesn't get any worse, I can check on her here," the doctor said. "Can I meet you in the foyer with further instructions?"

54

AT 11:15 A.M., KORD RECEIVED a call from the hospital that Youssof Dagher had regained consciousness. Still critical and receiving care for his injuries, but alive. Kord informed Prince Omar and Ali, but he wouldn't waken Monica. She'd not be happy to learn Youssof had been questioned without her. Yet she'd understand the nature of what they were doing. Their mission came first. He arranged for an agent to take his place at the mansion and wrote her a note before driving to the burn center at Memorial Hermann.

During the alone time, his thoughts turned to Monica. Last night he'd kissed her, and he'd welcome the chance to do it again. He laughed at recalling her reactions to being diagnosed with double pneumonia. She was one upset lady. No way would anyone hold her back from working a case. What would a future be like with a CIA operative?

Gorgeous. Skilled. Intelligent. Committed to her job.

Christian.

The God-Jesus thing had him rethinking his agnostic views. For too long he'd been searching for purpose and an answer for how this world came to be. He didn't believe he was a sack of chemicals, a being whose thoughts were merely electrical impulses. Was he a product of a big bang? The result of a huge fireball? Who or what set the standards for right and wrong? He'd read the Bible from cover to cover—twice. Also read the Quran twice. The Bible and archaeological proof had leverage. It was the grace thing that didn't fit into the human personality . . . or was grace what each person needed?

While Monica's family believed she was finding her way in the career world, she put her life on the line to keep them safe. But she didn't appear bitter about her family's view of her. Instead, she claimed they loved each other unconditionally. The strange part of her faith came in her conviction—totally out there, and nothing he'd ever experienced before.

Was it God who gave her courage? With her outstanding record, she had superior intelligence, and he'd always heard Christians were ignorant, needed a crutch. A professor from a prestigious university told him once that most Christians lived in the South, products of ignorance. Even as a college student, Kord had rejected those words.

Where did he fit in this universe? And why was the answer important to him?

Snatching his personal iPhone from the console, he spoke to Siri and requested connection to his mother's cell phone. Strange urge to reach out.

Kord waited. Uneasy. He hadn't talked to either

parent since his obligatory Christmas call. Hadn't seen them in over two years.

"Hello." His mother's smooth voice brought back memories of her impeccable hair, dress, and makeup, when she wasn't—"Whatcha want?"

She'd been drinking.

"This is Kord. Just called to say hi and see how you and Dad are doing." He had questions, but little good they'd do him now when she was wasted.

"We're partying. On a cruise somewhere. You know the Jamaican rum." She slurred every word.

"And Dad?"

"Passed out on the chair beside me. The older he gets, the less he can hold his liquor. How's the law business?"

"This is Kord."

"Oh, the cop wannabe."

What a mistake. "We can talk another time."

"No rush. We have lots of trips and little time for chitchat." She ended the call.

Some things never changed. His parents hadn't started out as drunks who couldn't wait until their two sons left home. When Kord was five and his brother eight, Mom and Dad seemed normal. They did family things: vacations, taking his brother to soccer and baseball. Whatever his parents had experienced that turned them into alcoholics had left Kord questioning the purpose of life and if a God existed who cared about humans.

This was why he'd steered clear of relationships. How could he father a child when he had no clue what being a good parent meant? He'd been scarred and recognized it. Why subject a wife or child to his confusion? But since meeting Monica, he wanted to try, make a difference.

What had blasted his parents' lives? The only person who might have an idea was his brother. Kord spoke into his iPhone for Siri to call Blake's private number at his law firm, and his brother answered on the second ring.

"This is Kord. Got a minute?"

"Fire away. Welcome the interruption from research."

"Tried to have a conversation with Mom, but she thought I was you. Peculiar question here, but what caused our parents to dive into the bottle?"

"Thought you knew."

"I was five."

"Right. You were five when Mom got pregnant. Twin girls. She and Dad were happy. Mom lost them and the doctor told her she couldn't have any more children. She had a nervous breakdown. Dad started drinking, and Mom climbed in there with him."

"That's how it all started?"

"Yep. Neither of them ever recovered."

"Sad," Kord said. "No purpose in life but the next drink."

"Sure says good things about how they felt about you and me. Smartest thing they ever did was give us the high road."

"Maybe we should try to help."

"Are you crazy? Trust me, they don't want it. Dad's brother tried years ago and gave up. The parents are pathetic."

"But they are our parents."

"Forget it. I have a law practice and a new girlfriend. Why the interest now?"

Great question. "To understand the dysfunction. Help them find quality of life."

"Leave that to professional shrinks."

He and Blake talked awhile longer about sports and the weather until they both grew tired of talking to a stranger.

Why had Kord chosen today to probe deeper into their parents' lives? If he admitted the truth, it was more about wanting proof of God. His parents' inability to handle a tragedy only left him feeling empty. The more he deliberated it, the more he felt like a kid wanting attention from Mom and Dad, embarrassed he'd wasted time on a hopeless cause. No one in this world looked out for another, unless they were trained.

55

KORD MET AGENT RICHARDSON in the waiting area of the ICU burn care unit. Together they walked to Youssof Dagher's room. The man had also suffered multiple fractures, a ruptured spleen, and a concussion.

Kord turned to Richardson. "Thanks for joining me on this one."

"Glad to. What's the status on this guy?"

"Barely alive. Treating him with aggressive pain management. Awake but hasn't spoken."

"He's in the best place for burn treatment."

"His attitude might be the determining factor. Not much of a future for him," Kord said. "An exchange of a hospital bed for a cell cot. And that's if his cohorts don't get to him first."

"With the charges against him, why would he want to live?"

"We can try a few promises."

"True. How's Miss Alden?"

"Sleeping."

"Will she be replaced?"

"Don't think so. By the time I get back to the Saud home, she'll be sprinting."

"Impressive. Odd, I hadn't met her before."

"From the DC office. You've seen what we have of Youssof Dagher's file?"

"Choice piece of work. Saudi living in Iraq and possibly working for the Iranians or Saudi conservatives in an assassination plot."

"We'll see if he's ready to open up."

The two agents showed their IDs to the officers guarding Dagher's room and stepped inside. Screens beeped in time to the man's heartbeat, displaying vitals and showing his oxygen levels. Two IV bags hung from a pole, providing antibiotics and fluids. Gauze covered some areas, while creams were spread over his exposed face and neck. Huge blisters and seared flesh were the biggest source of agony.

"Good afternoon, Mr. Dagher." Kord closed the door. "We're from the FBI, and we have a few questions about what led to your unfortunate accident. I'm Agent Davidson, and this is Agent Richardson." He spoke Arabic. "I'm recording our conversation, so I encourage you to cooperate. Would you like to talk in English or Arabic?"

He glared at Kord from charred flesh, a body that would never be the same. Surprising he was alive.

Kord and Richardson grabbed chairs and set them on each side of the bed. "English is my preference," Kord said. "Mr. Dagher, you've gotten yourself into serious trouble. Illegally entering the US, attempted murder, resisting arrest, and more. We'd like to help."

"No use for you," the man whispered in English.

"That's understandable, since you tried to kill my partner and me early this morning. But I'll give you a pass on the murder charges in exchange for information."

"Nothing."

"Your address?"

"You're FBI. You find out."

"What about your phone?"

"Burned."

"Your gun was uncovered but not a phone."

Youssof sneered through twisted lips. "Too bad."

"Targeting members of the Saudi royal family on American soil? Not smart."

The man spit at Kord, but the spittle fell a little short and landed on the white sheets. "*Alkalb algharbia.*"

"So you know what my enemies call me. But this Western dog is smart." Kord allowed silence to deepen the tension. "Listen closely. If I remove the guards outside and announce to the media you've given us names, you're a dead man."

No response.

"I could help you, but you have to work with us." When Youssof remained mute, Kord took his strategy up a notch. "Messing with you is a waste of time, and I'm tired of your games. We know you're part of a plot against Prince Omar and his family. Who else is involved?"

"No proof." Every word was forced and slow.

"Since Prince Omar arrived, we've discovered a few things. A sniper killed a bodyguard and a janitor at a high school. Someone killed the consul general's driver. We found a bomb designed to blow up the Saud family planted in a box of fruit and vegetables. In fact, one of your people, Parvin Shah, is dead. Bet you miss her—or him, depending on how she was dressed."

Silence.

"How did you gain access to the US?"

"Walked."

Prince Omar's words about how Saudi Arabia protected their borders swept across his mind. Kord sighed and looked at Youssof. "Prince Omar has requested the opportunity to question you alone, take you home to Riyadh, and I'm in the mood to agree. He has a private jet. Smooth ride all the way to Saudi Arabia. He'd throw you a nice welcome party."

"My father?"

"He's in Saudi custody."

"He doesn't know."

"Not my problem," Kord said. "This is the way your crimes have played out. You're under arrest and being charged with knowingly and intentionally conspiring, confederating, and agreeing to kill Saudi Prince Omar bin Talal while in the United States. You're also charged with three additional counts of murder and two counts of attempted murder of federal officers."

Richardson interrupted him. "Kord, you told me you wanted to reduce the charges, help our friend out here."

He shrugged. "Names of those involved would help. Youssof doesn't talk much. Too bad when the fate of his father and family is at stake."

"Parvin Shah," Youssof managed.

"She's dead, and we found evidence implicating her neatly arranged in her apartment. That's all over the media. Old news. Give us something else."

Youssof stared. "I have nothing—" he sucked in a breath—"to tell you."

"Your choice, given your father's facing execution for sedition."

He closed his eyes. "He's innocent."

"Then you'd better find the truth, along with names," Kord said. "Were you working with Parvin Shah?"

He nodded, eyes still clamped shut.

"Who recruited her?"

"I did."

"How?"

"Before she left Iran."

"You were active at thirteen and living in Iraq?"

"I started . . . young."

Kord wouldn't question this since suicide bombers were sometimes as young as eleven. "You recruited an Iranian woman?"

"Yes."

"Were you her lover, too?"

"Until she came here. Parvin traveled back and forth to Iraq."

"Who gave her orders?"

"Me." His words grew weaker, and Kord stood to ensure he caught every one.

"Who sent a virus to Prince Omar's phone?"

"I did."

"When?"

"In Riyadh."

"What about your cousin Malik?"

"Loyal to prince."

"Parvin Shah had two expensive men's suits in her closet. Who paid for them?"

"I did."

"Where were the purchases made?"

"I didn't ask."

"Who set her up, planted evidence in her apartment?"

Youssof gasped from a visible surge of pain. "Don't know."

"So she was set up?" Kord was pulling straws on this one, but he and Monica had noted Parvin's detail.

Youssof squeezed his eyes shut.

"Please clarify."

Richardson waved his hand. "Kord, we have better things to do. He's our man."

"I'm letting the charges stand, but I'll give him

one more chance tomorrow. If he changes his mind, he can let the police officers know."

"He could be dead then."

"So will his father."

While walking with Richardson through the hospital corridor, Kord received a text that gave both men Youssof's address at a Marriott property north of downtown.

"I've got the sweep," Richardson said. "I'll call as soon as I have something."

56

MONICA WOKE with the sensation of a tree lying across her chest. The familiar smell of her room at the Saud mansion told her she was safe—and sick. No point in opening her eyes until she remembered . . . Finding the mystery man on the café's security footage. The pouring rain. Shooters. HPD in pursuit of a getaway car. Youssof Dagher nearly dead. She battled the weakness. Head, throat, and chest pain. What had she missed? Her mind started to drift and she forced herself to figure out how she'd gotten into bed. Oh yes. Kord carried her from his car. A doctor told her she had double pneumonia. She moaned and hoped neither of the princesses had heard about it. Thank goodness her condition wasn't contagious.

God had taken care of her when the shooters first opened fire.

No other way to explain it. *Thank You.*

While in God territory, she thanked Him for sparing Kord's life too. A gentle tug at her spirit brought the unforgiveness of her past center point in her mind. How could she talk to Kord or anyone about God if she shoved aside what He asked of her? She listened when others complimented her skills and then brushed aside their accolades. Even appeared strong when others joked about her faith. But no one knew the real Monica E. Alden. The *E* stood for Elizabeth, not elite or exceptional.

She failed in the good-enough arena—for Kord or any man.

She'd gotten so far from God with Liam. Difficult to admit even to herself. Forgiveness had become an ocean she couldn't cross. She'd viewed Liam as her soul mate, her savior of sorts. Looks. Charm. Intelligence. The two worked missions others deemed impossible. Monica believed it was God blessing both of them, and Liam agreed.

Don't go there.

She took a journey in her mind to escape the nightmare, to a place she used to visit at her grandparents' farm. Instantly she relaxed. She and Granddad walked along the creek. He taught her about the different plants and types of trees on the green, rolling acres. Most times, his conversation moved to God. "Little girl, you can do in life what matters most as long as God's in it. He'll show you the way."

Her eyelids fluttered. An IV bag dripped into her veins.

"How are you feeling?"

Sounded like Fatima. Monica looked toward the voice to see the sisters on a sofa. "I'm better. How long have you been here?"

"Since you returned in the early hours of morning."

The shades were pulled. Had it been a few hours? This was awkward. Blinking to shove aside the drowsiness, she glanced at the time: 4:36 p.m. How had she slept so long? "It's Sunday afternoon. You've been here all this time?"

Yasmine walked to her bedside. "Mr. Davidson said you'd be upset at sleeping so long. He said 'cranky.' "

"He was right. I should talk to him."

"He's not here." Fatima reached into her pocket and produced a folded slip of paper. "He gave this to our brother for you."

She took the note.

Monica, Youssof Dagher wakened. I'm heading to the hospital. It's about 1 p.m. Call or text when you get this. Mind the doctor and the princesses.

Kord

She sighed and refolded it. Her cell was missing from the nightstand. "Do you know where my phone is?"

"It's in my room," Yasmine said. "We didn't want it bothering you."

Normally the vibration roused her.

Yasmine quickly brought it to her. No texts or

387

calls to return. She pressed in Kord's number. "Can you talk?"

"First off, how are you feeling?"

"Better."

"Medicine is on the nightstand."

She turned to see two bottles of prescription meds and a bottle of syrup that was probably for her cough. "I'll take it in a few minutes."

"I'm wrapping things up with Agent Richardson. On my way back there. Will give you an update then."

"Do we have enough info to close this case?"

"No."

"When will you be here?"

"Within thirty minutes. The doctor will be making another house call around five thirty."

She'd wasted far too many work hours. Yet she should be grateful. "Thanks for taking care of me."

"Get used to it."

But they didn't have a future together. She pressed End and placed her phone beside her. "The doctor is coming in less than an hour. I need to get cleaned up."

"We're here to help you," Fatima said. "The steam in the shower will be good for your lungs, and you can sit on the bench."

She didn't have the strength to get out of bed.

"You can't do this by yourself," Fatima said.

Yasmine shook her head. "We're afraid you'll fall."

A heavy dose of humiliation warmed her, not the first occurrence in this mission. "Not since my mother has anyone helped me bathe."

"Oh, we'll honor your modesty," Fatima said. "I'll start the water. Washing your hair will be the biggest obstacle. We can do this together."

She choked back emotion. "How can I thank you for tending to me like a baby?"

Fatima touched her face. "This is a small kindness for what you've done for us."

"Self-defense classes are on hold."

"Yasmine and I will practice."

Monica wanted to cry. Crazy medicine. Stupid pneumonia in both lungs. Since when did a CIA operative resort to tears because of a shower? They slipped down her cheeks despite the self-talk.

57

KORD PACED THE NATATORIUM while the doctor from the FBI examined Monica upstairs in the women's quarters. The trickling of water from the fountain might soothe Prince Omar, but it did nothing to ease Kord's stress and unanswered questions.

Prince Omar watched him. "Would it be easier for you and Ali if I asked Miss Alden to be wife number three?"

Kord startled. "Where did you come up with that? My mind's on Youssof Dagher."

"Maybe a little."

Kord wasn't going to admit he was right. "She's my partner."

"I see more."

"Ali and I are friends."

He nodded. "To you, friends are family. You're loyal."

Kord fished for something to say. "Not sure what you're seeing with Miss Alden."

"Personal matters are difficult for you."

How well the prince understood him. "I don't want to damage my friendship with Ali. What's important is keeping you and your family safe." He formed his words. "But you're right."

"I won't make you feel more uncomfortable

right now." Prince Omar gave his typical nod. "How did the questioning go with Youssof?"

"HPD recovered his weapon in the car. Not registered. We were missing his cell phone, but pieces of it have been found in what's left of his car. Doubtful anything can be salvaged. At the hotel, a change of clothing hung in the closet. A toothbrush in the bathroom."

"Saudi dress?"

"Yes."

Prince Omar muttered an oath in Arabic.

"Amir, he refused to cooperate even with the knowledge of your having his father in custody."

"I want to talk to him. I can be persuasive, and I have access to every member of his family."

Kord might insinuate such actions, but the prince would follow through. "A trip to the hospital could backfire. We have no idea who all is involved."

"I'm going with or without you."

Kord was tired of dealing with stubborn people. He ran his fingers through his hair. "You'll wear jeans? Sunglasses? I'll choose which limo to take?"

"Yes, and Ali will accompany us. The doctor should be finishing with Miss Alden. We'll learn how she's faring before we leave."

As if on cue, Ali entered the natatorium. "The doctor is waiting in the foyer."

"Tell him we're on our way," the prince said,

and the three met the FBI-sanctioned doctor, a white-haired man who wore a perfect bedside manner smile.

The doctor shook hands with the prince and then Ali and Kord.

"Is she responding to the medication?" Prince Omar said.

"I've prescribed a stronger antibiotic for Miss Alden. She needs one of you to ensure it's filled. She's doing well but needs rest. I hope you can influence her to not overdo it. She does need to walk a little, but with assistance and for short distances." He handed Prince Omar a prescription. "I've given her enough of these for two days, then this needs to be filled."

"I'll get it handled promptly. Thank you for coming. When do you need to see her again?"

"Is Tuesday morning all right, about ten? I asked her to call me if her fever spikes or if the pain doesn't subside in her chest. I don't want her out of the house for the next five days or so, or she'll be in the hospital."

"She'll miss the rodeo and concert on Thursday," Prince Omar said. "She'd have enjoyed it. Luckily we have plenty of body-guards."

Monica would be in his face if she heard the prince denying her the rodeo event. Although Prince Omar respected her, he still looked at her gender as the weaker sex.

"Kord," Prince Omar said, "I'll let you inform her about Thursday."

"Thanks." He smiled while thinking through what this would mean to her. She'd never allow her job to be neglected.

"I gave her something to help her sleep. Miss Alden is a trouper."

"We've seen her in action," Kord said.

Prince Omar chuckled. "Her spirit keeps her alive."

58

MONICA GAZED OUT THE WINDOW of her room into the early evening shadows. She fought sleep and her tummy growled. The best way to heal and climb out of the bed was to follow the doctor's advice. He'd said she needed a week inside the house. Right. She'd sleep, move around a bit, eat, and work this case from her head and laptop.

Fatima walked in carrying a golden tray of fruit, a type of soup, and bread.

"You are an angel," Monica whispered. "I'm embarrassed about how long it took in the shower. My tears. And your helping me into pajamas."

She set the tray across Monica's lap. "Humility builds inner strength."

"I'll not forget those words, and I'm grateful to be clean."

"My sister and I cried with you."

Yasmine entered the room. "Our brother, Mr. Davidson, and Ali would like a word with you. Fatima and I will wait in our rooms until they leave."

In her pajamas. Sleepy. Weak. Under the influence of a sleeping pill. But she smelled better, and her hair was clean. She glanced at the food and picked up a date. "I'm ready."

The men walked in stiffly and gathered at the foot of the bed. A rather comical procession.

"I'm not armed and dangerous," she said.

"Neither have you lost your sense of humor." Kord grinned, and her pulse sped.

"You look better than when you arrived." Ali spoke in the gentle tone he used only for her.

"Thank you all for taking care of me. I'm a horrible patient."

"We're not surprised, Miss Alden," the prince said. "High-level achievers have difficulty when situations slow them down."

"I'll try harder to be civil." A cough rose in her chest, and it went on far too long. Drat, it hurt.

"The doctor gave us your instructions, and we have an antibiotic prescription to fill. I'll talk to my sisters about a regimen to help you regain your energy."

Her eyes moistened, and she warred against her emotions. "Prince Omar, I'm supposed to be protecting you, not allowing you to hover over me. Would you rather I be replaced?"

"Not at all. I've grown fond of you. We all have." He looked at Kord. "I'll leave you to speak with Miss Alden while Ali and I prepare ourselves for the hospital trip."

"Is Princess Gharam okay?" If only she could crawl out of this bed and join them. But she had an idea, something she could accomplish while stuck recuperating.

"My mother is fair, but we're not visiting her. Youssof Dagher is conscious, and I have questions for him. Mind the doctor, Miss Alden. That's a royal order."

Prince Omar and Ali left her and Kord alone. She wanted answers, but he pointed to her plate.

"Eat, and I'll talk before you fall asleep."

She blew out her frustration, so unladylike. When had she ever second-guessed appropriate behavior? "I hate taking meds."

"So I've heard."

She bit into a piece of warm bread. "I'm listening."

"I recorded what little was said." He reached for his phone. "Sending it to you now."

She grasped the spoon for the soup. Her hands trembled like a decrepit old woman's, and she quickly laid it down. Kord would not see her this way.

"Monica—" his voice was soft—"I can help you."

She blinked. Despised herself. "No thanks."

"I won't tell anyone. You can depend on me, and you need nourishment."

She peered into his brown eyes and almost agreed. Almost. "Thanks, but I'll manage."

He laughed. "Do I make you nervous?"

"Always." The word slipped out before she could stop it.

He leaned over and kissed her lightly. "You

should be kissed every day. I'm heading out without my partner, and I don't like it. So eat, sleep, and take your meds."

"I appreciate your putting up with me." For a moment she forgot about the burden of this mission weighing on them.

Many times she wished she'd never set eyes on Kord, but he kept crawling closer to her heart. Pushing away was the only thing within her control, but she welcomed him at the same time.

She believed in the power of God working in the world. But why hadn't He stopped her before she made mistakes with Liam?

Before Monica fell asleep, she called Jeff. With her brain refusing to fire on all cylinders, she'd make more sense using the phone than typing meaningless words.

"How are you feeling?" Jeff said.

"That's one of the nicest things you've ever asked. Or is it because I have a job to do?"

"Monica, they destroyed the mold with you. You always find a way to fight back, no matter what's hit you."

"Aren't you glad?"

"Not when I hear you have double pneumonia. And I can't relax or concentrate for worrying. You should be in the hospital."

"Sorry and thanks. I'm okay. In bed at the Saud home. Taking meds, drinking liquids, and sleeping. The doctor brought in an IV bag and one of the princesses changes it."

He sighed. "What can I do for you?"

"Rashid Dagher is in Saudi custody. His son Youssof won't talk to Kord. Are the women in the family ready for their men to die?"

"They've been interrogated and said nothing."

"By another woman?"

"Not a bad idea. We don't have a woman on the ground there."

"What about me?"

"You can't travel in your condition."

"I'm not suggesting that. I'd like to conduct a video interview with Rashid Dagher's wife and daughters. Need to ask Prince Omar's permission and request he arrange it."

"And you feel confident in talking to these women?"

"We need answers before another person is killed."

"Or gets pneumonia in all this cold rain."

She smiled. "I'm working on it. Anyway, those women need a dose of reality."

"Go for it, Monica."

59

ALI DROVE PRINCE OMAR and Kord to Memorial Hermann hospital through light traffic. Rain no longer fell, and the weather forecasters claimed clear skies for the rest of the day. Kord could use the same positive forecast for this case.

He feared the prince and Ali would consider using strong-arm tactics to extract information from Youssof. Couldn't happen, although he didn't blame them.

His phone rang. Odd—it was Monica. He snatched it to his ear. "Why aren't you asleep?"

"Almost there. Can you put this on speaker?" she said, a little weakly in his estimation.

He pressed the button. "Done."

"Is Prince Omar beside you?"

"Yes, Miss Alden," the prince said.

"I'd like to request a video interview session with Rashid Dagher's wife and daughters. They've insisted they know nothing about the assassination attempt, but they might talk to another woman."

"We have thorough interrogators."

"Are any of them women?" she said.

"It could be arranged."

"Are any of them trained CIA operatives?" Her words grew slow. Yet the woman he cared about proved relentless.

"I feel confident we can convince Youssof Dagher to give us names and details."

"If he shuts down, I'd like an opportunity to talk to the women. My findings could confirm anything you learn."

"She has a good point," Kord said. "I'm hoping Youssof is willing to talk, but we need intel."

The prince glanced out the window. "All right. I'll make the arrangements if our efforts aren't successful."

"As soon as possible, Prince Omar. Just wake me." She disconnected the call.

"Thank you," Kord said.

"We'll see. My sisters are fond of her, and she has a way with women."

Neither Kord nor Ali said a word.

Kord observed Youssof in the hospital bed. His eyes seemed glued shut, the young man's flesh twisted and raw. More dead than alive. His vitals weren't positive, a drop in blood pressure and a temp of 99.9. Had he thought about the consequences of his actions? What kind of monster had recruited him as a child?

"Youssof," Kord said.

Silence.

"Youssof, this is Special Agent Kord Davidson."

His eyelids attempted to open. "I hear you." A hoarse whisper.

"Saudi Prince Omar bin Talal and his body-guard Ali Dukali are with me. The prince would like to speak with you."

"No."

"You're sending your father to his death," the prince said low. "We also have your mother and sisters. I can make the call for their deaths now. Your choice."

He dragged his tongue over blistered lips. "Innocent."

"Your mother? Sisters?"

He shook his head. "All."

"Then who's responsible?"

"Parvin Shah."

"You're wasting your breath. I could ask Mr. Davidson to step out of the room. You and my bodyguard could come to an agreement."

Youssof moaned.

"That's better. I'm assuming you're willing to save your family. Who's behind the assassination plot?"

"Iran."

"Interesting. Intel claims Saudi, but an Iranian was hired to carry out the plot."

A tall nurse entered the room, more like a Norwegian Helga. "This is the ICU, gentlemen. Your time for visiting is up." Kord showed his badge, but she'd not be persuaded. "I don't care who you are. This man needs rest." The woman was as big as Ali.

Prince Omar ignored her. "You're saying an Iranian?"

Youssof slightly nodded.

"Born in the US or naturalized?"

Youssof stared up as though mocking him. "You'll free my family?"

"Yes."

"Naturalized Iranian."

"Gentlemen." The nurse's voice rose. "Shall I call security?"

Kord whipped around. "We are federal security, and this man is in custody."

"Doesn't matter to me your business. My responsibility is the patient in my care."

"Houston?" Prince Omar said to Youssof.

Again he nodded.

Prince Omar leaned over Youssof's body. "For your father and family, a name?"

"Parvin Shah."

"Who else worked with her?"

"That does it," the nurse said. "I'm calling security."

Kord waved her away, and she huffed out of the room. Prince Omar repeated his question.

"Me. I initiated the plot."

"Why?"

"Conservatives."

The lease of oil and gas reserves.

"Who else is involved?"

"They will kill my family."

"I'm able to protect them."

"Parvin's brother took over. No name."

"What did he look like?"

"Never saw him."

"We're done here," Prince Omar said.

"My father? Family?"

"When we have the name of who you're working with, your family will be released and protected. You're a fool if you think I believe you spearheaded the plot." He exited the room with Kord and Ali, passed the nurses' station, and went to the elevators.

Inside the limo with Ali driving, Kord spoke. "Nasim died for what he knew, and he specifically said a Saudi initiated the assassination. The prince's source indicated Iranians were enlisted to carry it out. Parvin Shah and Youssof Dagher may be on the payroll, but they aren't the ones who put this scheme together."

Ali snorted. "Shows how much his family means to him. But we have a lead to run down. Shah's brother through a contact in Iran. Already notified our people."

"I've done the same," Kord said. "Prince Omar, give Monica a chance to interview the women. We're looking for possibly another shooter or shooters from late last night. The real killer or killers just might show up at Youssof's hospital door, and we'll be ready to make an arrest."

60

KORD THREW A SWEATY TOWEL into a bin at the workout room of the Saud mansion. He'd finished a five-mile run on the treadmill. His left arm protested from the flesh wound, and he couldn't lift weights. Exercise stoked his mind to work harder on the criminal activities surrounding Prince Omar. Yet firing neurons hadn't given him the answers he needed. Parvin Shah had died with answers, and Youssof Dagher's family was condemned if he breathed a word of truth. Did Shah have a brother here in Houston or was Youssof lying?

His phone alerted him to a call—HPD. "Special Agent Davidson."

The officer introduced himself as the one who'd reported a security cam picking up the license plate of a car that had left the area of the Coffee Gone Dark café. "Wanted to give you an update. Officers found the car abandoned in an alley three blocks from the incident. It was swept clean."

Kord thanked him before laying his phone aside. Youssof hadn't worked alone, and whoever else attacked him and Monica last night was still out there.

He'd hoped Prince Omar and Ali might scare

Youssof into spilling his guts. But the young man's brainwashing stopped him from exposing those who barked the orders. Kord walked into the workout room shower while his thoughts explored the who and why.

On the return trip from the hospital, the prince shared he'd be in Houston for at least three more weeks. Longer if his mother survived. With the attacks since the prince's arrival, every day brought new problems, deadly ones. Enemies in the Middle East ridiculed the US and Saudi Arabia for not ending the assassination attempts, calling their investigative skills inferior and laying groundwork for the two countries to turn against each other.

"With the investigation showing progress, I'm postponing sending my sisters home," the prince said. "Especially with my mother's dwindling health."

The word *indecisive* crossed Kord's mind.

Prince Omar had arranged the video interview with Youssof's mother and her two daughters for the following morning, evening in Riyadh.

Concern about Monica's health, her perfectionism, and especially what he'd learned about Liam Fielder hit hard. People and mistakes went hand in hand, a part of the human DNA. He'd made his share. For Monica, he saw a woman hurting and unable to forgive herself. Choices and consequences balanced the scales and forced a person to grow stronger or slide downhill.

Kord asked himself if he wanted to help her crawl out of the misery hidden behind those blue eyes. His attraction to her took him down a road he wanted to avoid—the thought of family. While he feared the temptation of turning to alcohol when life overwhelmed him, he also promised himself it wouldn't happen. He'd never tasted the stuff. Never intended to. The picture of a falling-down drunk out of control and making a fool of himself wasn't worth it.

He was hunting for the purpose of life. Like discovering the motivation of a criminal, he craved a reason to crawl out of bed each morning. One day, he wouldn't have this job, and he didn't want to be still searching, investing his self-worth in his work. God had become more real as he explored who or what set the standards for right and wrong. But he was plagued with confusion. The injustices in this world warred against the possibility of a loving God. He wanted to understand the origin of creation, and what it meant for him.

How many times had he deliberated the meaning of life? If all he had to look forward to was a cold grave, wouldn't it be better to have faith in a God who claimed life eternal?

Dealing with his feelings for Monica meant exploring why he wanted what he swore he didn't, a battle of his heart. Liam played a huge role as the fiancé who'd used her and spit her out. Yet Kord sensed her hurt went deeper than Liam—something else added mortar around her heart. Kord saw the guarded look that went beyond betrayal—a primal fear. He wanted to help even if he didn't understand the depth of why. For sure she wasn't aware of what he sensed or she'd unload her S&W on him.

He wanted to help her end the turmoil. Then he had to stop debating the reality of God. Stop putting it off.

God, if You're real, show me. I want to find meaning in my life. If it's not You, I don't know where to look.

At 7:30 p.m. Monica woke, groggy but stronger. Then reality choked her. The doctor had insisted the IVs be in place through Tuesday, and he stated it would be Friday or Saturday before she felt better. Not Thursday for the rodeo event. What a wrench in her protection detail.

No matter, she'd manage her responsibilities without the doctor's permission.

All the think time with no action hammered at her typical pace. Parvin Shah and Youssof Dagher . . . Neither appeared to have the aptitude to pull off the assassination. What had been determined after the second interview with Youssof?

She loathed lying in bed as an invalid. A knock sounded at the door in the common area. She heard Fatima and Prince Omar. A moment later, Kord stood alone in the doorway to her room.

"The prince is having coffee with his sisters, so we can talk."

"I could use the company."

"The company or me?" He grinned.

She treasured the sparkle in his eyes. "I wouldn't want to damage your ego."

"Let's start with the latest updates."

She'd like to capture his smile and bring it out on rainy days. "Same thing."

He moved into the room and pulled a chair to her bed. "How's the coughing?"

"Manageable."

He pointed to the meds on her nightstand. "Do you need—?"

She shook her head, then broke into a cough that ripped at her stomach muscles. Finally she could speak. "Tell me about Youssof."

"He's not doing well. My guess is he's given up the will to live. He's permanently disfigured and condemned to spend the rest of his life in jail."

"What happened with the prince?"

"Prince Omar talked to him, threatened his family. He confirmed what little we already have: internal Saudi with an Iranian assassin." Kord told her about the threat to Youssof's family if he revealed any names and about Parvin Shah's no-name brother.

"Hard to say if he told the truth." She coughed again, this time clutching her chest. "Has Prince Omar made the interview arrangements with the women?"

"In the morning at ten o'clock."

"That's 6 p.m. for them," she said. "But you know what? The evening means they could be tired, more prone to open up. What else?"

"Tell me about Liam Fielder."

She stiffened, couldn't help herself. "Why? We've had this conversation."

"I think it's interfering with your state of mind."

If she had the strength, she'd black his eyes. "No, it's not. What is it with you anyway? My personal life has nothing to do with this protection detail."

"Monica, you're lying to yourself if you remotely think his betrayal hasn't affected your role in the CIA or your personal life."

She would not face the reality about Liam with Kord. She needed an exit ramp. Now. Worse yet, she refused to admit the hurt and damage to her relationship with God. "It's inconceivable." Her words sounded disgustingly weak, like she felt.

"Isn't confession good for the soul?" He scooted the chair closer.

"Being inches away from me doesn't mean I'll

talk about Liam. Last I checked, you're not a shrink."

"I'm a friend."

A friend who'd kissed her multiple times. Carried her up the stairs when she collapsed with this disgusting pneumonia. The challenge of opening up about Liam meant revealing the extent of her hurt. How could Kord ever understand the depth of her mistakes when he didn't have a relationship with God?

"While you're debating it, here's my take," he said. "Monica Alden is a dynamic woman. She can go on being miserable, not trusting anyone. Or she can work through the past and shake it off."

"Since when have I given the impression of being miserable?"

"I can see it in your eyes when you think no one is looking."

Her heart thudded. "I'm fine."

"And I'm a world intellect. I'm surprised God has allowed you to get away with all the denial stuff. Doesn't He do the accountability thing?"

His words knocked at the wall around her heart. She choked back a lump in her raw throat. "Where is your firsthand info about God?"

"Closer than I've ever been. You and I have been through hell and landed on our feet several times. The last few days are part of it, and the danger's not over. Give me a chance to help you with this." The tenderness in his eyes should have spelled caution, but the hint of release nudged her forward. "You are the strongest woman I've ever met, but you've allowed someone to assume power in your life, someone who doesn't deserve it. What hit you so hard that you can't get past the punch?"

Her eyes watered. "I've never admitted all of the story to anyone."

"You value your privacy. I get your reasoning."

"Why, Kord? What's in it for you?"

"To see you happy."

Seemed like a lame excuse, but she really wanted to believe him. Dare she move forward when her insides curdled? Tell a man she barely knew the ugly truth? "Why do you care if I'm happy?"

"Because I don't understand this crazy attraction to you. Because I'm looking for God and what a Christian worldview means. Because I have a hard time figuring out life too." He took her hand, and she clung to his.

Maybe she could find an escape from the nightmares.

She'd move forward. "Liam's betrayal paralyzed me, especially when recalling his every word added another rung on the ladder of lies. I believed him. Put him higher in my life than he should have been. I thought we were a divine team destined to bring down enemies of the US. Then I picked up intel pointing to him as a monster, taking thousands of dollars from a known terrorist who'd been suspected of biological warfare. I followed it up. Confirmed his guilt. I tried to confront him, but he disappeared. I went to Jeff with the findings and led a team to bring him down." She squeezed his hand in an effort to keep her emotions intact. "The faces of the dead men, women, and children will never leave me. Not a day goes by that I don't see them again."

"I'm really sorry."

"There's more. From the moment he showed interest in me, I let my faith slip. Liam said he was a believer, but he preferred a motorcycle ride in the country or a walk in the park over a church service. At first, I protested. Wasn't long before I allowed him to dictate what I did not only on Sunday but every day of the week. The things I valued about my faith fizzled. We lived together, though I swore I'd never give myself to a man without the sanctity of marriage. I thought he loved me as much as I loved him." She stopped to breathe and manage the debilitating weakness hammering against her lungs. "I put Liam in God's place. When I realized my stupidity killed so many people, the guilt and shame rested on me for forsaking my faith."

"From what I've learned, God is forgiving."

"You've uncovered quite a bit."

He started to speak, then shook his head. "I'll tell that story on another day. Am I right in assuming you can't forgive yourself?"

Her stomach burned. "I pushed God aside for a man who was the devil incarnate."

"You blame yourself for something out of your control."

"Are you sure you're not a shrink?"

"I need one myself." His denial soothed her.

She glanced away, then back to him. "My actions won't leave me alone."

"Has your God indicated you aren't worth His time?"

"It's not Him."

"Are you a candidate for change?"

She wanted to be one. If only she could get past the blackness that mocked her. Had the time arrived for her to accept His forgiveness and herself? She looked into Kord's eyes, the man who'd offered to spoon-feed her when her hands trembled. The man who confused her in far too many ways. The man who'd found a place in her heart.

The worst needed to be said. "I'm afraid the shot I fired into Liam was more about my personal vengeance than preventing a man from killing others."

"Why?"

She thought about truth setting her free. "I've

often thought I should resign from the CIA. Taking a life to get even is motive for a criminal."

"What if you hadn't pulled the trigger? What would have happened?"

She'd considered the same thing. "He was on his way to take botulism to the Sudanese government when we caught up to him."

"I'm listening."

"You're not an interrogator. I've come this far. Might as well finish. Liam was hiding in a small village. We located the hut, and I asked for an opportunity to confront him. Thought I could talk him into surrendering. If we engaged him in a firefight, innocent people could be killed. Getting Liam to confess and give intel would've helped us stop those involved."

"So you approached him alone?"

The whole nightmare replayed, the villagers grabbing their children and scurrying to their huts. The heat and the smell of Africa. "I called out to him. Asked him to put down his weapon. No one else needed to die. He laughed. He reminded me of my weakness and stupidity." She recalled her threadbare faith and how she'd felt too undeserving to ask God for help. "I made it to the opening and walked inside. I was deadly calm. Filled with rage. He aimed his firearm at my chest. A rustle outside the hut caught his attention, giving me a moment to take the advantage. He lost his balance, and I dove after him. He fired into my shoulder. I sent a bullet to his head." She paused to rein in her emotions. "The blood covered both of us."

"His death was not your fault."

She swiped beneath her eyes, and he handed her a tissue from the nightstand. "I hated him for his lies."

"You loved him, and he tore out your heart. But if you hadn't pulled the trigger, you'd be dead along with probably countless others."

"That seems cold, callous."

"When we're hurt and don't understand the actions of those we love, nothing seems rational."

She feared dissolving into a puddle of despair, and she blamed her illness. But Kord was the voice of reason, although she had no idea how or why she'd unloaded the story. It must be to pave the road to freedom and peace.

He towered over her. "I'm leaving you alone to take care of business."

"Are you sure you're not a believer?"

"Working hard on it."

"You're a lot closer than you think." She bit into her lower lip. "Keep me updated."

"I will." He turned to leave.

"Kord, do my struggles deter your faith?"

"You have a grip on God, and I admire it. I think the problems you're experiencing are more about your perfectionism than the reality of a creator God. Your secret's safe with me."

When he left the room, she sensed a profound loneliness. Except the emptiness had nothing to do with Kord but about the condition of her soul. Perhaps the ugly past happened to draw her close to God again. And in the stillness, the pain in her body subsided to a renewal of spirit. The memories would remain, dim as time passed, but they'd always serve as a reminder of what evil people tried to accomplish.

61

MONDAY MORNING, Monica took a glimpse at the clock on the nightstand in her room. Nearly time for the video call with the Dagher women in Riyadh. Fatima and Yasmine had helped her to a chair and dressed her in traditional Saudi black. Although she was forced to wear the IV, by keeping her arm down, the camera shouldn't detect it. A small table held her laptop as though she were sitting at a desk.

The physical effort had sapped her, but she'd not admit it. By the time the day hit its end, she'd walk the upstairs hallway to build her strength.

In five minutes, the interview with Youssof Dagher's mother and sisters would take place. Kord sat across the room, ready to assist with his mic. He'd be giving Monica prompts or insights from the women's body language that she could hear through her earbud. He looked at her differently, softer, and it wasn't her imagination. Prior to dressing for the interview, she'd received his text.

With God all things r possible.

Have u chosen belief?

Yep.

Knowing his faith in God now had roots, she shouldn't fear her caring for him. How very

417

strange to fear a relationship while craving it at the same time. Later they'd talk. Most likely after the mission ended.

The computer screen came to life with four women wearing black from head to toe and seated in a bleak-looking room in total gray scale. The male translator did an audio test, and they were ready to go.

"Miss Alden, these women are aware you have questions for them."

"Thank you," she said in Arabic and gave a slight smile. "I'm sorry for the tragedies that have fallen upon your family. I understand the heartache of losing loved ones. My hope is to offer comfort and possibly address questions about Youssof and Rashid."

One of the women stiffened, but nothing was said.

"Good," Kord said into her earbud. "You've established your purpose."

"I'm so sorry about Youssof's car accident and your father being detained. We women treasure our relationships with the men in our families, and without them, life is unthinkable."

"The older woman's body language says she distrusts you," Kord said.

Monica interpreted the same reaction.

"How is my son?" the woman said.

Monica could only imagine how the woman's heart ached for her child. "He's critical with serious burns, broken bones, and a concussion. A friend spoke to him, and he expressed concern about his father, you, and his sisters."

"Are you a mother?" the woman said.

"Not yet."

"As a woman, what can you do for my husband and son?"

"I can bring truth to those looking for answers."

"Answers for what?" the woman said. "My husband and son are innocent of betraying our country. We are all loyal to Saudi Arabia."

"I hear concern in your voice, and I don't want to see you lose a family member. But evidence is mounting that either Rashid or Youssof has helped in an assassination plot against Saudi Prince Omar bin Talal. People are dead. Right now your husband and son look guilty, which means both face serious charges." Monica tilted her head. "Are you ready for both of them to face death?"

The woman rose from her chair. "They are innocent."

"Why was Youssof in the US illegally?"

"I didn't know he was there."

"Pay dirt," Kord said.

A younger woman shook her fist at the camera, her anger apparent in her tone. "Mother, you know Youssof believed his friends. Father tried to persuade him, but you saw how he treated Father."

"What happened?" Monica said.

The younger woman rose and took her mother's hand. "After we moved to Riyadh, Youssof and Father argued about him returning to Iraq. When Father blocked the door and would not let him pass, Youssof pushed him against a table. Father is loyal to Saudi Arabia, and it's wrong for him to take the blame for Youssof's actions."

The older woman buried her face in her hands. "What am I to do? Choose between my husband and son?"

"Mother, choose the truth and save my father."

"Who is guilty?" Monica waited.

The older woman looked up with a tearstained face. "My son. He has friends who are bad men."

"Why did he choose their ways?" Monica said.

"Youssof was a small boy. Weak. Many teased him about his size. The bad men promised him money and power."

"Do you have names of these men?"

"No. Rashid followed him a couple of times, but Youssof seemed to sense it and my husband learned nothing."

"Your sorrow must be great. What you've said will help your husband."

"And my son?" She heard the anguish in the mother's voice.

"I wish I had an answer for you. He's getting the best care available for his burns and injuries."

"How will we be informed about his condition?" the mother said.

"I'll make your request known to Prince Omar." Monica wished she had the power to ease their minds.

The mother whispered her thanks, and Monica ended the interview.

They had corroboration of Youssof's friendship with possible suspects, but no names. Would Rashid have discovered his son's friends? Would he go to his death protecting his son?

62

MONDAY AT NOON, Kord propped his feet on an ottoman on the rear patio and reviewed intel. A text from SAC Thomas stated Youssof Dagher died twenty minutes earlier. The young man's injuries overpowered any will to live. He'd become an enemy of the US and Saudi Arabia who'd faced the consequences of saddling up with a terrorist regime. What had convinced Youssof, like so many others, to forsake family and friends for a deadly cause? Kord saw how loners, criminals, and those who'd broken laws looked for companions with a united cause, a family. Youssof found acceptance when others turned him away because of his stature.

Kord typed into the secure FBI site for updates. The FIG was digging into the many unanswered questions. He texted SAC Thomas for the camera footage near and around the burn unit at Memorial Hermann. Although techs were on it, he needed to see for himself. If questionable visitors had attempted to gain entrance into Youssof's room, he wanted to identify them. Others involved could fear Youssof might talk and seek to eliminate him.

Was there an Iranian man in the city who had

agreed to help in the prince's assassination? And where was the intel linking the right people to the crime?

The camera footage from the hospital arrived. He phoned Monica, who was probably napping, but she'd want the info.

"What's happening?" The words were muffled from her obvious dreamworld.

"First off, Youssof died before noon. Richardson and another agent were there to see him at ten thirty. He was already unconscious."

"Some will view him as better off. But he might have survived and chosen to use his mind and heart for a noble purpose." She sounded more awake. "I'm a hopeful kinda gal."

More like she was complicated.

"Kord, hold on while I check CIA updates."

He heard a shuffle. "Aren't you supposed to be recuperating, which means staying in bed?"

"The mind never shuts down, and the IV pole has wheels. Fatima turns off my phone once I go to sleep."

"Should I come up there?"

"It's the women's quarters, remember?"

He chuckled.

"Finally," she said. "Jeff sent us something we can use. I'm sending it to you so we can discuss it together. Oh, you've sent me camera footage."

"We have time to discuss both." Pics sailed into his phone. "Got 'em."

"Youssof and Malik in Baghdad," she said. "And look at the time stamp."

"So what were they doing in Baghdad?"

"A question for Malik. Look at the men's body language. Youssof's shoulders are back. No strain in facial muscles. Definite lack of intimidation."

"Cousin-to-cousin conversation or instructions about a conspiracy?" he said.

"One of them or another person has computer knowledge."

"Youssof hinted toward Parvin being set up, and he confessed to planting the virus in Prince Omar's phone. What if he planted evidence in her apartment to incriminate the Iranians so the Saudis would look innocent?"

"The Iranian government has denied any knowledge, but they wouldn't admit to a crime that could destroy them," she said.

Neither said the obvious of the shadow that hung over their country if they lost Saudi Arabia as an ally.

"I wish I was overseas."

"We'd be dynamic." He thought of Liam. "And the past would be behind us."

"Maybe so. Shall we look at the hospital footage?"

He brought it up. "I haven't reviewed it yet. Might take a while."

"I'm looking." She coughed, and the sound of it hurt his gut. "Don't say a word. Fatima and Yasmine are my med police."

For the next fifteen minutes they reviewed the footage with questions here and there. She coughed a few times, but he kept his mouth shut. Fatima had told her brother that Monica was running a consistent hundred-degree fever.

"Nothing jumps out at me," he said.

She gave the location of a section of the burn unit's waiting area. "See the old woman near the nurses' desk? Glimpses of her have been in a few frames at different times."

"Where?"

She gave the points of interest. "Her sweater is a distinct gray, and I see flashes of it here and there. Can you zoom in?"

He obliged. "Olive-skinned. Not much else to go on, but I'll check it out." He texted the inquiry to the FIG.

"Patience is not a virtue for either of us. Anything turn up on Shah's brother?"

"Not yet. Investigators are following up on the places she visited."

"Like the library?"

He mulled her question. "That's a safe place."

"Yes, sir."

"I'm on it."

"If you'd let me out of this bed, I'd run it down."

"Even if you didn't sound like your cough came from your toes, our role is protection."

She laughed, and he savored the sound.

63

MONICA HAD MADE A USELESS attempt to fight sleep and explore the new findings. She fell asleep before three in the afternoon and didn't wake until her phone buzzed with a call from Kord. This time, she'd placed her cell beneath her blankets to keep Fatima from confiscating it.

"Woke you up?" he said.

"I refuse to answer that." She took a quick look at the time—9:00. What a shirker. "What have you learned?"

"The FBI held a press conference, encouraged the community to help."

"You've had positive responses with billboards and enlisting citizens' cooperation in the past. By the way, are you hungry?"

"I could be. Do you want me to bring you up something?"

"No, I need the exercise and I hate to eat alone."

"Aren't you still running a fever?"

"Low grade. Very low."

"What about your sidekick, the IV pole?"

"I can carry the bag. Please, anything to get out of this room."

"I'll meet you outside your door."

"But no help down the stairs unless I ask."

"I could carry you. After all, I carried you up there."

"So not laughing."

"On my way."

Maneuvering the IV bag in and out of the sleeve of a floor-length robe took more time than she thought. Then a scarf in case a Saudi man showed up. Nearly wore her out. Then she had a coughing spell. Fifteen minutes later, she shuffled out. "Sorry to keep you waiting."

"Sure this is a smart move?" he said.

"I'm going to the rodeo on Thursday. Have to start somewhere."

"Monica, you'll be watching Keith Urban from YouTube videos."

"A good mental attitude is the beginning of great things."

"Whose quote?"

"It's in the book of Monica. Sure hope there are leftovers in the fridge."

"If not, I'll whip up scrambled eggs."

"With lots of cheese."

She took slow, deliberate steps. Not since she'd caught malaria had she been this weak. Clinging to the smooth metal railing, she worked her way down the winding steps while he carried her medicine bag and supported her arm. "Keep talking to me," she whispered. "Keeps my mind off myself."

"What kind of a diamond do you want?"

"A little sure of yourself, aren't you?"

"I'm bedazzling you."

"Where did you get that word?"

"Found it in the dictionary."

She could get used to Kord Davidson. Seemed to take far too long to get to the kitchen.

Ali entered the room. "Thought I heard you two talking." He shook his head at her. "You need to be resting."

"I will once I get something to eat."

He wrapped his arms across his chest. "I'm staying until you do. And Jeff Carlton is at the gate."

Prince Omar walked in dressed in jeans. "I want to hear what Mr. Carlton has to say."

What were the odds of the kitchen being the most common meeting area?

Oh, well, there went her idea of having Kord all to herself.

A short time later, Jeff sat at the kitchen table, while Kord scrambled eggs with chives and cheese for her. Coffee brewed. Maybe it would keep her awake.

"Are you checking on my progress or are you bringing info?" she said.

"How's the pneumonia?"

"Better." If only the fever would break. Kord set the eggs before her, and she picked up a fork. Needed nutrition to work smart. "Tell us what you've learned."

Jeff smiled, his scruffy beard causing him to look like a college kid. "Figured you'd say that. We have a lead on Parvin Shah's brother, a man who's lived here in Houston for eight years. Works as a librarian at the downtown branch of the library she frequented. He didn't pop up on the initial search for Shah's family because they don't share the same last name."

She perked. "You have him in custody?"

"On it. A follow-up earlier this evening with the library director shows he hasn't been at work for the past two days. Neither has he called in or responded to his phone. Not his habit. Well liked and dependable. He's a naturalized citizen, lived in Houston since his arrival to the US."

"Address?"

"The apartment was cleaned out. We've got a BOLO out now with his photo. Viewing security video from his apartment complex as we speak."

"Anything left behind we can use?"

"He has a strong resemblance to his sister. Sending pic of Jafar Turan to your and Kord's phones."

"Mine and Ali's," Prince Omar said.

"Yes, sir. Jafar Turan has a clean background."

"Definitely not the kingpin?" she said.

"Doubt it," Jeff said.

"Just received my info from the FBI," Kord said. "Every investigator in the city is on it."

Jeff turned to her. "We need your photographic memory expertise."

She pulled up pics of the brother and sister. "Aside from techs comparing Parvin's and Jafar's facial recognition to what we already have, I have nothing." She longed to help in identifying the suspects. "Parvin had lifted eyebrows, higher cheekbones, and fuller lips. I'm thinking through the footage at Paramount High School, the attempt on Consul General al-Fakeeh at MD Anderson, the bomb left here, Parvin's apartment, and the various other clips. Jafar is in none of them. Sure of it." She looked at Kord. "Did you see anyone at the hospital who caused suspicion?"

Kord shook his head. "If involved, he must be behind the scenes."

"Prince Omar?"

"Nothing, Miss Alden."

"Ali?" She studied the big man's features. He took a breath.

"In the waiting room of the burn unit, I remember an old woman. Dressed Iranian. Wearing gray."

Ali didn't need to say more. She wanted to run the leads herself, especially with the woman wearing gray. She pulled up the burn unit waiting room footage and pointed to the woman in a few pics. "Is this her?"

"Yes," Ali said. "I remember she stared at us."

"Could be the woman was Westernized," Monica said.

"Or she could have been Jafar Turan," Ali said.

"Possibly so."

Jeff typed into his phone. "Having techs examine the hospital footage. Jafar's face will be splattered worldwide." He glanced up. "He can't hide long. The job isn't done, so he's in the city." Jeff finished his coffee. "Will call with updates." He shook Prince Omar's hand. "Don't go anywhere. Whoever's behind this is getting desperate."

"I can't promise that. I refuse to cancel my plans like a coward."

Couldn't the prince see he put them all in danger with his actions? Or did his honor and self-sacrifice supersede common sense?

64

TUESDAY MORNING, Monica rolled out of bed in a fetal position—the most comfortable—and found maneuvering to the bathroom and dressing a little easier than the previous day. Dragging the IV pole irritated her. She unhooked the bag. The doctor claimed he'd remove it today. Couldn't happen soon enough.

Last night's kitchen meeting had sapped her. How long until she was back to full speed? She swallowed her meds and slid the thermometer into her mouth: 100.2.

What was wrong with her body? The doctor said exhaustion had weakened her, but she was tired of the temp game.

Three Tylenol to curb the heat.

Now to brush her teeth. She bent and gasped at the ache in her stomach from all the coughing. Yesterday she'd managed the task standing up. Sending a brush through her hair proved equally hard on muscles she normally took for granted. At least she was ambidextrous.

After hooking back to the IV pole, she moved to the common area, but the princesses weren't there. They'd long since finished breakfast, but a plate of fruit, bread, and coffee awaited her. A text flew into her phone from Ali.

Prince Omar would like to see you.

B right down.

I'll be in the hallway.

Best the meeting be now. A nap would chase her until she gave in. Outside the women's quarters, Ali waited. "Good morning, Miss Alden."

She returned the greeting. "Did Kord tell you not to help me with the stairs?"

He smiled. "Said you might shoot me."

"You're a wise man." She liked Ali. He had charm. Except she'd kill him because of his temper. Or vice versa.

But this morning she allowed him to hover over her. Falling face-first down the stairs might stop her from attending the rodeo on Thursday.

In the prince's office, she sat beside Kord. Coffee was served, and she desperately needed a second cup. The prince gave her his attention.

"Miss Alden, you look feverish."

"I'm much better, Prince Omar."

"Following doctor's orders by multiple ascents and descents of the stairs?"

Ouch. "I'm taking the antibiotics and sleeping."

"So my sisters tell me." He rested his cup on a saucer. "During the night, Kord and I requested information. Kord, would you fill her in?"

"Jafar has not left the States since his arrival in 2009. Legally, that is. I sent a request for sources inside Iran to learn about Parvin Shah and Jafar Turan with ties to anyone in Saudi Arabia, specifically Rashid and Youssof Dagher and Malik al-Kazaz."

The prince's phone sounded, and she paused to listen. He spoke in Arabic to someone she believed was the director of Saudi security. Out of respect, she rose to leave.

"Miss Alden, wait." The prince immediately returned to his native language.

Ali gestured for her to sit, and she did.

"Are you certain?" The prince listened for a few moments longer. "Arrange a live interrogation with Malik. I want to pose questions. Dig into his mother's death. Also I want more on Youssof Dagher's companions in Iraq. We need answers."

The conversation ended, and Prince Omar set his phone on a side table. "You heard my part of the conversation. I'll let you know when the interrogation takes place." He eased back in his chair. "We have additional intel. Jafar Turan had military training before entering the United States. He's not associated with any Iranian government official. We don't know who recruited his sister, trained her, or what the motive behind their actions is in connection with Saudi Arabia."

"Youssof claimed to have recruited Parvin, but where does Jafar fit? A sleeper cell doesn't make sense. We assume the ultimate goal of the plot is to eliminate Prince Omar, but why Parvin, Youssof, and Jafar?" Kord said. "And the consistent question is what Saudi paid an Iranian to assassinate Prince Omar?"

"We're researching a plot by the conservatives," Prince Omar said. "I've read the reports and shared them with Saudi officials. We need to find Jafar alive. If he's killed, we'll have a difficult time stopping the enemy from sending another assassin or suicide bombers into my country or here."

"Would you cancel the rodeo event on Thursday?" Kord said.

"Not at all. Jafar may have slipped out of the country since he's a fugitive, but I'm prepared to hire additional security to protect my family here and friends at the rodeo."

"I intend to accompany you," Monica said.

"Miss Alden, the doctor will have a few things to say about that decision."

"I heal quickly."

"What about your fever?"

She might have to pull a trigger on Kord for that question. "I'm sure it's normal now."

Prince Omar huffed. "We'll allow the doctor to deny or permit your participation."

She'd not let anything or anyone deter her. Including the doctor.

"I'll escort Miss Alden to her room," Ali said.

"Good. I need a word with Kord."

Exhaustion seemed to take a chunk out of her normal vibrancy.

"May I encourage you to stay in bed," the prince said.

She rose and slowly moved to the doorway. A bit of dizziness swept over her, and Ali grabbed her arm.

"Last night's meeting in the kitchen weakened you," the prince said.

He might be right, but she'd not admit it. A raw throat from the cursed cough plagued her. No time to sleep when she wanted to follow up on the same info as Kord and Saudi security.

Inside the women's quarters, Fatima and Yasmine were reading in the common area. At times Monica wished for a more leisurely lifestyle, but it never lasted more than a few minutes. She'd be bored out of her mind.

"Good morning," she said to the sisters.

"We're good. You're pale," Fatima said. "Did you take your morning medications?"

"Absolutely." The word had become a joke between them.

Fatima stood and examined her IV bag while Yasmine retrieved her pole from Monica's bedroom. Sweet ladies. She'd never forget their kindness. She wanted to talk to Yasmine, see if she unknowingly had vital information.

Monica sank into a chair. "While you two slept last night, I walked down the stairs."

Fatima touched her heart. "By yourself?"

"Kord met me in the upper hallway. I was hungry."

Yasmine giggled. "Ali helped you walk down midmorning. Congratulations."

"Slow but sure. Before you know it, we'll start back with self-defense classes. Actually a child could take me out right now."

"You have many tricks," Fatima said. "I think no matter what you face, you'd be triumphant."

She laughed. "I doubt it. Do you mind if we chat?"

"Of course." Fatima pointed to a comfy chair. "Rest and talk. Is this about my brother's safety?"

"Your entire family," Monica said. "Has Prince Omar spoken with you about the latest findings?"

Fatima put her book aside. "He told us our people and the Americans are looking for a man named Jafar Turan, brother to Parvin Shah."

"It's not my role to give you any more information than the prince has shared. My question is about another subject, one we've discussed before. Mostly for Yasmine."

"Malik?" Yasmine said. "Has he done something else?"

"I'm just working on making pieces fit. Did Malik mention Youssof Dagher to you?"

"He looked forward to spending time with him in Riyadh."

"What happened when the family moved?"

"He encouraged my brother to meet with Rashid and Youssof."

"Why?"

"He said to build good relations between the men. He was proud of Youssof and hoped he gained favor with Prince Omar to secure a position within the family."

"Were there other times Malik met with the younger man?"

She shrugged. "He never told me."

Fatima took Yasmine's hand.

"If there is anything at all you remember that can help us end this nightmare, tell me now. When Malik returned home, he called you right away?"

Yasmine shook her head. "Not until the next day. That's when he told me about the trip."

"Did Malik speak of your brother's business dealings here in Houston?"

She tilted her head. "Only that Omar believed he was doing the best for our country."

"And Malik shared the same conviction?"

"I assumed so. Monica, I've told all I can remember. I hate him. He's not who I thought he was at all."

65

KORD SPENT THE REMAINDER of Tuesday morning reviewing security footage from every venue in which Jafar or Parvin might have been present. FBI and CIA techs were on it, but he wanted insight now, which meant doggedly pursuing every angle. The FIG beat him to the find— Parvin visited Jafar twice after the prince landed in Houston. Both trips at night to his apartment. She appeared to avoid one camera, as though knowing where it was located, but missed a second one. Didn't mean Jafar was guilty of conspiracy—only that he and his sister had met.

Shortly after lunch, Kord sat in Prince Omar's office with Ali and the prince awaiting a live feed from Riyadh. Monica slept, but she could view it later. A protective nature for her had him concerned for her weakened condition.

Kord mulled over the connection points for the plot. Information about the conservatives lacked clarity. None of them would own up to an assassination attempt to reinforce their views of how the country should handle natural resources. Monica believed Malik held a critical role, while Kord wavered. Could the former press secretary be innocent and simply have done his father's bidding and tried to help Youssof, a wayward cousin?

"Prince Omar, Malik is in place to answer your questions," Ali said.

Malik faced a plea for his life. His white *thobe* was streaked with dirt and bloodstains, and bruises marred his features.

"Malik," Prince Omar said, "your story hasn't changed."

He lifted his head and stared into the camera. "Because it is the truth."

"I have new questions, ones that might jar your mind and help you remember."

Malik closed his eyes. "I doubt I can help, but I will answer."

"What were the dates of your trip to Iraq?"

"January 3 to the thirteenth. Prince Omar, I've answered this before."

"Ten days is a long time."

"My cousin, Rashid Dagher, took a while to make a decision about returning home."

"What was his delay?"

"His wife's family didn't want them to leave."

"I see," the prince said. "You know Parvin Shah was killed in an assassination attempt. But we've uncovered more. She worked with Youssof Dagher, and he's dead."

Malik startled.

"Are you surprised at the death of your cousin?"

"I have no knowledge of this woman. I thought Youssof lived here with his family."

"Not so. He left for Iraq and ended up in Houston. He attempted to kill Miss Alden and Kord but failed. He sped away but sustained serious burns and injuries in a car explosion that resulted in his death."

Malik rubbed his face. "I spent time with Youssof. I thought he'd be fine once in Riyadh."

"Why did the two of you spend three days in Baghdad?"

"When I broached the subject of wanting to get to know him better, he suggested a short trip. I asked where, and he said Baghdad."

Prince Omar crossed his arms over his chest. "Why?"

"I asked the same, and he claimed to like the city."

"What happened there?"

"Visited mosques. Talked for hours."

"Weren't you fearful of bombings? Shootings?"

Malik moistened his lips. "Encouraging my cousin to be a good man was more important."

"Whom did you meet with there?"

"Neither of us saw anyone we knew."

"Were the two of you ever separated?"

Malik blinked. "Twice he went for food, and I stayed behind."

"Unusual?"

"He was insistent I rest."

"Were you ill?"

"A stomach problem from bad food."

"How convenient he was unaffected."

"Prince Omar, when can I leave this wretched place?"

"When I have the truth. If it's a comfort, you will leave. How remains to be seen." Prince Omar turned to Kord. "What would you like to ask?"

Kord wished this was face-to-face. "Did Youssof have unsavory friends? Did you see any of them?"

"No."

"Names?"

"No."

"What was Rashid's argument with these men?"

"They stressed violence against enemies."

"I see," Kord said. "Had Youssof participated in any of their activities?"

"Rashid wasn't aware, but he worried his son might soon embrace their ways. I asked Youssof about his friends, and he claimed they were fine and his father was suspicious of every Iraqi or Iranian."

The first bit of information that Malik had offered on his own. Truth? Lies? "Were they Iraqis or Iranians?"

"I have no idea."

"Did you hear any statements termed as treason?"

"If so, I'd have told Prince Omar."

The prince huffed. "Like you told me about my sister?"

Malik lifted his chin. "I am not a traitor. I'd give my life for you."

And he might if evidence proved otherwise soon. Kord posed a question. "Who is Jafar Turan?"

"I have no idea. Never heard the name."

Prince Omar indicated he wished to speak. "Do you side with the conservatives?"

"I'm loyal to you."

"My final question—are you prepared to die for your crimes, or do you wish to provide names in exchange for your life?"

"I have never betrayed you or any member of the Saud family. If you choose to execute me, know you are killing an innocent man."

Monica's phone rang late afternoon after a nap. A call from Mom while on a mission was seldom a good thing. Except this time Monica didn't mind, and she was in the mood to chat. Closing her eyes, she breathed in and out while willing her lungs to work properly.

"Hi." Mom's cheery voice greeted her. "Hope I'm not catching you at a bad time. I thought the coffee shop would be closed for the day."

"It is, so talk away. Love hearing your voice."

"Are you in the middle of dinner?"

"No, and it wouldn't be a problem if I was."

"Your dad and I want to see you. Wondering when you'd be available for us to visit."

"Were you reading my mind? I was thinking of a trip home."

"I'm so excited. When?"

Monica touched her chest. The cough would most likely linger. "In six weeks. I can take a few days then, like a Thursday through Sunday afternoon."

"Before Memorial Day?"

"Yes, unless you want me to wait until then and take two more days."

Her mother squealed.

"Okay, that settles it. I'll be home on Friday the twenty-fifth and fly back on June 3." She'd put in for leave now before getting a new assignment.

"I can hardly wait. We'll have a new foal then." While Mom talked about farm life, Dad's refusal to slow down, and her brothers and their families, she longed to join them. But only for the planned week.

She'd go nuts after that, but she'd never tell them so. Her dear family meant too much to hurt them.

"I'm going to have all your favorite foods. The rhubarb should be ready then too. Have you saved up enough to buy your own coffee shop?"

"Not sure I want the responsibility of ownership."

"My winsome daughter. I don't care. Do what makes you happy. Is there a special young man?"

Monica thought about saying yes, but the complications from it might snowball. "Maybe."

"Bring him with you. He can have your brother's room."

"No promises." Now why did she offer such a thing?

66

THE DOCTOR ARRIVED AT 5:00 P.M. to see Monica. Not a moment too soon as far as she was concerned. He removed the IV and took her temp.

"Still running a fever," he said. "Let me check your lungs." He listened and she prayed, but he frowned. "Neither lung is clear. I'll be back on Friday."

It was what he didn't say that bothered her the most.

"Stay on the bronchodilators and antibiotics. Don't attempt any strenuous activities. A little walking is good. Rest often."

"Yes, sir. I'll do my best."

She hadn't requested the doctor's approval about attending the rodeo, and she hoped the prince hadn't either. Priorities meant a few sacrifices.

During a short evening walk outside the Saud home, Kord enjoyed Monica's grip on his arm. He hadn't talked to the doctor after her appointment due to another meeting with Prince Omar and Ali.

She leaned into him and slipped her arm into the crook of his.

"Have you given in to my charms?" he said.

"No, Agent Davidson. Just maintaining my balance. Sorry for burdening you."

"You're overdoing it." Telling her he enjoyed it might not be a good idea. "Like the scarf, by the way."

"It makes the prince happy."

"So would resting more."

"The fresh air is good medicine, and the scent of spring flowers boosts my morale."

"As long as you don't have a relapse. What did the doctor say?"

"That I'm a good patient."

"Why don't I believe you?"

She laughed. "Tell me about your meeting with Prince Omar this afternoon."

"You inspired him."

"How?"

He told her about the live video with Malik. "You were asleep. Saw no need to wake you. Not one sign of deceit in Malik's words or body language. Threw me."

"He's playing the role of his life."

"And he's trained."

"Does the prince know we believe Malik is still a suspect in the conspiracy?"

"He does. But he needs more proof and names."

"In all that we've discovered about the suspects, we have two outsiders who can be questioned—a distraught father, whom I believe, and an Iranian national. The FBI and CIA are gathering more intel, but we're missing an important piece that links them all."

Kord reached for his phone and pointed to the marble bench. "Perfect time to check in again with my Iranian contact."

Once seated, she removed her arm from his. "Everyone likes to be wakened at 2:30 a.m. Can you put the call on speaker?"

He glanced around before tapping in Rere's number. The informant answered on the first ring. "That was quick."

"Just picked up my phone to call you. Learned something tonight. Hold on while I make sure no one is around."

When Rere indicated he was in place, Kord urged him to share all the details.

"My source points to Malik al-Kazaz as the originator of the assassination plot against Prince Omar," Rere said.

"Is the source reliable?"

"The man has a connection inside Saudi with the conservatives. Malik arranged for Parvin Shah to handle the kill, offered to pay her $500,000 once the job was complete."

"How did he recruit her?"

"We don't know."

"Where does her brother Jafar Turan fit?"

"No mention of him."

"Youssof Dagher?"

"Malik recruited him."

"Is Malik the leader of the conservatives?"

"That hasn't been confirmed. I'm working on names."

"Malik's motivation?"

"Unclear. I heard a story about him slitting his mother's throat when she learned he was meeting secretly with an Iranian. He blamed an intruder who was never found for the attack."

"That was over two years ago, and he told Prince Omar she'd been attacked in her home, claimed she was murdered. Doesn't fit with the current scheme unless he had designs to bring down Prince Omar then." Images darted across his mind of the prince and his family in a pool of blood. "Maybe the mother's murder is what ties it all together. We'll work through it here. Anything else?"

"Another of my sources inside Iraq has photos of Malik with Parvin taken about six months ago. I'm sending them to your phone."

"Which means she sneaked in and out of the US."

"You need the why, and I'm working on it."

"Dig more into the Saudi conservatives," Kord said. "Thanks. Be safe."

"No worries. I'm a good liar."

Kord dropped his phone into his pocket and turned to Monica. "ASAP to Prince Omar. You were right. Should have listened. Remember when I said, 'You know nothing about a brother-hood of loyalty'?"

"Doesn't mean I like hearing a man is a killer. What can I do?" she said.

"Get better." He kissed her cheek.

"I'm doing my best." She yawned.

"Need to get you back inside. While we walk back, I'm contacting SAC Thomas. See how quickly we can confirm Jafar's whereabouts."

"I'll text Jeff. Malik won't live past the hour unless Saudi authorities think they can extract more information."

"Either way, he's a dead man."

67

KORD EXPLAINED TO PRINCE OMAR what he and
Monica had learned from Rere and encouraged
him to refrain from executing Malik until they
had more information. She stood beside him, and
he could feel her silent support.

"Until we have confirmation of who's behind
the plot, Malik is worth more to us alive than
dead." Kord was aware Prince Omar would be
sending a team to Iran to find out who else might
be suspected in working for Malik. But a formal
declaration meant chaos in a world already fueled
by violence.

Fury lined every visible muscle in Prince
Omar's face and body. Nothing came from
his mouth. He picked up his phone and called
Riyadh. "Intel points to Malik as our man.
We must discover who else is involved before
executing all the traitors."

Kord caught a glimpse of relief from Monica.
But without names, Prince Omar and his family
still faced danger.

Prince Omar clenched his fists and requested
his bodyguards and staff to meet him in the
natatorium.

When seated, the prince glared at each man.
"Malik is responsible for the death of Zain, a

friend and good man. Too many others have been killed by his orders. If any of you suspect another man or woman, now is the time to speak up."

Nothing.

"Allah has seen fit to show us the truth. We will not relax but keep our eyes open for the next man or woman to carry out orders. Our plans in Houston will remain intact. The Saud family has built an empire on power and courage. We will not run home in the midst of adversity. We will hunt down these men and destroy them."

Back in his room, Kord sank into a chair, his mind weary. This assignment had tested his skills as an agent, and it wasn't over yet. But finding faith in God, and the sense of purpose beyond the FBI, made it all worth it. He'd read in Christian literature and the Bible about the power of grace. Until he'd experienced it, the concept seemed like a fairy tale. Then there was Monica—wherever that led.

Wednesday arrived and Monica's temp dropped to 99.6. Reason to celebrate. The cough was a nuisance. She had sore stomach muscles, ones she never knew existed.

Houston's security camera footage indicated Youssof had been in the city twenty-eight hours after his family believed he'd left for Iraq.

Footage showed him alone, but the search for accomplices continued.

Fatima and Yasmine visited their mother during the morning hours while Monica stayed at the Saud home like an invalid. The two young women confided in Monica about the steady decline of their mother's health. Their good-byes were tearful, as though each time might be the last. Princess Gharam fought hard, but her strength waned.

After returning from the hospital, Kord accompanied Prince Omar along with three bodyguards to Saudi Aramco. The meeting ran smoothly, according to Kord.

She despised this wretched healing process.

She studied secure CIA websites to catch the latest news since the revelation of Malik's involvement in the assassination plot. A coughing spasm hit, and she clutched her chest. Then took a dose of medicine before diving back into her research. The CIA, along with the Saudis, had people on the ground in Iran running down names and suspects. None of it had hit the media forefront. Yet.

The one thing cementing her sanity came with the rodeo event on Thursday. She'd be out of the house and working again. Prince Omar had reservations about her participation. Serious ones. But it would take cuffs, chains, and a locked cell to keep her from being at NRG Stadium.

A few positives—no further attempts on the

prince's life, and she was determined to see this mission through to the end.

The negatives took a frightful stand. Jafar was hiding. Rere fled Iran to Saudi Arabia due to death threats. Malik refused to talk. Only a fool would believe the turmoil had ended.

Late afternoon, she made her way to the common area, where Fatima and Yasmine were busy with their phones. The younger woman glanced up, wearing despair like another veil. Monica recognized the immaturity.

"Yasmine, if you let Malik's treachery wall up your heart, he won in destroying at least one member of the Saud family." From Monica's experience, that kind of bitterness did no one any good. Perhaps it was only a temporary defense mechanism. "If you fuel your soul with hate, your heart will blacken."

"How do I rid myself of it?"

"Forgive him and yourself," Monica said.

"I'm trying. Never thought I'd feel so much hate and pain."

"I'm praying for you."

Yasmine thanked her. She kept her head high and not a tear was shed.

The quiet in the house was like living in the eye of a storm.

When she woke on Thursday morning, her temp held steady at 99.2. She had one thought on her mind—that afternoon was Prince Omar's rodeo event. He'd invited a group of oil and gas businessmen to fill a private suite with catered food and nonalcoholic beverages. No expense spared. In fact, the prince had to pay extra because of not serving alcohol.

Friday morning he had an appointment with Shell to discuss leasing Saudi oil reserves.

Jafar had disappeared, and the reality made her nervous. While today's guests would dine on fine food, watch rodeo activities, and listen to the rich voice of country-western star Keith Urban, those entrusted to the prince's protection stood by on alert.

For sure she'd not be bored, and what she needed was energy and strength.

Snatching her phone from the nightstand, she pressed in Kord's number. "Got a minute?" she said.

"What's up?"

"My guess is Jafar knows what I look like, as well as any other players. I can balance the situation in our favor by letting them think I stayed behind. You go on without me, and I'll meet you there."

"I don't think that's a good idea. It's supposed to rain, and your lungs aren't clear."

"Says who? I don't have a fever."

"How can I talk you out of this?"

"Impossible."

"Figured so." He sighed, and she knew it was for her benefit. "Will I recognize your getup?"

"Never know. Arrange for a pass at will call under the name of Kay Bronson. I've used it before and have ID. Can you request a car and driver from the FBI?"

"On it. Your being there isn't necessary. We have law enforcement swarming the place."

"If Jafar shows up, I want to see the look on his face when he's arrested."

The customary breakfast with Fatima and Yasmine energized her while they chatted. In truth, her mind swarmed with scenarios of what could go wrong. She'd learned from the past how to survive, but every mission had its twists. Mentally she was ready. Physically, another few days of healing would have given her more confidence. Spiritually, she was learning to forgive herself and allowing God to work through her. A wrist mic, an earbud, and her weapon lay on her bed.

Had she been cooped up too long, or was the nudging in her spirit a warning to be prepared for the worst?

A different pair of limos were scheduled to leave at 3:45 with the prince and his entourage to ensure catering, preparations, and security had perfection stamped on them. From NRG Stadium's layout online, Monica had memorized the private suite's location and the nearest exits.

She calculated how many steps to the men's room, elevator, and stairway. Her car would arrive at 4:00, driven by FBI Agent Richardson.

Prince Omar expected guests by 5:00, all ushered by HPD from the entrance to where the prince and the festivities awaited them.

"I hope you enjoy the rodeo," Fatima said. "You're leaving with my brother?"

"Actually I'm leaving in a separate car a few minutes later."

"Do you need help getting ready?"

Monica took a sip of her coffee. "If I can't shower and dress myself, then I need to stay here."

"Tell us all about the concert when you return," Yasmine said.

"You can watch a collection of Keith Urban music videos from right here. Great view."

"Not exactly the same," Yasmine said.

"I doubt I'll have time to listen and watch anything except what's going on around your brother and his guests."

"True."

The morning passed more quickly than Monica anticipated. A brief nap late morning added energy to her pitiful body. When the time came, she grabbed a tote bag from the closet and dumped the items on the bed—a short, wispy auburn wig, a pair of brown contacts, cinnamon-colored lipstick, ID for Kay Bronson, a navy-blue pantsuit, white silk blouse, gold stud earrings, and comfortable flats with good arch supports—in case she had to run. Jeans would have allowed her to blend in, but the prince wouldn't have agreed to it for his guests. After dressing, she tucked her weapon in her back waistband and inserted the earbud, covering it in a mass of auburn hair.

As she opened the door to the common area, Fatima's eyes widened. "I don't think the doctor will approve what you're about to do. I thought you were going to enjoy the concert."

Monica smiled. "A girl can always use a different look."

A text informed her Agent Richardson waited outside.

68

MONICA BELIEVED the mood of a Texas rodeo was as unique as the state. Food vendors dished up pickle fries, barbecue, bacon cotton candy, nachos smothered in cheese and jalapeños, macaroni-stuffed baked potatoes, and anything that could be deep-fried, including strawberry shortcake. The smells zoomed straight out of heaven.

The amusement park section bustled with activity, and for a split second she gave the Ferris wheel and roller coaster a longing glance.

The latest country-western hits blared from loudspeakers, and the sound of laughter from all ages proved just as entertaining. A crowd dressed in boots, jeans, and cowboy hats blended in a sea of Texas pride.

If only she had the opportunity to explore the livestock ribbon winners, from cattle to chickens. But today was a workday.

Monica hurried on to the stadium, where police officers hovered in front of the entrance. She presented her Kay Bronson ID, and an officer escorted her to the elevator and on to where Prince Omar awaited his guests. She sealed every person's face to memory and counted the steps from various markers to ensure she'd been correct in her original estimation.

Inside the huge private suite with its glass wall facing the arena, Kord greeted her. Ali gave her a double take, and Prince Omar laughed.

"I warned the prince, but not Ali," Kord said.

"Shame on you." She waved at Ali. Glancing at her watch, she figured guests would be arriving within ten minutes.

"Do you live by your watch?"

"It's an OCD thing."

He chuckled. "I've noticed."

"Everything set?"

"Appears so. FBI has cameras positioned inside and outside the building. HPD is in place."

She nodded. "If Jafar is here, he'll be dodging security like his sister."

White-jacketed caterers loaded a serving table with buffet warming trays filled with food. A chef examined a station where he would slice prime rib according to each guest's specifications. A designated area contained traditional Middle Eastern foods. Another table held cold dishes, and still another had additional hot Texas favorites and breads. Nonalcoholic drinks were on ice. The aroma of freshly ground coffee swirled about the room. Certainly more food than the twenty guests would eat. Two rectangular tables, each large enough to serve twelve people, were covered in white linen, crystal, china, and more silver alongside the plates than she owned.

The elegance and wealth bothered her, especially when she'd seen starving nations. Shaking her head, she chose to dwell on the men enjoying every moment of the event. And keeping every person there safe.

Consul General Nasser al-Fakeeh and two of his bodyguards arrived. She hadn't been aware of their invitations. But not surprised.

She joined Kord and Ali. "I'll be in the background with you." Premonition caused her to shiver. "I'm nervous."

"I haven't seen you so . . . concentrated," Ali said.

His description made her smile. Like she'd been condensed into a frozen orange juice can. "I'm worried I might miss something. Meds aren't my best friend when I'm working."

"You're not alone," Kord whispered. "None of us are once we accept God's sacrifice."

"You've found Jesus?"

"I have and will show you from this moment on."

The sincerity in his voice shoved aside her doubts about his new faith.

Kord handed Ali an earbud. "This way the three of us can keep in touch on a separate network. I don't trust anyone today."

Within minutes, guests arrived. Oil oozed from the handshakes of those greeting the prince, well-known figures in Houston hailed for their contributions in keeping Texas floating above the prosperity of many other states.

Monica memorized every face. No one hostile or suspicious. Nothing spoken alerted her. Body language appeared appropriate. She'd maintain a watchful stance and do what she did best: look for a man—or a woman—who plotted murder.

After the meal, Prince Omar rose to give a short speech before the rodeo portion of the entertainment began. He lifted his arms, a figure of wealth and power, and reiterated a few of his statements from the previous press conference. "By cooperating together, we are the future. By sharing knowledge and resources, our countries can flourish while creating job opportunities for all our people. Please enjoy tonight's rodeo. Thank you for taking time out of your busy schedules to be a part of this event."

The guests applauded, and she didn't detect hostility. Prince Omar toured the tables and shook each man's hand.

The meal concluded, guests mingled and the rodeo readied to start before the concert. Perhaps the prince's goodwill intentions would continue. The world's ability to shrink brought races and cultures into close quarters. Peace for all stayed on her heart. Definitely her prayer life would stay busy.

The rodeo began with cowboys riding broncs

and bulls, marking up records and dollars, followed by a race of horses and wagons setting the stage for a glimpse of the Wild West. The next event brought schoolchildren into the arena along with several calves. Each child who caught a calf not only received the animal to raise but also secured an educational scholarship. All the while, her gaze darted about.

Exhaustion soon hit. Prince Omar said something to Kord, then left the box with Ali and Wasi.

Five minutes passed.

Then five more.

Monica joined Kord. "Where are Prince Omar, Ali, and Wasi?"

69

JAFAR STARED UP at the Ferris wheel at the rodeo. He'd prepared himself mentally for revenge in the death of his sister. He understood Parvin's reasons for wanting to kill Prince Omar. Like every good Iranian, he hated the Saudis. Parvin was drawn into the assassination plot by the love of money and sweet words of devotion from Malik al-Kazaz. Jafar held back, not sure he wanted to get involved when so much could go wrong. To encourage his sister, he'd continued her training once she was in the US. Few knew of his skills obtained inside Iran as a dark agent.

Then Parvin was gunned down, and honor took over Jafar's very being.

Youssof Dagher contacted him within minutes of her death. Together they'd bring down the woman who'd pulled the trigger and her FBI partner, then finish what Parvin started.

A smile tugged at his mouth. The US and Saudi Arabia were headed for historic disaster. Within a few short hours, Prince Omar would be dead. The Saudis would sever ties with the US. No longer would the US have an ally in the Middle East, and Jafar intended to inflict all the damage possible and, if necessary, die a hero.

He and Youssof had designed a plan. The stupid

Saudi had gotten caught up in his own ego and died. No matter. Jafar would now carry it out. Youssof had informed him of the prince's rodeo event. They falsified gold volunteer badges, which made access to any part of the rodeo doable.

This afternoon he wore loose jeans and an oversize shirt to store needed items and a vest with his volunteer badge. To anyone who glanced his way, he looked like a Hispanic who was volunteering for the rodeo.

He even had two sets of security credentials.

A baby Glock with a silencer.

A bomb strapped under his shirt and vest.

And a dead-man switch in his left hand.

A foolproof plan was not easy, and his confidence had worn thin with past failures. For Parvin, he'd do this.

Jafar entered the men's room not far from Prince Omar's private suite, knowing the prince would leave for the bathroom at some point with only two bodyguards. He picked the lock of a built-in janitors' closet and found a few cleaning supplies.

Within fifty minutes, the bodyguard Ali Dukali stepped into the men's room. Jafar greeted him.

"Sir, this area must be cleared immediately by order of the rodeo management and HPD," Ali said. "I'm in the company of a Saudi prince who is under tight security."

Jafar stiffened his shoulders and swung into action. He added a limp to his stride, then pulled two signs that said Closed and placed them outside the entrances.

The men using the restroom finished and exited. When the area had been vacated, Prince Omar entered with a phone in his hand. His features were drawn.

"I'm sorry, Amir," Ali said. "We were all hopeful of Princess Gharam's recovery."

A second bodyguard offered condolences. The prince headed for the handicap stall. The others must not suit his royal blood.

"*Perdone, señor.* No clean there." Jafar moved behind Ali, closer to the prince, reached up, and shoved a syringe into the bodyguard's neck. He let go of the syringe, then grabbed his gun with the same hand. Ali struggled to yank it out, but the needle did its job and the big man fell. The second guard pulled his weapon, but Jafar fired into the man's shoulder and turned the gun on Prince Omar. "Step into the stall or you're a dead man."

Jafar fumbled with his gun as he pulled out another syringe. He sent it into the second bodyguard's neck.

Prince Omar lifted an arm, but Jafar slammed the butt of his weapon into the side of the prince's head, hard enough to draw blood. The prince stumbled inside the handicap stall.

Jafar pulled the second volunteer badge, a baseball cap, sunglasses, and a black T-shirt from inside his own shirt. "Your phone, now. Into these clothes and give me everything. One word, and it's over." Jafar showed his bomb strapped to his body and raised his left hand holding the dead-man switch. "I'm watching, Prince Omar."

In less than forty-five seconds, the prince was ready. Jafar stepped on the prince's phone, smashed it, and dropped the pieces along with the prince's Saudi clothes into the trash. He yanked out paper towels and covered them.

"We'll walk out together. You'll not look at any law enforcement. One word, and the bomb goes off."

Prince Omar didn't utter a word.

70

KORD'S ATTENTION SWUNG UP and down the corridor. People walked by, but not the men he was looking for. He turned to Monica. "The prince received a phone call from the hospital and headed to the restroom. From there he'd find a private place to talk." He touched his earbud. "Ali, everything okay?"

No response.

"Ali?" Kord broke into a run.

He hurried toward the restroom and Monica followed. Signs at both entrances indicated the facility was closed. Correct procedure for Ali and Wasi to clear the area. He entered with Monica on his heels. Ali lay facedown on the floor. He moaned and lifted his head. Wasi had a bleeding upper shoulder wound, and he looked unconscious.

"Find the prince," Ali whispered.

"Where is he?" Kord bent to his side while Monica called 911 and checked Wasi.

"Don't know. A man got me with a needle. I remember him pulling a weapon before I blacked out."

Ali should be glad he was alive. Must not have been a big enough dose for such a huge man. "Did you recognize him?"

Ali rubbed the back of his neck. "From the size, could have been Jafar Turan. But he sounded like a Hispanic."

"Another disguise," Kord said.

Monica poked through the trash. "Prince Omar's *thobe* and *ghutra* are here."

"Stay here," Kord said. "I'm going after Prince Omar. You're in no shape to help."

"Don't think so." She bolted out an entrance as though she weren't recovering from pneumonia.

Kord alerted the other bodyguards and HPD security. "Shut down all exits. At least one man, maybe more. Armed." Saad and Inman entered the men's room. "Help is coming. I've got to find the prince."

Ali stopped him before he could rush after Monica. "Prince Omar learned his mother died. I don't think it has any bearing on Jafar taking him, but I wanted you to know."

Kord thanked him and raced from the building before speaking into his wrist mic to Monica. "Did you hear Prince Omar's mother died?"

"Very sad."

"Where are you? We'll do this together."

"I'm not waiting on you."

His thoughts spun as he pushed forward. The prince had been wearing Western clothes under his Saudi garments, which meant he could mix in with the crowd and whoever had abducted him.

How could they find Prince Omar in time?

• • •

When Monica didn't see the prince, she rushed outside NRG Stadium and scanned the crowd in every direction. Didn't help that her five-foot-two frame left her shorter than most people. Adrenaline fueled her because her lungs ached.

Stop.

Focus.

Think like a killer.

Monica looked for a less crowded area and moved toward the pavilion housing the many animals. Two men caught her attention. One shorter than the other and wearing a volunteer badge. The second man wore a baseball cap and sunglasses. He was also a volunteer. She recognized the height and build of Prince Omar, and the slighter man resembled Jafar.

She broke into a run, drawing her firearm while speaking into her mic. "Kord, I have eyes on the prince and Jafar. Southwest corner of the livestock building."

Jafar's head jerked up—obviously he'd sensed her. He forced the prince into the building. By the time she made it to the entrance, the pair had blended into a large crowd.

The smell of animals hit her nostrils while she moved through the many people. Children shouted. Animals called out. No doubt Jafar would exit at the other side. Her chest ached, but she pushed on.

Prince Omar would overpower his abductor if given the opportunity.

Two familiar men emerged from an exit, and she elbowed toward them. Outside, a navy sky rolled in. A jagged slice of lightning in the distance followed by rumbling thunder added to the imminent danger.

The two men hurried into the amusement ride section, Jafar walking beside the prince. Did Jafar have a gun stuck in the prince's ribs? Where were they going?

And where were Kord and the bodyguards? To her far left, she caught a glimpse of HPD officers. She saw Kord and other bodyguards gaining speed. All of them were faster than one puny girl, and they could overpower Jafar. In her condition she couldn't take him out alone.

Up ahead, the Ferris wheel unloaded passengers. The splattering rain and the darkening sky dictated the ride should cease operation. Jafar pulled his gun and spoke to the man assisting the passengers. Neither Monica nor Kord and the HPD officers got to the prince and Jafar before the two men slid into an empty gondola.

"Mommy, that lady has a gun," a nearby child said.

"Whoa. Whatcha doin' with a piece?" came from a teen.

A woman screamed. "Call the police."

People moved aside, clearing a path to the

Ferris wheel. The wheel jerked into action and took the gondola upward, coming to a halt when Jafar and the prince were at the twelve o'clock position.

Monica hurried to the operator. "I'm FBI. Bring that gondola down."

The rough-whiskered man shook his head. "That guy's wearing a bomb. And he had his left hand wrapped around what looked like a dead-man switch."

Thunder resounded.

HPD officers urged the crowd to move back several yards.

Kord joined her at the Ferris wheel. "We need a bomb specialist."

Agony in her chest caused her breathing to come in short, painful spurts. Why was she doing this?

Clenching her fist, she turned and plodded to the far end of the 150-foot-tall Ferris wheel, barely able to put one foot in front of the other. Let someone else take over.

No way could she help the prince when every breath hurt.

Who cared anyway?

Coward slammed into her mind.

The word penetrated her soul—what it meant, the color of giving up, not who she was and what she stood for. Her faith. Her being.

A war within herself.

A splattering of heavy raindrops beat against her, enforcing the desire to find shelter. At the rear of the Ferris wheel, a roller coaster jutted up against a threatening sky.

Whom do you serve?

God wasn't fair.

The sound of Kord calling her name caused her to whirl around.

"Are you okay?"

She blew out a burst of agony, mental . . . physical. "Did you see what happened?"

"Jafar has the prince trapped at the top of the Ferris wheel."

"And I've got to finish my job." She half walked, half ran to the roller coaster, where she reached for the metal and started an ascent.

"Are you crazy?"

She smiled back at him. "Has there ever been any doubt?"

Lightning sliced across the sky, so close the back of her neck tingled.

"Monica, you'll be killed."

"Then get a sniper in place to take out Jafar. You've got to have my back. Promise?" She swung him one last look and jerked out her earbud. He'd distract her climb, and she had to concentrate on what lay ahead.

"Whatever it takes. Monica, I'm not letting you do this alone."

She ignored him because she feared what he

was about to do. He mattered, but protecting the prince came first.

Water soaked her and made the climb slippery, but the raging storm did not match her will to stop Jafar before he killed Prince Omar and many other innocent people. She'd not fail a second time. A quick look down showed Kord moving upward behind her on a parallel metal support beam.

She loved that man.

71

JAFAR WANTED TO STAND and shout his success from the gondola. After Parvin's, Youssof's, and Malik's failures, he'd succeeded in trapping Prince Omar. Surviving this was impossible for either of them, but it didn't matter when he would have vengeance for his sister's death.

"Down on the floorboard," he said.

Prince Omar squeezed into the narrow space at their feet, and Jafar lowered himself beside the man. He held his gun to the prince's head with one hand, his other hand on the dead-man switch. "I claim victory for all those who seek your death."

"What is this about?"

"Your press secretary and his conservative following sold you out to the highest bidder."

"Parvin Shah. Malik paid her."

Jafar fought to keep from triggering the bomb. "Malik will be executed, but you don't know the names of the others in your country against you."

"Saudi security has every name, every opposition to moving our country ahead. Neither the conservatives nor our enemies will stop progress."

Jafar slammed a fist into Omar's jaw. "Youssof

told me about Malik. He had big plans for your sister."

The prince's face reddened.

"Move, and I trigger the bomb." Jafar laughed. "If Malik slit his own mother's throat, what would he do to Yasmine? He was one step ahead of you for so long." He stared up at the dark sky, ready to strike before he ended it for himself and the prince.

"He was caught before he touched my sister."

"Ah, but by then they had access to all Malik knew about you."

"Who recruited Parvin?"

Why not tell Omar the truth? They both were about to die. "Malik. He enlisted Youssof's help too. Got him to send a virus to your phone. Money talks, Prince." He spat the title. "When he shorted Parvin on the advance, she sent the e-mail that implicated him." Jafar laughed. "I tried to get to Youssof when he was in the hospital. Dressed as an old woman. But Allah saw fit to take his life and end Malik's."

Prince Omar dragged his tongue across his lips. "This is between us, not all these innocent people."

"My only regret is not spending more time at the library. There I read so many books about the US." Jafar smirked. "The best way to have victory over the enemy is to learn all about them."

"Who—?"

"Shut up. We're done talking." He lifted a small pair of binoculars to his eyes. "Your bodyguards and cops are moving into place. Just what I wanted." He held up the dead-man switch. "Are you ready?"

72

IN THE TORRENTIAL RAIN, Kord stared up at Monica struggling to reach the top of the roller coaster. "Let me do this. You aren't in any shape to take down the killer."

"No thanks."

"Between the lightning and pneumonia—"

"Kord, hush. I'm going to finish this."

"Correction: we are."

Ali spoke to him in the earbud. "Allah be with you both."

"God is. Both of us," Kord said. "I'm sure of it." He joined Monica about ten feet from where the cars traveled to the top of the tallest hill. From there, one of them would have a clear shot at Jafar. Both men were crouched on the floorboard of the gondola.

Why hadn't Jafar detonated the bomb? Could the man possibly be afraid? Kord prayed so.

A chill settled on Kord. The storm only added to the difficulty of taking the killer down and increased the risk of him blowing himself up and others. If he or Monica were able to take a shot at Jafar, Prince Omar must immediately hold the dead-man switch down. The prince was no stranger to the stakes, and Kord believed he'd be ready.

Kord's attention swerved to the tiny woman climbing higher on the roller-coaster tracks. He followed while keeping his sights on Jafar and Prince Omar. Sirens wailed and thunder pounded along with the rain. What chance did they have?

"You care for Miss Alden," Ali said into his earbud. "Together you can do this."

"You have feelings too."

"I care for what she represents and her beauty. You love her heart. It's in your face when you look at her."

Later Kord would talk to Monica. "Who's with you?"

"Saad, Inman, and Wasi."

"Wasi needs a doctor."

"The prince's welfare comes first."

All a force to be reckoned with, but none of them were in a position to prevent the bomb from going off once Kord or Monica put a bullet in Jafar's head.

"I keep going over it in my head," Kord said. "We don't have a choice but to believe Prince Omar will do everything he can to stop Jafar from detonating the bomb."

Ali's voice rang over his earbud. "If we do nothing, the prince and all of us are killed."

Lightning struck several yards away, followed by an explosion of thunder.

"Monica, we have to take Jafar out. Pray the prince is able to stop the bomb."

He watched her put her earbud into place. "Ali, tell the others to take cover."

"We're here to support you," he said.

"You'll get yourself killed. Kord, I need to be higher up the track before I can take a shot. Cover me."

He shielded his eyes in the blinding rain, barely able to make out her form. "You got it. Monica, the lightning is worse."

"Hush. I need quiet. Do you like to ride horses?"

She hadn't lost it, only calming herself. "Every chance I get."

She crawled to an incline where the ride took a plunge, and he moved up too. "My parents have horses," she said. "Promised Mom I'd visit over Memorial Day."

"Can I come?"

"They will think we're together."

"We are."

God, I'm new at this. But please take care of Monica.

"Jafar sees her," Ali said.

Kord's attention flew to the Ferris wheel. Jafar and Prince Omar struggled.

Monica took her shot.

Jafar's head jerked back, and he slumped over the side of the gondola. The prince wrapped his own hand around Jafar's left.

Thank You.

The rain beat harder.
Lightning flashed.
Thunder roared.
Prince Omar was alive.

73

KORD AND MONICA CLIMBED DOWN the metal support beam to the ground. He couldn't get to her fast enough. Knowing her, she'd have a gunshot wound and not tell him. He reached for her, and she fell into his embrace. Neither was concerned about anyone watching.

"Don't ever scare me like that again," he said, his fingers weaving through her wet hair.

"I don't want to scare myself like that again." Her words were light, but she trembled. Her body shook with a cough.

He refused to comment. The FBI doctor would be making another house call.

They made their way to the Ferris wheel operator, who lowered Prince Omar and Jafar's body to ground level. The prince held tight to Jafar's left hand until the bomb squad stepped in to disarm the explosives.

Free of the bomb, Prince Omar stepped off the gondola, his head high and his shirt stained with blood. A bruise discolored the right side of his face. "I'm fine. The blood is Jafar's." He reached out and gripped Kord's hand. "My friend, it is good to be alive. We have information to help us stop the plot." He turned to Ali and repeated the gesture and words. With a smile he greeted his other bodyguards one by one. "Miss Alden, you saved my life."

She was drenched, her breathing ragged. "I'm relieved you're safe." She averted her eyes. Kord's girl honored the prince, although without her, he'd be dead.

"Thanks to you, the nightmare is over."

"Everyone did their part. Mine was small. It's been an honor to serve you."

"How can I repay the sacrifices you've made?"

A smile touched her lips. "Perhaps not getting pneumonia in this weather." A cough broke, and she clenched her chest. Kord held her tightly.

"You need medical care immediately." The prince gestured to Kord and pointed to an ambulance. "Perhaps a paramedic can help."

She nodded. "I'm sorry about Princess Gharam."

"She is at peace. I'll be escorting her body home to Riyadh as soon as arrangements are made. She fought courageously."

"I'll always remember her strength."

Kord helped her walk toward the ambulance. "Are you ready to consider us?"

"I am. Scared."

"Me too. I'm thinking an operative and an agent would be a dynamic team."

"I'd take another round of double pneumonia to hear those words."

He bent to kiss her. "Not necessary."

"Remember when you said I should be kissed every day?"

"Yep."

"I want to take you up on it."

Kord had little to say during dinner. Exhaustion and relief left him craving sleep. When the meal was over, Prince Omar invited Kord, Monica, his sisters, Ali, and his other bodyguards and staff to the natatorium. Quiet conversation accompanied strong coffee, fruit, and dates while the pool's fountain offered soft sounds. They spoke of Princess Gharam and how much she'd be missed.

Fatima and Yasmine hosted tear-filled eyes with Monica nestled between them. She should be in bed, but Kord knew his girl and the priority of her responsibilities. The doctor requested hospitalization, but Prince Omar insisted she be treated at his home as before, at least for tonight.

"Miss Alden, do you remember when I suggested we discuss our faiths?" the prince said.

"Yes."

What did this mean? A conversation now?

"Thank you for showing me what yours means to you."

Whoa. Kord hadn't expected that comment.

"Jafar told me a few things while on the . . . ride this afternoon," Prince Omar said and repeated Malik's treachery. "Fatima and Yasmine, for tonight only, I give you permission to ask questions. I've shielded you from many things, and I will continue. But you may speak." Lines fanned from his eyes. "I wouldn't want either of you using self-defense on me." He rose, took both their hands, then resumed his position.

"I'm thankful this is over," Fatima said, "and you're safe."

"I'm so fortunate to have you for my brother," Yasmine said. "I will study hard and make my family proud."

"I can hear it in your voice," he said.

"Did he say what lured Youssof?" Yasmine said. "I met his sisters in Riyadh, and they were kind."

"Youth are drawn into causes, especially when those with wealth and power are depicted as the enemy. Instead of searching for reasons why actions and laws are in place, they choose rebellion. The relief is Rashid and his wife and daughters were not aware of how deeply Youssof was involved. I ordered their release earlier and spoke to Rashid."

"Brother," Yasmine said, "after severing the conservatives' plot, how soon will it take for them to regroup?"

Prince Omar shook his head. "I'd say as soon as they receive word of the fate of those who are dead. Security is questioning those in power among the conservatives. They will suffer. I'm more determined to continue my plan of leasing our oil reserves. I'm sending you and Fatima home with our mother tomorrow. I'll accompany you and return in a few days to finish my work."

Tonight Kord refused to think of warring countries, assassination attempts, the innocent caught up in the middle of bloodshed, or one beautiful lady dodging lightning to save a man who might never fully value her gender.

Tonight he held on to peace and all he'd learned over the past two weeks about a real God, friendship, and new love.

EPILOGUE

7 Months Later

SOFT MUSIC FLOATED FROM the church's sanctuary, and Monica counted twenty minutes and forty-five seconds before Dad walked her down the aisle. With the way her stomach fluttered, she might need a skateboard. Dad had eight more minutes before he knocked on the door.

"You look like a princess." Lori fussed with her bridal train.

"I feel like a blundering idiot."

"Just think about who's meeting you at the altar."

Monica giggled. "I know. I'm so lucky." Kord had entered her life as the least likely candidate for a future husband. But they'd fallen in love. A fairy tale for a woman who believed happiness and family might never happen. Definitely a God thing.

"I think he's the lucky one." Lori stood back and gave her a head-to-toe once-over. "Sure glad you're settling down. The business with the Saudis was far too dangerous."

"Yes, ma'am." Monica and Kord had no intentions of giving up their careers. She'd continue until they had children. Neither would they stop showing Prince Omar what a Christian looked like.

A text landed in her phone. She knew it was Kord without looking.

Send a pic of yourself?

"Don't think so, my love." She typed, Bad luck.

"Is he wanting to see you?" Lori said.

"What do you think?" Another text arrived.

UR tearing my heart out.

U need a hobby.

I have 1 - U.

"What am I going to do with him?" she said.

"Marry him."

"Good idea." Monica typed. B nice & I'll marry U.

I Luv U.

Luv U 2. Is UR best man close?

In all his regalia. Ali's right beside him and Blake. And Pastor.

UR parents?

Sitting in church. Just need u.

Who would have ever thought when she took that call in March, she'd find peace with God. A mission completed. And Kord Davidson to love for the rest of her life.

A NOTE FROM THE AUTHOR

Dear Reader,

The characters in *High Treason* captured my heart the moment the story crept into my mind. My goal was to show the reader that although culture and race may separate us, we can get along and model Jesus to all we meet.

CIA Operative Monica Alden's skills and intelligence were a solid fit for the task force, but her gender fought Saudi Arabian tradition. She overcame a nightmare past to find the blessings of acceptance and love.

FBI Special Agent Kord Davidson valued his relationship with Prince Omar. They were as close as brothers. All the while Kord searched for meaning and purpose until he found it.

Like so many of us have experienced, life doesn't play fair. When we are faced with tragedy and injustice, the blame game enters our hearts. Sometimes God allows us to walk through fire to make us stronger.

Monica and Kord were more than survivors; they are characters we think about long after the book is closed.

Thank you, my friend, for reading *High Treason*.

DiAnn

DISCUSSION QUESTIONS

1. FBI Agent Kord Davidson seems initially reluctant to accept help from his CIA counterpart. Monica Alden, meanwhile, has her own hesitancies about working with a partner. For what reasons do both Kord and Monica want to work alone? How do their skills complement each other? When given the option of working alone or with a team, what's your preference? What advantages and challenges are inherent with teamwork?

2. Kord has forged a strong bond with the Saudi men in the prince's detail, but Monica and Kord's superiors fear he might be blind to an inside threat. Is he able to look at this investigation objectively? Do you tend to err on the side of trusting those around you or being suspicious? What can you do to set aside your emotions and remain unbiased?

3. In joining the Saudi prince's security detail, Monica faces some cultural gender inequalities. How does she handle the discrimination? When encountering cultural differences, when is it appropriate to stand up for your perceived rights and when is it better to step back?

4. As a CIA agent, at times Monica feels forced

to lie to her friends and family. How does this affect her relationships? Her emotional health? Are there situations where not revealing the truth is completely justified?

5. Kord's family history left him searching for answers in the Bible and the Quran, as well as Hindu and Buddhist teachings, and ultimately becoming an agnostic. What causes him to revisit his thoughts about the existence of God? How do you approach someone who's well-read or well-versed in world religions but doesn't see the truth?

6. After Monica catches Princess Yasmine meeting secretly with the prince's press secretary, she worries that telling Prince Omar the truth could have dire consequences. Is her concern justified? Does she do the right thing?

7. Ali is a rather passionate man—swinging from extremes of being bloodthirsty at the possible betrayal within the prince's inner circle to sharing a lighthearted moment with Monica. What was your favorite moment for this character? Do you think he was significantly changed after this trip to the States?

8. Monica struggles to forgive herself after Liam's betrayal. What happens to convince her to begin the process of forgiveness? Have you ever felt stuck in a similar state of being

unable to forgive yourself? What steps could you take to get unstuck?

9. When Monica shares her story about Liam with the princesses, she briefly worries that the prince might not approve of her words but rationalizes, "What good was her faith if she didn't stand for it?" Describe a time when you stood for your faith or when you could have taken a stand and didn't. What happened as a result?

10. Kord wonders why, if God is good and in control, innocent people suffer in the face of evil. What would you tell him? What does he learn about grace?

11. In chapter 44, when Yasmine declines to learn self-defense techniques, Monica has some harsh words for the young woman. Does she go too far in what she says, essentially telling the princess to stop being selfish? How would you respond in that situation?

12. Monica's perfectionism becomes a barrier to her spiritual growth. What would you say to someone struggling to "let go and let God" work in their life?

ABOUT THE AUTHOR

DiANN MILLS is a bestselling author who believes her readers should expect an adventure. She combines unforgettable characters with unpredictable plots to create action-packed, suspense-filled novels.

Her titles have appeared on the CBA and ECPA bestseller lists; won two Christy Awards; and been finalists for the RITA, Daphne du Maurier, Inspirational Reader's Choice, and Carol Award contests. *Firewall*, the first book in her Houston: FBI series, was listed by *Library Journal* as one of the best Christian fiction books of 2014.

DiAnn is a founding board member of the American Christian Fiction Writers and a member of Advanced Writers and Speakers Association, Sisters in Crime, and International Thriller Writers. She is codirector of the Blue Ridge Mountains Christian Writers Conference, where she continues her passion of helping other writers be successful. She speaks to various groups and teaches writing workshops around the country.

DiAnn has been termed a coffee snob and roasts her own coffee beans. She's an avid reader, loves to cook, and believes her grandchildren are the smartest kids in the universe. She and her husband live in sunny Houston, Texas.

DiAnn is very active online and would love to connect with readers on Facebook: www.facebook.com/DiAnnMills, Twitter: @diannmills, or any of the social media platforms listed at www.diannmills.com.

Books are produced in the United States using U.S.-based materials

Books are printed using a revolutionary new process called THINKtech™ that lowers energy usage by 70% and increases overall quality

Books are durable and flexible because of smythe-sewing

Paper is sourced using environmentally responsible foresting methods and the paper is acid-free

Center Point Large Print
600 Brooks Road / PO Box 1
Thorndike, ME 04986-0001 USA

(207) 568-3717

US & Canada:
1 800 929-9108
www.centerpointlargeprint.com